I feel a shiver down my spine. Imagine someone whose voice you've heard a hundred times before suddenly singing right in front of you. No, he's actually singing *to* me, word-perfect, with some of the deep growl of Johnny Cash but a smoothness overlaying it. He has an absolutely amazingly fabulous voice. Then I start laughing. Even though I hardly know him and I'm returning home in a couple of days, even though I'm about to lose my job and I'll probably end up marrying Stephen because no one else is going to ask me, in spite of all these things, I'm laughing in a way that is truly carefree, a way I haven't laughed for years.

British born Rosie Wilde now lives in Ohio, where she is perfecting the art of baking cupcakes.

Life's Too Short
to Frost a Cupcake

ROSIE WILDE

First published in Great Britain in 2008
by Orion,
an imprint of the Orion Publishing Group Ltd,
Orion House, 5 Upper Saint Martin's Lane,
London, WC2H 9EA

An Hachette Livre UK company

1 3 5 7 9 10 8 6 4 2

A CIP catalogue record for this book
is available from the British Library.

ISBN 978-1-4091-0208-3

Set in Abode Sabon by Input Data Services Ltd,
Bridgwater, Somerset

Printed and bound in the UK by
CPI Mackays, Chatham ME5 8TD

The Orion Publishing Group's policy is to use papers
that are natural, renewable and recyclable products and
made from wood grown in sustainable forests. The logging
and manufacturing processes are expected to conform to
the environmental regulations of the country of origin.

www.orionbooks.co.uk

For Fiona

PART ONE

London, England

CHAPTER 1

I had no idea what I was letting myself in for. I want to make that clear at the start. Some people have hinted that I engineered this whole thing – even implying that I had a master plan in place before I left London. The truth is I had no clue what was happening, and by the time I did realize, I think you'll agree that it was too late to do anything about it.

Everything else that followed – the incident inside the Barnsley Corn Maze, the fracas at the stay-at-home young mothers' group and my involvement with the Dairy Prize at the Ohio State Show – none of it, trust me, was planned. And for the record, I never claimed to be a recovering alcoholic.

I simply assumed that it was a Monday morning like any other. Stephen had already left for work. He's a solicitor in the property department of a London law firm, and if you're not at your desk by seven-thirty a.m., they reclassify you as a part-timer.

Stephen and I are boyfriend and girlfriend, but virtually engaged, and we live in Southfields, which is a suburb of south London for people who would like to live in nearby Wimbledon but can't afford it. In July the Wimbledon tennis tournament is held at the famous All England Lawn Tennis &

Croquet Club, which is situated just half a mile from our flat. It's very exciting: lots of the roads are closed, and once I stood next to Chris Evert in the queue at the Southfield's Starbucks. People with gardens lining the route to the tennis championships set up stalls selling home-grown strawberries and home-made lemonade. Stephen and I don't have a garden because we live in a very small one-bedroom top-floor flat.

Graham, who is my boss, always starts late on a Monday because that's his day to take his grandchildren to school. He's very nice, underneath his no-nonsense exterior, and lets me start late, too. So I took the opportunity to run my Dettol wipes over the kitchen counters, washed the floor, which doesn't take long because it's about the size of a bath towel, and ordered our Internet shopping from Tesco because I had a feeling that I would be working till all hours that week. And since I would be stuck at my computer all day, and I didn't have any meetings scheduled, I put on my comfy Marks & Spencer's black corduroy jeans and my Dorothy Perkins thick-knit mauve crochet cardigan. I work at Carmichael Music, where Graham is the boss of the UK office and I'm his assistant. In two days' time Phoebe Carmichael – the daughter of our firm's founder Terry Carmichael – will be arriving for a week-long review of the London operation. I had a nasty feeling that Phoebe meant 'review' in the sense of 'firing people'.

I log off from the Tesco website – it doesn't take long because Stephen and I are creatures of habit and order the same things every week – and take a moment to stand in front of the bathroom mirror and put on some lipstick and a bit of matte face-powder. I'm one of those women whose make-up has remained unchanged for twenty years. I buy it all from Valerie, Dad's long-term girlfriend, who is an Avon lady in her spare time.

Right now I do look a bit pasty – there has been no sun in Southfields for several months now – and so I take my courage in my hands and apply some of my new mineral powder, a free sample from Valerie, which helpfully performs the three tasks of foundation, blusher and powder all in one. Dad says that Valerie has found her vocation as an Avon lady. She expertly applies tons of make-up, whereas when I put on foundation and the works, I often find, staring at the mirror in the ladies' loo, that, far from being blended, my make-up has formed a tide-mark along the jaw-line and I'm sporting two uneven panda eyes.

Hmm. It's hard to judge because our bathroom has no natural light and Stephen only buys low-wattage, energy-saving light bulbs. I shouldn't have been so liberal with the special brush, £2.99 with every purchase. Also I think it may be at least two shades too dark. I turn the pot over and am alarmed to see that it's 'Beautiful Bronze'. I'm always Ivory. I have pale skin, which does tan if we ever get any sun. Perhaps it'll make me look like I have a healthy tan, like I've just got back from a ski-ing holiday.

The basin is now sprinkled with mineral powder, so I give it a quick wipe-down. I like to clean the bathroom every day: with the advent of MRSA you can't be too careful. I favour Tesco's bleach-based spray for basin and lavatory and Windolene-brand wipes for the bathroom mirror. The extra expense of Windolene is well worth it in terms of convenience and a smear-free finish. It's important to keep on top of the cleaning, though given the size of our flat, this is not too difficult. Our flat is, depending on whom you listen to, best described as bijou (the estate agent), cosy (me) or poky (my sister Teresa). There is one white-walled bedroom, a tiny square shower-only bathroom and an open-plan living room with a dining area leading on to a tired

1980s galley kitchen. At our flat-warming party my sister Teresa shook her head at the chunky white Provençal kitchen tiles. 'Very dated, Alice. You could have got a proper house in Surbiton for your money,' she sniffed. But later Dad gave me a hug and congratulated me on 'getting on the property ladder at last' – and because Teresa was standing next to us I didn't tell him that the house is actually in Stephen's name only.

Then all that's left is to lace up my Clarks moulded-sole lace-up shoes – as I say, we haven't got any meetings today and it's forecast to rain – pull on my coat and grab my handbag. I don't brush my hair at the moment as I find that it makes the frizz even worse. Instead I'm experimenting with towel-drying it and standing with my head between my knees fluffing it out. But I found out when I woke up this morning that this doesn't work so well if you do it the night before and go to sleep with it slightly damp.

The coat is a Per Una puffy number which was a present from Dad for Christmas. He worries about me catching a chill on the Tube-station platform. Teresa calls it the sleeping bag. 'Very useful if the train breaks down, Alice. You could provide warmth and shelter for four commuters.' My handbag is actually my trusty Karrimor rucksack (technically a daysack because it doesn't have a metal frame), which contains my purse, keys, paperback, antiseptic hand wipes and thermos of coffee. Stephen and I gave up Starbucks three weeks ago in order to save both cash and calories. Imagine, after just one week we have saved enough to purchase the one-handed kitchen-roll dispenser from the Scotts of Stow catalogue. In time, I'm hopeful of acquiring a complete set of Dorma bedding, including curtains. As for the calories, I'm still waiting for progress on that front. Dad says that I'm just right as I am, but I could definitely do with losing a few pounds. Like a bear, I put down fat for the winter.

I head out of the flat, carefully double-lock the flat door – the deadlock first, then the Yale – then descend the three flights of stairs, pulling my Karrimor rucksack over my shoulders. I then repeat the double-locking procedure with the house front door, even though Stephen and I are the only people who do this, despite several reminder notices to the owners of the other flats. The notices were in large capitals – Stephen bought a thick black marker pen especially – but even that didn't make a difference. Stephen is very good like that – he's responsibility personified.

I started going out with Stephen after something of a dry spell in my dating life. To be accurate, it was a two-year drought. I'm not one for blind dates, speed-dating or Internet chat. Before I met Stephen I was working at Kingston Council, where I met Paul, a junior planning enforcement officer, with whom I endured a tumultuous on off relationship for two years. Paul wasn't tall, dark or handsome, but he did kiss very proficiently and he was great at stir-fries. We enjoyed a three-month honeymoon period, but our relationship began to come under pressure when he was seconded to night work as part of the Noise Abatement Task Force, and took a further turn for the worse when he went back to college to do a degree in Town Planning. He got really sniffy then. 'I'm sorry, Alice,' he said after the first term. 'I think I need to find someone who's my intellectual equal.' You've heard of men who dump you after you've slept with them. Paul was cut from the same cloth: he waited until after I had typed his term paper – *Pavement Layout: Meeting the Challenges of the 21st Century* – to tell me.

It was a relief to meet Stephen, a man who, unlike Paul, has never once been late or forgotten my birthday (he has a reminder programme set up on his email). He's also very supportive of my career. I was very nervous indeed when I went for my job interview at Carmichael Music, but Stephen had ensured that I was thoroughly prepared. He made flash-cards with key statistics about top performers of the last four decades. When I was asked about key trends in the recording industry, I could talk for five minutes without hesitation or deviation about digital download technology. They stopped me after three. Donny Osmond made his first television performance aged only four singing 'You Are My Sunshine', by the way.

Physically I would describe Stephen as bookish or, better still, intellectual-looking. He's tall, nearly six foot one, which I think is good on a man. He's of very slim build with fine, sandy hair which he has swept back at the sides and short on top, just like Andrew Ridgeley, one half of the now defunct 1980s pop group Wham! He also has what I think is a very distinguished Roman nose. Teresa says that contacts and a decent haircut would take ten years off him, but he's been going to junior-stylist night round the corner for a while now and sees no reason to change.

Outside I zip up my coat against the harsh March wind blowing down the street. About half the three-storey houses have been converted into flats, while the rest are invariably described as substantial and much-sought-after family homes. The houses have lovely stained-glass front doors and window boxes, which in the summer will be full of tastefully coordinated geraniums. They are barren containers of soil right now. Our neighbours in Southfields are married with two children and one dog per couple. The mothers have Volvo estates and the husbands drive those fast Audis. The dogs come in three makes: Labradors, scotties or spaniels. We wave hello, but they don't socialize with us because Stephen and I are childless, dogless cohabitees.

I turn into Replingham Road, walk up past Budgen's and hasten past Starbucks, lest I'm tempted to grab a hot chocolate. Then I go into the Tube station to wait for a District Line train to Kensington High Street. Standing on the platform, where the overhead monitor displays a three-minute wait until the next train, I'm depressed to find that I can no longer put off thinking about Phoebe Carmichael.

CHAPTER 2

I already knew all about Phoebe. Dad had sent me an article. It was about a year ago, cut out from *Vanity Fair* with a Post-It note stuck on the front. Dad had written, 'Valerie saw this in the hairdresser so we splashed out on a copy'. He's always doing things like that – trying too hard to make us all one big happy family, even though I've told him a hundred times that I like Valerie and I haven't got a problem with them being together. Dad was alone for five years after Mum died, but that wasn't long enough for my sister Teresa.

The title of the *Vanity Fair* article was 'Daddy's Girls – Ten Women Step Out From Their Famous Fathers' Shadows'. Underneath there was a double-spread Annie Leibovitz photograph taken at night-time on the empty floor of the New York Stock Exchange. Ten super-serious young women stood in a semicircle.

Dad had drawn an arrow pointing at Phoebe Carmichael's head. She was dressed in a Michael Kors strapless black jumpsuit, brunette hair glossily brushed over one shoulder. She sort of glared at the camera, standing with one hand on her hip, elbowing a senator's daughter out of the way.

She looked made-up, rich and altogether pretty scary.

When Phoebe Carmichael enters the Fifth Avenue head-quarters of Carmichael Music, heels click and interns scatter. First in her class at Brown, she started her career by restructuring the firm's Chicago office – a process described by one industry insider as 'brutal'.

Here Dad had written a note in the margin. 'Be careful, Sugar Plum!!!' Even though I'm thirty-five, nearly a home-owner and, as I say, almost married, he likes to 'lend a hand'.

Ms Carmichael smiles at the memory. 'I prefer to say streamlined rather than downsized. I learnt this business at my father's knee. He taught me the value of five hours' sleep a night and no whining.'

Insiders say she is tugging the reins of the business away from her father. Her mission is updating the Car-michael Music brand, fending off criticism of the label's old-fashioned business methods.

As for her personal life, at thirty-six Ms Carmichael says she is happily single. She is tight-lipped on the subject of her father's marriage. Last year Terry Carmichael married for the second time after a combative divorce from Phoebe's mother. He met his second wife Olga when she was employed as his private nurse following his coronary bypass.

'We all get along fine now,' Phoebe comments succinctly.

That was a year ago. In the interests of corporate loyalty I pinned the article to my pinboard, but folded so that I couldn't see Phoebe. Then I tried to forget about her. Maybe the London office would slip her mind, or she'd decide to leave it in Graham's hands ... But she didn't forget all about us. Apparently she has spent the intervening year streamlining New York.

By the time the train had reached High Street Kensington station it was packed. As I emerged on to the High Street in the stream of hurrying commuters, dodging the people handing out free newspapers and flyers for cheap airfares, I looked to the grey sky, and as I set out on my walk to the office I couldn't help but feel worried about the week ahead.

Part of this is Brent's fault. Brent is Phoebe's assistant. He calls several times a day from New York to repeat himself. 'Alice, please tell me that Ms Carmichael definitely has a park-facing room at the Dorchester Hotel.' Brent talks in a fast, nervy voice, emphasizing every other word, and since I'm somewhat highly strung myself, I find that I get panicky too.

Meanwhile Phoebe's reputation has spread through the London office, and lately I have been interrupted every day by worried Carmichael Music employees tapping on my door confiding details of their horrendous mortgage payments and asking plaintively if I know anything about redundancy plans. Even Graham is feeling the strain, wandering into my office and peering over my shoulder as I type – which, if you have experienced it, you will know is very irritating.

I walk down the High Street, narrowly missing men in suits late for the office and the odd out-of-season tourist. The shops windows are already displaying summer dresses despite the fact that's it's bloody freezing. I force myself to concentrate on my breathing – slow on the exhale – and remind myself that Phoebe Carmichael couldn't fire Graham even if she wanted to. Her father wouldn't let her. Graham has known Terry Carmichael for nearly forty years, ever since Graham left his family's two-up, two-down terraced house in Manchester, took a hitch-hiking trip across America, met Terry in a Nashville bar and got talking about music. In a stroke of genius, Terry employed Graham on the spot to set up the UK arm of Carmichael Music. Terry was always the boss, but they're two of a kind. While Terry sat in bars across America listening to high-school dropouts, somehow discerning that one in a thousand who would go all the way, Graham sat in smoky pubs signing up bands from Glasgow to Bristol.

Graham is one of *Billboard*'s hundred most influential people in British music. But you wouldn't know it to look at him. That's part of the secret of his success – his fatherly persona of grey hair, bald patch and bit of a paunch, plus his Marks & Spencer's wardrobe of wash 'n' wear suits. Graham thinks dry-cleaning is a shameful extravagance. Not that he's mean. Last Christmas he gave me a bonus big enough for a holiday in Barbados. 'Get some sun, love. Live a bit,' he said, handing me an envelope with the cheque. We didn't actually go. Stephen spent hours going through the financial pages of the *Sunday Times* to help me choose the best-performing Tax-Efficient Retirement Plan.

Graham is one of those 'work hard, play hard' people, and likes to spend the weekends sailing his yacht across the Channel or nipping over to New York on Virgin Upper Class for a bit of shopping with his very tanned wife, Maureen. They recently celebrated their silver wedding anniversary with a cruise around the Caribbean, taking their three sons and their wives and seven grandchildren. I know all about it because I organized it. I don't mind doing stuff like that for Graham. I enjoy it, actually. Oh, how the other half live. Graham's cabin had its own butler and jacuzzi, and every night they put a real Godiva chocolate on the pillow.

Graham wasn't supposed to call me, but he sneaked off twice a day to use the super-expensive satellite telephone, telling Maureen he was going to check the weather charts outside the bridge.

By day four I started to wonder if Graham wasn't quite as family-orientated as I had hitherto imagined. He began to sound a bit desperate. 'Have you got *Billboard*?'

'Yes.'

'Read something out to me.'

'What?'

'Anything!'

Even though he's been signing up bands for ever, he's still hungry for success. To be honest, he can get quite tetchy from time to time, but it's worth it because I've learnt so much from him. Last month Firestorm came to the office to renegotiate their contract. Firestorm – black leather, crazy hair – are our headline band in the heavy-metal charts. Graham sat them down, passed them a plate of chocolate digestive biscuits and managed to persuade them not to take a rival deal with Sony.

'Now, lads, do you really want to be five little minnows in a very big pond?'

Firestorm thought about it, looked at each other and shook their heads meekly. Graham casually reached for the contract papers. 'Now, just put your paw prints here.'

Graham believes that bands do best when they write their own songs, play live venues and work on turning out 'cracking' albums. Graham still hankers after albums, and in truth he has never really got to grips with what the music press always calls 'the digital music revolution'. He's only just bought a BlackBerry, and anyone who mentions 'sharing' music is liable to provoke a pop-eyed rant. 'Sharing is theft!'

Graham listens to Johnny Cash, Rod Stewart and, when he's feeling risqué, a bit of early Eric Clapton. 'All the greats write their own songs, Alice. Wyatt did.' On my office wall there is a huge poster of Wyatt Brown's first album cover – *Moonshine*.

'That's what we need,' Graham will sigh at the end of a hard day. 'Another *Moonshine*. Wyatt made us millions in the nineties.'

Once I asked him, 'Do you think you could persuade him to record again?'

Graham shrugged. 'He's still under contract. We've tried to get him revved up again. But he passed out in Montreal five years ago blind drunk and hasn't sung since.' Graham pauses in a moment of reverent silence. 'Wyatt had it all, you know. Country, rock and a little bit of pop spun together.' He sighed. 'Universal appeal.'

Because it's Monday I stop off at Pret A Manger: a yoghurt and pecan muffin for me, plus a medium cappuccino and a cinnamon and raisin pastry for Graham. Graham and I would never have an affair, but we do keep our patisserie habit hidden from our partners. Graham's wife thinks he's on a low-GI diet, and Stephen didn't make an allowance for take-away items in our monthly budget.

It's nine-fifteen and Graham won't be in until ten. I walk the last five minutes to the Carmichael Music headquarters located in a side street around the corner from the Kensington Odeon, enter the glass revolving doors into the foyer and wave to Lisa on Reception, who is talking on the telephone. She waves back energetically as I dash for the lift, and as the doors close behind me I think I hear her call out my name. But as usual there is no time to locate the 'open door' button before the lift begins its ascent to the top-floor offices. In the bright lighting of the lift I check my reflection in the mirror and am alarmed to see that I don't look suntanned at all. I resemble a radiation victim with odd pigmented patches over my nose, chin and forehead where I didn't wipe hard enough with the loo roll. But there is no time to pull out one of my Kleenex pocket-pack tissues, because simultaneously an email appears on my BlackBerry from an address I don't recognize.

Sender: sharingistheft@biznet.com
Subject: alice i wont be in
Message: *obviously wont be in today ring me on the mobile graham ps watch your back love*

Before I can work out what Graham means – or jot down a memo to myself to tell him how to do caps – the lift doors open. In front of me stand four people in dark business suits – three I don't recognize and one that I do. Nervously I emerge from the lift.

The shortest of the three strangers bustles forward, clutching a clipboard. 'Name?'

'Alice Fisher.'

Before I have a chance to say any more, Phoebe Carmichael turns to face me. For a moment her gaze alights on my comfy jeans, falls to my Clarks lace-ups and rises to take in my puffy coat. Finally she looks at my face. For a moment she loses her composure and actually stares. Phoebe, the tall and elegant Brown graduate, stands before me without a hair out of place in a perfectly fitting dark red trouser suit and glossy black high-heeled shoes – a woman who, in the words of *Vanity Fair*, effortlessly combines leadership and glamour – while next to her I shuffle out of the lift like a dishevelled caterpillar.

She appears to pull herself back to the moment.

'Alice. We've been waiting for you.' She looks at her watch. 'Since seven a.m.'

Our eyes meet. Oh, bloody hell – I'm about to be streamlined.

CHAPTER 3

The boardroom of Carmichael Music looks out over the pigeon-populated rooftops of west London. It's formal, but in a hip, music-business sort of way, with black leather high-backed chairs and a teak oval boardroom table. On the walls are rows of platinum, gold and silver albums plus our number-one singles. Unfortunately our last number-one single was over three years ago, a freak Christmas hit by the Kingston Grammar School Rowing Squad with their cover version of Bette Midler's 'Wind Beneath My Wings'.

Phoebe marches us into the boardroom and briskly introduces us.

'Alice, this is my team.' I hate it when people say that. Graham always says 'our team'.

She points. 'Brent, my assistant.'

Brent, who I had already suspected was the clipboard man, nods briefly to me as if we have never spoken before.

'And Jason, my intern.' Poor Jason. Not only is he owned by Phoebe, he doesn't even get a surname. 'Jason, water, please.' There is a pause while Jason gets crystal tumblers and Evian and Phoebe takes out papers from a black leather document folder.

My first thought is, What have they done to Graham, closely followed by, What the hell is Stephen going to say

('How about Sainsbury's as a temporary option?'); and then, What is Dad going to say ('Sue them!'); and then my sister Teresa, who's always been jealous of my job ('That's what you get for flying too high').

Stephen is going to take it the worst. Rather than worry him, I've not said too much about Phoebe and her visit, so the news that I've been fired is going to come as a shock. I imagine Stephen sinking on to our IKEA cream calico sofa, clutching his hand to his forehead. 'If only you'd warned me, Alice,' he will say, the hurt showing in his eyes, 'I would never have increased my voluntary pension contributions.'

Dad, I believe, will be more indignant. 'That Phoebe's made a terrible mistake, Alice. The place will collapse without you.' Then there will be a long silence as I sit facing them in their 1930s New Malden semi. He will be wearing his beige slacks and a Pringle golf sweater. Next, Valerie will constructively suggest looking through the ads in the local paper while Dad shakes his head and quotes randomly from the History Channel. 'Time will tell, you mark my words. Marie Antoinette treated people shabbily, and look what happened to her.'

As for Teresa, she'll be unbearable. Teresa lives in Surbiton with her long-suffering husband Richard, a BT engineer and amateur birdwatcher, and her twin four-year-old boys. 'This is what I've been trying to tell you, Alice. A career won't keep you warm at night.'

Then she will become faux sympathetic. It was the same on her wedding day. She turned to me right before she went down the aisle, lifting her veil to address me. 'I know this must be hard for you, Alice – you are the older sister. It's natural for you to feel that it should have been you.' Then she squeezed my arm. 'You mustn't lose hope that you will meet someone one day.'

I look at Phoebe, who is now reading a typed sheet of paper and sighing from time to time. Phoebe knows how to apply eyeliner so both eyes look the same, and how to blow-dry her hair like they do in the commercials – it's full of volume, movement and shine. I wonder if I can take this moment to surreptitiously pull out a Kleenex and wipe my nose, chin and forehead, but decide that any movement may antagonize Phoebe into attacking me. So I sit bolt upright and look at the wall, the office-worker equivalent of playing dead.

Phoebe clears her throat, but just as I think she's about to speak, she reaches over for a dark green folder. Oh my God, it's my personnel folder. I recognize the photograph pinned to the CV she pulls out. Phoebe looks at it and glances over at me as if to check we are the same person. My hair was normal then, and blonder, because it was taken in the summer. In fact, now I come to think of it, it looked really nice; I'm not sure Teresa's suggestion of a perm was ever going to be in my best interests. Teresa used to be a hairdresser and she still cuts kids' hair in her kitchen. She's always on at me to let her do my hair, and before Christmas, filled with Yuletide goodwill, I agreed.

'It'll be a very light perm, Alice,' she assured me. 'It will add volume, that's all. Your hair's so mousy and thin,' she sighed, picking up a lock and letting it fall with a disdainful look. 'You need something to give it some body. This way you'll be all set for your office Christmas party.'

After she blow-dried me, Teresa continued to insist that it was a light perm. 'Just dry it straight, Alice,' she said airily.

'I look like a Cabbage Patch doll,' I squealed, pulling at the dense ringlets sprouting from my head.

'No,' said Teresa. 'Their hair is much shorter. Yours is shoulder-length. It'll drop in a few days,' she said dismissively, putting her combs in sterilizing solution. 'Now, I expect you'll be getting something new for your party. I do hope so. I'd go a size larger than last year if I were you.'

It didn't drop, and, if anything, the damp weather of recent weeks has made it curl up even tighter. My hair has taken on a mind of its own, and I'm only truly comfortable going outside when I'm wearing my Shetland wool pom-pom hat. Four months later there is a flat patch of regrowth on the top of my head giving way to the splayed mass below. Teresa says it will take two years to grow out completely, but if I get desperate she could do a Jamie Lee Curtis.

As I watch Phoebe thumb through my file, occasionally shaking her head, I feel a black cloud of depression settle over me. I should have ordered the Scotts of Stow one-handed kitchen-roll dispenser when I had the chance. I'll never own one now: Stephen will impose an emergency budget. Meanwhile, Teresa will suggest giving up work and having a baby. Then she'll turn her mouth down at the edges. 'Whoops! Sorry, I forgot. Stephen has commitment issues, doesn't he? It's so hard to keep track of them all.'

The only person who will be any use at all is my best friend Carolyn, and I resolve to go and see her as soon as Brent has escorted me off the premises. She lives in Fulham with her new baby, and even though she has given up a high-flying career to be a full-time middle-class mother, she won't try to advise me to give up work and have a baby, too. We were at school together and have seen each other through thick and thin. Carolyn is the only person who knows the truth about how Stephen and I met. But that's a story for another time.

Oh, all right. We met at the Chelsea and Westminster Hospital's Anxiety Sufferers Support Group.

Now, as Jason tops up Phoebe's crystal tumbler and

ignores mine, I realize that I'm feeling strangely calm. This has happened before. When you live in a state of perpetual expectation of unspecified harm – as Dr Vaizey, the anxiety specialist, calls it – then when something really bad does happen it's almost a relief. It's as if you can finally tell all the happy-go-lucky people in your life that you were right to worry.

Dr Vaizey is a world-renowned anxiety specialist and once appeared on the GMTV morning show to talk about nervous mums. I stayed at home to watch him, telling Graham I had overslept. I felt guilty but it was worth it. Dr Vaizey really put that Lorraine Kelly in her place when she said nervous mums should take more exercise. 'That certainly helps, Lorraine, but cognitive behavioural therapy is the essential therapeutic tool.'

The ten-week session of classes ended years ago, but a few of us still meet up once a month for coffee at the hospital Starbucks. Naturally everyone gets there early. Not Stephen, though – he says he doesn't need it any more.

So now I look at Phoebe and I don't feel worried at all. Go ahead. Fire me. In fact, the second time she looks up to tut and exchange knowing glances with Brent, I realize I have nothing to lose. I feel suddenly quite brazen.

'Where's Graham?'

Phoebe looks a little surprised at this, but then she smiles at me in a way that is only slightly feline. 'I'm glad you asked that. Graham has spoken very highly of you, Alice. He has every confidence in your abilities.'

She closes my file and nods at Brent as if prompting him to speak. Brent continues, 'Graham has decided to step down. We arrived this weekend to do some preparatory work and things moved a little faster than planned.' He shoots me a fake smile at this point and I notice that he has really white, big American teeth. Not like British teeth, which are generally yellowish and a bit cramped. At my side Jason is furiously taking notes on an A4 legal pad.

Phoebe takes over. It's almost as if they have rehearsed this. 'Alice, you will be aware that the performance of the UK operation gives severe cause for concern. Revenue is falling. Hip-hop has passed you by. World music is barely represented. Worst of all, you haven't so much as a *Pop Idol* reject signed up.'

Brent sighs and gives a little grimace of disapproval.

It's hard not to stare at Phoebe. She has really long, red nails with huge diamond rings stacked up on her fingers, big pearl drop earrings and lots and lots of gold bracelets that clatter when she waves her hand around imperiously.

She leans forward. Instinctively I lean back.

'You have made virtually no inroads into the vital ringtone market.' She glares at me. 'Some of your artists aren't even available on iTunes.'

Brent gives a sniggering little laugh. Jason turns over a page. Phoebe's voice rises. 'Alice, do you comprehend that we are in a make-or-break situation?'

I'm not quite sure what I'm supposed to do about this. And now that I understand that Graham has gone, I don't think I care very much anyway. But it turns out that an answer is not required. Phoebe has hit her stride. 'That's why I'm going to stay – in order to take charge of the London office. Brent will be my second-in-command. We will implement a raft of new ideas.'

'A raft of new ideas,' repeats Brent.

Phoebe's taking an awfully long time to fire me. Perhaps they're going to make me Brent's assistant, starting tomorrow at six a.m.

'However, we remain committed to interface with our US

headquarters.' Phoebe pauses as if to allow time for this to sink in.

'In Fifth Avenue,' I add helpfully, appreciating too late that she doesn't need to be told this.

But she ignores me anyway. 'And as such, we are looking to recruit someone to replace Brent as a member of our US team.'

'Graham suggested you,' says Brent.

It takes a moment before my head starts spinning.

New York! I have never been to New York – for the obvious reason that you have to fly to get there – but I was a huge fan of *NYPD Blue*, so I know all about it: Don't Walk signs, Reuben sandwiches and those yellow things that spout water all over the street.

But how am I going to get there? Flying is out of the question.

Phoebe has started talking again. 'The selected candidate will be based out of the New York office and assume special responsibility for artist development.'

I can take a boat!

'We think that there are a number of non-productive artists who could be reactivated into music production. We need a fresh eye to look at the backlist.'

And Stephen can take a boat to come and visit me!

'For example, Wyatt Brown. He's under contract until the end of the year and we're very keen to capitalize on this narrow window of opportunity.'

Dr Vaizey was always telling the group to live in the moment – 'It's your imagination that gets you into trouble, Alice,' he would say sternly – but this is good imagining, so I only half listen as Phoebe drones on about the backlist. I shall have a cosy but chic apartment on the Upper West Side, wherever that is, unless it's more chic to be in that Tribeca place. Yes, definitely Tribeca. Every day I will get my lunch from the local deli, the same one Robert De Niro patronizes.

I force myself to pay attention as Phoebe reads aloud. 'We also think that The Raptors could be persuaded to re-form.'

I will have a new wardrobe of Jackie O-style suits. All the scattering interns will love me. After a little while word will get round about my Friday night Fish 'n' Chip suppers – Manhattan's hottest invitation.

'Does that appeal, Alice?' asks Phoebe eventually. 'Do you have any questions?'

I would like to ask her what's in a Reuben sandwich. Instead I say, 'When would I start?'

'Next week,' says Phoebe. 'We're very keen to wrap this up.' She exchanges a pleased look with Brent. I realize that I have just accidentally accepted a job on the other side of the world. 'Good. Graham said that we could rely on you.'

CHAPTER 4

The rest of the day passes in a blur. Phoebe spends the day meeting 'her new staff', while Brent takes up position next to my office computer taking notes on our handover. He has absolutely no sense of irony. I have just finished showing him how to print the weekly chart sales spreadsheet.

'Just don't press the tab key while the printer's running,' I say, mock seriously. 'It makes the computer explode.'

Brent's eyes widen. 'Oh my gosh! Is that a trade espionage security function?'

At lunchtime I manage to shake Brent off and call Graham's home number while locked inside a cubicle in the ladies' loo.

Graham answers after one ring. 'I've been waiting for you.'

'I can't talk for long.' I'm whispering and, even though he's at home, Graham is whispering too.

'Is everything all right?'

'Fine. Phoebe called everyone in this morning and said that there would be no staff changes for three months. She's going to do a review. But what about you?'

'She offered to let me work alongside her, love. So early retirement seemed like the best option.' In the background I can hear screaming. 'And it gives me the chance to spend

26

more time with the grandchildren,' adds Graham without much enthusiasm. 'Are you staying on?'

'Actually, I'm going to New York.'

'New York?'

'Hmm. She wants more interface with the American operation.'

'Well I'll be damned.' There is a thud and a wail in the background. 'Got to go, love. Keep me posted.'

I fully expect to be working through the night, but at six o'clock Phoebe appears at my office door to summon Brent to go and look at a penthouse apartment in Chelsea Harbour. For some reason I don't feel like rushing home, and Stephen is working late at the office on a new case (he hasn't told me much about it because it's top secret, but he did say it could have major implications for the tractor-tyre industry, so I hop on a bus and go and see Carolyn.

Carolyn lives in a tree-lined street in Fulham in a tiny brick terraced house that cost a bomb. You can tell it's more expensive than Southfields because most of the houses have neat topiary trees on either side of the front door, and in the summer they put those miniature cabbages in their window boxes. Every third house has the builders in.

Carolyn answers the door with a muslin cloth over her shoulder, holding a small bundle who is her four-month-old baby, Maisie. They are both in head-to-toe Boden: Carolyn in moleskin jeans and a jersey shirt; Maisie in corduroy baggies. I follow them, squeezing past the red Bugaboo Cameleon which takes up most of the narrow hallway.

In the kitchen – redone last year in cream Smallbone units, so it's good that I'm not the envious type – I tell her about my New York news, and in response Carolyn lets out a small scream of excitement. 'Oh my God! That's fabulous.'

I'm touched, because Carolyn is obviously genuinely

pleased for me despite the fact that she has given up her job as a financial analyst in a City bank. Carolyn went back for a week before she and her breast pump broke down in the bathroom. Luckily for Carolyn, her husband still works as a financial analyst in a City bank.

'You're leaving next week,' she exclaims, pouring me a glass of wine and making a Red Zinger herbal tea for herself. 'What about your visa?'

'Phoebe has contacts,' I explain. 'Apparently I'm getting a Platinum Green card.'

Carolyn looks at me hopefully. 'So you'll be flying to New York?' That's one of the good and bad things about old friends. They know your weaknesses.

'No. We need to find an alternative.'

Within minutes I'm inexpertly holding Maisie – who is adorably fat and smells of Johnson's baby shampoo – and Carolyn has set to work on the Internet. For weeks I was too scared to hold her, and even now I have the giveaway pose of the non-mother with my elevated elbow bent at ninety degrees. Maisie is stretching her chubby legs and I'm blowing air-kisses back at her. The living room, which used to be London-couple-minimalist in design – white sofas and Indonesian hardwood occasional tables – is now crowded with a yellow and blue plastic swing, a lime-green bouncer seat and an animal-print playmat where the coffee table used to be.

Carolyn looks up from her computer. 'The bad news is there's no cruise line operating from Europe to the USA this month on account of the March tides. The good news is you could possibly go across on a commercial ship.' She turns back to the computer and reads out from myfreebeez.com, the website for the budget-conscious traveller.

Intrepid voyagers can hoist the mainsail and work their passage as a temporary merchant seaman – or woman. Working passengers travel at the grace of the Captain, living with the crew and assisting with duties on or below deck. Accommodation is usually a separate cabin. Go to the docks a few days prior to sailing and approach the Captain direct.

Carolyn clears her throat. 'I've found a Liberian-registered cargo vessel crossing from the Netherlands on 2 April and arriving in Nova Scotia ten days later.'

'Brilliant! I can take a train from there.'

(I'll return to the subject of driving at a later time. For now I will summarize the current position: journeys of under twenty-five miles along previously travelled routes.)

Carolyn gets up and gently takes Maisie, who has begun to cry, probably because she senses that she's in the aching arm of an amateur. 'Alice,' she says coaxingly, 'how about flying?'

I shake my head. I went to Jersey once on a little propeller plane. But I was ten then, and not yet scared of anything.

'Alice,' Carolyn persists, 'there's a reason that no cruise lines cross the Atlantic in March.'

I nod. 'I know.' My head is already filled with images of fifty-foot waves and drunken Liberian sailors.

But the truth is that I'm already having second thoughts about this whole enterprise. All day long, worries have begun to pop up in my head. Dad will hate the idea of me being so far away. Stephen may meet someone else while I'm gone – though I concede that this is unlikely. Brent has been vague about my job description, my salary and where I'm going to be living. 'A hotel to start with. Obviously,' he snapped dismissively when I tried to get more details out of him this afternoon.

I watch Carolyn as she holds Maisie with relaxed skill. 'I think she's got wind,' she says confidently. I detect that Carolyn, fearing I may one day become a mother, has begun to try to educate me on the subject of babies, dropping educational snippets into our conversations. 'The baby is crying! When did she last have a feed?'

She gets up and begins pacing around the room, cooing, 'Poor little windbag.' She looks at me and a frown crosses her brow. 'The next major decision is whether to start her on solids.'

I hope I look interested, but it's not a good sign when Carolyn begins to talk about feeding, one subject on which I have to say she can get quite nutty. Take a tip from me: never helpfully suggest to a Fulham new mother that breast milk and formula are basically just the same.

Carolyn is talking about organic baby rice and how to freeze puréed carrots in ice-cube containers. I do try to pay attention, but my mind is now drifting to the subject of my future life in New York. It has taken just a few hours for my East Coast daydream to take a darker turn. Now the scene is somewhere in the Bronx. I lie awake listening to couples arguing, muffled televisions and random gunfire. At work, no one returns my calls, no one apart from a drunken Wyatt. 'Darn it, woman, I ain't never singing again.' Italian Tony in the deli is my only friend. One day he comes round to the front of the counter and takes my hand. 'Bambina. I see the sadness in your eyes. Go home to your people ...' Teresa meets me at Heathrow airport where my plane has just made an emergency landing after its undercarriage fails to descend. 'Successful trip, Alice?'

Carolyn's voice cuts into my thoughts. 'What do you think?'

'Sorry?'

'Baby rice or carrot?'

'How about a nice boiled egg?'

Carolyn looks as if she's about to say something, then closes her mouth. Instead Maisie burps and we congratulate her for a full minute. Then Carolyn turns to me and says slowly, 'Promise me you won't let Stephen talk you out of this.'

I'm surprised. 'Of course not.'

It hadn't occurred to me that Stephen might try to talk me out of going. If anyone is going to do that, it's Dad. Dad, since he took early retirement from British Gas, where he was Home Counties Residential Sales Manager, has switched from worrying about gas leaks to fussing about his family. He means well, but since he learnt how to send email attachments, it's got increasingly hard to keep up. I get emails all day long of the 'Warning!!! – New Identity Fraud Scam Alert!!!' variety.

Doing Valerie's Avon accounts, collecting Teresa's twins from school and volunteering at the New Malden Citizen's Advice Bureau every Friday still leaves him a lot of time to fill. As well as sending me articles cut out of the papers, he also likes to videotape television programmes that he thinks will be of interest to me, and then pesters me about whether I have watched them. Then I feel guilty and have to stay up late on a marathon VHS session, fast-forwarding *The Antiques Roadshow*.

Carolyn hesitates. 'There's no doubt you've changed, Alice. You've worked so hard to get out there and do things. It would be a shame to stop now.'

'I know,' I say quickly. I know she's got my best interests at heart, but I feel compelled to defend Stephen. 'He's always helped me in my career.' I think back to my job interview and Stephen's flashcards. Not only that, but he gave himself temporary tinnitus listening to Firestorm.

'Hmm. He certainly likes to be involved in everything you do,' she says, and though this might be read as a compliment, something in her voice tells me it isn't. I know what she's getting at: I admit that Stephen's attention to detail and love of routine is in part a way of avoiding difficult emotions. After I initiate our 'When are we going to have a baby' talk every month, he generally gets up and cleans the oven.

'I'm sure he'll be thrilled,' I say brightly, now wanting to reassure both her and myself.

But Carolyn isn't fooled. She fixes me with a no-nonsense stare. 'Alice, you have to go to New York. After everything that's happened, you deserve this. It's the opportunity of a lifetime.'

CHAPTER 5

L ater that evening, I do bear in mind Carolyn's words as
I watch Stephen sink on to our IKEA cream calico sofa.

'You're going to New York,' he repeats breathlessly.
'Why?'

'Because it's the opportunity of a lifetime. And because I
think the alternative of working with Brent is unbearable.'

I notice Stephen's eyes dart backwards and forwards as
he analyses these two options. 'Have you accepted?'

I'm a hopeless liar. 'Sort of.'

'Sort of!'

'It wasn't an opportunity of a lifetime that they were going
to hold open for me.'

Stephen struggles with change. He joined the Anxiety
Support Group after an ill-fated flirtation with criminal law.
One day, on the second day of jury deliberations in a minor
fraud trial, Stephen's client was forced to clamp a brown
paper bag over his mouth and count him through his breathing. When the client was sentenced to eighteen months,
Stephen collapsed. But thanks to Dr Vaizey, who I believe is
destined for greatness, Stephen was dissuaded from retrain-
ing as an insurance assessor. Instead, he switched to property
law and it has been a huge success. He's now something
of a leading light in the world of agricultural restrictive

covenants. His *Farming Law Journal* article 'Ploughing rights – the case for piecemeal reform' was described by his boss as 'very methodical'.

'Even if you were to go,' he says beseechingly, 'what about your salary, benefits, health insurance and the employer contribution to your TERP?'

I nod. Stephen is right, of course. I know what people think of him. Dad says he's solid, Carolyn says he's reliable and Teresa says he's a total saddo, but they don't know the real Stephen. Not only is he very supportive but he's also kind and thoughtful. Anxiety sufferers spend days shopping for the perfect birthday present, and we all gabble exactly the same thing when you open it: *If you don't like it, you can change it – I've got the receipt.* Stephen is no exception. As his Internet research disclosed, one breadmaker is not just like another (as Teresa insisted). The one he gave me for my last birthday was state-of-the-art. 'Alice, it's something for you *and* something for the home.'

He's also a lot like me: he pays off all his credit cards at the end of the month, respects the speed limit and hangs up his clothes on identical white plastic hangers facing in the same direction. Plus Stephen has made huge strides with his 'issues – money and fear of failure – which began in child-hood when his parents' restaurant went bust. Haltingly he said to the group, 'Imagine everything in your life changing overnight. We lost the business, the house and my dad was never the same. Going bankrupt broke his spirit. I never felt safe again – because I knew then that bad things didn't always happen to other people. They could happen to me.'

I ached for Stephen when he said that. It's easy to pick at someone's faults, but when you know where they've come from and what they've been through, it makes you see things from their perspective. We have been together for almost four years now, which is a long time to invest in a relationship, particularly if you are not very confident of your chances of meeting anyone else. Most people don't understand anxiety issues – they think that telling you to relax because it will all be OK is useful advice. 'Oh, really,' I want to say, 'I never thought of that.' I don't say it, of course, because I'm afraid of offending them. Donny Osmond would understand – he has gone public with his anxiety issues on www.donny.com; but he's married with several children and lives in the USA.

When you understand the whole story, it's easier to see why Stephen writes down everything he spends in a spiral notebook and why he can't yet commit to getting married or having a baby. 'I do love you, Alice,' he said when he asked me to move in after three years together. 'I just need to take things slowly.'

Now Stephen rubs his temples. 'This is terrible timing. I'm under enormous stress with my tractor-tyre preparatory reading.'

'I'm sorry, I really couldn't help it,' I say, trying to soften it all.

He looks up at me with pleading eyes. 'Don't go, Alice. It's too far for too long.' He spreads his hands wide. 'In time you and Brent might hit it off.' He catches sight of my expression. 'And if not, there are loads of jobs out there for someone like you. Graham would give you a great reference.'

I look around the house at everything that's safe and familiar: at our Brontë mug, brought back from our first holiday hiking in the Lake District; the stainless-steel kitchen bin we chose together in Homebase; the souvenir photograph of the two of us on the London Eye (a big breakthrough given our mutual fear of heights. We held hands and did our breathing while a group of Austrian teenagers laughed at us). I know that, given more time, Stephen will commit to getting married and having a baby – though God knows how I'm going to get him through the delivery.

'We could book a holiday,' he says earnestly. 'Anywhere you like.' He takes a deep breath. 'And we could raid the rainy-day fund and put in a new kitchen.'

I do a double-take. 'Really?'

He nods decisively. 'Cabinets, counters – even new tiles.'

I hesitate. I can see that for Stephen this is a huge step, like jumping out of an aeroplane on a parachute jump for a normal person. But I can't help but remember Carolyn's warning to me – *you deserve this*.

'But I'll never have a chance like this again,' I say quietly.

'Unless we take a trip to New York together,' he says intensely. 'After we've done the kitchen.'

The tension is unbearable.

But then, in a dramatic gesture, Stephen reaches for the Scotts of Stow catalogue sitting on the coffee table. My heart misses a beat. I like to flick through it most evenings and escape into a fantasy world of kitchen islands. He picks it up and turns quickly to page four. 'We could make a start now,' he says commandingly. 'Look, the one-handed kitchen-roll dispenser. Let's go online and order it.'

He jumps up, ready for action. I don't know what to say or do. Stephen has never ordered anything online – he and Dad remain constantly vigilant against identity theft. I watch in shock as he pulls out his wallet and gets out his credit card. 'Nothing ventured, nothing gained.' But wait, there's more. He turns another page. 'We could get the cordless swivel sweeper at the same time.' His voice is low and tempting. 'No more getting out the hoover for those little clear-ups, Alice.'

Stephen is offering to buy me not one but two cleaning-related products, with the promise of a brand-new kitchen and a holiday to New York.

Faced with that, what else could I say? 'All right. I'll tell them I'm not going.'

CHAPTER 6

I'm going to be honest here. The next morning, after my conversation with Stephen, I probably would have gone straight into the office and handed in my notice if Stephen hadn't paused in the middle of drinking his breakfast decaffeinated tea, peered at the Provençal white kitchen tiles and uttered the fateful words, 'Maybe we could get away with regrouting.'

'What!'

He looks at me with an expression of pure reasonableness. 'There's no point spending money for the sake of it, Alice.'

'You said we could do the tiles.'

'Obviously I meant subject to budgetary constraints.'

'Oh, for God's sake, Stephen. We're ordering a kitchen, not commissioning a warship.'

'Actually, I think the same principles apply. Let's see how we feel after the Scotts of Stow order has arrived.'

He looks at his watch. 'I'm going to be late,' he mutters, reaching for his cycle helmet. He knows there is nothing I can say to that.

So I go to work, and instead of handing in my notice I check out Italian marble tiles online whenever Brent is called to see Phoebe. After one day, things at Carmichael Music are already changing. At lunch I sit with Lisa from Reception, the girls from Accounts and Bob from Technical Support. Graham made a point of having lunch in the canteen whenever he was in, sitting with different departments. He knew everyone by name. But Phoebe and Brent are upstairs in her office eating ordered-in sushi from Itsu.

Lisa the receptionist is packing half her lunch into a Tupperware container. She's a single parent and I suspect that is her dinner. 'Graham was always so understanding. Anytime Kayla got sick, he let me stay at home. I expect that's all going to change.'

No one contradicts her.

Betty from Accounts jerks her head at the publicity girls sitting by the window. 'If those girls have got a job at the end of the summer, then I'm a banana. That Phoebe will close 'em down and use an outside firm.'

Bob nods sagely. 'It'll be a skeleton staff soon.' Bob from Technical Support is also Dad and Valerie's neighbour, and, thanks to him recommending me to Graham, the reason I have a job at Carmichael Music. Bob's been here since Graham employed him to set up our Internet access. He only works here to fund his real passion, writing his novel, a medieval romantic comedy. He's very highly educated.

Lisa leans towards me. 'So is it true, Alice? There's a rumour you're going to the Big Apple.'

I shake my head. 'Nothing's definite.'

After work I go to the monthly meeting of the Anxiety Support Group. Andy, Jennifer and Zara are already there. Andy is an ex-airline pilot who lost his nerve after a storm in the Bay of Biscay forced him to make an emergency landing outside Santiago. He still has his grey hair cut in a crew cut, and he wears those white pilot shirts with pockets. Jennifer is a housewife who, before she came to Dr Vaizey's group, hadn't left the house for ten years except to go to

Spar. As for Zara, let's just say that she's a twentysomething aspiring poetess with waist-length hair and an awful lot of problems.

I wave hello, then join the queue at the counter. I'm careful to ask for a take-away paper cup for my semi-skimmed latte. Germs – and how to avoid them – is a popular subject on these occasions. Jennifer and I never go anywhere without our antiseptic hand wipes, and Zara – who was once handed a cup with a partially removed lipstick stain – now only drinks through a straw.

As I sit down, Andy is in the middle of talking about depression. 'Fucking depressives. They get all the attention.' He counted off on his fingers. 'They don't work, don't wash and sleep all day. Then they expect everyone to feel sorry for them. Tell your GP you've got anxiety and what do you get – twenty Ativan and a meditation tape.'

Jennifer nods in agreement. I notice that she's had blonde highlights put in her hair and she's showing more cleavage with every month that passes. Today she's wearing a V-neck, pale pink, mohair jumper. Lately I have begun to wonder if there is something going on between her and Andy, despite the fact that her husband, a traffic policeman, drives her everywhere. I see him sometimes, parked in a side street with an unrestricted view of Starbucks, reading the *Daily Express*.

Zara takes her knitting out of a holey plastic bag. Zara can get tasks done, but only if she carries them out in a particular order. Any deviation and she has to start again. In consequence, her last job on the checkout at Tesco turned pretty nasty on Christmas Eve. She'll start talking once she gets her knitting under way.

'I've been offered a job in New York,' I announce.

Andy claps me on the back and Jennifer looks as if she's

about to cry. 'Oh, I've always wanted to go there.' She blinks at Andy. 'Maybe one day . . .'

'What will you be doing there?' asks Zara, going click, click, click.

'Still working for Carmichael Music.' I take a sip of my coffee. 'The thing is, I'm not sure about going. I mean, I'd have to fly.'

I was expecting some sympathy – in the world of the anxious, boarding an aeroplane is second only to undergoing a general anaesthetic – but oh no.

'But you drive,' says Jennifer.

'You go on the Tube,' says Zara.

'You're a bloody idiot if you turn that down,' says Andy. He slams down his chai latte. (Dr Vaizey banned us all from coffee, but I relapsed.) 'Come on, Alice, you've always been top of the class.' Andy has always had a soft spot for me and – I suspect – a bit of an attitude towards Stephen. For example, he never uses Stephen's name. 'Is this down to that bloke of yours?'

'Ooh,' inhales Jennifer. 'Is he against it?' She exchanges glances with Andy. 'Is he taking away your power on account of his own control issues?' she says knowingly.

'Shame,' says Zara dreamily.

I feel obliged to defend Stephen. 'No. He cares about me.'

Jennifer has now locked eyes with Andy and they are nodding simultaneously. 'That's always the justification, dear,' snaps Jennifer.

'He stopped coming to the group, didn't he?' says Andy. 'Once he started running your life he thought he didn't need it. Chivvying you about gave him something to think about.'

'Oh yes,' chimes in Jennifer authoritatively. 'By focusing on you, Stephen didn't have to address his own inner-child pain.'

'For goodness' sake,' I say irritably, 'can we stop talking about Stephen? I'm the one who needs some moral support.'

'Look. Just go, Alice,' says Andy with a wave of the hand.

'But the flight,' I say miserably.

'It's the safest form of travel,' barks Andy dismissively.

'But you . . .' I begin.

'That's different. I had to keep the bloody thing in the air. All you have to do is get drunk.'

Thank goodness Dr Vaizey can't hear us now. He fought a war against our little crutches: drink, ciggies, Kit Kats and all our crazy rituals. I would hate to let him down.

Zara is lost in thought. 'I took a train once. I was fine until I ran out of wool.'

Later, Andy takes me aside. 'Alice, life is short. Enjoy the journey.'

When I get home, I lie to Stephen when he asks me if I told them I wasn't going to New York.

'Phoebe was out of the office all day.'

Any guilt I feel fades away when Stephen fails to mention the kitchen. That night we sleep on opposite sides of the bed.

The next day, Andy's advice keeps replaying in my mind. Besides, the rumours of my New York posting have now taken on a life of their own. I'm a bit of a celebrity at Carmichael Music. Betty gives me a congratulatory bear hug in the corridor, and Lisa looks at me with longing. 'Oh, Alice, you're soooo lucky.' I feel guilty about throwing away my good fortune. I summon up the courage to call Dad, and, far from being worried, he's delighted. 'So you'll be leaving Stephen behind, eh!' Meanwhile Bob catches me in the queue at lunch. His eyes dart around. 'Changes are afoot.' He lowers his voice. 'Ask not for whom the bell tolls, Alice. It tolls for thee and me.'

Besides, how bad can an eight-hour flight be?

So I fob Stephen off, and by the end of the week I'm almost convinced. It's Teresa's call that pushes me over the edge.

'I had to call you, Alice. Dad's just told me. New York!' She gives a peal of laughter. 'What are you going to do? Flap your arms through the flight to keep the plane in the air? Seriously, Alice. Whatever were they thinking of, offering that job to *you*!'

That was when I finally decided to go.

CHAPTER 7

'The job market isn't good, Stephen,' I say, shaking my head. 'Redundancies are looming at Carmichael Music, and at my age I could well lose out to a younger person. Going to New York may be the only viable way that we can safeguard our financial future.'

I have decided to worry Stephen into letting me go to America, and I think my plan is working. Anxiety sufferers are predictable in this way, because they worry about everything. He's leaning forward on his chair at the Wimbledon Village Pizza Express. This location is another part of my strategy – spending money in restaurants always makes Stephen nervous. He puts down his menu and clasps his hands together. The mention of our financial future has brought a hint of fear to his eyes.

'Just think, Stephen,' I run on, trying to sound despondent, 'it could be months before I get another job. The longer you've been out of work the harder it is. I expect I'll have to join one of those job clubs where people who used to run multinational banks get clapped by the group when they come back from their interview at Asda.'

'Do you really think it could come to that?' he says, shocked.

'If I even make it to the job club,' I say, wide-eyed.

'Depression could set in and I might end up spending all day on the sofa ordering things from QVC.' I pause. 'With the heating turned up.' I sigh. 'I probably won't have the motivation to cook, so we'll have to live on take-aways.'

Stephen's mouth drops open as the waitress comes to take our order.

'A four seasons pizza, please,' I say.

'A four seasons pizza, please,' Stephen says. 'And one garlic bread and one side salad to share and half a bottle of your house wine and two glasses of tap water.'

You see, that's another benefit of living with another anxiety sufferer – no unexpected surprises or changes in behaviour.

'But you are a qualified PA,' he says, frowning as the waitress leaves. 'I'm sure there are loads of jobs out there for people like you.'

'Nope. PAs are a dying breed. I blame computers,' I respond, shaking my head. 'And Third World outsourcing. And global warming,' I throw in for good measure.

I can see that Stephen is contemplating the situation. He takes his glasses off, cleans them with his Pizza Express paper napkin and puts them back on, a telltale sign that he's under stress. I start to feel a bit bad at this point for putting him through this. But everyone is nagging me all the time about not pulling out and sort of assuming that I will – it's a bit insulting. Andy texted me today – 'Go 2 NY. Chnce of lftme. Dnt fck up!!!' Really.

I take a sip of my wine. We are not big drinkers – our wine box lasts us for months. We are surrounded by young couples on dates and good-looking families with children who eat bruschetta. Outside it's cold and raining, but inside it's warm and loud in the high-ceilinged, modern-design restaurant. I could get used to living like this, but we don't often partake of restaurant meals – kitchen hygiene is a concern of mine, and Stephen can't help but point out that we could eat for a week for the price of one meal – but Pizza Express has a spotless open-plan kitchen and a value-for-money menu.

'But it's a long time for us to be apart,' he says. 'I'd have to spend six months in the flat alone without you.'

I have anticipated this. 'I'll call you and email and I'll get a webcam set up. Plus we can instant-message. Keeping in touch won't be a problem.' I take a deep breath. 'You could come out and visit me.'

'Visit you,' he says weakly.

'With the aid of prescription tranquillizers,' I add hastily. 'You'll fall asleep at Heathrow and wake up in New York.'

The garlic bread arrives and Stephen divides it down the middle.

Meanwhile I describe our imaginary tour of New York, one that misses out the boat trip round the Statue of Liberty and the part where you step out on to that really windy platform at the top of the Empire State building. 'The museums are world-class,' I declare.

'It would also give us more time to plan the new kitchen,' I remark casually. I have not given up on my kitchen, oh no. But I think it would be better to wait until I get back rather than risk Stephen choosing the cabinets, counters and fittings.

'OK,' he says slowly. 'I suppose if you're saying that there's no alternative ...' His voice trails off and his face is a picture of misery. 'I just don't know how I'm going to manage without you.'

Oh my God. I reach for his hand and squeeze it, though I'm forced to let go almost immediately because the waitress arrives with our pizzas. I'm choked up by Stephen's loyalty.

Let's face it, Stephen may have his quirks of personality, but I'm not the easiest person to live with either. There's a lid for every saucepan, which in our case means I'm the mis-shapen lid for Stephen's dented pan.

'We'll just have to make very detailed plans for all eventualities,' he says bravely. 'That's how the SAS do these things.' Stephen's favourite author is Andy McNab, the former SAS soldier turned best-selling novelist.

I look at him with a surge of love as he begins eating his pizza methodically, crust first, working inwards in a clockwise direction. I follow suit. It was one of the first things I noticed about us – on our first date at Pizza Hut – that told me we were destined to be together. Oh, what fun we had on that first night, swapping notes! Stephen agreed that horses are very scary indeed from whichever end you approach them. As for that habit people have of tasting food off your plate with their fork, we tutted that it was both insanitary and bad manners. Over coffee we confided our mutual horror of swimming pools – the insanitary communal water, the threat of verrucas and the danger that they have added too much chlorine, resulting in one being overcome by fumes and then drowning.

As cohabitees we are ideally suited. He knows that I can't stand soft-boiled eggs – even the sight of the runny bit in the centre makes me squirm – and boils them faithfully for ten minutes. We both have very sensitive ears – Stephen and I have the volume turned so low on the television that we often have to guess crucial lines of dialogue. And we both always wash new clothes before wearing them because you don't know who's tried them on before you.

We eat in silence for a few moments, then Stephen puts down his knife and fork. 'We'll call it Operation USA,' he announces. 'We'll need to start planning tonight.'

I reach out to clasp his hand again, but he has already picked up his knife and fork and is cutting the five o'clock section of his crust.

So instead I content myself with an image of us in New York, Stephen wild and carefree on account of the long-lasting effect of his aeroplane tranquillizers. There we are, hand in hand, skipping down Fifth Avenue, dining at soon-to-be-discovered restaurants and rowing round that lake in Central Park. Manfully, Stephen steers our little boat to the middle of the lake and then stops. I look puzzled, even though I have a suspicion of what is to come. Sure enough, Stephen pulls a Tiffany box from his pocket. I tilt my head coquettishly. As I open it I'm dazzled by the diamond within. 'Will you do me the honour of becoming my wife?' he whispers. 'Yes,' I say proudly. American bystanders watching this romantic scene from the shoreline shout 'Yankee Doodle Dandy!' as they throw their baseball caps in the air. For-tuitously a few have fireworks which they let off. It all causes quite a stir, and later that evening we are interviewed on WKTZYB television news. 'Central Park saw some good old-fashioned romance today when an intrepid Brit came to the Big Apple to pop the Big Question!' Stephen is filmed holding me close. 'I found the most wonderful woman in the world and I can't wait to devote my life to her happiness!' Donald Trump calls up while we are on air and offers us a free honeymoon at his Palm Beach hotel.

I feel a surge of love for Stephen as he starts the second lap of his pizza. Yes, I know where I stand with Stephen. He's what old people call 'good husband material'. Stephen would never sign us up for one of those too-good-to-be-true mortgages – cheap for two years then after that you can't afford to eat – or fail to renew our RAC membership: one breakdown and it pays for itself. As a father he would ask

48

searching questions at parents' evenings, man the barbecue at the summer fête and help coach the school football team. As a schoolboy, Stephen played in goal; given his build he had a tendency to be knocked over on the pitch.

We finish our meal as Stephen fills me in on the latest developments in his Dorset coastal footpath dispute, then he catches the waitress's eye for the bill. 'Let's have coffee at home,' he says as normal. (You can buy a whole pack of coffee for the price of one froth-filled cup of cappuccino.) As I wait for him to pay, I feel warm, happy and secure and I continue to feel that way for the five minutes it takes Stephen to add up the restaurant bill and fill out his Master-Card receipt, because it's his turn to pay. Truly, I am a lucky, lucky woman.

CHAPTER 8

At five o'clock on Friday I arrive at Phoebe's office for what Brent has called my executive briefing. In less than a week, Graham's office has been refitted in Japanese style. I have a good look round at the paper screens, mountain-scene prints and extra-big potted plants while Phoebe checks her email. There are also lots of photographs of Phoebe – ski-ing, horse-riding, shaking hands with the President; and the *Vanity Fair* article has been framed on the wall.

(Perhaps, I wonder, *Vanity Fair* might wish to commission a 'Top Ten British Ex-Pats Taking Manhattan By Storm' feature. 'You're naturally photogenic, Alice,' comments Annie Leibovitz casually.)

Phoebe finishes checking her email and reaches for a sheaf of papers on her desk, which she begins to peruse leisurely. I know the Japanese foggy mountain scenes quite well by now, so I surreptitiously turn my attention to Phoebe herself. She's wearing a close-fitting black Chanel suit (I know this because it has those Chanel gold buttons) over a simple red silk T-shirt. Teresa would like Phoebe. Teresa dresses a bit like Phoebe, only from TK Maxx. She likes matching trousers and jackets, silk-effect blouses and heels, but not stilettos as she says these are tarty. I glance down at Phoebe's feet.

She's wearing black ballet pumps. I tried them once, but they kept falling off my feet.

Finally Phoebe looks up from her file and swings towards me in the brown suede chair which has replaced Graham's black leather one. Phoebe's is bigger, though.

I decide to take the initiative. 'I wanted to say how grateful I am for the opportunity to go to New York.'

Phoebe stares at me for a moment, probably wrong-footed by my new-found self-assurance.

'And I want to say thank you,' I continue purposefully.

Her expression clears. 'Say nothing of it.'

'And I will not let you down.'

She bestows a little smile on me. 'Alice, we wouldn't send you if we didn't think you were *exactly* the right person for the job.'

She opens the file again, takes out some papers and slides them across the desk towards me. 'This is your US contract of employment. It's for six months. And this is the paperwork for Wyatt Brown. We want you to deal with him first. He had another relapse, but I'm sure he's as right as rain now.'

I feel an inkling of unease. Relapse? Is he in one of those luxury rehabs? 'So where will we be working?'

'At his home,' she says, as if it was self-evident.

I relax. A palatial rock-star pad overlooking Central Park, no doubt: one of those places with a liveried doorman, a red carpet to the street and a canopy to stop you getting wet as you step out of your stretch limo. It could also be very convenient for my English afternoon teas with Annie Leibovitz. 'You've taught me so much about European culture, Alice. Would you be offended if I called you my muse?'

Phoebe continues. 'On the thirtieth of September, Wyatt's

contract with us expires, Alice. So you need to apply a little pressure on him to send us some demo tapes as soon as possible.'

It's not at all unlikely that some pretty famous people are going to be living in Wyatt's block. Perhaps I could rope them in for an informal 'jamming session' to inspire him to record again. Paul Simon on keyboard, Paul McCartney on guitar and Robert De Niro working the tape recorder.

Phoebe gets up, and it's clear that our meeting is over. 'I'm sure you'll come up with a raft of ideas,' she says, her gaze distracted by something out of the window. It's a pigeon. She turns back to me. 'All that remains for me to say is good luck, Alice.' She gestures to the door. 'Brent has your ticket and travel papers.'

I'm filled with gratitude for the chance she has taken, sending someone she barely knows to the company's head-quarters. I'm almost in tears as she opens the door to usher me out of her office. 'Thank you so much!'

As she closes the door behind me, I feel the momentous opening of a new chapter in my life. Friday afternoon – London. Monday morning – New York. More than that, I feel a psychic connection to the millions of immigrants who have passed before me, my fellow travellers to the New World. I, too, will forge a new life on those faraway shores before coming home again.

I go down to my office, where Brent is busy stacking the boxes filled with my belongings in the corridor.

'I'm here for my tickets. My tickets to *New York*,' I add in a fake American accent, and I can't help but do a little shuffle from side to side as I wave my hands in the air.

'New York?' says Brent, executing a pirouette and catching the last of my dance. He recovers after a few seconds. 'Oh dear me, no. You'll be *based* out of New York. But you'll be *flying* to Ohio.' Brent goes over to the desk and picks up an airline ticket. 'To be exact, you're going to the town of Barnsley, Ohio. That's where Wyatt Brown lives.'

He gives a little laugh as he hands me the ticket.

'I don't think he's left there for years.'

CHAPTER 9

It's Saturday evening and in less than twelve hours from now I will be airborne. Dad and Valerie are hosting my farewell party in their 1930s New Malden semi-detached home. It's situated close to the A3 arterial road into London, but is very effectively double-glazed. Dad has strung the lounge with red, white and blue paper chains and a Bon Voyage helium balloon as a centrepiece. Valerie has spent all day making party food – cheese straws, prawn toasts and a guacamole dip that is grey in colour but delicious nonetheless. I'm touched by the obvious effort they have made.

Dad and Valerie are sitting on the sofa, and Teresa has grabbed the new recliner. Richard, her husband, is not there on account of a telecommunications system overload in Uxbridge which has reduced broadband speed in west London to a snail's pace. Saturday night is apparently a big night for Internet traffic, so Teresa has informed us, on account of single people online-dating. 'Useful to know that, isn't it, Alice?' As this is a party in my honour, she's dressed down in her velour two-piece in pink with sparkling white trainers. She does her own hair like Farrah Fawcett, with little wings brushed back from her face and sprayed into position with extra-hold Harmony hairspray. Her hair never moves, even in high winds.

I'm on the G-plan easy-chair, and Stephen's on my old bedroom beanbag. Bob is reaching forward to grab a mini Scotch egg – that's Bob from Technical Support, Dad and Valerie's neighbour.

Dad clears his throat. 'So, Alice, tell us all about your new responsibilities.'

It might be my imagination, but I see Teresa flinch at this.

'I'm in charge of artist development for North America,' I exaggerate. Stephen looks up at me, but I ignore him.

'I always said you'd go far in that job,' says Dad, even though at the time he was obsessed with the drug culture infesting the music industry and tried to persuade me to stay at Kingston Council.

Dad has put on his smart-casual outfit of ex-British Gas white shirt teamed with a Marks & Spencer lambswool V-neck in sage green. Valerie has tried to get him into Lacoste golf shirts, but to no avail. He's quite vain about his hair, though, and sometimes remarks that people say he bears a striking resemblance to Michael Parkinson.

'I expect there'll be quite a lot of international travel involved,' I continue with a sigh, 'but I'll just have to cope with that. I think many four-star hotels have spas now to help stressed executives unwind. Most nights I expect I'll just get a massage and order room service.'

Dad rubs his hands together. 'Just fancy that. My Alice joining the jet set!'

I look at Teresa out of the corner of my eye. She's examining her fingernails intently. I endured years of Teresa's comments during my time at Kingston Council – *At least the Council offers you a good pension scheme. You'll need that as a single retired woman* – and I'm savouring this moment.

'I suppose you'll be flying in a Boeing 747?' Dad asks.

'I don't know,' I say grandly. 'My assistant Brent made the arrangements.'

'Actually, I'm not sure it is a 747,' interrupts Stephen. 'The type of aircraft is specified on the ticket, but is subject to change.' He's honest to a fault. Stephen gets out my transatlantic itinerary, which is at the front of my multi-sectioned document folder. Once he got over the initial shock of my leaving, he's been a tower of strength and a slave to our label-maker.

'I think in all likelihood it will be a 747 but I wouldn't rule out the Airbus,' he says in the considered tone that makes him so respected in his profession.

My document folder contains sections for each stage of my travel, my briefing paper on Wyatt and even one marked 'Alcoholism' for my background reading material. This is a copy of '*Enable YOU – strategies for dealing with the alcoholic in your life.*' Earlier this afternoon Stephen and I had a very intimate moment as we sat together and ticked off my suitcase and flight-bag packing list. Valerie has lent me her aquamarine Samsonite wheeled suitcase and matching flight bag, so I look quite the seasoned traveller.

Stephen clears his throat. 'The flight leaves at seven-fifteen a.m. Given the requirement of a minimum period of three hours prior to check-in at four-fifteen a.m., and the possibility of auto-mechanical failure and overnight motorway maintenance, we felt it was wiser to go straight to the airport after we leave here.'

'Don't you think you ought to be getting going?' says Teresa, coming to life and tapping her watch. 'I'd say you were cutting it fine.'

Honestly, I don't know why Teresa bothered to come. It's always tense when Teresa and Valerie are in the same room, Dad smiling uneasily from one to the other. Dad met Valerie, who is a school secretary, at the New Malden Leisure Centre swimming pool. It took months of swimming laps side by side before Dad moved beyond nodding to saying good morning, and another six weeks before they went for a coffee. Dad made me tell Teresa that they were moving in together.

Teresa thinks that Dad has forgotten Mum. But I know he hasn't; he just got too lonely.

Teresa was thirteen when Mum died, and she always says that because of her sensitive personality it affected her the worst. I was eighteen and it didn't seem right to go away to university straight away, so I decided to take a gap year and get a temporary job at the Kingston Council civic centre giving secretarial support. The rest, as they say, is history. Sometimes I think about going back to get a degree, but as Stephen says, at my age would I ever recoup the considerable investment of time and money?

Teresa and I are at that age when women's magazines say sisters are supposed to become closer. Let's just say I'm not holding my breath. If anything, relations between us got worse when I landed the job at Carmichael Music. ('I expect they're all very cool there, Alice. Will you fit in?') Teresa likes to portray herself as the creative genius of the family because she belongs to a book club and her kitchen walls are stencilled with bunches of grapes. But the truth is that we're a lot alike. We both wash our kitchen floors on our hands and knees and start ticking off our Christmas shopping lists in August. Teresa's twins are dressed identically and only allowed to use washable felt tips. Right now they are enclosed in the kitchen in case they make a mess.

Bob takes advantage of the awkward silence to give us an update on the progress of his medieval romantic comedy. 'In the rom-com genre there are always a series of obstacles to

57

the couple getting together. In my novel the first problem is the tithe.'

'Sounds like a book you'd enjoy, Stephen,' says Teresa, smirking, and Dad laughs disloyally.

'Unless our hero can pay the ten per cent of his meagre earnings to the Lord of the Manor he cannot get permission to marry, you see.'

I counter-attack. 'Teresa, how's the house? Any progress with your plans for an extension?' The extension was a big topic for a while, but lately Teresa's gone quiet. .

She doesn't miss a beat. 'We may just move to something much bigger now that Richard's got his new promotion. He's a wonderful provider – so important in a *husband*, Alice.'

'How's he getting on with that lady boss?' says Dad, shaking his head. Dad still struggles with the notion of women in positions of leadership, though it would be OK if it were me, if you see what I mean.

'Sandra gave him a very positive end-of-year appraisal, actually,' says Teresa. 'I wouldn't be surprised if he's promoted again this year to regional level. Richard is scaling the British Telecom corporate ladder,' she says proudly.

'Wouldn't that be the British Telecom corporate *telegraph pole*?' says Dad in a very laboured voice. 'Careful he doesn't fall off the top!'

'Boom boom,' I add in my Basil Brush voice, which is our family tradition follow-up to Dad's awful jokes.

'He'd have some explaining to do if he landed on his lady boss!' Dad chortles, as Valerie tries in vain to shush him.

Teresa purses her lips. 'For goodness sake, Dad,' she snaps as he and I collapse with mirth. 'No one talks about "lady bosses" any more. The glass ceiling has been well and truly smashed.'

'Well, let's hope there was a woman there with a dustpan and brush to clear up the glass!' says Dad, virtually wetting himself laughing. Poor Teresa, she never did have much sense of humour. It was Dad and I who sat together watching Benny Hill. When she was fifteen, Teresa called a family meeting to announce that she was a feminist. When Benny Hill came on she used to make a big fuss of getting up, huffing around and then stomping upstairs to read her Fay Weldon novels. No one took any notice, and at sixteen she got a boyfriend and forgot all about being empowered.

Bob pipes up, seemingly unaware that the conversation has moved on. 'Once that obstacle is overcome, I intensify the drama by introducing the prospect of plague in chapter six.' He turns to Dad. 'But in a light-hearted manner.'

'So, Alice, I expect you're planning lots of sightseeing in New York?' asks Valerie, passing round a plate of prawn-toast triangles.

I haven't told them I'm not actually going to New York, and I've told Stephen not to tell them either. He's not very happy about it, but I'm hoping he can hold his nerve. Brent and I had a slightly tense conversation after he handed me the tickets, and I asked him why I was going to Ohio when I was supposed to be based in New York. 'You are based *out of* New York: any problems, call them. Besides, that's where your email server is located.'

I take a prawn-toast triangle and start chewing. 'Hmm.'

'Prawn-toast triangle, Teresa?' asks Valerie politely.

'No thank you, Valerie,' responds Teresa stiffly.

'Ooh, I forgot the vol-au-vents!' Valerie gets up and goes into the kitchen. I take advantage of her temporary absence to glare at Teresa. She gives me a 'What have I done wrong?' look.

'Valerie,' I mouth silently, jerking my head in the direction of the kitchen. 'What?' she mouths back silently with exaggerated puzzlement, as if she doesn't know what I mean.

'You could make an effort,' I counter in this increasingly long silent conversation.

Valerie is a good sort, and I wouldn't mind at all if she married Dad. She makes him happy and looks after him. She doesn't have any children herself; her first husband didn't want them, to her lasting sadness. She's always on at me to let her do an Avon makeover, but in a nice way. 'I could show you how to blend your Cocoa Glow four-shade eye-colour palette,' she says enthusiastically. 'Your green eyes lend themselves to something really dramatic!' Valerie and I have different tastes. Valerie is to turquoise polyester what I am to beige fleece.

'Let me get a pen and paper,' says Dad, levering himself up. 'I need your address and phone number.'

'I don't have those yet,' I say, trying to sound nonchalant.

Dad looks alarmed. 'Well, where are you staying when you arrive?'

'I'm going straight to the office.'

'Alice ...' Stephen begins nervously. I can see from his expression that he thinks I'm living on the edge here.

I ignore him. 'They'll tell me when I arrive where I'm going next.'

'Oh, Alice,' says Teresa. 'Like *Mission Impossible*.' She points at my document folder. 'Careful with your ticket. It might spontaneously combust.'

Dad frowns. 'We do need a number.'

I've anticipated that. 'The BlackBerry works in New York.'

'What are you going to do when you arrive?' Teresa splays out her arms and legs in a starfish shape. 'Suspend yourself over your desk and await further instructions?'

'For emergencies,' Dad continues.

That does it. Stephen cracks, reaching into the 'Ohio Residence' section of my document folder. 'Here. This is the address.'

Teresa, seeing me shake my head frantically, grabs the paper from him.

Bob, who clearly has little natural sense of drama, starts up again, despite the fact that I'm trying to grab the sheet from Teresa by doing a playful Chinese burn on her wrist. 'Crop failure was another hazard of medieval living. Of course that might be a little dark.'

Dad is always encouraging. 'They do say that tragedy is the flip-side of comedy.'

Teresa reads out loud, pulling my hair. 'Buckle & Braid Farm,' she exclaims. 'Barnsley,' she says confused. 'Ohio?'

'Is that a suburb of New York?' enquires Valerie.

'No,' Stephen says, correcting her. He looked up Ohio online this morning while I did my ironing. 'Ohio is a mid-western state located approximately five hundred miles from New York and three hundred and fifty miles from Chicago.'

'Is it close to Hollywood, then?' Valerie asks hopefully.

Stephen could have been a teacher. He's very patient. 'No, Valerie. If you imagine a map of the United States, it's slightly to the right of the centre.'

Dad looks perplexed. 'What are you doing there?'

I attempt to rescue the situation. 'I'm going to see Wyatt Brown. He's my first project. That's his home address.' I have to make it sound more impressive. 'And the location of his recording studio.'

'I expect all the stars hang out there,' says Teresa. 'Say hello to P. Diddy for me.'

'Then I'll be going to New York,' I say firmly.

Stephen has hit his stride. 'Ohio is the home state of the

famous astronaut John Glenn and a major producer of sweetcorn and soybeans.'

'Sounds like one long party,' sniggers Teresa. 'Who's this famous John Glenn then?'

'He was the first American to orbit the earth,' Stephen informs her, but Teresa is now preoccupied with her sleep mime.

I don't give up. I try to ignore Teresa and address my remarks to Dad and Valerie. 'I'm based out of New York, but I'm sort of a roving ambassador for the company. I could go anywhere,' I say airily.

Teresa comes to life. 'Roving ambassador,' she hoots. 'Watch out Angelina Jolie. I'll look out for you on the six o'clock news.' Then she does that thing with your hands where you make a square, and pretends to take a picture of me.

We leave soon afterwards. Dad gives me a long hug and reminds me to drive on the right side of the road. Valerie presses a Body Shop Travel Pack into my hand, Bob claps me on the back, the twins are let out of the kitchen to kiss me goodbye and Teresa softens for a moment. 'Give me a call. Oh, wait a minute. Do they have electricity where you're going?'

Then all that remains is for us to climb into the Honda and proceed to the M25, stage one of my trip of a lifetime.

CHAPTER 10

The M25 is completely clear of traffic and we arrive at Gatwick airport at 11 p.m. It's a little over six hours until the check-in for my flight opens, so we take my wheeled Samsonite suitcase and matching flight bag and wait in Costa Coffee. The airport is all but deserted as I begin my international jet-set life.

I can tell when we sit down that Stephen is not himself. He looks nervous, twisting his watch strap and continually reaching into the pocket of his Lands' End khaki squall parka.

'Is everything all right?' I ask him.

'Fine,' he answers too quickly.

'Is this about me leaving?'

He nods. 'Yes,' he says miserably.

He takes hold of my hand and gently rubs my fingers.

'What is it?' I have an inkling that Stephen may be leading up to saying something.

He reaches into his pocket. 'I've been doing some thinking, Alice. About us. I know that things between us have always been on an informal basis. But you going away for six months has made me reconsider that.' He looks at me intently. 'It's a long time apart, Alice.'

I know what an enormous step this is for him. I feel a

rush of protective love for him as I take his other hand. 'Stephen, the miles may separate us but you will always be in my thoughts.' I take a surreptitious look around. The scene is not promising. Two elderly men are cleaning out the near-empty pastry cabinet. If Stephen does propose, we're going to have to split a celebratory Danish pastry.

He takes a deep breath. 'Your job offer took me by surprise. It's forced me to re-evaluate some fundamental things. And I know I should have asked you earlier – and I know you probably think that it's a bit late in the day ...'

I tilt my head coquettishly. 'No,' I simper.

'But it took me a while to figure it out.' He takes his hand out of his pocket and I now see that he's holding his spiral notebook, into which an A4 sheet has been carefully folded. I'm baffled as I watch him unfold it. Has he written a poem?

No, it's a spreadsheet.

'You see, Alice, there's the question of your contribution to the household bills while you're away.'

'What?'

'I know. There is the argument that because you are not in physical residence you shouldn't be liable. But the counter-argument is the common understanding with which we moved in together – that we would share the bills. And the fact is, I haven't budgeted to pay all the bills myself while you're away.'

I'm speechless.

Stephen takes my silence as a sign to continue, which he does with more confidence. 'Now, I concede that while you are away you will not be consuming resources like electricity, gas and water. Nor will you receive the benefit of domestic refuse collection. But those services will be waiting for you when you return! So I think the fairest thing would be for you to pay one half of the standing charge for each utility.'

'Each utility?'

'Plus half the television licence, obviously.'

If the bloody check-in was open I would get up and leave there and then. It's just a few hours before I board a flight – which I have very little confidence that I will survive – and arrive in the middle of nowhere to try to persuade a reclusive drunk to sing again. I admit that it had crossed my mind before now that Stephen might be jogged by my departure into proposing. But those hopes have been cruelly dashed by a man more concerned with his bank balance than my lengthy absence.

'You earn a fortune,' I say bitterly.

He looks askance. 'I don't see how that's relevant.'

'I'm going to have a lot of expenses while I'm away.'

'I'm sorry you're taking it like this, Alice,' he says stiffly. 'I'm just trying to do what's right.'

'For you, maybe. But what about us?' I'm feeling really upset now. 'Sometimes I think you care more about money than you do about me.'

(I have a flashback to one of Dr Vaizey's sessions. Stephen had just finished explaining why he couldn't let go and spend more than twenty-five pounds on a Christmas present. Dr Vaizey was nodding sympathetically. Then Andy said sort of under his voice but not really, 'So, Doc, is there a pill you can take for being a tight-fisted twat?')

Stephen says what he always says on these occasions. 'I can't help it.'

I have lost patience. 'You could try!'

At this point I can feel that we're being watched. I look up at the two Costa Coffee staff, who look away embarrassed and recommence talking in Italian.

'I think you'd better go,' I say bitterly, staring into my cup.

'Alice.'

But I don't respond.

OK, I admit it: I really, really thought that he was going to propose, and I feel like a disappointed idiot. Everything has changed now: I'm seeing Stephen in a different light – the cold, harsh light of Gatwick airport industrial lighting, to be exact – and it isn't flattering. All the little things Stephen has done in the past that I made excuses for have come flooding back. I thought I had let these incidents go, but really they were there all the time, stored away in the 'archived files' part of my subconscious. My Christmas solar-powered calculator. My birthday Lakeland Plastics salad spinner. And, I don't care what Stephen says, our John Lewis bedroom chandelier light fitting just doesn't look right with energy-saving light bulbs.

Stephen looks downcast. 'Look. Why don't we compromise?' he says, trying to sound jovial. 'I'll pay the bills, and you can settle up when you get back.'

'Bugger off!'

My resentful thoughts gather steam. He's never bought me a ring of any description. The best he managed in the jewellery department was a set of nine-carat gold aquamarine earrings which he got with his MasterCard reward points. I suddenly realize that actually I would like some bloody Valentine roses, and I don't care if they double in price the day before.

He rises to his feet. 'I didn't think you'd react like this,' he says petulantly.

He hovers, waiting for me to back down. But I don't, and after a few awkward seconds he begins to walk away.

Instinctively, I reach for my case to get up, catch Stephen and repair our argument. I rise to my feet.

I know exactly what will happen next – it's the same old

story every time. Stephen will faithfully promise to change, I will believe him and everything will stay exactly the same.

Stephen is heading for the exit. He hasn't even looked round.

I'm standing holding my case. But I don't think I can bear things staying the same any longer. It strikes me that I don't have time for this. I'm thirty-five, with the odds of me getting married in time to have a baby getting worse every day.

Stephen has reached the glass doors. At last he turns round. He raises an eyebrow as if to say *Are you coming?* But he doesn't take a step towards me. It seems symbolic. Stephen looks aghast as I sit down and take my hand off my case. I'm pretty surprised myself. I watch as Stephen's mouth hardens and he turns on his heel and marches off into the night.

Miserably I concede to myself that perhaps Teresa was right when she turned to me after the toast at my thirtieth birthday party, 'Have you thought about freezing your eggs, Alice?'

A wave of reality washes over me. I have no husband, no home of my own – and no real job. It's finally time to admit to myself that Phoebe's sent me to Ohio to get me out of the way. It's a set-up. They know Wyatt will never sing again, and when I fail in my mission I'll be sacked. That's if I make it back at all. '*Enable YOU – Strategies for dealing with the alcoholic in your life*' has been quite an eye-opener. Each chapter ends with a case study of a real-life alcoholic.

I can see the scene clearly. I turn up at Wyatt's ramshackle farm, bits of rusty tractor littering the yard and chickens pecking. Loudly I bang on the peeling door, but there's no reply. Slowly I push at the creaking front door. It's unlocked but hard to open on account of the post, warrants and free newspapers littering the floor. I step gingerly inside the darkened room, following the sound of snoring from the living room. Wyatt is sprawled on the sofa, a guitar and several empty bottles of Jack Daniel's on the floor beside him, an LP clicking silently on the turntable. I go over and lift the needle. It's *Moonshine*, which he listens to every night as he drinks to forget the memories of better days. I shake him awake. It's then that I see the shotgun by his side. 'We shoot trespassers in the US of A,' he growls. Boom! There is a white light and I'm floating, looking down at the earth below. Teresa is standing over my grave. 'Who's the favourite now, Alice?'

I'm startled out of my Country Star Murder Tragedy daydream by a thick Italian accent. 'You finished with the cup?'

I look up to see one of the elderly Costa Coffee staff pointing at my paper cup. Stephen, of course, took his with him when he left. I nod.

As he reaches forward to take the cup, I notice his name-tag: *Tony*. Oh my gosh, as Brent would say. It's Italian Tony!

'You look sad, lady,' he says, wiping the table.

What the hell. 'I've just broken up with my boyfriend, my job is going nowhere and I'm supposed to get on a plane in eight hours and I'm terrified of flying.' My voice breaks and I have to hurriedly blow my nose to stop myself from crying.

Tony doesn't seem at all fazed by this. He looks at me in an understanding way as if he hears this type of thing every day. 'Why you break up with boyfriend?'

'Because he's a tight-fisted twat who cares more about money than he does about me.'

Tony looks horrified. 'Boyfriend is fool! He not deserve beautiful lady.'

I agree. Tony has to be sixty if he's a day, but I need this right now.

He leans on his cleaning cart. 'If I knew very special lady like you, I would never let her out of my sight.' Tony gets going. 'Maybe this all work out for the best. Maybe you meet someone nice on plane. Good man who will look after you.' Tony sighs. 'Take my advice. Forget boyfriend.' He claps his hand across his chest. 'If he is mean with his money, he will be mean with his heart.'

'So you think I should go?'

'Plane not crash,' he says confidently. 'And if it does, then it's your time.'

He catches sight of my expression. 'Wait there. I get you panacotta. No charge! It just a little bit stale.' He opens his arm expansively. 'Then you go look round the shops, buy yourself something nice.'

Tony heads off behind the counter. 'I get you coffee, too,' he calls out. 'On the house.'

I sit back in my chair and think how it's the sympathy of strangers that's often the most affecting, the words and gestures of people who have no reason to be kind that touch us the most. Then, as they always do when I feel alone in the world, my thoughts turn to Mum and how it was only years later that I understood how much she hid from us and what she really meant when she said certain things. 'You should see the world, Alice. While you're still young.' Now I grasp that she wanted me to do the things she didn't have time to do – and not to wait and think that there's always time in the future because sometimes, for some people, there isn't.

I wish more than anything that she was with me now, and I close my eyes and try to see her face.

After a few seconds I have her in my mind. But it's what I hear next that shocks me. I make out the sound of a few familiar bars of music coming over the airport loudspeaker system. It's a song everyone knows, joining in together to shout out the last line of the chorus. It's played at every wedding, every birthday disco, and every event at which the DJ has a choice between this or 'Dancing Queen' to get everyone on the dance floor.

> Take a little trip in the moonlit dew
> Down by the creek
> Thinkin' it through
> Maybe come and see you
> Maybe come and see you
> Hell, I've got the Moonshine Blues

It's Wyatt Brown singing 'Moonshine'.

I'm going to America.

PART TWO

Barnsley, Ohio

CHAPTER 11

I feel as though I've been travelling for ever. There is no time here to describe my interview with US Immigration or all the details of my unscheduled night at the Columbus Airport Budget-Beater Motel. Just take it from me: if an immigration officer asks you when you intend to leave the USA, do not, under any circumstances, say, 'I don't know, it depends on how things go'. You may find yourself detained in a small, white, windowless room. There was nothing to do but reread *'Enable YOU – Strategies for dealing with the alcoholic in your life'* and Brent's briefing paper on Wyatt Brown, which must have taken him five minutes to write.

'Wyatt Brown was signed to Carmichael Music under a five-album contract. Four top-selling albums followed:
   Moonshine
   Takin' It Slow
   All I Have
   Losing You
The fifth album is due by September 30th of this year.
Address: Buckle & Braid Farm, Hunter Hill, Barnsley, Ohio, USA.
   Any queries email admin@carmichaelmusicny.com

Brent also paid very little attention to my itinerary. If he had, he wouldn't have booked me on to the back row of a flight from Gatwick to Indianapolis with a six-hour wait before my connecting flight to Columbus, Ohio. It was a 737 by the way, one that doesn't have individual television screens. But I did take Italian Tony's advice and buy myself a present at Gatwick airport to mark my passage into lifelong spinsterhood. Since I'm clearly never going to get engaged, I decided to buy myself a consolation ring with a large zirconia diamond and two synthetic sapphires on either side. The woman in the shop where it was on special offer for £99.99 said it was the same kind that Charles gave Lady Di. I took it out of the box standing in the Gatwick airport toilets and put it on the third finger of my right hand.

I'm now one day late, due to my unscheduled stop at the Budget-Beater Motel following my Ativan overdose. Bump, bump, bump we went across the Atlantic, but that was nothing compared with the flight to Columbus – in a propeller-driven plane presumably on loan from a crop-spraying company – at the end of which we were encouraged by the captain to give a round of applause for the first officer's inaugural landing.

There is no way I can fly back to the UK, so I'm either going to have to become an illegal immigrant in the USA or circumnavigate the globe via the polar ice cap.

It's now Tuesday morning and thus technically day four of my journey.

But I'm now at the entrance to Wyatt's farm. Ahead of me is an open gate with a sign overhead, *Buckle & Braid*. I crawl up the bumpy gravel driveway in my Avis Ford Focus. On either side of me are bare ploughed fields covered with an icy film, a sight with which I have become quite familiar in the hours since I left Columbus airport, stopping every twenty-five miles to do my breathing and check my Black-Berry for emails from Stephen. So far there have been five, each one increasingly more desperate in tone, the subject lines reading:

Payment Plan
Discounted Payment Plan
Mediation Options
Our Scotts of Stow order has arrived!!!
Whatever You Want, Alice.

But I can't think about Stephen right now. All my attention is focused on Wyatt and the task ahead. I have decided that it's crucial to win his trust. Now that I'm actually here in the USA, I'm feeling much more confident about our first meeting. I now imagine this as the encounter which Wyatt will later credit with changing the whole direction of his life. He says so when he writes his autobiography. In this lengthy tome our meeting takes up a whole chapter, but to sum-marize, Wyatt will describe movingly how he awakened from what was his last ever hangover. He looked up and there I was, a damp flannel in my hand. 'Are you an angel?' he rasped as I dabbed his brow. 'No, Wyatt,' I whispered softly. 'But I have travelled from a far land to save you.'

Naturally I will never publicly claim credit for changing the whole direction of Wyatt's life, and reviewers will forever puzzle about the book's title – *Darlin', I Owe It All To You* (a bit like they puzzle over that mystery woman in Shakespeare's sonnets).

I proceed slowly for about a quarter of a mile along the driveway, turn a corner and see a cluster of buildings surrounded by pristine white-fenced fields and, in the dis-tance, a dense wood. I park the car in front of the neat, wooden-sided farmhouse. Smoke is rising from the chimneys at either end of the gabled roof. I notice a stable block, a red-painted barn and a cottage. Stiffly I get out of the car. I have made such slow progress from Columbus that it's a wonder there isn't a slimy trail behind me. It's freezing cold: an icy wind cuts my face and I see that I have arrived just in time, because snow from the white-grey sky has begun to settle on the ground.

I'm taking my Samsonite suitcase on wheels out of the boot, my matching flight bag slung across my body, when I'm approached by a man in green overalls carrying a broom, swaddled against the cold.

'What do you want?' he says, his voice muffled by his scarf.

He's obviously a labourer and not privy to the information that I'm expected. 'I'm here to see Wyatt Brown.'

'You a journalist?' he says suspiciously.

'No! I'm Alice Fisher from Carmichael Music,' I say authoritatively. 'I'm a day late but he's expecting me.'

'No he isn't.'

'Yes he is.'

'No he isn't.'

'Oh, for goodness sake.' I unzip my flight bag, reach into my multi-sectioned document folder and pull out Brent's briefing sheet from the 'Wyatt Brown' section. The snow is falling in big, soft flakes. Thank God I'm wearing my Lands' End khaki squall parka (buy two and you qualify for free postage and packing). And then I remember with a sick jolt that I can't actually recall seeing any sentence in Brent's paper that read, 'We have informed Wyatt Brown of your arrival.'

The farm person seems to be able to read my dismayed

expression. 'You best call your office. There's a phone down in the town.'

The snow is settling on the car, my hands are sore from gripping the steering wheel and I have a headache from remembering to drive on the wrong side of the road. More driving is an impossibility.

'Wait! He needs to see me.' I have to impress this idiot farmhand with the importance of my assignment. 'I'm here to produce his next album.'

That shuts him up. 'Album?' he says eventually.

I seize the initiative, assertively signalling my intention to stay by extending the handle of my Samsonite. 'I've come with a raft of ideas. So I think you'll find that he wants to see me.'

There is a very long pause. 'What's this album about then?'

Damn! I search for inspiration as the snow falls. 'The seasons.' We are surrounded by trees and fields. 'Nature.' I look around desperately, 'And barns.'

'Barns?'

'Yes. In all their guises.'

From what I can see of his face, he continues to look unimpressed.

I decide to play for time. 'Look, I'm freezing. If you let me come in I can explain everything.'

'I don't think so.'

Oh God. What can I say? 'Will you please go and tell Wyatt that the boss of the London office sends his regards.'

'The boss?'

I can see from the flicker in his eyes, which is all I can see, actually, that I have his attention. 'Yes. His name's Graham and he's in charge of the London office. Well, he used to be in charge. And I was his right-hand woman. And I know that Graham would be very cross if he knew that I had come all this way and not even met Wyatt. Graham is one of the top one hundred most important people in the music industry,' I say, trying to sound a bit threatening.

He jerks his head at the farmhouse. 'You'd better come in.'

It's worked! This is what is must be like to be Phoebe, scaring people into doing what you want. I follow him, wheeling my suitcase behind me. He takes it from me wordlessly and pushes open the front door.

We step into a spacious high-beamed room with a huge stone fireplace in which a log fire is burning. It's not at all what I'm expecting. There are no empty bottles, pizza boxes or overflowing ashtrays in sight. In fact, it's very clean – the two large windows are spotless and the floors are gleaming, and I speak as something of an expert in the area of domestic hygiene. There is an antique bow and arrow mounted above the fireplace, a state-of-the-art sound system housed in an oak cabinet and photographs of Wyatt with his family and his band. Three huge sofas are arranged at right-angles to each other round the fire, and on the far wall there is an enormous flat-screen television. A golden Labrador is snoozing on a sheepskin dog bed placed to the side of the fire.

There is a smell of apple wood from the fire and beeswax from the wide, dark, polished floorboards. Obviously Wyatt can pay for a housekeeper.

The farm person has pulled off his gloves and unbuttoned his overalls.

'Shouldn't you call Wyatt?' I ask irritably.

He pauses in the middle of unwrapping his scarf and begins hollering up into the rafters. 'Wyatt. Hey! Wyatt.' Then he ambles into the kitchen and I follow him. For a moment I'm nonplussed. It's the kitchen of my dreams.

Granite countertops, an island, two sinks, a six-ring chef's stove, copper pans hanging from one of those rack things and a built-in microwave. But in the midst of this luxury I'm saddened to see that Wyatt has lost the respect of his employees – a common situation amongst alcoholics – because the farmhand is now making a pot of coffee and preparing himself a packet of Quaker instant hot apple oat cereal in the microwave.

I decide to make some light conversation to put him at his ease while we wait for Wyatt. Perhaps he's a little intimidated by me. I expect he has met very few executive women. 'So, are you busy on the farm at the moment?' I ask in a friendly but purposeful manner.

'No.'

Hmm. He's clearly one of those types happiest on his own on a tractor.

'I expect you'll be getting ready for ploughing soon,' I venture.

'No. Ground's frozen.'

'Silage?' I say a little more randomly.

'No. Silage's frozen.'

'Painting the barn?'

'No. Paint's frozen.'

Honestly, if he wasn't a country person unfamiliar with the ways of the world I'd think he was making fun of me.

There's a pause. Then he asks, 'What do you do in London?'

I'm tempted to say that that is none of his business. But I want to put him at his ease. He has probably never left Barnsley, so I decide to answer in terms he can relate to. I slow my voice. 'I work in a big office in the middle of London. I go there on the train. Have you ever been to a big city?'

79

He says nothing, instead taking the bowl out of the micro-wave. Maybe these simple tasks take all his concentration.

'Or do you prefer to stay here on the farm?'

'Yep.'

'Very wise,' I say patronizingly. 'It's easy to get lost in those big airports.'

'So Graham's not there any more?' he asks.

Graham. Oh, I get it. I mentioned that Graham has lost his job and because of his country values he's concerned about this stranger. How noble. Probably this farm life in Barnsley is all he has ever known. I expect there's just a small village school here with all the children taught in one room like *Little House on the Prairie*.

'Graham is very well and happy,' I say. 'He has left his job but he isn't sad. No, he's happy. He will play with his grandchildren.' I remember that he likes animals. 'Perhaps they will get a little puppy. They could call it Max. The children will stroke Max.'

I stop, but there is no response. He hasn't offered me anything to eat or drink – clearly social skills are a bit basic here in Ohio. My hands are tingling and I'm getting a little anxious about frostbite. I push them into my pockets. I search for something to say.

'My name is Alice,' I say. 'What is your name?'

There's a brief hesitation as if he's having trouble recalling his own name.

'Dork.'

Wow. Dork is something of an insult in Britain. Thank goodness he doesn't know that. Fortunately I'm saved from thinking of a response to this because the Labrador, pre-sumably alerted by the sound of the microwave pinging, has joined us in the kitchen and is nuzzling Dork the farmhand. Is this the attention-seeking behaviour of a neglected animal?

I guess it's a long time since Wyatt has taken that poor creature for a walk or played ball with him. I resolve there and then to love the dog back to emotional wellness.

Still there is no sound from upstairs. It doesn't look promising. I may as well try to get some background information. 'Is he sleeping it off?'

He still has his back to me. 'Sleeping what off?'

I must not be afraid to speak the unpalatable truth. 'The alcohol,' I proclaim loudly.

(*Enable YOU* is very keen on saying the word *alcohol* as much as possible. 'When the alcoholic in your life says that he is 'quenching his thirst' or 'having a tipple', gently but firmly correct him. 'No, you are taking a drink of alcohol.')

'Does he drink?' he says flatly.

I must not expect too much of him. 'Look, Dork, I know that you probably want to protect Wyatt. But I'm here to help,' I say firmly. 'Denial of the problem will only worsen the situation.'

'The situation,' he says blankly.

'His issues with alcohol,' I hiss. 'Not to mention the hidden cross-addictions that probably exist as well.' I've read *Enable YOU* twice so I'm pretty knowledgeable about all this. 'Cigarettes, gambling, food ...'

'Food,' he interrupts me. 'You mean Quaker hot apple oat cereal could be a problem?' He looks askance at the bowl as he takes it out of the microwave.

I'm beginning to lose patience. 'I'm sure Quaker hot apple oat cereal isn't a problem.'

'How can you be sure? What if he had to have it?' He reaches into the drawer for a spoon. 'What if he was eating it secretly? What if he knocked back a six-packet of oat cereal a day?'

Why is Dork suddenly so articulate? How did he know

where to find that spoon? Who exactly is Dork?

'Between you and me,' he says, turning round, 'I've heard he's hopelessly addicted to breakfast cereal.'

And it's then, in the bright halogen light of the kitchen, that I finally realize to whom I'm speaking.

CHAPTER 12

Wyatt stands staring at me. I'm still sitting on one of his kitchen chairs. I can't get up and run screaming from the kitchen, much as I want to, because my legs would give out. My mouth is dry, a massive red blush has spread across both my cheeks and I'm feeling really sick. I can't hold Wyatt's eye. Instead I sneak a peek in Wyatt's direction. Then I see the expression on his face and hastily look away. So now I'm staring intently at the bottom of a copper frying pan. It's very clean and shiny.

'What the hell are you doing here?' he says eventually, and believe me, his tone is far from conversational. But I'm so mortified I cannot reply. Even Dr Vaizey couldn't help me now. Instead I pick at the toggle of my parka and try to keep breathing. I watch as Wyatt takes off his farm labourer's garb and throws it on a chair.

It's quite clear to me that Wyatt is stone-cold sober. He's also clean-shaven, properly dressed in Wranglers and a dark grey work shirt and not in possession of a firearm. His mouth is set in a hard line and he looks really, really pissed off. He looks a bit like Bruce Willis before he's about to kill the baddie. But he's not bald: he has thick, longish brown hair that looks as though it hasn't been combed for a while, weather-beaten skin that looks tanned even in the winter, a hint of stubble and dark brown eyes that are glaring at me.

'How do I even know you're from Carmichael?' he says, leaning back against the kitchen counter with his arms folded.

Oh hell, he's going to phone them. I can imagine Phoebe's response. It will be short and crisp. 'Wyatt, I'm so sorry. Hand Alice the phone. Alice, you're fired.'

Then I have a brainwave. 'I've got my London office ID card,' I say quickly. 'I begin rummaging in my flight bag, which fortunately I still have strapped across my body. 'Here.'

I hold it out to him. After a pause that seems to last for ever, probably because I'm holding my breath, he comes and takes it from me. He looks at the photo – it's the same as the one on my personnel file, the good one – and then gives me the identical look Phoebe gave me. *Are you this person or a new Muppet character?* I should mention here that the snow has made my perm even springier.

He hands it back to me. 'You've had a wasted trip. If you'd called first, you could have saved yourself the journey.'

'But I thought they had called,' I protest. To hell with corporate loyalty; I'm desperate to save my own skin here.

'They?'

'Phoebe Carmichael's assistant Brent. I assumed you knew I was coming.'

'No,' he says flatly, 'and if you thought you could doorstep me, you're wrong.' It's obvious from his sceptical expression that he doesn't believe a word I'm saying.

'I didn't think that!'

He appears not to have heard me. 'I've made it clear to Carmichael I'm not recording. They know I'm not interested.'

I'm not in a strong position to argue with this. I've broken the first rule of the successful music producer – correctly identify your artist. There is a long pause while I think of another approach.

I know! Let's move it away from the personal. 'Do you have any thoughts about your contract?' I say conversationally.

He looks even more pissed off. 'So you think you can quote my contract at me to force me to record?'

'No.'

'Yes, you think you can come in here and strong-arm me. My God, you people,' he interrupts me. 'If you want to talk contracts, fine,' he spits out. 'I'll give you my lawyer's number.'

No, no, no. I don't want to talk to Wyatt's lawyer because he will definitely be even worse than Wyatt. Oh my God, if I'm not careful I will soon have embroiled Carmichael Music in a multi million-dollar lawsuit. Phoebe will be forced to make a statement on the steps of the US Supreme Court shortly before Carmichael Music Inc. declares bankruptcy. 'Alice Fisher was acting alone and without the authority of Carmichael Music. She is what is termed a rogue PA and has been eliminated.'

I think desperately. I have to try to redeem this situation somehow.

'Look. I'm sorry if I surprised you.' I must make him realize that I'm not trying to threaten him with his contract. 'And I'm deeply sorry if anything I have said has caused offence.'

'You mean about the drinking,' he says incredulously. 'You think you can breeze in here, accuse me of God knows what, then say sorry and that's OK?'

'No, I didn't mean the drinking. I meant the contract.'

But he's off now. 'My private life is none of your goddamn business. I'm clean, I'm sober and I don't need advice from you on how to stay that way. And I don't smoke,' he adds snippily.

'I really didn't mean about the drinking.'

'Well, you had plenty to say about it before,' he barks.

'I was only trying to help,' I squeak.

He gives a humourless laugh. 'No offence, but I think I'll struggle on on my own.'

Is there anything I can say that will calm him down a bit? He's glaring at me now, still with his arms folded, and it occurs to me that at over six feet, with a farm labourer's build, it was a reasonable mistake on my part.

'Look, I didn't realize that it was you.'

'Really? You thought that I'd open the door and invite a complete stranger in? Have you any idea how much hassle I get from journalists?'

'I'm sure,' I say, now thinking it best to agree with everything he says.

'Then you'll appreciate that I have to be careful.'

If being careful means impersonating a farmhand called Dork, then personally I would just install an entryphone system. But this is not the time to enter into that debate.

'Fine,' I say, 'but now that I'm here, we might as well discuss the Carmichael proposal.' Calling it a proposal is a bit of an exaggeration: it's some notes I jotted down in the Columbus airport Budget-Beater Motel about how Wyatt and I would proceed:

Write song
Write tune
Practise song and tune together
Add more instruments

86

But Wyatt just shakes his head. 'No way. I don't want to write, I don't want to record and I don't want to tour.'

I wonder if this leaves me any room for manoeuvre. I have to come away with something to report to Phoebe.

'How about some informal jamming?' I say brightly.

'What?'

'Or a reissue of some old material. Donny Osmond has had a lot of success with that.'

He seems stumped for a moment. Maybe I've stopped him in his tracks. He unfolds his arms. 'We're finished.'

He strides out into the hall and I hear the sound of the front door opening. I hurry out after him.

'Look, I think we've got off to a bad start here,' I say with exaggerated reasonableness.

'Start?' he repeats in a who-are-you-kidding voice. 'I've given you all the time I've got.'

'Will you at least let me tell you what Carmichael Music think about you and your wonderful music,' I say earnestly, as the snow blows in. I feel bad about the polished wood floor getting wet, but this is my last, all-or-nothing chance to save my job. 'Let me assure you how committed Carmichael are to your career.'

'I'm not interested.'

'The whole company is dedicated to your success.'

'I'm not interested.'

'You are the lynchpin of our entire ten-year worldwide plan,' I say, making it up as I go along.

He just looks bored. Meanwhile, the snow is blowing in and forming little melted puddles on the floor. Oh hell. As you can imagine, my anxiety levels are off the scale right now, and seeing that water melt around me is unbearable. I can't help myself. 'You need to close the door,' I say urgently, 'or you could get indelible water marks on your floor.'

For a moment he's struck dumb. 'Indelible water marks?' he repeats, confused.

'Hmm.' I point at the puddles one by one. 'Unless it's sealed, in which case it will be OK and I could just wipe it dry with some paper towel.' That would make me feel a bit better, I know it. 'I saw you had some in the kitchen.'

He looks at me as if I'm a lunatic. 'Lady, we're done here.'

'But I've flown all the way from England to speak to you!' I cry out.

'That's not my problem.' There's a pause. 'I'll put your suitcase in the car for you.'

Something finally snaps. I know I've screwed this up about as thoroughly as it's possible to do. I know I've handled this meeting so badly that I will never be able to work in the music industry again. I know that my relationship with Teresa will be defined by this moment for the rest of my life. It will be the same story at every family gathering for the next forty years. 'Alice, do tell us about that time you worked in America for a day.'

But I'm damned if he's going to escort me to my car.

'No thank you,' I say. 'I can manage.'

For a millisecond there is just a flicker of surprise across his face. Then it's gone. 'Suit yourself.'

'I will.' I want to sound proudly defiant, but it comes out sounding like a five-year-old.

Then there is nothing for it but to extend my Samsonite handle, step out on to the snowy drive and slide to my car, to the sound of Wyatt's front door slamming.

CHAPTER 13

Outside, the sky is grey, the air is thick with snow and a blizzard is howling. As I look out across the bare fields, it's like a setting from a really depressing Russian novel, and like most Russian fictional heroines, I have lost the will to live. Right now, as I drive and skid down Wyatt Brown's driveway, death from hypothermia in a snowbound Ford Focus seems a reasonable option. I have a pen and paper with me, so I'll be fine. I'll tell Dad that I love him, Teresa that I forgive her and Stephen that he can sell all my stuff on eBay. Then I will recline my seat and die in Ohio, the Siberia of the USA.

I make it down the driveway and about half a mile down the road before pulling in to do some emergency meditation. The snow is falling so thickly now that it's like a sheet. I search in my bag for my lavender oil and apply it to my temples and take my 'soul music' CD out of my flight bag, a soothing medley of plink-plonk piano, running water and pan pipes. It sounds as if it's been recorded in someone's garage. Then I close my eyes and begin assertively to repeat to myself, 'I am a strong and confident executive woman. Whatever happens, I'll handle it.' I repeat it twice, then I burst into tears.

How has it come to this? How did my dreams of a new

life come to such a swift and bitter end – and what will become of me now? I'm a failure. Dr Vaizey liked to talk to us about the role played in our decision-making by our critical inner voice. Right now, as I weep piteously by the side of the road, mine is enthusiastically reciting a catalogue of my past failings.

Part of sheep in nursery school nativity play: fell over.

Windsurfing in the canaries aged nineteen: could not even pull up sail.

Strappy sandals which women's magazines say are a summer essential purchase: feet always splay out at sides.

Salsa dancing class at Kingston Sports Centre: who were you kidding?

Maybe you could go back to the Council and beg to get your old job back, my critical inner voice concludes with a sigh.

I'm all cried out after ten minutes, so I blow my nose and turn off the soul music, which I think is making my depression worse. It occurs to me that if I sit here much longer, I will get snowed in and actually die here. At this I feel my survival instincts kick in. I decide that I definitely don't want to die, and I'm beginning to panic a bit. So I take a deep breath, tell my critical inner child to go away, and do what I find most helpful when I'm feeling particularly anxious. I ask myself the following question: *In this situation, what would Dr Vaizey do?*

Oh, all right, I did have a bit of a crush on him, but not as embarrassingly as Zara, who once knitted him a scarf. 'I cannot accept your gift, Zara,' he said assertively. 'It would be inappropriate.' My heart skipped a beat when he said that. He was so confident and in control. Zara sniffed and put it back in her ancient Harrods carrier bag, as if bringing it in that would impress him!

Dr Vaizey wears brown brogues, thick navy cords and cream checked Viyella shirts. I'm sure he's privately educated. He's what Dad would call very well spoken. We knew nothing at all about him; he was very professional like that. I decided he lives in a flat in Chelsea, spends most evenings reading and listening to opera, and despairs of ever finding the right woman – a woman who would support him both emotionally and secretarially. Jennifer thinks he must be married to a gorgeous nurse, one of those blonde, busty types. I'm sure that's not right.

Anyway, Dr Vaizey used to tell us to do what was in front of us rather than worrying about the future implications of our decision for our lives in twenty years' time. I close my eyes and focus until I hear Dr Vaizey's voice. Yes, I have it. 'Take proactive action to safeguard your employment. Then drive to a place of safety and seek medical attention.' I know I shouldn't, but I keep my eyes closed. 'I always looked upon you differently from the other patients, Alice,' Dr Vaizey continues. 'You were special. And now that you're not in my group, I'm at liberty to ask you to come and have dinner with me at my flat in Chelsea. As well as being a successful doctor with a flourishing private practice, I'm also the beneficiary of a family trust, so it's spacious and tastefully furnished with a newly fitted kitchen. I have been alone for far too long.'

Reluctantly I open my eyes and bring myself back to the present. If I go into the dinner-date daydream, I could be here for a very long time. With Dr Vaizey next to me, I feel renewed. I pull out my BlackBerry and follow Brent's instructions to email admin@carmichaelmusicny.com in case of any problems. It takes me ten minutes to painstakingly compose a grammatically correct email with a somewhat edited version of today's events, in which I comprehensively stated the position of Carmichael Music and Wyatt foolishly turned down my offer. Next I decide to go back to Columbus, book into somewhere other than the Budget-Beater Motel and take an Ativan, which will have to do for the seeking-medical-attention side of things.

As I set off again, I'm feeling a little better. To be on the safe side, I've switched on all my lights, including the blinking hazard lights. Now I come to think of it, there's a small glimmer of hope that Wyatt might not ring Phoebe: he doesn't give the impression of being the most communicative person. He seems more the sort to sit down at the kitchen table and brood in silence for a couple of hours before striding out on a long, windswept walk across the frozen wastes.

But then the thought of Wyatt brings vividly to mind a whole series of unbearable images and I start feeling worse again. Each image is more horrifying than the last: there is the part where I said 'alcohol' really loudly, the bit where I invented Max the puppy, and last but not least the bit when I lowered my voice in a really friendly way and said, 'Look, Dork ...' I try to erase these images, they are too excruciating; but I know that they will be there for ever, like an indelible water mark, ready to haunt me in the early hours of the morning. They are too shameful ever to share. Only Wyatt and I will know – until he writes his autobiography! Oh my God.

I've had some pretty funny encounters in my time. Rodeo bulls, wild women and howling coyotes, to name but a few. But I ain't never met a woman like that crazy, crazy gal Alice Fisher from Carmichael Music. Let me tell you what happened one snowy day in Barnsley, Ohio ...'

Teresa will buy everyone in the family a copy and read it out during Christmas Dinner.

> No offence, but she was some nutty-looking girl. I've seen bears with better haircuts. I didn't know whether to make her a cup of coffee or take down my bow and arrow ...

I'm making slow but steady progress – they salt the roads here before it snows, which is a good idea – when I see the lights of a police car ahead of me. A man in a sheriff's uniform is waving his arms for me to stop at the crossroads where I need to turn to get back on to the motorway. As I come to a very slow halt, he shuffles over and I wind down the window.

'The interstate's closed, ma'am.'

'But I have a flight to catch!'

I don't, but I have a great desire to get away from Barnsley. Who knows, if Wyatt doesn't call Phoebe and I can get to the New York office, I might be able to live there unnoticed for the next six months.

The police officer shakes his head. 'Blizzard. You won't be getting to the airport today. Maybe not for a week.' He peers at me. 'Where are you from?'

'England.'

He looks pleased with himself. 'Nearly! I would have said you were Australian.'

I'm about to tell him stiffly that Australia is a former British colony on the other side of the world when I catch sight of the gun attached to his belt. 'It's all the same really,' I agree.

He leans against the car. 'My wife loves England. We went once for her cousin's wedding. Cup of tea!' he chortles in a terrible cockney accent.

'So where can I stay?'

'Pint of bitter! Cream tea!' He laughs to himself for a bit, then looks puzzled. 'What are you doing in Barnsley?'

'I've been to see Wyatt Brown.'

'Up at the Buckle and Braid?' He jerks his head behind us. Of course, Barnsley is one of those places where everyone knows everyone else's business and no one locks their doors. 'Wyatt's all right, but you don't want to get on the wrong side of him.'

You don't say. 'Is there a hotel I can stay at?' I ask, keen to change the subject.

'Hotel? In Barnsley?' he says as if I had asked for the Ritz. 'There's a bed and breakfast. Your best bet's to go to the Blue Ribbon and ask for directions.' He points down the road. 'Five minutes, you can't miss it.' He rubs his chin, seemingly oblivious to the biting wind and snow that is falling on me through the open window. 'We went to Leicester. Let me see if I can remember the name of the wife's cousin.' He pauses and looks at me as if he's doing me a favour. Then his expression lights up. 'I've got it! Bernie Smith. That's his name. Bernie and Maureen. I don't suppose you know them,' he asks hopefully.

I say nothing for a moment as if to consider this, then say regretfully, 'Afraid not.'

'Wait a minute. I'll put up my sign then I'll escort you to Barnsley. I'm Billy, by the way. Everyone calls me Sheriff Billy.'

I wait as he puts up a Road Closed sign at the crossroads. Then he signals to me to follow him, all lights blazing, and we proceed to Barnsley. It's not ideal, but I'm going to go with the flow. Dr Vaizey was always telling us to let go and enjoy the journey. Right now I don't have much choice. At least, I console myself, I will never have to see Wyatt again.

94

I'm driving further and further away from the Buckle and Braid farm, and if I'm lucky it won't be more than a day until I'm out of this place.

CHAPTER 14

I'm too worried about driving into the back of Sheriff Billy to notice much about the journey into Barnsley. Out of the corner of my eye I glimpse more fields and neat houses spaced every quarter-mile or so, most with a flagpole in the front garden. As we drive into the town itself we pass a white-painted church, and a little further on a giant sign saying 'Home of Barnsley High School. Ohio State Bowling Champions.'

We turn into a small town square with a statue in the middle. The shops are neat brick, and although it's only midday, all the lights are on, burning yellow through the thick falling snow. There is a general store and post office, a drugstore, a doughnut shop and an old-fashioned barber shop with a red and white pole outside.

Sheriff Billy parks in front of a glass-fronted restaurant with half-height blue gingham curtains hanging in the two plate-glass windows. 'The Blue Ribbon Diner' is painted in an arc on each window. Above the door is a lit-up sign in the shape of a blue rosette. I skid to a halt beside him. In England the roads would be deserted by now, but here everyone seems to carry on regardless of the weather.

'No need to lock it,' he laughs, seeing me fumble with my key fob.

We hurry in, Sheriff Billy taking off his hat as he enters the door. It chimes, thanks to the large cow-bell tied to the top.

Inside there is a long counter, behind which two white-aproned cooks are grilling bacon, tossing pancakes and joking with the customers who are seated on tall stools at the counter, which is set with cakes and pies under glass-domed cake stands. Two rows of booths with navy-blue vinyl seats run down the other side of the room.

Sheriff Billy calls out. 'Celeste!'

A pin-thin waitress in a frilly apron and bright red lipstick hurries up.

'This is my wife Celeste,' he says, pecking her on the cheek.

She beams at me. 'You're very welcome, hon. Cup of coffee?'

She doesn't wait to hear my reply. I hope it's not too strong. I can get a little overwrought if I have too much.

Then Sheriff Billy goes over to the door, reaches up and takes hold of the cow-bell. In a fraction of a second I have a hideous premonition of what may follow. It does.

Clang, clang, clang goes the cow-bell. Everyone turns to stare at me.

'Hey!' Sheriff Billy calls out. He points at me. 'This young lady's come all the way from England to visit with us at the Blue Ribbon.'

He turns to me. 'What's your name, honey?'

'Alice,' I mumble.

'Alan,' he shouts out. It's awful. The customers do a sort of communal wave. This must be what it's like to be Madonna.

Sheriff Billy looks thoughtful. 'That's interesting. In America, Alan's a guy's name.'

97

'Yes,' I begin to explain, 'it is in England, too,'

But he's not listening because he's already headed off towards the counter. 'I'll introduce you,' he calls back to me.

Then we're off.

'This is Jim. He owns the bowling alley.

'This is Paul. He's your man for any termite problems.' There's no time to ask what a termite problem is.

'And this is Gerry.' Sheriff Billy doesn't say what Gerry does, and by the look of him I think he may not need to work. He's wearing an expensive-looking brown leather jacket and I notice his car keys on the counter have a Mercedes key fob. He has swept-back straw-coloured hair and very intense blue eyes. He shakes my hand, holding mine for a little too long. 'How you doing, Alan?'

'Alice.'

'Alice,' he repeats slowly, holding my eye.

He really is very good-looking. But the moment is broken by Sheriff Billy. 'Break it up, you two!'

We meet the cooks, Nancy and Dolores, then start down the centre aisle of the two rows of booths, stopping to say hello to every one of the lunchtime customers: farmer types in overalls, two elderly blue-rinse ladies and the four members of the Scott County Road Maintenance crew, one of whom winks at me in a rather overfamiliar manner. 'The Trail Tavern's got karaoke tonight.'

Everyone loves my accent and wants to visit England. All I want is to be alone, and I'm relieved to see, as we near the end of our walkabout, that at the far end of the diner there are two empty booths. I need to collect my thoughts – none of us anxious types is good at meeting new people.

But Sheriff Billy has stopped by a booth occupied by a young mother and her crying baby. 'Alan, I expect you want some company. This is Rachel and this is Baby Dale.' Then he turns to an older man in the booth opposite. 'And this is Mr Horner, our retired high-school principal.'

Mr Horner is the only person in the diner wearing a jacket and tie: tweed jacket, knitted tie. He looks up from reading the back page of the *Barnsley Messenger*. 'Good-day.'

I've barely sat down before Rachel starts talking. 'Delighted to meet you, Alan.'

'Actually, it's Alice,' I say, but she can't hear me because Baby Dale has started bawling even louder.

We are interrupted by Celeste, who has come to take my order. I start to read the menu, but Celeste, who clearly doesn't have time for ditherers, makes up my mind for me. 'I'd recommend the Farmer's All-Day Breakfast.'

Dale's crying has gathered pace and Rachel is jigging him up and down just like Carolyn does with Maisie. Dale looks about the same size as Maisie. And Rachel has that distracted new-mother look that Carolyn gets when Maisie isn't doing what the baby book says she should. Rachel has thick auburn hair tied back in a schoolgirl ponytail, and she's wearing a white turtle-neck under what I recognize instantly as a Lands' End half-zip fleece in poppy red. She's obviously a very nice person.

'Four months?' I guess.

'Yep.' She frowns. 'He's very fussy today.'

Dale is crying just like Maisie, too.

'Maybe he's got wind,' I suggest.

Rachel looks doubtful. But she lifts Dale up to her shoulder and a few seconds later he gives a huge burp.

Rachel's expression brightens. 'You've got a gift for babies.'

Celeste arrives with the coffee I haven't ordered.

'She's got a gift with babies,' Rachel says to Celeste.

'They call me the Southfields Baby Whisperer,' I joke.

'Really?' they chorus.

'No,' I say, but Celeste has already turned to the retired high-school principal Mr Horner. 'She's called the Southfields Baby Whisperer.'

'Oh. Don't you have a book?' Then Mr Horner sighs. 'Or these days would that be a television show?' Mr Horner speaks the universal language of headmasters all over the world – carefully articulating every disapproving syllable.

Rachel looks up from ransacking her baby bag for a muslin square. 'A television show!' Rachel clearly doesn't get out much, because she's desperate to talk. 'I bet you have such a glamorous life.' She looks puzzled. 'So what are you doing in Barnsley?'

'Research,' I say non-committally. I have no intention of bringing up the subject of Wyatt and my humiliating encounter.

'For your programme,' she says. 'Do you know that Supernanny, then?'

'No, I don't actually have a—'

'Have you ever met the Queen?'

'No. And I don't—'

'Simon Cowell?'

She's unstoppable.

I can't help but boast a bit here. Last year Graham took Lisa, the receptionist, and me to the drinks party before the Brit Awards. 'I met him once at an awards ceremony. He's very nice in real life.'

Rachel calls out to the old ladies. 'Alan says Simon Cowell's very nice in real life.'

Mr Horner looks up. 'I gather Simon Cowell's quite a cultural icon amongst the young.' He wipes his mouth primly with his napkin. 'Rumour has it that they're proposing a "Barnsley Idol" competition at this year's town festival.'

'Town festival?' I repeat.

'It's like a fair,' Rachel explains. 'All the towns have one. Every festival has a theme.' She begins reeling off a list. 'Enon has apples, Fairborn has sweetcorn. And Barnsley has the cupcake.'

'Cupcake?'

'We used to celebrate the soybean,' Mr Horner explains. 'But despite our best efforts and the introduction of a Bean Queen beauty pageant, attendance was disappointing. So we changed it to cupcakes five years ago.'

'Now it's one of the biggest fairs in the county,' Rachel says. 'You ought to come back for it. It's in September.'

I don't want to disappoint Rachel by telling her that I will be in London or New York by then.

The diner is now close to full, the floor wet from melted snow and the windows steamed up. It's impossible not to unwind a little amid the aroma of coffee, the laughter of Celeste and the door with its cow-bell ringing out. I have my back to the door with a view of the far wall, which is decorated with dried-flower wreaths, photographs of prize-winning cows and jokey hand-painted signs: *In 1892 on this spot nothing happened.*

Celeste arrives with my Farmer's All-Day Breakfast. There are three enormous pancakes surrounded by bacon, sausages, hash browns and a pile of toast.

'Alan's friends with Simon Cowell,' Rachel informs Celeste.

'We used to get all the celebrities coming in here when Wyatt was singing,' says Celeste, exchanging glances with Rachel. 'They needed a good square meal after the shenanigans at those parties.'

Rachel rolls her eyes. 'A zillion years ago.'

'That young man needs to get back in the recording

studio,' comments Mr Horner. 'Hard work never hurt anyone.'

I guess that Mr Horner was once Wyatt's teacher. I think about asking more, but I'm sure that the warm-hearted people of this small hamlet will be loyally protective of Wyatt's privacy.

'Stupid fool,' says Celeste, refilling my cup. 'Shutting himself up there at the Buckle and Braid.'

'We've all tried to persuade him to sing again,' says Rachel. 'But he's stubborn as a mule.'

For a moment Rachel is lost in silent thought. But only until her eye falls on my £99.99 zirconia and fake sapphire ring. 'Ooh, look at that ring. That's lovely.'

She turns to Mr Horner. 'That's how they do it over in Europe. I remember that from when we went to Paris with the school. They wear their rings on the wrong hand. When are you getting married?'

I feel obliged not to disappoint Rachel, which means I cannot tell her the truth – that I bought it for myself at the airport because my boyfriend didn't propose. And since I'm never going to see her or this town after the snow thaws, how much does it really matter? 'We haven't set a date,' I say which, strictly speaking, is true.

'A long engagement, then. Very traditional,' she says approvingly. 'What does he do?'

'He's a lawyer.'

Rachel looks impressed. She looks at me eagerly, clearly wanting more information.

'He's something of a leading light in the world of restrict-ive covenants,' I continue, taking a bite of my toast in order to play for time.

'Yes …'

I finish chewing very slowly. 'And next month he's a panel

member at the afternoon session of the Law Society's One-Day Agricultural Law Conference in Manchester.'

'Manchester,' Rachel repeats.

But I'm saved from further elaboration by Celeste arriving. She looks at my plate worriedly. 'Is everything all right?'

'Yes. Delicious.'

'You've hardly eaten anything,' she says accusingly.

I have eaten quite a bit; I just haven't made much of an impact.

Something catches Celeste's eye out of the window. 'Watch out,' she says under her breath to Rachel, jerking her head towards the window. 'The Queen Bee's parking her car.'

'Heidi,' Rachel says glumly. 'Don't worry. She'll be nice to you.'

I force myself not to turn round at the clang of the door opening. Besides, I'm worried about offending Celeste, Nancy and Dolores by not eating enough, so I set to work on my pancakes.

'Heidi and I were at school together,' Rachel whispers, but there's no time for her to tell me more before an elegant figure appears at our table dressed in a body-hugging white ski-jacket, elegant wool skirt and black leather boots. Heidi has shoulder-length blonde hair which is carefully curled up at the ends, her foundation is perfect and she's wearing tons of pink lipgloss.

Rachel introduces us just as I swallow a huge chunk of pancake. Heidi shoots me a broad smile.

'How terrible for you being stuck here. They say the blizzard's going to get worse. We've just closed the school for the afternoon so the children can get home.'

'Heidi teaches English at the high school,' Rachel explains.

Heidi has begun cooing at Baby Dale. 'Such a big boy, aren't you, Dale!' She glances at Rachel. 'You're making such progress getting rid of the baby weight, Rachel. Only a few more stubborn pounds to go.'

It's odd, but though I've only just met Heidi, she seems strangely familiar.

But there's no time to ponder this, because the door opens and shuts with a bang. I notice Heidi glance up and touch her hair self-consciously. Rachel waves and Mr Horner looks up from his newspaper.

'It's my brother,' says Rachel. 'He usually comes in about now.'

I'm tackling a second mouthful of pancake when Wyatt walks up to our table.

Rachel babbles excitedly. 'Wyatt, this is Alan from London, England. She's called the Southfields Baby Whisperer. She's got her own TV show. And she's engaged to a top international attorney.'

Wyatt looks at me quizzically, absorbing everything Rachel has just said. 'Alan?'

I have to finish eating. 'It's a nickname,' I explain eventually, staring at the table. I cannot believe that barely an hour after fleeing the most humiliating encounter of my life, I'm face to face with the man I once called Dork.

Rachel looks at Wyatt proudly. 'This is my brother Wyatt.' She looks from me to him. 'You two have so much in common. Wyatt's been all over the world.'

'Yes,' he says evenly, 'as long as I don't get lost in those big airports.'

Suddenly I've lost my appetite. I push my plate away. Right, I'm going to stay silent. That way nothing else can go wrong.

Heidi moves over and stands close to Wyatt. 'I'm sure you've got lots of interesting stories about England, Alice.'

She looks me up and down. 'I thought everyone from London was very fashionable?'

Rachel looks daggers at her. 'So where are you staying, Alice?'

I have no choice but to reply. 'At the bed and breakfast,' I say quickly. I'm keen to get out of here as soon as possible. I reach for my parka and begin pulling it on.

Rachel frowns. 'I've got a much better idea. Alan can stay at the guest cottage,' she says enthusiastically.

What guest cottage?

She turns to Wyatt. 'Alan can stay at your cottage.'

Whose guest cottage?

'Is that a good idea?' Heidi cuts in, sounding very concerned about my welfare. 'It hasn't been used for years.'

'It'll be perfect,' Rachel says. 'It just needs a bit of a clean-up.'

She looks at Wyatt, who has pointedly said nothing. I relax: there's no way he's going to let me go back with him to the Buckle & Braid.

Then I hear another voice. 'Is there anything I can do to help?' It's Gerry, the Mercedes man in the brown leather jacket. 'Why don't you come back to my family's place, Alice? I can make you very comfortable.'

'That won't be necessary,' says Wyatt a little sharply, and I see the two of them lock eyes for a moment. 'I'll drive her to the b—'

But before Wyatt can say any more he's interrupted. 'Splendid!' It's Mr Horner. 'Well done, Wyatt. You'll drive her to the Buckle and Braid, then.' He stands up, takes his newspaper and carefully folds it. 'This lady has travelled here all the way from England.' He turns to me, putting on a fur hat with ear flaps. 'As if we would send you to a bed and breakfast. No, we weren't raised that way in Barnsley,

Ohio. Wyatt here will take you back to his home and treat you like royalty. English royalty,' he chuckles to himself. He turns to Wyatt. 'That's settled, then.'

Wyatt says nothing and then, eventually, given that everyone in the diner is now looking at him, gives the briefest nod.

Mr Horner touches his hat. 'Good-day to you all.'

'Good-day,' we chorus.

I look at the group: Gerry grins at me, Rachel seems delighted, Heidi looks a little put out and Wyatt's expression is impossible to read.

CHAPTER 15

'I would like to go to the bed and breakfast,' I say firmly. Wyatt and I are standing in the icy cold outside the Blue Ribbon.

Wyatt looks at me. 'Yeah. But I have my orders.'

'You mean Mr Horner,' I say.

'That's how it works round here. We're hospitable,' he says coldly.

Wyatt looks at my Ford Focus, which is the smallest car in the town square. 'The ground's freezing over. Let's take the Chevy. You can come back for it when the snow thaws.'

Before I have a chance to object, he has taken my suitcase out of the car and thrown it in the back of the truck, where it lands in a pile of snow and hay bales.

'Excuse me ...' I protest, but he's already gone round to the driver's side, leaving me to open the passenger door and climb in. The Labrador is in the back, and when I get in he tries to snuggle on to my lap. Wyatt pushes him back gently.

'Get back, Travis. He thinks you're in his place,' says Wyatt in a tone that implies Travis is right about that.

Wyatt starts the engine. Clearly he has no intention of making conversation, because he turns on the radio, which is tuned to a station called Scott County Country. The announcer promises us 'forty minutes of non-stop country –

new hits and all your old favourites with no dirty talk'. Travis is nudging my shoulder and I'm rubbing his ears. I wonder what it must be like to hear your own voice over the radio, and for a moment I contemplate asking Wyatt before deciding that I've said enough today without asking him saddo questions that he's been asked a million times before.

Besides, Wyatt is concentrating on driving as we plough through the snow. I've noticed that most people round here drive pick-up trucks, except for the old ladies who drive big old Cadillacs, and the children who ride around in bright yellow school buses.

The man on the radio is singing about working as a farmhand for a young widow woman and what happens after dark when the thunder roars. But it's all very tastefully done.

We turn into the driveway down which I careered just a few hours earlier to make my escape from Barnsley. Ahead of us is a small figure trudging through the snow.

'Casey,' says Wyatt. He slows down and draws level, winding down the window. 'In you get.'

Casey climbs in the back. 'This is Alice,' says Wyatt. 'She's from England. She's staying for one night.'

'Pleased to meet you, ma'am,' says Casey, taking off a man's leather glove to shake my hand. He's sweet, I guess about twelve years old, green-eyed and freckled, muffled up to his eyeballs in a red hand-knitted scarf and a coat that's two sizes too big for him.

'You have Friesians in England, don't you?' says Casey. 'And Jerseys. I've seen pictures.' And then he's off. 'I keep my cow in Wyatt's barn. Her name's Mary Lou. I live at the next-door farm. We used to have a huge herd but they got sold. My Grandpa makes the best corn maze in Ohio.'

I'm trying to work this out. Is Mary Lou a pet? Is a corn maze what I think it is?

'Mary Lou's a prize-winner,' says Casey proudly. 'She won Champion Dairy Cow at the Scott County Show last year. Mary Lou likes going to shows, she's ace in the ring. She really enjoys it. Next year she could go to the Ohio State Show.'

Before Casey can say more, we pull up at Wyatt's yard. 'Are you going to come and see her?' asks Casey breathlessly.

'Later,' cuts in Wyatt.

At this, Casey jumps straight out and heads for the barn.

'There's new straw in there,' Wyatt shouts after him. 'I picked it up this morning.'

'Thanks,' yells Casey. 'See you later, Miss Alice,' he shouts over his shoulder, hurrying towards the red-painted barn.

Wyatt takes my case and we make our way through the snow to the guest cottage.

'It's been a while since anyone's stayed here,' says Wyatt, pushing open the door.

We have stepped into a neat living room with two small red-checked sofas, some woven rugs and a small fireplace with an empty log basket to one side. Immediately I notice that all the antique oak furniture is covered with a layer of dust. A large cobweb is laced around the brass ceiling-light, and when I go over to check I see that there are ashes in the fireplace.

'Don't you ever clean in here?' I say before I can stop myself.

'No one stays here any more,' Wyatt says, and for the first time since we met he sounds a bit defensive. 'It just needs a bit of a dust.'

'It needs a deep-clean,' I retort crossly. 'I'll need a dust-pan and brush, dusters, all-purpose polish and plenty of disinfectant spray,' I say commandingly as I size up the task. There's a curved wooden staircase leading up to a galleried bedroom above us with a wood-framed double bed covered with a patchwork quilt of reds, whites and blues. But this is no time to admire the interior decor. 'Plus fresh bedding and some Windolene wipes for the windows.'

'Will Windex do?' Wyatt says, a trifle taken aback.

'As long as it's brand-name,' I say crisply.

'Anything else?' he says sarcastically.

'A Swiffer if you have one.'

He opens his mouth and then closes it again.

I go through the open brick archway to the kitchen. I encounter a dust-strewn pine table, counters and a sink that hasn't been bleached in years.

'I need to get started,' I say, taking off my parka and rolling up my sleeves, which I then regret because it's pretty cold in here.

Fortunately Wyatt is fiddling with the thermostat, and after a few seconds there's the welcome sound of the heating coming to life.

Wyatt hesitates. 'You really don't need to clean,' he says. Gosh, he actually sounds a little bit apologetic.

'I think I do,' I say briskly. 'If you could just get me those cleaning supplies.'

'Right.' He heads for the door.

'Don't forget the vacuum cleaner,' I call after him.

By the time Wyatt returns I've already started on the living room. The kitchen would be the logical place to start, I know, but I'm waiting for hot water. Instead I give the rugs a good shake-out and make a pile of old newspapers and magazines.

'I think this is everything you asked for,' he says, setting down a box on the floor together with a top-of-the-range

Dyson vacuum cleaner. How exciting! I've always wanted to use one of those.

I look in the box. Oh my goodness! They have Pledge multisurface polish in the USA. And Swiffers. This just keeps getting better. The Pledge is multisurface orange-scented, my favourite. I get to work spraying and dusting the furniture. Oh yes, I feel like a new woman. Wyatt disappears out of the door and I don't imagine I'll see him again. He's sure to avoid me for the rest of my short stay. With a bit of luck I'll get going in the morning without even having to see him.

By the time I've done the windows, I'm almost relaxed. I'll be just fine here, holed up with my BlackBerry. Dad has emailed several times wanting to know 'how things are panning out across the pond'. Less good is the news that my email to admin@carmichaelmusicnyc.com explaining my predicament in Barnsley has been answered by an automatically generated server response. 'Regrettably none of our employees can assist you with your enquiry. Please refer to the FAQ section of our website.' I'm going to have to contact Brent and ask him why on earth the email address he gave me doesn't work.

But ten minutes later Wyatt is back with a big basket of logs.

'You need a fire in here,' he says curtly. 'It'll warm it up quicker.' He starts expertly making a fire, sorting out little bits of wood for kindling and piling the logs on top. Meanwhile I get up on a chair and get down all the pesky cobwebs. We're working side by side in silence, but I don't care because I'm happily occupied.

I go into the kitchen and get started with my disinfectant spray. Fortunately the water's getting hot now.

After a few minutes I hear Wyatt curse. 'Damn fire. This wood's damp.'

'Can you get it going?' I call out politely.

'Yes,' he says a bit huffily. Of course. Round here, if you can't get a fire started you're not a real man. I expect he can lasso a herd of cattle and chop down a tree as well.

I'm on my hands and knees wiping the kitchen chair legs and surveying the floor when I hear Wyatt say, 'There. It's caught now.'

It would seem rude not to go and look.

It's a very nice fire. The large logs are beginning to burn, giving off the same smell of apple wood that fills Wyatt's house. The wind is whistling round the cottage, but I'm warm and a little bit sleepy from my enormous breakfast and frenetic cleaning. I'm beginning to understand why you might choose to live here and not in some ritzy apartment in New York.

I catch the faint sound of a cow mooing.

'She does that when Casey grooms her,' says Wyatt, shifting one of the logs slightly.

'He grooms the cow?'

'Yep. And oils her hooves and spends quality time with her every day.'

'Doesn't she miss the rest of the herd?' I say.

'She has Billy.'

'Billy?'

'The goat,' he says as if it was self-evident. 'Casey's grandfather had to sell the rest of the herd. It's a pretty sad story. Casey's parents were killed in a car wreck a couple of years ago. Since then the farm's gone downhill. The grandfather tries, but he can't keep it up.'

Wyatt doesn't say anything about how he's taking care of Mary Lou. I have to admit that I like that about him. I think about how Stephen and I do nothing for our neighbours. We don't even know most of their names.

The fire has taken hold now and Wyatt gets up. For a moment there's an awkward pause. I can see his problem: he has as a house guest a woman who veers between grievously insulting him, acting like an imbecile and being afflicted with obsessive–compulsive disorder.

He coughs. 'I'll show you how everything works. There's wireless Internet in here.' Then he shows me how to operate the TV remote and the music system. There's a big stack of CDs next to the Bose system. They need dusting, but the Swiffer will make short work of that. I glance over them: Bob Marley, Jimi Hendrix, Stevie Nicks, BB King and what I guess are lots of country stars because I don't recognize any of the names. I think about Stephen's and my CD collection, arranged alphabetically in our IKEA CD stand. James Blunt, Coldplay, Enya and David Gray are well represented. Stephen can't play music with too much bass in case it gives him a migraine.

'I'm going out tonight,' Wyatt says. 'Do you want me to call Rachel and get her to keep you company?'

'I'm pretty tired,' I say truthfully. 'I think I'm a bit jet-lagged.'

The thought crosses my mind that Wyatt might be going to see Heidi, the blonde girl from the diner.

'They'll have the local roads cleared,' he continues. 'The salt trucks and snow ploughs work through the night.' He hesitates. 'The forecast says there's more snow coming to the south of us. The interstate to the airport might take longer.'

He heads for the door. 'I'll leave a box of groceries on the doorstep.'

Good Lord, he actually sounded a bit friendly.

And then he's gone, leaving me to ponder how long exactly I'm going to be stuck in the middle of nowhere.

CHAPTER 16

I finish the kitchen, give the bathroom a good scrub and settle down to spend a pleasant evening in front of the fire in my British Home Stores rose-print brushed-cotton pyjamas. Thanks to Wyatt, I have delicious supper of meat-loaf, some fried potatoes, green beans and a piece of cherry pie. I suppose someone cooks for him – Heidi? I also savour a cup of Boston Stoker coffee, which must be expensive because it comes in a brown-paper packet with 'Costa Rican Blend' printed on the front.

Then I get to work on my laptop. Stephen is clearly making an effort – his latest email includes a link to a design-your-own-kitchen website – but I'm still in no mood to respond. Instead I write to Dad, giving him an edited version of events in which I'm staying with Wyatt and having long conversations about his musical future. I give much the same story to Jennifer from the Wednesday-night group, who sent a good-luck email from her new email address – jennitsanewstart@freewhizz.net – with a PS in which she asked if I knew any good lawyers.

At the same time I listen to several hours of country music. All the songs are about lovin', lyin', cheatin' or dyin'. Someone called Toby Keith spends nearly a whole album on a bar stool after successive women are unfaithful, though lots of the other singers find it more useful in times of crisis to get Mama to pray for them. But try as I might to be sophisticated and a bit sneering towards 'country', as they call it, sometimes the raw emotion of the music gets to me. I have to turn off Wyatt's 'Losing You', which is on a 1990s compilation album, because it makes me think of Mum.

> *Taking the time to think of you*
> *Turning away from the day*
> *Taking a walk down that steep old path*
> *Letting the memories play.*
> *If losing you was hard*
> *Living like this is breaking me.*

I can't help but wonder whom Wyatt loved so much to write that way.

By nine-thirty the jet lag is catching up with me and I go upstairs to bed. The bedroom has a beautifully carved mahogany wardrobe and a matching chest of drawers, and thanks to me it's all gleaming, with a fresh set of sheets and blankets on the bed. The last thing I remember is looking at my watch at ten o'clock.

I'm wide awake at five a.m. There's nothing for it but to get up, make a cup of Wyatt's coffee and switch on the television in time to hear the forecast. Barnsley and the surrounding area, I'm alarmed to see, is the subject of a severe weather alert. Sure enough, the motorway is closed and everyone is being urged to go and check on their neighbours. Imagine if that happened in Britain – half of us would assume we were being burgled.

At least this gives me time to do the refrigerator – the seals are in a dreadful state – and defrost the freezer section, which is filled with a giant iceberg. At ten o'clock Wyatt interrupts me. He finds me defrosting a stubborn section of ice with my travel hairdryer.

He looks around. 'How long have you been cleaning?' He has to raise his voice on account of the hairdryer.

'Oh, just last night and a couple of hours this morning.' I point to the fridge. 'You need to get one of those bicarbonate of soda odour-eating things. It'll keep it nice and fresh.'

'I'll ask Dolores,' he shouts. 'She cleans the house.'

The name sounds familiar. 'The cook from the diner?'

He nods. I recall her now – a red-cheeked, heavy-set lady.

'But she can't clean in here.' He gestures at the spiral staircase. 'Her knees are bad.'

I switch off the hairdryer. There's another one of those awkward pauses.

Then we both speak at once.

'Thanks for cleaning it up in here.'

'Thanks for putting me up.'

Wyatt leans back against the kitchen counter. 'No problem.' I get the impression that he's trying to be hospitable. Maybe Mr Horner has only given him a D+ so far. 'I guess it's quite a change for you coming to a small town like this.'

This is not the time to tell him that I accepted the job because I thought I was going to New York. 'I've always wanted to visit Ohio,' I say earnestly.

'Really?'

'Oh yes. It's a childhood dream of mine.'

He doesn't seem to know what to say to this. Eventually he says, 'How does your fiancé feel about you being so far away?'

I know that now is the time to correct this misapprehension and simply explain that my ring is a present I bought for myself. I also need to tell him that I'm not the

Southfields Baby Whisperer and I do not have my own television show.

'Stephen's very supportive of my career . . .' I begin, choosing my words carefully.

Wyatt gives a low whistle. 'He's an international attorney, right? I dealt with some high-powered legal guys when we were thrashing out my contracts. Those boys work hard and live fast. Hell, I reckon they live on straight whiskey and Cuban cigars.'

Oh yes, that's Stephen all right. I picture him downing his morning Actimel before fastening his cycle helmet.

'He certainly works hard,' I mutter. Then I summon up my courage. 'I'm not the Southfields Baby Whisperer, by the way.'

He raises an eyebrow. 'No kidding.'

'I said it as a joke and they took me seriously.'

'I know, Alice.'

'Please, call me Alan.'

I'm astonished to see his mouth curl up very slightly at the corner, which I think is what passes for a Wyatt smile. Rather than risk this major breakthrough, I decide to tell him about the ring later – or maybe not at all. I'm going to be gone soon, after all, and for once in my life it's quite exciting to enjoy the experience of having a high-powered, cigar-smoking fiancé. Perhaps he drives a Porsche. No, he drives an Aston Martin. We go to polo matches and private views of art exhibitions. 'Miss Fisher,' says the curator, taking my arm, 'may I have your opinion on our new Renoir?' Sadly my fiancé sometimes has to work at the weekends, saving small countries from bankruptcy. But he always brings me back a nice present. 'I saw it in the airport shop in Geneva,' he says, fastening a diamond bracelet around my wrist. 'I hope it's not too over-the-top?' My fiancé pulls me closer. 'I thought it would go with your wedding-day tiara.'

Wyatt clears his throat. 'Well, let me know if there's anything you need. I'll bring some wood in later.'

After Wyatt leaves, the rest of the day is filled with non-stop socializing. First Mr Horner calls in with a selection of pamphlets published by the Barnsley Historical Society, a lot of which are written by him. 'Alice, I think you might especially enjoy "Farming and Family: Barnsley at the turn of the nineteenth century".'

After Mr Horner leaves, Rachel arrives with Baby Dale in his red Lands' End snowsuit. We sit over coffee and the apple streusel cake which Rachel has brought along with my dinner for this evening: a whole roast chicken and four different vegetables plus a pecan pie.

Rachel beams at me. 'I want you to come to talk to the Barnsley Mom's Group. They'd love you! We meet every Monday.'

'I think I'll probably be gone by then.'

Rachel sounds deflated. 'But I've told everyone about you.'

I try to let her down gently. 'I'm only the Southfields Baby Whisperer on a part-time basis. South-west London babies are generally very easy-going,' I add airily. 'I have a day job with Carmichael Music. That's why I'm here, actually, to review Wyatt's contract.'

'Oh my gosh,' Rachel says. 'That's so exciting. We all thought his record company had forgotten all about him.'

Graham never did. 'No, not at all. Actually there's a poster of him on my office wall.'

Rachel gives a shriek of excitement. 'Do you think you can persuade him?'

'I think he has to want to do it,' I say.

Then she's off with tales of Wyatt's musical childhood.

He played piano in the church every Sunday. I conjure up a picture of Wyatt's mother in a black wool dress and white bonnet rapping Wyatt's fingers with a ruler every time he makes a mistake on the church piano. In the end Rachel stays all morning, because Baby Dale has fallen asleep in his pushchair, or stroller, as they call it in American, and we're too scared to move him. We exchange confidences – me about how much I hate my hair and Rachel about how much she loathes Heidi ever since Heidi accidentally-on-purpose dropped her in their final ever high-school cheerleading display. Then Rachel insists on getting to work with my hair, dampening it and painstakingly drying and smoothing it. 'You just need to dry and straighten each section, Alice,' she explains. 'Then you get volume, not frizz.'

Now why didn't Teresa tell me that?

After Rachel leaves, Casey arrives, finishes the apple streusel cake, has a huge slice of pecan pie and drags me out to meet the horses – Rascal and Flatts – and then Mary Lou. She's a beautiful cow with big, dreamy eyes. Casey points out the quality of her rib cage and udder. 'That's what makes her a champion. That and her star quality,' he says gravely.

We hang out sitting on the hay bales, swapping stories about cows and pop groups.

'Wyatt's friends with Mick Jagger,' Casey tells me. 'That old guy.'

It's early evening when Wyatt calls back with a basket of logs. He does a double-take when he sees me (my hair is 100 per cent improved), but doesn't say anything. Instead he gets to work making the fire.

'I hear you've had visitors today,' he says, striking a match.

I wonder what they've told him.

'Rachel said she had a great time with you.' He clears his throat. 'Look, about the other day.' He's still working at the fire. 'I'm sorry if I was a bit of a jerk. And I didn't mean to pretend to be someone else. It was just when you assumed—'

'It's OK,' I interrupt. 'Forget about it.'

He hesitates. 'I have breakfast late. Call in tomorrow if you're hungry.'

So Mr Horner has given him a D+ and he's trying to improve his grade. Obviously I won't go: he's just being politely hospitable.

Before I have a chance to reply, I hear the front door open. 'Anyone at home?' It's a slightly nasal male voice. A relative of Wyatt's?

A tall figure in a navy-blue hooded raincoat comes in. He stares at us with surprise. 'I'm looking for you, Wyatt,' he says. 'I saw the lights were on in here.'

He looks quite put out at the sight of me. He has a thin goatee beard and hair combed across his bald patch. I guess he's about forty. He's carrying a stack of books under his arm.

'Hey, Bruce!' Wyatt looks up. 'This is Alice from Carmichael Music in London.'

At this, Bruce curls his lip slightly and looks at me suspiciously.

'Alice, this is Bruce, my sponsor.'

Oh my gosh! I've now met a real-life alcoholic and a genuine sponsor. *Enable YOU* is very keen on sponsors. The sponsor is an alcoholic who's managed to stay sober. They take the new alcoholic under their wing, escort them to AA meetings and make them read lots of books.

Bruce says sternly, 'We ought to get to work, Wyatt.'

'Yep,' says Wyatt distractedly as the fire goes out. 'I need more matches. I'll get some from the house.' I can see that Wyatt doesn't take orders from anyone, and I glimpse a bit of the rebellious side of Wyatt that's got him into trouble in the past.

With Wyatt gone, Bruce puts down the books on the oak coffee table and takes a step towards me. 'I hope you're not going to derail Wyatt.'

I imagine Wyatt the Tank Engine toppling over.

Bruce points at the books. The top one is called *Step Up to Strategies for Lifelong Sobriety'*. Not a thrill-a-minute page-turner, then. 'Wyatt has a great deal of work to do looking at his issues,' Bruce says prissily. 'I don't want him distracted by your people putting pressure on him to record.'

'No,' I say, shaking my head very vigorously. 'Believe me,' I say, very slowly, for emphasis. 'I'm on your side.'

I decide to quote some *Enable YOU* at Bruce to persuade him of my sincerity. 'Sobriety is the foundation stone of everything in the recovering alcoholic's life – one day at a time.'

Sure enough, Bruce looks impressed. 'You're familiar with our AA slogan?'

'Very,' I say self-assuredly.

'I see,' says Bruce, rubbing his goatee. 'So that's presumably why Carmichael sent you – someone who could really understand.'

'Carmichael put a great deal of thought into choosing exactly the right person for this job.'

Bruce looks impressed. 'So often employers are awkward about allowing time off.'

'Actually, my old boss was always really nice about it.' From time to time it's necessary for me to see Dr Vaizey on an emergency basis. I last saw him before we moved house – a very stressful time. Stephen got hives and it culminated in my computer crashing and the devastating loss of my box-by-box packing list.

'So you belong to a group?' Bruce says, a little more friendly now.

'Oh yes. I started going after I finished the outpatient programme. We meet on a Wednesday.'

Bruce nods his head. 'Good, good. A home group is so important. Right now I'm trying to get Wyatt to as many different meetings as possible. We go to one a day all over the county.'

He looks at me apologetically.

'I'd invite you, but it's a men-only meeting today.'

Some AA meetings are secret, for proper alcoholics only, but others allow visitors.

'Maybe another time,' I say gaily.

Bruce shakes my hand. 'Imagine – you coming here all the way from England and us having this conversation. That's the miracle of sobriety. It's a perfect example of what I always say to Wyatt – everything happens for a reason.'

We're interrupted by Wyatt returning with the matches.

Bruce looks much happier now. 'Alice and I were just having a most interesting conversation. It turns out she started off in an outpatient programme.'

Wyatt looks at me surprised. 'Really?'

I nod.

'It just goes to show, Wyatt,' says Bruce. '*Everything happens for a reason.*'

CHAPTER 17

It's Day Two in Wyatt's cottage, and it's four o'clock in the morning. I'm wide awake. Not because of jet lag, but because the telephone is ringing. It's Dad.

'Hello,' he shouts. 'Having a good day?'

'What?'

'I calculate it's three p.m.,' he says cheerfully.

'It's four a.m.'

There's a rustling of paper. 'You're behind us? I must have written it down wrong.'

'Yes.'

'Now I've got you on the line, let's hear all your news,' Dad says, unabashed.

I rouse myself to fill Dad in. It's not easy, because I have to try to remember what I told him in my upbeat email. 'So Wyatt and I are getting on brilliantly. He's even invited me to breakfast later.' I leave out the fact that this is just a polite invitation and I'm too scared to go because I can't face the memories of the last time in that kitchen.

'Great,' says Dad. 'He wouldn't do that if he wasn't raring to record.'

I have to deflate Dad a little. 'I think he has some reservations.'

Dad interrupts. 'Just emphasize that you've travelled all

this way to see him and that he's crucial to Carmichael Music's strategy.'

'Really? I never would have thought of that.'

'Oh yes,' says Dad smugly. 'I didn't spend thirty years with British Gas without learning something about human nature. Trust me, if he's inviting you into his home, he's definitely ready to work with you. Now, I want you to email me after you have breakfast. Then we can work out the next phase of the plan.'

Dad rings off then. 'It's an expensive call, Sugar Plum.'

It looks as if I have no choice but to go. Dad is like a terrier once he gets an idea in his head. He was the same when he had the idea to knock a serving hatch between the kitchen and dining room. Valerie was worried about the dust and possible structural damage, but Dad wore her down in the end.

I's several hours before breakfast, so I get up, make coffee, watch television for a while, then spend about two hours getting ready. I'm determined to create a good impression. The Rachel hair-drying technique really works, as does applying the correct tone of make-up in natural daylight. I pull on my Next jeans – I keep them for best – and my Marks & Spencer pink Oxford casual shirt (a Christmas present from Valerie).

I dash across the yard with my coat pulled over my head and scoot into the house, slamming the door behind me against the freezing wind. There's already a delicious smell of coffee and something sweet. Maybe Wyatt's mother has dropped by with some home-made blueberry muffins on her way to arrange the flowers at the church? Wyatt and I will enjoy breakfast by the fire as he tells me stories from his days on the road. Who knows, my empathetic listening could one day bear fruit. Perchance in a few years' time I'll switch on the radio and hear Wyatt's new single – 'Girl From Afar'.

Girl from afar
Not mine for lovin'
I see her now
Eatin' a muffin.

So I'm in a jolly frame of mind as I call out, 'yoo-hoo' and skip into the kitchen. Heidi is leaning against the sink sipping a cup of coffee, and Wyatt is sitting at the table reading the newspaper.

'Alice,' she says warmly, taking in my startled expression. 'Did you sleep well?'

'Yes, thanks,' I manage to say.

Wyatt looks up and raises a hand in greeting. So he did spend the night with Heidi. She's probably planning to stay all day.

'Is the school still closed?' I ask, in what I hope is a more casual tone.

'No,' she says, and I think I hear a note of annoyance in her voice. 'We start two hours later, that's all, to give the school bus more time to get round.' Heidi is giving me a hard look up and down. Her expression is a little puzzled.

Wyatt looks up. 'I was just watching the news earlier. The interstate's totally blocked.'

Is it my imagination or does Heidi darken slightly at this?

'Looks like you'll be with us a little longer.' Heidi looks at her watch. 'I ought to get going.'

She walks over to Wyatt and leans down to give him a kiss on the cheek. 'See you later.'

'Thanks for dropping by,' he says.

Wow, Wyatt is pretty offhand with his women. What a thing to say to someone you've just spent the night with!

But just as she pulls on her jacket, I see that it's damp with melted snow and I realize that Heidi hasn't been here all night. Then she pulls on her boots, which I now notice are standing in a wet puddle by the kitchen door.

Heidi looks up and says, apparently spontaneously, 'I've just had a really good idea.' She moves closer. 'Alice, my class would *love* to hear all about England. Why don't you come in and talk to them?'

My all-purpose excuse comes to mind. 'I think I'll be gone by then.'

She ignores me. 'They're quite a handful,' she says, laughing, 'but you'll cope.'

I'm not quite sure I like the sound of this.

Heidi has turned to Wyatt. 'What do you think? It seems like such a wonderful opportunity for a cultural exchange.'

Wyatt, who is eating a piece of toast, nods distractedly. 'Hmm.'

'That's settled then,' says Heidi decisively, putting her hand on the door. 'Alice, I'll have a look at my timetable and call you.'

I hear her car start up. I slip over to the kitchen window in order to be friendly and wave goodbye – and see, from the defrosted windows, that her car hasn't been parked here overnight.

'Heidi brought an apple pie,' Wyatt says, gesturing to a dish on the counter.

It seems awful eating another woman's pie, but I manage a hefty slice along with a cup of coffee and a glass of orange juice that Wyatt pours for me.

'It's still pretty nasty out there,' he says. 'You might want to wait until later on to get your car.'

'That's fine.' I've already worked out my plans for the morning. First I need to call Brent. Then I need to do my washing. There are three days' worth of dirty clothes and I don't like to let things get out of hand.

'Bruce is coming over later,' says Wyatt. He gets up and rinses out his mug. 'Bruce is a good man.'

'Does he have a job?' I can't help but ask.

'Apart from baby-sitting me? Yep, he's a chef. Really good, actually. He trained in New York. Now he works an early shift as a breakfast cook so he can go to meetings and help ne'er-do-wells.'

'So he takes it really seriously,' I say.

'I think you need to,' says Wyatt. 'That was my problem in the past. I did the expensive rehab routine. Then six weeks later I was back to my old habits. So now I'm trying it the old-fashioned way.'

It's odd, but this conversation doesn't feel too bad. 'Which is?'

'Stay home, work on the farm, keep out of trouble. So far it seems to be working.'

'Was it singing that caused the problems?'

'No. It's the whole lifestyle. It presents a lot of temptations.' He stops abruptly.

I know that Wyatt has what gossip magazines call a chequered love life – at least one ex-wife that I can recall, and lots of pretty girls who drink more than they eat.

Normally I wouldn't dare ask Wyatt personal questions, but I'm leaving soon and I'll never see him again and my curiosity is getting the better of me.

'I was listening to "Losing You",' I say. 'Who's it about?'

'Who?' he says, surprised. 'It's not about anyone.' He pauses. 'I wrote it the first time I tried to quit drinking.'

'Oh. Sorry.' There we are. I've just made yet another fundamental mistake as a music producer – completely misunderstanding the artist's song.

His expression softens. 'Don't worry about it. Everyone thinks that. And I don't usually talk about it.'

So Wyatt has shared a small confidence with me. I replay 'Losing You' in my mind: *'If losing you was hard, Living like this is breaking me.'*

'Did you like it?' he says.

I do a double-take. But his expression is deadly serious.

'I loved it,' I say. 'Any chance of a sequel?'

What! Where did that come from? The Tropicana must have gone to my head.

But to my amazement Wyatt grins at me, for the first time ever. 'You're full of surprises, Alice. I never would have—'

But just then the telephone rings. Wyatt stops talking and reaches for the receiver mounted on the kitchen wall.

'Yes.' He sounds a little curt. He turns to me. 'Yes, she is. I'll hand you over.'

Wyatt's mouth hardens a little. 'It's for you.'

He hands me the telephone and walks out to the hallway.

'Alice. It's Gerry. We met at the Blue Ribbon Diner.'

It takes me a moment to place him. Then I recall that Gerry is Mr Brown Leather Jacket Mercedes Key Fob Man.

'Listen, how would you like to come and see the sights of Barnsley?' he says.

Before I have a chance to respond he adds, 'That'll take about five minutes. Then we can have dinner.'

I hear the front door close as Wyatt leaves the house.

'I don't know any historical trivia,' he continues, 'but I can read a restaurant menu.' He gives me a description of a couple of the local restaurants. 'I know it's not London,' he says, 'but hell, Alice, you might get to like possum and cornbread.'

He does sound like fun. Why not go? Wyatt will be going to a meeting with Bruce. I've no doubt that Heidi will turn

128

up later. As for Stephen, my eye alights on Wyatt's granite counter and I recall a line in his last email about our new kitchen. 'I propose synthetic composite granite-lookalike in one of three standard colours as an all-round value product.'

'I'd love to,' I say.

'Great! I'll pick you up about seven.'

I replace the receiver, and for a moment I feel a small pang of guilt about Stephen. I know he's making an effort. But sometimes in my darker moments I doubt if he will ever change. A vision of our future life appears before me, a life we embark on after our wedding reception at the Holiday Inn Express Tolworth where Stephen has opted for the light sandwich buffet menu (includes one complimentary soft drink). In time we have two children, Brian and Mabel, whom I dress in identical boys' clothing handed down by Teresa. Once a week Stephen counts out my housekeeping money. Thank God for jumbo bags of lentils. I try to shield the children from the endless rows. 'How can I ever trust you again,' yells Stephen furiously, pointing at the thermostat. 'One degree higher I could forgive. But two!' At Christmas we put up the table-top miniature tree and switch on the lights for half an hour before Dad gets home.

Right now Stephen seems a long way away. So does England, and everything that is safe and familiar. I feel a wave of homesickness and I'm glad that Gerry called and that I'm not going to spend the evening alone.

CHAPTER 18

It's later the same afternoon and I'm in the small utility room of the guest cottage. It's equipped with a huge Maytag washing machine and matching tumble dryer. Everything is spotless: I've mopped the floor – including behind the washing machine and dryer – and spent a happy half-hour shining the stainless-steel sink and draining board. The lint filter on the dryer is completely free of fluff and the fabric-conditioner dispenser in the washing machine is as clean as a whistle. I can't abide that blue, slimy sludge that gathers after just a few washes.

I put on my first load of washing – I always separate my whites from my coloureds – and sit down in the living room to call Brent. I dial my own office number and remember with a pang that it isn't my office any longer.

'Brent, it's Alice.'

'Who?'

'Alice Fisher. Graham's secretary.'

'Hold on. I'm just watering the plants.' There's a very long delay which I finally grasp must be caused by Brent leaving the office to fill up his miniature watering can. When he comes back he still seems to be having trouble remembering who I am. 'What can I do for you?' he asks off-handedly.

'I'm here at Wyatt's house in Ohio. He doesn't want to do another album.'

Brent sighs. 'But that's your job, Alice. To persuade him.'

'I've tried persuading him.'

'I'm sure he'll come round,' says Brent distractedly. I can hear him splashing water on his pot plants. 'Just give it time.'

'I can't stay here at his house indefinitely,' I protest.

'Has he asked you to leave?'

'Well, no.'

'There you are, then. Chip away at his defences. Hold on. Miss Carmichael's just come in.'

Brent must have put his hand over the receiver because there's the sound of muffled voices. I think I can make out Phoebe hissing the words 'idiot', 'out of my way' and 'at all costs'.

Hmm. I supply the missing words to piece the sentence together. 'Wyatt's an idiot and I'm prepared to go out of my way to get that album at all costs.'

Then Phoebe comes on the line. 'Alice. I hear you're doing wonderful work in Ohio. Keep it up.'

'I need to come back,' I interject. 'There's nothing for me to do here.'

'Now come on, Alice,' says Phoebe briskly. 'No whining! Where would we be today if my father had walked out of Nashville saying, "There's nothing for me to do here"?'

'But that was Nashville,' I begin.

'Sometimes these small country towns are havens of talent. Barber-shop quartets, families with umpteen children, singing dogs.'

'Dogs?'

'Yes, you know the kind of thing. They bark in unison. Scout around and see what you can find.'

'I need to come back to London,' I say firmly. 'Also, my email to New York got returned.'

Phoebe ignores me. 'Just think, Alice – you could discover the next Partridge Family. What a feather in your cap that would be. Let me hand you back to Brent.'

Maybe he will listen.

Brent comes on the line. 'Let's talk in a month.'

The line goes dead.

There's nothing for it but to dry and fold my washing and iron my jeans.

At lunchtime Wyatt and I drive down to the town to collect my car. We're in the pick-up truck for about a minute before Wyatt says a little tersely, 'So Gerry called.'

'Yes. He's taking me sightseeing.'

'Really.'

Wyatt switches on the radio and we don't speak for the rest of the journey. Is it my imagination or does he take a hard look at my fake engagement ring as I get out of the truck? Oh no! I'm filled with shame. He thinks that I'm going on a date despite being the fiancée of a top international attorney. I know exactly how that type of behaviour is dealt with in these small American towns. As I get into my car I look around the town square. If I'm still here on Sunday this is where they'll hold my public trial. The Barnsley elders will sit at a long table dressed in black suits with frilly white collars as I'm brought before them, my hair in a bun.

'Alice Fisher,' Mr Horner announces. 'Thou standst accused of bawdy thoughts and licentious deeds.'

The jeering crowd begins to throw tomatoes at me. Wyatt's mother sits knitting at the foot of the dock. Heidi argues passionately for me to be dunked in the Barnsley pond. 'If she floats then she's guilty.' After the sentence is pronounced – one day in the stocks – Heidi comes forward and deftly stitches a scarlet 'A' to my smocked dress. 'Trollop,' she hisses. 'Now take thine foreign eyes from Wyatt and cast them down.' Then she cuts my hair off.

I drive home along the route which is now quite familiar, past the low, ranch-style houses on the outskirts of town to the open fields, up the long uphill road to the crossroads and another mile beyond that to the entrance to Wyatt's farm. Along the way I wave as I pass Sheriff Billy – there's next to no crime in Barnsley so he spends a lot of time just driving around. When I get home I see that Wyatt's pick-up truck is not in the yard.

I go into the cottage, put on my next load of washing and go upstairs to get my dress, the only one I brought with me, a Monsoon black velvet from three years ago. Stephen has never been keen on it on account of the low neckline, which he thinks is 'a little young'. I bought it for Dad's sixtieth birthday party, which was held at the New Malden Golf Club. 'Very nice, Alice,' said Teresa, looking me up and down, 'and very sensible of you to opt for black. It's the most slimming colour.' I was half expecting Dad to announce that he and Valerie were getting married, but he didn't.

At about four o'clock I look out of the window to see Casey going into the barn. There's still no sign of Wyatt. I decide to visit Casey. I find him sitting next to Mary Lou.

I can tell straight away that something's wrong. He's slumped, staring at the floor, and I have the feeling that I've interrupted his conversation with Mary Lou because he looks startled and a little embarrassed when he sees me. Next to him is his school bag, and I realize that he must have come here straight from school. I expect he's hungry.

'There's some apple pie in the kitchen.' I'm sure Wyatt won't mind me feeding Casey.

133

Wordlessly he gets up, picks up his bag and, after patting Mary Lou, follows me out.

He's still not speaking as I warm him a slice in the microwave and get him a glass of milk. It's not until he's finished his second slice that we start talking.

'It's a project,' he says with a sigh. 'It's for the end of term, which is next week.'

How exciting! I always loved projects at school. Sometimes in the holidays I would set myself a project, spending many happy hours cutting and sticking pictures from Mum's *Woman's Own* into my WH Smith scrapbook.

'What's it about?'

There's another sigh. 'The fifty states and their flags. Every state has its own flag,' he explains wearily. 'You have to choose a state and then do a presentation to the class.'

I can't see how this poses a problem. 'It sounds like fun,' I say cheerily.

He gives me a look which is difficult to read. 'It has to be on PowerPoint. And I don't have a computer. We used to have one but it broke.'

Casey speaks as if there's no prospect of the computer being repaired.

'Actually,' I say, 'I have a computer and the very latest edition of PowerPoint.' I could add that I'm something of an aficionado when it comes to presentations, but I don't want to boast.

Casey's face lights up. 'I want to do Kentucky. That's where Mom was born.'

I can't help myself. 'Hold on. I'll get my laptop.'

One hour later Wyatt returns to find us planning out each of our ten slides. He closes the kitchen door, hangs up his coat and unlaces his boots. I wonder where he's been, but I know it would look nosy to ask. If he's surprised to find his kitchen taken over by Casey and me he doesn't show it.

'Homework?' he asks, going over to make a pot of coffee. At least I was right about one addiction.

'Yep.' Casey doesn't look up. He's reading his American Studies school textbook. 'Alice is lending me her laptop.'

'Do you need a printer?' asks Wyatt helpfully.

Casey and I roll our eyes at each other. 'He puts it on a disk and takes it into school, then loads it on to the classroom computer,' I explain.

'Sorry,' says Wyatt, holding his hands up in mock surrender.

Casey is full of enthusiasm. 'Alice can do really awesome graphics.'

'Is she supposed to be doing it for you?' says Wyatt doubtfully. He's a famous rock-pop-country star, but right now he sounds like everyone's dad.

'I'm not doing it,' I say briskly. 'I'm just the consultant.'

Wyatt goes over to the cake tin and takes off the lid. 'Where did all the pie go?'

I wink at Casey. 'Travis got to it. We tried to save it for you but we were too late.'

Wyatt takes down a plate. 'Amazing ability that dog has to open cake tins.' He turns back to Casey.

'I think I need to say something about famous things in Kentucky,' Casey says, chewing the end of his pencil. Schoolchildren, like headmasters, are the same the world over.

'I can't help you there.' Up until an hour ago I didn't even know where Kentucky was. Now I know it's to the south of Ohio.

Casey reads aloud from his textbook. 'It's famous for horse-racing. It's the location of the Appalachian mountains and it's the home state of Johnny Depp.'

135

Wyatt looks over his shoulder. 'Shouldn't you say something about Kentucky bluegrass music?'

Wyatt can't see me as I mime a yawn at Casey. 'Good idea,' I say, crossing my eyes, at which point Casey gives the game away by collapsing in giggles.

'I get it,' says Wyatt, sitting down. 'By the way, Casey, I may be getting another horse.'

Casey looks up with interest.

'She's a Clydesdale. I went to see her today. The owner's selling up and moving to Florida. She's an old girl, but she'd be company for Rascal and Flatts.'

Casey nods. 'The older horse will calm him down,' says Casey sagely.

He's just so sweet. Wyatt and I exchange glances. Then I pull myself back to the task at hand. I think Bob from Technical Support has some old promo photographs on disk of Johnny Depp taken at a Carmichael Music party from a few years ago that we've never used. 'How would you like to use an exclusive, never-before-seen photo of Johnny Depp?' I say to Casey, whose mouth drops open.

'You ought to come and hear some Kentucky bluegrass bands, Alice,' says Wyatt, putting his feet up on a kitchen chair.

I'm not really paying attention because I've set to work on the animation toolbar and I'm sending the Kentucky State Seal spinning and flipping over the screen.

'Hmm,' I reply. Then I have an idea. 'Hey, Casey,' I say. 'Are you doing a handout for the class?'

He shrugs. 'Don't know.'

'You could do a "Fun Facts" handout. Look, I can show you some of the fonts you could use.'

Casey gets up and looks over my shoulder.

'George Clooney was born in Kentucky,' says Wyatt, obviously joking.

We both look at him disbelievingly. 'He was not!' we chorus.

Wyatt shrugs his shoulders.

Casey and I exchange glances as if to say to each other that it's time to get back to work. 'Why don't you look up some Kentucky trivia on the Internet,' I suggest to Casey. I save the PowerPoint presentation, log on and swap seats.

'George Clooney *was* born in Kentucky,' says Wyatt. There's a pause. 'Want a bet?' he adds devilishly in a low voice. Then he looks over each shoulder and whispers, 'You'll have to promise not to tell Bruce.'

I'm very sure that George Clooney is the son of Rosemary Clooney, a famous singer, and that he was therefore born in Hollywood or somewhere glamorous like that. 'I wouldn't want you to lose your money,' I say coolly.

At that he shoots me a smile, which, if our relationship wasn't purely professional, might be judged a little flirtatious.

'It doesn't have to be money.' He's now looking at me wide-eyed. 'It could be for that last slice of pie.'

We both turn to the last slice sitting on a white china plate. I will concede at this point that Heidi makes quite good apple pie (presumably the main reason he's going out with her), and I had mentally already reserved that last piece for myself. I sit back confidently. Fortunately, my reading of *Enable YOU* has educated me about the reckless personality of the alcoholic, many of whom frequent illegal gambling dens and other locations of vice.

Wyatt, up for a bet, however ridiculous, is clearly calling my bluff.

'It's a deal,' I say, holding his gaze.

In response he puts his hands behind his head and leans back in his chair.

A few seconds later Casey looks up at me forlornly from the computer. 'George Clooney was born in Kentucky.'

'What!' I exclaim, horrified.

Wyatt raises an eyebrow at me and shakes his head. 'If I didn't know you better, Alice, I'd think you were a born gambler.' His expression is dead-pan. 'I've got some books on gambling addiction I could lend you.'

I'm saved from thinking of a cool retort to this by Casey reading out George Clooney's online biography. 'He was born in the town of Lexington, Kentucky.' Wyatt gets up and saunters towards the pie. 'He went to high school in Augusta, Kentucky.' Wyatt makes a big fuss of getting a fork out of the drawer. Then Casey starts on his early show-business career. 'George had family connections. His aunt is the famous singer Rosemary Clooney.'

Aunt!

I'm absorbing this when something really unexpected happens. Wyatt begins to sing quietly. It's Don Maclean's 'American Pie'.

'Bye, bye, Miss American Pie ...'

I feel a shiver down my spine. Imagine someone whose voice you've heard a hundred times before suddenly singing right in front of you. No, he's actually singing *to* me, word-perfect, with some of the deep growl of Johnny Cash but a smoothness overlaying it. He has an absolutely amazingly fabulous voice. Then I start laughing. Even though I hardly know him and I'm returning home in a couple of days, even though I'm about to lose my job and I'll probably end up marrying Stephen because no one else is going to ask me, in spite of all these things, I'm laughing in a way that is truly carefree, a way I haven't laughed for years.

CHAPTER 19

I'm sitting with Gerry at The Winds restaurant in the town of Yellow Springs. It's very sophisticated with white napkins and big wine glasses. Gerry, I guess, is a regular here because we have the best table, overlooking the street outside. We drove for quite a while to get here in Gerry's huge Mercedes with black leather seats. Before we left, Gerry reached across me to show me how to operate the heated seat button. He smelt of expensive aftershave and cigarettes, but not in a bad way. Not at all. I didn't see Wyatt as I left the guest cottage, which was just as well because I was wearing my Lands' End parka, the only coat I brought with me, over my Monsoon black dress.

'Red or white?' Gerry says, looking at the wine list.

It's so nice to be given a choice.

'Red,' I say, savouring the moment.

He grins at me. 'I was hoping you would say that.'

Gerry has the knack of making you feel that everything you say is just right and he's hanging on your every word. That's another welcome change. Stephen likes to tell me all about his day at the office. 'There's a very real danger that my Northumberland footpath dispute could go all the way to the Court of Appeal.'

'Yellow Springs is a bit of a novelty round here,' explains

Gerry. 'It's an arts community and there's a small university. Quite a few filmmakers and writers live in the town.'

It seemed different as we walked from the car, the main street lined with shops selling second-hand books, tie-dyed T-shirts and global-trade plant pots. The Winds is full, the conversation loud and there's an enticing aroma of warm bread. Outside, passers-by hurry through the snow still lying thick on the pavement. Even though this is a date, I don't feel in the least anxious, though this may have something to do with the large martini – Gerry's suggestion – that I had in the bar before we sat down.

The waitress comes. I order wood-grilled blue-fin tuna (specially flown in from Florida) and Gerry orders steak. 'And a bottle of Zinfandel,' he adds.

She leaves and he says, 'I hope you like Californian wines.' I'm sure I do.

'So, Alice, what do you think of Barnsley?'

True to his word, Gerry showed me the high school, the library and the famous Barnsley Native Indian burial mound. That was about it. He also explained that the statue in the square was of William Armstrong, an immigrant from Barnsley, England, who founded the town back in the late 1800s.

'I'm sure a London girl like you must find us very dull,' he continues.

'No,' I shake my head. 'I like it here. It's very friendly. London can be very impersonal.'

He nods. 'I lived in New York for a while,' he says. 'It was the same.'

'What were you doing there?'

'Business. We have a local family business, but we've diversified. I was working on that.' He pauses.

'So,' he says casually, 'is there anyone special back home?'

Gerry is certainly a fast worker. I had resolved before I left this evening to be totally truthful with Gerry. No more lies, no more ironic comments, nothing that might be misinterpreted.

'There is someone,' I say carefully. 'But we had an argument at the airport before I left.'

'He didn't want you to go?'

Clearly Gerry has in mind a distraught boyfriend begging me not to leave as I check in my bags. It's too humiliating to reveal the full details. I still have that bloody spreadsheet in my parka pocket.

'We split up,' I say succinctly.

'I ought to say I'm sorry.' Gerry leans forward. 'But I'm not.'

I can feel myself blush at this point, just as the waitress brings the wine and pours two glasses.

'And I ought to let this breathe,' says Gerry, raising his glass. 'But I'm not.'

Gerry is a lot of fun. He's also very good-looking, manly, and he drives in a calm, decisive manner that is extremely refreshing.

'What brought you back to Barnsley?' I ask.

'Family commitments. I would like to have stayed in New York, but I was needed here.'

'Was it hard coming back?'

'You do what you have to do,' he shrugs. 'I have some business interests in Las Vegas, so I fly out there most weeks.'

I would like to know more, but he changes the subject to talk about me and my work. I've already told him that I work in the music industry, without going into details about exactly why I'm here.

'So who are the up-and-coming bands?' he asks.

Probably not anyone who's recently been signed by

Carmichael Music, I'm tempted to say. Our track record recently hasn't been great, on account of all Graham's recommendations being turned down by the New York head office. So I talk about some of the bands I've read about in *Billboard*, and before long I'm on to my famous trip to the Brit Awards.

'Joss Stone looks totally different in person,' I inform him, 'and Sharon Osbourne is very down-to-earth.'

He touches my hand. 'Alice, I can see you're a real live wire.'

Before I know it we've moved on to discussing our favourite films, we've finished our main course, and Gerry is persuading me to order dessert. 'I'm sure you never put on a pound.'

I'm really enjoying myself. I can even see myself having a pre-midlife fling with Gerry. In years to come, when I'm living boring married life with Stephen, I shall look back on these days. Occasionally my children will find me looking wistfully out of the window as the snow falls. I'm remembering Gerry, the dashing American I left behind when duty called me back to my country. I'm dressed in a 1940s flower-print dress, my hair neatly curled, my red lipstick flawless. In the background the music from *Brief Encounter* is playing. 'Mummy, what is it?' Mabel says, in her cut-glass accent. 'Are you sad?' I give a high little laugh. 'No, darling,' I reply bravely, wiping a single tear away with a freshly laundered linen handkerchief. I take her hand and say gaily, 'Let's toast some crumpets on the fire!'

Back at The Winds, I choose Red Berry Pancakes with Whipped Cream and Gerry orders cheese. I allow him to refill my glass, my second, and also allow him to rest his leg against mine. He runs his fingers over my hand in a very sensual manner.

'Alice,' he says, leaning towards me, 'you are a very attractive woman.' He takes a sip of wine. 'I'd like to get to know you better.'

Right now I think I could skip the getting to know each other bit altogether and get right on to the biblical-type knowing. Gerry clearly feels the same, because he presses his leg harder against mine. I reach for my glass of red wine. I feel Gerry's free hand gently squeeze my knee under the table. Gerry squeezes for a second time. Our eyes lock.

'I think we could be very good together,' whispers Gerry seductively. 'We could give international relations a new meaning.'

I'm now blushing terribly. I raise my glass to my lips and take a large sip, looking away to regain my composure. I glance to the side of me out of the window. There, standing right in front of me, wearing a hooded raincoat and looking at me with an expression of horror, is Bruce. And standing a few paces behind him is Wyatt.

Stunned, I put down the glass.

'Is everything all right?' says Gerry, concerned.

'Fine,' I say, utterly confused. What are Bruce and Wyatt doing in Yellow Springs? And why was Bruce looking at me like that?

Before I have a chance to consider this further, there's a bellowing yell from the entrance to the restaurant. 'Alice, *stop*!'

I purposefully don't look round. Perhaps there's another Alice in the restaurant.

Seconds later Bruce appears at the side of our table. Wyatt is following more slowly behind him. Bruce snatches the glass from my hand. 'Alice, you don't have to live this way any longer!'

He holds my glass aloft, swinging round to address Gerry. 'This woman is a recovering alcoholic.'

Gerry stares at me, aghast. 'Alice, you didn't tell me that.'

'I'm not!' I protest.

'Everything happens for a reason,' proclaims Bruce, ignoring me and talking to Wyatt. 'We come to an AA meeting in Yellow Springs, and look who we find here,' he says, pointing at me.

Yellow Springs may be a community of alternative-minded artistic spirits, but that hasn't stopped everyone in the restaurant from gawping at us.

'Young woman, the time has come for you to sober up,' says Bruce sternly.

'But I'm not drunk,' I say indignantly.

Bruce sighs and shakes his head. Then he says to Wyatt, 'You see here a prime example of denial of the problem of alcoholism.'

'But I'm really not an alcoholic,' I say. 'I drink very occasionally and I can stop whenever I want to.'

Bruce looks at me with an expression of exaggerated understanding. 'I think we've all told ourselves those lies at one time or another, Alice.'

'I do not have a problem,' I say, nearly shouting now.

Bruce shakes his head sadly. 'Is that what you believe, Alice? Just a couple of days ago you told me you went to meetings.' He lays a hand on my shoulder. 'Isn't it the case that you were at one stage hospitalized because of your alcoholism?'

Gerry has gone pale. 'Is this true?'

I recollect my previous conversation with Bruce, and it's dawning on me what has happened. 'Yes. No.'

Bruce turns to Wyatt. 'She doesn't know her own mind, you see.' He waves a waitress over. 'A large glass of water,

144

please.' He turns back to Wyatt. 'We need to start her detox right away.'

'Oh, shut up.' I have to clear this up. 'It wasn't an out-patient clinic for addiction. It was something else.' I have no intention of discussing my anxiety issues with half of Yellow Springs. 'Something private.'

'You went to a clinic for something private?' says Gerry, recoiling.

'Not that,' I snap.

Bruce takes a step closer. 'Alice, I'm going to escort you to an AA meeting.' He turns to Gerry. 'This is the end of your evening.'

'Hold on a minute,' says Gerry, bristling. 'I think I'll be the judge of that.'

Bruce bristles back. He looks like he's ready to take the gloves off. 'According to Wyatt, this young woman is engaged to be married,' he says, drawing closer to Gerry.

Gerry shoots Bruce a triumphant look. 'Not any more, buddy.' His tone clearly implies that this is as a result of meeting him.

Just as I think they're about to come to blows, Wyatt lays a restraining hand on Bruce's shoulder. 'Let's leave it, shall we?'

Gerry is still spoiling for a fight. 'That's right, Wyatt.' He looks at his watch. 'If you leave now, you'll be home in time for cocoa.'

I see Wyatt give Gerry a long, hard look, then swallow and finally turn away. After a few seconds Bruce reluctantly follows him out of the restaurant.

It takes a few moments for both Gerry and I to regain our composure. Then he leans back. 'I was going to suggest a brandy. But let's make that two coffees.'

We drink them as quickly as possible and Gerry calls over the waitress to pay. When he pulls out his American Express card, I notice his surname. Gerry Armstrong.

CHAPTER 20

It's nearly midnight when Gerry and I arrive back at the cottage. Wyatt's pick-up truck is parked in the driveway, but there are no lights on in the house.

'Let's have a nightcap,' Gerry purrs, turning off the engine.

'I'm very jet-lagged,' I say.

He's not put off. 'That's fine. When you wake up in the middle of the night, I'd be more than happy to keep you company.'

I give a nervous laugh. He seems to take this as encouragement, because he leans over, runs his hand through my hair and before I know it we're kissing. I know that doesn't sound very convincing – accidentally kissing someone – but that's how it was. I will draw a veil over subsequent events in the Mercedes, though I will say that Gerry is an accomplished kisser (and very different from Stephen, who favours the darting tongue style).

I make my escape from the car – after promising Gerry I'll see him before I leave – and dash into the cottage. I half expect Gerry to follow me, and it's with some relief that after a little while I hear the engine start up.

The following day I decide to hide in the cottage and avoid Wyatt altogether. Perhaps the snow on the interstate will be cleared today and I can escape without seeing him again. Scenes from last night's Yellow Spring's drama replay through my mind. Bruce holding my glass aloft. The way the waitress not so discreetly removed it when she brought us coffee, winking at Gerry as she did so. And the old man sitting with his wife by the door who said in a very loud voice as we left, 'Is that the drunkard?'

Obviously I cannot ring Stephen and cry on his shoulder. So I make do with calling pilot Andy from the Wednesday-night group instead. He's always good in a crisis. But there's no reply on his mobile. Instead there's a message saying that the number is no longer in service. Very odd. Then I remember that I had promised Casey I would call Bob about the Johnny Depp photos for his school project.

'Bob. It's Alice,' I say as cheerfully as I can manage. I do have a bit of a hangover.

'Alice,' he repeats furtively. 'I can't talk right now. I'll call you back in five minutes.'

True to his word, five minutes later he calls me from his mobile. By the sound of it he's standing in the street.

'I have to take certain precautions,' says Bob when he comes on the line. 'The office lines aren't safe.'

'Safe?'

'Phoebe listens in to the calls. She's paranoid about losing artists to Graham.'

'Graham?'

'Hmm. There's a rumour that he's starting his own independent label. These are uncertain times, Alice. My advice is to stay where you are.'

'How do you know about Graham?' I ask, intrigued.

'I have my sources,' says Bob curtly. 'Those of us in Technical Support are something of an elite, Alice. Think of us as the MI5 of the office world. Our influence extends much wider than you would imagine. Graham is in my sights,' he concludes.

'I'm glad to hear he's OK,' I say.

'Graham is sorely missed,' says Bob, as if he'd died. 'He took good care of you when he left.'

'He did?'

'One of his conditions for retiring was that Phoebe kept you on for at least six months.'

'I see.' I have a sinking feeling. So I was right that this Ohio assignment was nothing but an excuse to get me out of the way. 'How do you know all this?'

'I read all Phoebe's emails,' says Bob.

'What!'

'I set up the system,' he says casually. 'I have a master password. All us techies read the office emails.' He chuckles to himself. 'My goodness. I remember when you came back from the Lake District with Stephen. All that fuss about the cash expenses!'

I really don't want to hear any more. 'So what is Phoebe planning?'

'To shut the London office down. This review's just a smokescreen for her global takeover plan,' he says dramatically. 'She's going to run everything from New York just as soon as she's met all the UK artists and got them on board.'

'Who else knows about this?'

There's a pause. 'No one else apart from Betty in Accounts.' The penny drops – that's why they always sit together at lunch. 'And I've been dropping hints to Lisa on Reception. I have to be careful not to say too much until I get another job. Or a book deal. I've abandoned the medieval rom-com and I've started a thriller. It's about a ruthless woman tycoon and her evil sidekick and how they want to make lots of money at the expense of the loyal employees. The hero's called Rob.'

I feel a wave of aloneness wash over me. I have nothing to do here and nothing to do back home. I liked working for Graham, and I don't want to look for another job. Interviews have always posed a particular challenge for me (though not as big a challenge as they do for Zara, who had to be given oxygen after the Marks & Spencer's basic maths test). Then there are the new people to meet, new routines to learn and the agony of hoping there will be someone to sit next to in the canteen. I'm sure that's the real reason so many people eat lunch at their desk.

I pull myself back to the present and ask about the photographs, which Bob promises to email me.

'Look, I have to go now,' says Bob. 'I'll email you if there are any developments. I can cover my tracks. But don't email back. I think Brent may be trying to hack into the system.'

I switch on the television and wait for the news and weather forecast. Apparently a thaw is due to begin this afternoon, so I call the airline to change my flight, get put on hold for half an hour on account of the backlog of stranded passengers, and eventually manage to get a flight out on Saturday. There's nothing for it but to go back to the London office, look for another job and put up with Brent in the meantime. Then I go up to the bedroom and start my packing. In my experience you can never do too much preparation in advance.

At just before noon there's a knock on the cottage door. It's Wyatt.

'I came to invite you to brunch,' he says. 'If you're up to eating?' he adds, grinning at me.

I'm very hungry. 'I'll get my coat.'

We go in by the kitchen door, which I suppose means that I'm no longer a formal visitor.

'I saw on the news that the road to the airport should be cleared tonight,' I say as I take off my parka and hang it over the back of my chair. 'So I'll be gone on Saturday.'

Wyatt doesn't reply. Instead, he takes down a cast-iron skillet from the hanging rack – I've always wanted to do that – and takes a pack of bacon out of the stainless-steel double-door Maytag refrigerator.

I sit down at the kitchen table. 'About last night,' I say nervously. 'It was all a big misunderstanding. Somehow Bruce got the wrong idea.'

Wyatt puts the skillet on the double range and begins adding bacon to the pan.

'I never told him I was in AA.'

'Yes. I think we worked that out.'

Wyatt pours me a glass of Tropicana orange juice (which, needless to say, I'm not permitted to purchase at home. We're limited to supermarket own-brands only).Then he begins making mix for waffles. Travis is pacing up and down in front of the range, sniffing for bacon.

I'm leaving soon. What the hell, I may as well come clean.

'The thing is, I do go to a group and I was in an outpatient programme. But not for alcoholism.'

Wyatt nods.

'I have ...' My voice trails off. 'Sometimes I get a bit anxious about things.'

Wyatt still isn't saying anything.

'Like driving. Or flying. Or things I have to do at work.'

Wyatt turns to me, frowning. 'But you do all those things.'

'Well, yes. I haven't had any choice here, have I?'

It's odd, but now he points it out, I have been feeling much better recently. By a strange coincidence, this improvement has coincided with me leaving Stephen behind in England.

I need to give him some concrete examples.

'Before I go to bed, I clean the kitchen sink, make a list of everything I have to do the next day and disinfect my BlackBerry.'

'Your BlackBerry?'

'PDAs are a haven for germs,' I assure him. 'So that's my life,' I say lightly. 'Tick, tick, tick. Tidy, tidy, tidy.'

Oh God, what the hell induced me to say that?

But I've started this conversation now, so I may as well finish it.

'My boyfriend's the same.'

'Boyfriend?'

'We're not engaged. In fact we had a big row at the airport.' I take a deep breath. I point at my ring. 'I was so cross that I went and bought this for myself. It's not a real diamond. It's zirconia.'

'No one would ever know,' says Wyatt gallantly.

'Thank you.' It's vital that I don't stop talking. Otherwise the sheer idiocy of much of what I'm saying will hit home and I'll never speak again. 'You see, I thought he was going to propose. He pulled out a sheet of paper and I thought he'd written a poem. But he hadn't. He handed me a spreadsheet.'

Wyatt is now looking incredulous. He recaps. 'You're his girlfriend. You're leaving for six months. And he hands you a spreadsheet?' He looks at me as if he can't quite believe this.

'Yes. Here it is.' I rummage in my parka pocket and hand it to Wyatt.

'Stephen and Alice Projected Household Expenditure Budget,' he reads out. He tosses it on the kitchen table. 'Sorry, Alice, but this guy sounds a jerk.'

I'm not in the least offended. 'You're not the first person to say something like that,' I sigh. I know I must defend Stephen at this point. 'Stephen's very sensible,' I say. As I look at Wyatt, a thought pops into my head from nowhere. *Stephen's also really boring in bed.* I can't think why that topic would come to mind right now.

I push the thought aside and hurry on. 'So that's it. I'm not the Southfields Baby Whisperer. I don't have a TV show. I'm not engaged. I'm not a recovering alcoholic.' Is there anything I've left out? 'And Stephen isn't a cigar-smoking international attorney. Actually he's mildly asthmatic.'

Wyatt must have been around some really nutty people in his life, because he doesn't look in the least fazed by this.

'Alice, it's OK,' he says. 'I came to apologize on Bruce's behalf. He gets carried away sometimes.'

He comes and sits down at the table.

'Bruce seems a bit over the top. But it's because he really cares about getting people to sober up.'

'Is that because of what happened to him?'

'You'll have to ask him. Let's say that a lot of chefs in top kitchens rely on alcohol and cocaine to keep them going.' Wyatt pauses. 'I was in a pretty bad state last Christmas. Bruce kept faith with me.'

'Is that why he doesn't want you to sing?'

'So he warned you off, did he? He's worried that I'll slip back into the old lifestyle.'

I can't stop myself. 'But you could write,' I say. I've been listening to a lot of Wyatt's songs lately on *Scott Country* – one even came on the radio as I was driving to Yellow Springs with Gerry. I heard the first few bars before Gerry changed the station. 'And you could record without touring.'

'You have to tour, Alice. The promotion's half the work.'

I know this, but I don't want to give up. 'Maybe you

could just write songs,' I say. Surely Bruce couldn't find anything to complain about with that? 'They could be uplifting, sober lyrics.'

I don't want to see Wyatt relapse. But I also feel it's a shame that all the talent he has should go to waste.

'Maybe.'

It's not much, but it's progress.

> *Girl from afar*
> *She's sort of taken*
> *I see her now*
> *Eatin' some bacon.*

Also, I know that I'm not the only one who feels this way. I remember Rachel and Celeste talking in the diner on the day I arrived. And I know Rachel is desperate for Wyatt to sing again.

I decide to take a chance. If Wyatt gets offended, too bad. I take a deep breath. 'It's seems a pity to have all that talent and let it go to waste.'

'Is that what you really think?' Wyatt says evenly.

'Yes! I came here to get you to record again. But I don't care about that any more.' I really don't. 'I just think that it's something you should do for yourself, even if you never make another record in your life.'

Wyatt gives me an apologetic look. 'I don't want to get you into trouble with Carmichael Music.'

I roll my eyes. 'Hey, it's only my job on the line.'

'What!'

'Only joking,' I say unconvincingly.

Wyatt is giving me a hard stare. 'What do you mean?'

'Nothing.'

'Alice!'

'Oh, all right. It's all very hush-hush, but Phoebe's planning to shut down the London office and we're all going to be out of a job.' I take a sip of my Tropicana, savouring the pulp. 'To be honest, I think Phoebe sent me over here to get me out of the way.' Too late I realize how this sounds. 'Not that they don't want you to record again!' I say hurriedly. 'In fact, they're paying me to stay here for six months. But now that you've decided not to write, there's nothing else for me to do here. Though Phoebe did suggest I look for some local talent.'

'What local talent?' Wyatt asks, puzzled.

'Singing dogs and families with umpteen children. She thought I might find the next Partridge Family.'

Wyatt says nothing to this. Instead we lapse into a comfortable silence as he serves up breakfast, waving away my offers of help, and bringing me over a plate of bacon, eggs and waffles and refilling my glass with Tropicana. It's a world of luxury here.

He sits down and we eat companionably for a few minutes, Travis padding up and down between us hoping for bacon bits.

'It's a terrible habit, begging at the table,' says Wyatt. 'I can't think where he got it from.' He reaches down. 'He's named after Randy Travis. Poor guy spent years trying to get me sober.'

Then we talk about Casey and his project, which I've promised to help him with again this afternoon.

'Are you going to get it finished?' asks Wyatt.

'Most of it. I haven't received the Johnny Depp photos yet. If they don't arrive by the time I leave, maybe I could send them to you?'

'Yes,' says Wyatt slowly. 'But wouldn't it be better if . . .'

At that moment Wyatt is interrupted by the sound of the telephone ringing. He gets up.

'Hey. Yep. Yes, she's here.'

Oh God, I hope it's not Gerry. Enjoyable though parts of yesterday evening were, I think it would be better for all concerned if we didn't meet again.

Wyatt looks at his watch. 'Just over an hour. OK, I'll tell her.'

'That was Heidi,' says Wyatt, replacing the receiver. 'She was calling to remind you that you're speaking to her high-school class this afternoon. First period after lunch.'

I put down my knife and fork. What talk? What class? *When?*

CHAPTER 21

Barnsley High School is a 1970s sprawling brick building situated at the top of a hill and surrounded by farmland. Across from the car park there are six tennis courts and a full-size running track in a proper stadium. As I step into the school lobby, there is row upon row of photographs of sports teams and wall-mounted cabinets stuffed with trophies – I see Barnsley High is a force to be reckoned with in the world of Ohio ten-pin bowling.

At the school office I'm directed a very long way away to Heidi's classroom. As I go down the corridor I hear that there's one class making a lot of noise. And as I reach the classroom door I realize it's Heidi's.

It's also boiling hot in here. Why are schools always so overheated?

I feel sick with nerves. But what could I do? Heidi obviously told Wyatt that my talk had already been agreed between us. With barely an hour's notice I have no notes, no slides and not so much as a list of topics. I'm going to have to do something I've never before done in my life – make it up as I go along. There was also no time to get changed, so I'm dressed informally in my Marks & Spencer regular-fit jeans and my trusty Lands' End fleece.

Hesitantly I knock on the door. Then I knock again. Still

there's no response, so I walk in and the class turns to stare at me. Right away I grasp that everything you've seen in those high-school movies is true. At the back are the sporty boys and in front of them are the gorgeous girls. By the window to the side are the alienated Goth teenagers – a scowling boy and girl dressed in black with lots of chain jewellery – and to the front are my people, the nerds. They sit with pencils sharpened, notebooks opened and intense expressions. There are three of them: a girl with plaits, a boy in a neatly ironed check shirt and a very thin girl who looks like she could benefit from my Wednesday-night anxiety support group.

Heidi is wearing a navy-blue suit and high-heeled shoes. Her hair is even more rigidly curled up at the ends. She gets up from her desk and embraces me like a long-lost friend. Then she turns to the class.

'I'd like to give a warm welcome to Alice, who has come to talk to you today about life in England. I do hope you will take full advantage of this valuable cross-cultural opportunity and ask plenty of searching questions.'

I hope that my legs are going to support me. My mouth is dry but I can't risk reaching for the bottled water I brought with me because then they'll see my hand shaking with nerves. I'm also bright red from the heat. I think I may pass out unless I cool down. There's nothing for it but to remove my Lands' End fleece to reveal my '*I walked the Pennine Way*' souvenir T-shirt.

'Good afternoon,' I say.

There's no response.

'It's a great pleasure to be invited here today to Barnsley High School to talk about the United Kingdom.'

In the front row the plait girl whispers worriedly to the shirt boy, 'I thought it was England.'

I continue. 'The United Kingdom comprises England, Scotland, Northern Ireland and Wales.'

From the back of the classroom there's a whale noise and lots of spluttering.

'Many immigrants to the United States came from England seeking religious freedom and new economic opportunities.' I must engage with them. 'Do any of you have English ancestors?'

No one answers. I notice a spotty boy in the middle of the room surreptitiously take out his phone and start sending a text message.

'Or Ireland, perhaps?' I say desperately.

Still no one answers.

Plait girl, shirt boy and the girl who's very thin are writing everything down. The honking whale noises are continuing in the back row amid a great deal of flirtatious whispering between the best-looking sporty boy and the prettiest, blondest girl sitting in front of him. He's wearing a Barnsley High School football shirt and she's in a plunge-neck stretch top.

'Madison, are you staying over after my party?'

Madison rolls her eyes. 'Get over yourself, Logan.'

I try not to be distracted. I stop trying to engage and launch into an explanation of the system of government of the United Kingdom. 'The House of Commons is comprised of six hundred and fifty-six MPs. That stands for Members of Parliament,' I explain.

From what I can overhear, I work out that Madison is sitting next to her friends Brittany and Leeanne, that they are all going to the party, and that Logan's older brother has promised to buy beer.

I summarize the role of MPs in the UK legislative system. At the back of the classroom I'm heartened to see that

Brittany is now writing keenly. Logan is throwing rolled-up bits of paper at Madison's head and Leeanne is applying lipgloss. The Goth boy is stabbing at his arm with a bunch of keys and a number of people have their eyes fixed on the wall clock.

'The Queen is the head of the government. After an election, the party leader with the most votes goes to Buckingham Palace to meet the Queen. Although the party leader has won the election, it's the Queen who asks him or her to form a government. It's an interesting piece of constitutional detail,' I say with a light laugh.

Brittany passes her notes to Leeanne, who for some reason collapses with laughter. At last Heidi takes action. She walks up to the back of the classroom.

Plait girl shoots me a worried expression. 'What if the Queen said she wanted someone else. Like a friend of hers?'

'That wouldn't happen,' I say reassuringly.

'But what if it did?' calls out Heidi from the back.

I have no idea. 'There would be a referendum,' I say confidently.

'I think it's sick that you have a Queen,' says Goth boy, coming to life. 'It's all about power and control and oppression.' His girlfriend, who must get through an awful lot of black eyeliner, nods in agreement and shoots me a look that implies I am personally responsible for global injustice.

'I don't think the Queen has ever oppressed anyone,' I say huffily.

Puzzlingly, Heidi is walking back to the front of the class holding Brittany's notes. But at least she seems to be coming on board to help me here. 'Would you say that the Queen is loved by her subjects?'

'Very much so,' I say firmly.

'So you're a patriotic nation,' says Heidi, coming to my assistance at last.

'Extremely,' I confirm.

Heidi gives a little smile. She casually tosses Brittany's confiscated notes on to the desk in front of me.

Oh my God. It's a drawing of me. I have a huge head, lank hair, stick arms and a speech bubble coming out of my mouth that says, 'Help me! I need a makeover!'

Logan is now miming sleep in the back row. I have to do something. Perhaps they would like to hear about some museums they could visit if they come to London. 'The British Museum has a fascinating array of Roman artifacts,' I tell them.

Logan mimes hanging himself, his head lolling lifelessly to one side.

I give up. 'Are there any questions?'

There's an agonizing silence.

Then a hitherto unnoticed boy with long, purple-streaked hair and a skateboard sweatshirt calls out, 'What age can you drink in England?'

'Eighteen,' I say.

Finally there's a response. They start chattering like birds. 'That's how it should be here.'

I must look confused, because plait girl says to me, 'You have to be twenty-one to drink alcohol legally in the USA.'

The questions are now starting to flow.

'What are pubs like?'

'What's the speed limit?'

'What beer do you like?'

'Can you smoke dope?'

'Do you have to wear a crash helmet on a motorcycle?'

I finally catch on to what's required here.

Heidi interjects. 'Alice, perhaps you'd like to talk a little bit about religious customs in England in the sixteen hundreds?'

No way. I know exactly what I'm going to talk about. My eye has fallen on Goth girl's T-shirt. If I'm not mistaken, it's a Firestorm World Tour T-shirt from last year.

'In my job at Carmichael Music I get to meet many of the most famous artists and bands in the world.'

They've all shut up!

'Last year at the Brit Awards, I mixed with Madonna, Beyoncé and Green Day.' I didn't actually meet them, but I was in the same room, so that counts.

Madison is entranced. Logan whispers something to her. She waves him away. 'Shut up, you moron.'

'Also, I met Joss Stone and Sharon Osbourne, who's very nice in person, and Simon Cowell.'

'Simon Cowell,' mouths Madison to Brittany. They look at me as if I'm a goddess.

I'm getting into my stride here. 'I was personally responsible for signing Firestorm to Carmichael Music.' This is technically true. I typed the contract and fetched the pens from the stationery cupboard.

'You've met *Jez*?' says Goth girl wonderingly. Jez is the Firestorm lead singer. He's actually called Jeremy and went to Eton, but Graham thought it would be better if we renamed him Jez.

I pull out my BlackBerry. There's a group murmur. 'Let's see if we can get hold of him in London.'

What the hell, it's worth a try. I dial Jez's mobile, then melodramatically lift the BlackBerry to my ear.

Jez answers! 'Hey, Alice, how are you?' He has such nice manners.

We exchange banter for a few moments as I'm watched

by twenty-five open-mouthed teenagers and Heidi, who's looking really pissed off.

'Jez, I have someone here who'd like to talk to you.'

Several girls chorus in unison, 'Oh my gosh,' as I pass the phone to Goth girl.

She listens for a few moments then shrieks to the class, 'It's him!'

Pandemonium breaks out. Heidi gets up and shouts at them. 'Be quiet!'

Goth girl finishes her conversation and hands me back the BlackBerry. 'How much does it cost to fly to London?' she says desperately.

I'm about to tell her when Heidi folds her arms and moves almost in front of me, blocking my view of the class.

'I'm sure we'd all like to thank Alice for her most informative talk.'

She turns back to me. Only I can see her expression. I begin to feel a little scared.

'We have ten minutes left.' She's looking at me with unconcealed dislike. 'Now, Alice, you said earlier that you are very patriotic, with a great affection for the Queen.'

She pauses as if waiting for me to confirm this.

'Yes,' I say slowly. This is leading somewhere bad, I can feel it.

She walks over to a cupboard and takes out a boom-box portable stereo.

No, it can't be that.

'It would be wonderful, given your impressive musical background,' she says heavily, 'if you would sing for us the British National Anthem.'

I open my mouth to object, but no sound comes out.

'Here are the words,' she says briskly, handing me a

photocopied sheet. 'Just in case you need reminding. I've managed to track down a recording of the music.'

I look out at the class. I can't sing to save my life. I have one of those warbling voices that breaks all the time.

Heidi is talking to the class as she sets up the stereo. 'You should all recognize the tune. It's the same as "Sweet Land of Liberty", our own American patriotic song. Probably the British stole the melody from us.'

Worse still, my previously bored audience is looking back at me with eager expectation. Plait girl leans forward and whispers, 'Miss Alice, could I have your email address, please? I'd love to have a life like yours!'

But then a miracle happens.

Madison gets up from her seat, revealing an inch of bare midriff, and sashays to the front of the class. 'I know that tune.' She turns to me. 'I'll sing it with you.'

She's an angel in low-rise Gap jeans!

'My Mom says I could win *American Idol*,' Madison confides to me as Heidi rewinds the tape. 'We're going to Chicago for the auditions as soon as I'm sixteen.'

Heidi looks up. 'Madison, sit down!'

Madison stares back at her. 'I'm doing a cultural opportunity,' she says sullenly.

Heidi glares. 'I'm sure Alice can manage on her own.'

'Oh, the more the merrier,' I say quickly.

Heidi has no choice but to start the music. Madison takes the paper with the words and begins to sing. She's really very good.

> *God save our gracious Queen,*
> *Long live our noble Queen*
> *God save the Queen.*

If she didn't have a huge white smile, you'd almost think she was British. Meanwhile I lip-synch by her side. When she finishes, Logan starts cheering at the back, and after a few moments the rest of the class joins in. Madison and I give little bows. Then the bell sounds and they all get up, scraping their chairs.

I turn to Madison. 'What can I do to thank you?'

She doesn't miss a beat. 'I want Simon Cowell's phone number.'

I don't have it, but I know someone who can get it. 'I'll speak to my contact, Bob.'

'Bob?'

'He knows everyone who's anyone,' I assure her.

Madison gives me a hug and joins the rest of the class as they leave the classroom. I pick up my handbag and pull on my fleece and go to say a quick goodbye to Heidi. I have no intention of being left on my own with her.

But Heidi clearly has other ideas, because as her last pupil leaves the class she goes over, closes the door and stands there, barring my exit.

'So I expect you have plans to leave soon,' she says.

'Saturday.'

Her expression clears. 'Good.' She takes a step towards me. 'I'm sure you wouldn't want to outstay your welcome.'

'No.' I feel obliged to stand up for myself. 'I don't think there's any danger of that.'

Heidi laughs. 'Oh, you mean Wyatt putting you up at the cottage? I wouldn't read anything into that if I were you. Wyatt has a thing for taking in waifs and strays.' She gives a louder laugh. 'He took in Mary Lou, didn't he? A *cow*.' She looks me up and down. 'I think that rather proves my point.'

Heidi takes another step closer. 'Wyatt and I go back a

long way. We have a history. We understand each other. You belong in London, Alice.'

Before I have a chance to tell her what I think of her, she puts her hand on the door handle and opens it, gesturing for me to leave. 'My advice to you is to pack your bags, get in your car and go back to where you came from.'

CHAPTER 22

It's seven o'clock in the evening and I'm still trying to get the image of Brittany's stick-woman drawing out of my mind. I'm focusing on doing my washing. I'm very behind schedule. I should have finished my packing by now – it's only seventeen hours until I'm due to leave for the airport – but somehow I just can't motivate myself to start. Instead I switch on the Maytag and embark on giving the cottage a mini-spring clean. It's as I'm on my hands and knees, polishing the bedroom floor with my Pledge multisurface orange spray (unfortunately I don't have any wax floor polish), that Gerry walks in.

'Hey, princess,' he calls out. 'Where are you?'

I emerge from under the bed and hurry down the spiral staircase.

Gerry is standing at the foot of the stairs holding a pizza in one hand and a bottle of wine in the other. 'I could come up there,' he says with a little-boy grin.

'That won't be necessary,' I say sternly.

Gerry pretends to collapse at the knees. 'I bet those English guys go crazy when you talk like that.'

I make do with an enigmatic smile rather than point out that my accent isn't really a novelty in the United Kingdom.

Gerry goes off into the kitchen, presumably in search of

a corkscrew. 'Couldn't leave a beautiful woman all on her own,' he calls out. 'I just passed Wyatt going down the drive with that beardy guy.'

'Bruce.'

Gerry comes back into the living room and opens the wine. I guess Wyatt and Bruce are off to an AA meeting, but I don't disclose this to Gerry. Thanks to *Enable YOU* I take the principle of anonymity very seriously.

Fortunately Gerry doesn't say any more about it. Instead, he flings his brown leather jacket across a chair, grabs my hand, lowers me on to the sofa and kisses me for five minutes before passing me a glass and feeding me pizza. Then he gets up and makes a fire, emptying out the log basket in the process. I notice that Gerry's fire is a lot bigger than Wyatt's. I think this fire-lighting must be a symbolic macho-man rite for American men. Gerry gives a low whistle of satisfaction as the fire takes hold. Then he gets up and puts on some light jazz. It's now just like a scene from a romantic film in here! A few flakes of snow are even falling outside.

Gerry puts his hand on my knee. 'I think you should stay, Alice. I'm leaving for Vegas next week. Come with me.'

'I really couldn't.'

He ignores me. 'I'm working on a very big deal. We could go to the Bellagio.'

I have no idea what the Bellagio is, but I'm sure it's very nice.

I shake my head. 'I'm sure Wyatt wouldn't want me to outstay my welcome.'

'Stay at my place!' he exclaims. Then he leans forward, takes a sip of wine and shrugs his shoulders. 'I know what you mean about Wyatt. He helps his neighbour ... up to a point.' His voice trails off.

I'm intrigued. 'What do you mean – up to a point?'

He shakes his head. 'It's nothing. Wyatt's a nice guy.' Gerry puts his arm around me and begins kissing my neck. 'Let's talk about you,' he murmurs.

Pleasant though this is, I can't let the subject of Wyatt's neighbourliness rest. Gently I push him away. 'Tell me.'

He sits back. 'Nothing, honey.' He waves his hand around the room. 'I'm not going to come here and bad-mouth Wyatt. You can't blame him for using his money to get what he wants.'

'How did he use his money?' I persist.

Gerry sounds casual. 'When it comes to business, he likes to win. Lots of people would say there's nothing wrong with that. I'm just old-fashioned, I guess.'

'What business?' I pull away from Gerry so that I'm sitting on the edge of the sofa. 'You have to tell me.' I can't imagine Wyatt doing anything that wasn't straight. 'He seems so good-hearted.'

Gerry gives me a sharp look and raises his eyebrows.

'This farm was in the same family for generations. The farmhouse, the barn, the land. When the farmer died, it passed to his two daughters. They were missionaries and they didn't want it, so they put it up for sale.' Gerry moves back to me and pulls me close. 'Of course, this cottage wasn't here then. Wyatt built it for his girlfriends to stay in.' He gives a sigh. 'Wyatt's the love'em and leave'em type. He likes his space.'

I have a churning feeling in my stomach. That makes sense.

'Anyhow, they decided to sell it at auction. That's a proper auction – out in the open air in the yard. Now, we're talking all the buildings and two hundred acres of prime farmland. This is farming country, Alice. There were a lot of decent, hard-working farming folks hoping to get it. They needed the land to make a livelihood. There were pick-up trucks parked all the way down that driveway and people spilling out of the yard. First they sold off the farm machinery. But everyone was waiting for the land. People had begged and borrowed to have a chance of getting it.' Gerry pauses. 'Well, ten minutes before the land comes up for sale, Wyatt rolls up out of the blue. He hadn't set foot in Barnsley for years. Folks looked like they'd seen a ghost. Then he outbid them all. See, he pushed the bidding right up till no one could beat him. How could they? They're ordinary farmers and he's a big star. So Wyatt got the land, moved in and announced he'd rent out half the land to the farmers.'

Gerry pauses.

'Why only half the land?'

'Said he wanted his privacy.' Gerry gestures out of the window. 'Take a look tomorrow at all that land down in the valley. It's not farmed. Wyatt won't let anyone on it.'

It's true. Since the snow has melted I've noticed that land covered in long meadow grass.

Gerry strokes my neck. 'Wyatt's not bad – he looks out for people – but when it comes to business, he doesn't take any prisoners.'

It rings horribly true. I think back to how Wyatt was on the day I met him: throwing me out of the house, acting like he hated visitors, then flinging my suitcase in the back of his truck. He only took me in because of Mr Horner.

'But that's enough about Wyatt, Alice. You're doing the right thing – keeping it purely business. I'd hate for him to use you.'

'There's no danger of that,' I say primly before sinking into Gerry's arms. Yes, I've had a lucky escape. I could have got quite fond of Wyatt, but now I know better.

The next couple of hours pass in a haze of pizza, wine

and what British teenagers used to call necking.

'You are an amazing woman, Alice,' whispers Gerry. 'I've never met anyone like you.' He undoes the top button on my Lands' End long-sleeved polo in sage green.

'Really?' I say hopefully, putting my hand over his.

'You have that English class and reserve. You're irresistible.'

I lighten my touch to allow him to continue. Gerry now moves his weight on top of mine so that I have no option but to lie flat on my back.

'Not that I'm trying to resist you.'

It's very tempting. I'm warm, woozy and I'm not feeling at all guilty about Stephen, which is odd, given that we've been going out for three years.

Gerry is doing that thing where he kisses my neck, and I literally have shivers going up my spine. He's stroking my hair with one hand and massaging my bottom with the other. He's very good at multi-tasking. 'I think we were meant to be together, Alice,' he breathes. 'It wasn't an accident you came into the diner. What were the chances of us meeting?'

'Remote,' I guess.

'Hmm.' He moves his hand from my bottom, slips it under my long-sleeved polo and dexterously undoes my bra strap. It takes him a nanosecond. In three years Stephen has never managed that. 'Let's go upstairs,' he whispers.

I unbutton his shirt. 'I don't know about that.'

Gerry slips his hand around my breast. 'I do. And the answer is an unequivocal yes.'

I can't reply to that because Gerry is kissing me very forcefully. I give up and surrender. I am, after all, a beautiful and classy Englishwoman – I must expect to have this effect on American men.

Gerry gets up and pulls me gently to my feet. I note that

he does not pause to take the leftover pizza into the kitchen and wrap it in clingfilm for his packed lunch. Instead, Gerry draws me to the stairs and silently leads the way up. Manfully he throws my British Home Stores pyjamas on the floor. 'You won't be needing those.'

He takes my hand and pulls me on to the bed.

I look over at the bedside light and reach for it.

'You don't need to turn out the light,' says Gerry. 'You're perfect.'

'Oh, I wasn't turning it off,' I exclaim. 'I just noticed a bit of dust on the lampshade. I must have missed it earlier. These pleated lampshades are a bugger to clean,' I tell him, dabbing at it with a pocket Kleenex.

'They are?'

'Hmm. I wonder if Dyson make a mini-brush attachment? They're useful for computer keyboards, too.'

Gerry looks at me with a hint of puzzlement. 'Hell, Alice, you really aren't like any woman I've ever met.'

Gerry has unbuttoned his shirt and tossed it on to the floor. He's definitely not British: he has proper pecs, abs and biceps and he's got a golden suntan. Also his Levi jeans fit properly. I feel a stirring in my nether regions. I haven't felt this level of excitement for years.

I watch him with pleasurable anticipation as he bends down to unlace his shoes. And then he disappears. Literally. He's there one minute and gone the next. I hear a yelp of surprise, an awful crunch and then a gasp of pain.

I think Gerry's slipped on the floor.

I should mention at this point that when I said earlier that I didn't have any wax floor polish so I made do with Pledge, I ignored the warning on the can that says *Do not spray or use on floors as it could make them slippery*. I really didn't think it would be a problem.

I scamper across and look over the side of the bed. Gerry is lying there holding his foot, his face wracked with pain. 'I think it's broken,' he says. 'I hit the end of the bed.'

I spring into action. 'We need to get you to a hospital. I'll see if Wyatt's back. He went to his AA meeting with Bruce but he should be home by now.'

Damn! I've just broken the anonymity of two AA members. This is very serious unless there's an exception for medical emergencies. I'm sure there is.

'No!' splutters Gerry, writhing on the floor. 'Don't call Wyatt.'

I ignore him. If only I had some frozen peas! 'Rest and elevate,' I call out over my shoulder as I hurry down the spiral staircase. I was a Kingston Council first-aider – the training never leaves you.

I run out into the yard and almost collide with Bruce, who's making his way to his car. 'Help!' I say. 'I need urgent medical assistance.'

'Alice, I knew you'd see sense one day.'

'Not for me. For Gerry. He's upstairs.'

'Should I bring my literature—'

I grab Bruce's sleeve and tug him inside. Unfortunately there's no choice but to lead Bruce through the living room with the debris of pizza boxes, an empty wine bottle and an ashtray. Bruce looks on disapprovingly. 'He's passed out, I suppose,' he says sadly.

'No, he's fully conscious,' I say over my shoulder, hurrying up the stairs.

Gerry is now lying on the bed, but his face is still wracked with pain.

'It's all going to be OK,' I say soothingly. 'This is Bruce.' I put on my best hostess voice. 'Bruce, you remember Gerry. You met at The Winds restaurant.' Bruce leans over and prises Gerry's hand away from his foot. I give a gasp of horror. Gerry's little toe is bright red and swollen to twice the normal size. Bruce kneels down, looks at it appraisingly, then gets hold of it and twists it.

'*AAAAH*!' yells Gerry. '*What the fuck?*'

'Probably broken,' says Bruce flatly, rising to his feet. 'But I don't think a doctor would do anything to it. I'll drive you home and you can see how it is in the morning.'

Gerry looks mutinous, but Bruce passes him his shirt. 'Technically, this is an alcohol-related accident. Something to think about, Gerry.'

'Yeah. If I'd had more to drink it wouldn't hurt so much,' mutters Gerry.

I can't help it. *Enable YOU* drones on and on about being honest in all situations. 'Actually, it was Pledge,' I pipe up.

Bruce does a double-take. 'You were sniffing Pledge?'

'No! I was cleaning the floor with it.'

Gerry is pulling on his shirt. As he buttons it up he casts me a woeful look. 'You see, Alice, you have to stay in Barnsley now. I need a nurse.'

I follow behind as Gerry hops down the stairs and out into the living room where I retrieve his jacket and drape it over his shoulders. Then Bruce helps him out to his Volvo. I look around and see that the downstairs lights are off in Wyatt's house – presumably Bruce sent him to bed with a pile of sober homework.

Gerry clambers into the car. As Bruce starts the engine, Gerry winds down the window. 'I'll probably need a bed-bath tomorrow, Alice.'

I feel awful. I can't help but kiss Gerry on the cheek, at which point he grabs my face and snogs me. 'Better than morphine,' he proclaims.

'It's frigging freezing in here,' barks Bruce, putting the car into gear and pulling away.

'Tally-ho,' shouts Gerry in a terrible British accent as they drive off.

I stand in the cold, watching until I can no longer see the lights of the car. I look up at the cloudless sky for a moment and out across the darkness to the lights of Barnsley. Somehow I know that after I leave tomorrow, I'll never come back here again. I feel an ache of regret. If only things were different: if only Wyatt was writing and wanted me to stay. I could go to Las Vegas with Gerry; I could see Casey's project through to the end; I could go with Rachel to the Lands' End shop at the mall and see their full summer range. And I could get those curtains down in the cottage and have them professionally dry-cleaned.

I wonder what Mum would say if she could talk to me now. Funny, but I think she would quite like Wyatt. Actually, I know what she would say, because she said it before.

'*You should see the world, Alice. While you're still young.*' Then I go inside to look up the Bellagio on the Internet. Just for fun, you understand. I'm sure I'll feel more positive about going home when I wake up tomorrow.

CHAPTER 23

It's Saturday morning, the day of my departure, and I'm feeling thoroughly depressed. I'm going to miss Barnsley, Ohio. I look around the little cottage and out of the bedroom window with its view of the fields and the woods beyond. I imagine walking there in the summer beneath the cool shade of the pines. It's so open and wild here. Unlike my flat in Southfields. This morning I telephoned Stephen to tell him that I would be arriving early on Sunday morning at Gatwick airport.

'Oh.' There was no mistaking the dismay in his voice.

'What is it?'

'Nothing,' he said too quickly.

'Stephen?'

'The thing is, there's been a small change in the domestic arrangements around here.' He pauses. 'We've got a lodger.'

I don't understand how. 'Stephen, we have a one-bedroom flat.'

'I'm sleeping on the sofa. It's perfectly satisfactory.'

'Who is it?'

'It's pilot Andy from the Wednesday-night group. He's been here since Tuesday.'

'But Andy doesn't like you,' I blurt out.

'He didn't have a lot of choice. Andy and Jennifer are in

hiding from her husband. He found out about them and broke into Andy's flat. Unfortunately he stole a good many portable valuables.'

'But why is Andy staying with you?' I ask, mystified.

'It was Jennifer's idea. She said no one would ever imagine that they'd choose to live with me.'

I'm almost screeching. '*Jennifer's there as well?*'

'Yes. Fortunately she had our home number. We thought about telling you, but we didn't want you to worry.'

'Don't you think you might have consulted me?' I say bitterly.

'There's nothing to be concerned about. We sat down and worked out a fair split of all the bills. And I label everything in the fridge so there's no confusion. Besides, their rent will more than make up for the shortfall caused by your departure. It's a win-win situation.'

'Until I come back.'

'Obviously we'll have to review the situation then,' says Stephen morosely. 'I wasn't expecting you back for six months. The loss of income will be significant.' He perks up. 'It works very well. The only time it gets a bit cramped is when Zara stays over.'

'Why does Zara stay over?' I say weakly.

'You know she can't go out after dusk.'

'How many times has this happened?'

'Twice. Wednesday night we played Scrabble. We lost track of time. Last night we reconvened for Monopoly. Jennifer and Zara sleep in the bed and Andy and I take turns on the sofa.'

I rang off soon after that. I think it's not unlikely that I will end up living with Dad and Valerie. That's it, then. No job, no home and an on-off boyfriend. Of course, things won't stay like that for ever. In time I'll get a job as a librarian, a bedsit in Surbiton and a cat. I'll sellotape large hand written signs to the other residents of the crumbling house – *Please ask guests to leave quietly, others are trying to sleep!!!* Every week I'll write a resentful letter to the local paper in spidery writing on my Basildon Bond lined blue pad. I'll start wearing my grey hair in a long ponytail, dress in Dad's cast-offs and talk to myself. Schoolchildren will shout at me, but only while riding past very fast on their bicycles. At least I'll have some racy memories to discuss with the cat.

I carry my suitcase down the stairs and lay my parka on top of it. As I look around the cosy living room, I feel, unaccountably, like bursting into tears. This is silly! I remind myself that clerical employment at Kingston Council offers job security, four weeks' paid holiday and a very nice self-serve salad bar in the staff restaurant.

Out of the window I see Wyatt and Casey coming out of the stables. Casey is manoeuvring a wheelbarrow full of straw. Wyatt is dressed as he was when I first met him, wrapped up against the cold, carrying a tin bucket across to the outside tap. Even though I've been here for less than a week, the farm feels like ... home. That's ridiculous, of course. Wyatt certainly doesn't want me to hang around. As Gerry says, he values his privacy.

I can picture the scene: after I leave, Heidi's car turns into the drive and she makes her way up the hill. She lets herself into the house. Wyatt is upstairs talking on the telephone to his other girlfriend. 'I'm busy,' he shouts out, 'and hungry.' Heidi occupies herself by making a three-course meal and washing Wyatt's pick-up truck. 'OK. I've got five minutes,' Wyatt shouts from the bedroom. After making love to her, Wyatt pushes her out of bed. 'See you next week. Maybe.' Then he falls asleep.

I almost feel sorry for Heidi. Unless of course she's the woman to cure Wyatt of his womanizing ways. I can picture the scene: after I leave, Heidi turns into the drive and makes her way up the hill. Wyatt greets her on the doorstep. 'After spending time with that imbecile, I've come to appreciate you and your incomparable apple pie even more. Heidi, will you marry me!'

I straighten the sofa cushions, clean out the fireplace and take out the Dyson to vacuum the rugs. It's as I'm pushing it up and down in parallel lines that I hear Wyatt's voice shouting above the noise of the vacuum cleaner.

'Alice!'

I switch it off.

Wyatt comes in looking stony-faced. I wonder if that's the expression he adopts when he's driving a hard business bargain, immune to the pleas of the honest farmer and his crying wife, who stands in the rain with a baby wrapped in a shawl as Wyatt's henchmen carry out all their worldly possessions. 'A contract is a contract,' says Wyatt, waving a sheaf of papers at them. Then he throws the baby's Moses basket into the back of his pick-up truck.

Wyatt peers around the cottage. 'Where is he?'

'Who?'

'Gerry,' he snaps. 'His car's parked outside.'

'Oh, he went home with Bruce last night.'

Wyatt's expression changes. He looks a bit happier. 'Why?'

'He broke his foot. He slipped on the floor.'

'Oh. I see.' For some reason Wyatt gives a half-smile at the news of Gerry's unfortunate accident. 'Painful, I guess?'

'Very.' I straighten out the rug and neaten the magazines on the coffee table.

'You don't need to do that, Alice.'

'I couldn't leave it dirty.'

'No, of course not,' he says resignedly. 'I forgot.'

He gestures to my suitcase. 'Is there anything I can say to make you stay?' he says. I recall Heidi's words to me. Obviously Wyatt is being characteristically polite. Either that or he wants to charge me rent.

'Afraid not. I have to get back to my jet-set lifestyle.'

He looks at his watch. 'Well, you can't leave without coming down to the Blue Ribbon.' He seems quite animated all of a sudden.

I look at my watch too. My flight leaves at six that evening. That's only seven hours from now, and the drive could take as long as two hours, maybe even two and a half.

I shake my head. 'I don't think I've got time.'

'Come on,' Wyatt says, grabbing my hand. 'Let's go.'

He goes out into the yard and calls for Casey. 'We're going to the Blue Ribbon.'

Casey appears like a shot and soon we're barrelling down the driveway in Wyatt's pick-up, Travis in the back with Casey but trying to wriggle his way into the front. Gosh, I hope Wyatt isn't charging Casey for the use of the barn and the straw. Maybe he writes all the expenses down in a little notebook. When Casey is eighteen Wyatt will present him with a bill. 'That's five years' of stabling and feed at eighty-nine per cent compounded interest. One million dollars, please.'

We reach the end of the driveway and turn on to the main road.

'It's a shame Alice is leaving today, isn't it, Casey?' says Wyatt conversationally. 'She won't get to see your project.'

'Yes,' mumbles Casey.

'You could email it to me,' I suggest brightly.

'I expect you've got a lot of projects coming up, Casey,'

says Wyatt, ignoring my very sensible suggestion. 'Bet you could do with some input from Alice?'

'Yes,' says Casey resignedly. 'Next term we have to do a huge project on plants and animals of Ohio.'

'I'm afraid I don't know much about that,' I say regretfully. 'I wouldn't be any help at all.'

'But you didn't know anything about Kentucky,' observes Casey. 'And that went really well.'

'It's a pity you won't be here to hear from Casey how his presentation goes next week,' chips in Wyatt. He's looking straight ahead at the road. 'Or for Casey's birthday in the summer,' he continues. He's really not helping the situation at all with these tactless comments.

'It would be cool if you were here, Alice,' says Casey wistfully.

Oh, really. I shoot Wyatt a questioning glance but he responds with a wide-eyed 'What have I said wrong' look. I remind myself that Wyatt is a good-hearted Ohio native brought up in the pioneer tradition of offering help to all. Heidi's words come back to me: *Wyatt always does the right thing, even for total strangers ... He took in Mary Lou, didn't he?* I picture Wyatt in the summer in a covered horse-drawn wagon just like on *Little House on the Prairie*, going round Barnsley helping build barns for people. At lunchtime he'll drink home-made lemonade and talk about how the coming of the railroad has changed everything round here. Then he'll drive a hard business bargain with them and two months later they'll be bankrupt.

We park outside the diner, pulling in at the same time as the Scott County Road Maintenance Crew, who look as if they've been out clearing the melting snow.

'This is Chris,' says Wyatt, introducing me. 'We used to have a band in high school.'

'Some of us still do,' Chris responds, lightly punching Wyatt on the arm.

Casey has run ahead of us into the Blue Ribbon. 'You could have made him a birthday cake,' whispers Wyatt, holding open the door for me.

The diner is full. All the seats at the counter are taken. Gerry is in one of them. He looks up from his newspaper and waves at me. I feel myself colour slightly. Before I have a chance to go over, I hear Rachel's voice. 'Wyatt! Alice! Over here.' She's in the same booth as before, with Baby Dale. And Mr Horner is sitting across from her. Presumably there's a riot if anyone sits in a different place.

Casey dives in first and I sit next to him. Wyatt squeezes in next to Rachel, Baby Dale and Rachel's bulging baby bag. Like Carolyn, she appears to leave home with supplies for a two-week holiday.

Baby Dale is asleep on Rachel's shoulder. 'Alice, we could go to the mall next week,' says Rachel.

'I'm sorry, I'm leaving today.'

Rachel's face falls. 'Oh no. I thought we could have lunch afterwards.'

'I've tried persuading Alice to stay, but she won't listen to me,' says Wyatt.

'If you want people to listen to you, Wyatt, you ought to make a record,' says Celeste curtly before taking our orders: three All-Day Breakfasts.

'Do you have to go so soon?' asks Rachel.

'I don't think there's anything left for me to do here,' I say.

'Rubbish,' says Wyatt. 'What about looking for local talent?' He shifts in his seat and calls out to the four members of the Scott County Road Maintenance Crew now sitting by the window. 'Alice here's looking for local talent.'

'Local talent? Why's she talking to you, then? We're your boys!'

'Then there's the *Barnsley Idol* competition,' adds Wyatt even more loudly to the diner in general.

'Goodness me, yes,' says Mr Horner. 'We would be honoured to have you as a judge.'

'Who said *Barnsley Idol*?' It's Dolores the cook. She hurries out from behind the counter, or as fast as she can go, given that her bad knee is making her limp. 'I heard about your talk at the high school.'

'Yes, I gather you were most enlightening on the subject of the British constitution,' says Mr Horner.

How do they know all this?

'Madison's my niece,' says Dolores. 'She had a lot of complimentary things to say about you.'

'As did my grandson,' says Mr Horner. 'He sits in the front row.'

'Madison's going to be the next *American Idol*,' Dolores says confidently.

'There you are,' says Wyatt. 'Alice could be Madison's voice coach.'

Dolores' hands fly to her face. 'I'll call her now!'

'Wait ...' I say, but she's already gone.

Celeste arrives in a little while with our three plates and Casey tucks in enthusiastically. I wonder how much he gets to eat at home. He's a little thin. Now that I come to think of it, perhaps there really is no one to make him a birthday cake. Perhaps he looks after his grandparents as well as Mary Lou? My thoughts are interrupted by Gerry arriving at our table. He's so sexy. Even on crutches with his foot in a plastic boot contraption he oozes sex appeal. He and Wyatt eye each other.

'How's the foot?' says Wyatt.

'Fine,' says Gerry curtly.

'I've heard those pinkie fractures can be really nasty,' says Wyatt. 'Though I've never heard of a man get one.' He sounds very sympathetic, so I don't know why Gerry gives him a dirty look. Then Gerry sits down opposite Mr Horner, who sniffs disapprovingly.

'How are you, Gerry?' I ask, trying to sound cool.

'All the better for seeing you. I'm definitely in need of some tender loving care.'

Out of the corner of my eye I see Rachel pass Baby Dale to Wyatt, who starts lifting him gently up and down. Thank goodness they're occupied, because Gerry has reached across the aisle to squeeze my knee.

'Does this mean that you won't be able to go on your business trip to Las Vegas?' I enquire.

Baby Dale must have done a trick, because opposite me Wyatt and Rachel burst out laughing.

Gerry frowns. 'Postponed. I'll just have to occupy myself in Barnsley.'

Mr Horner looks up from his newspaper and shoots Gerry a stern glance. 'If you're looking for a productive way to spend your time, Alice, we have a vacancy for the secretary's position at the Barnsley Historical Society.'

'Alice is the perfect candidate,' Wyatt announces. 'She could design a website for you.'

Mr Horner puts down his knife and fork. 'Splendid.'

I have to put a stop to all this. 'My flight's booked,' I state firmly.

'But what about my mothers' group?' says Rachel. 'I've told them all you're going to come and give a talk.'

'What about my project?' says Casey.

'What about me?' says Gerry suggestively.

'What have you got to lose?' says Wyatt quietly.

Everyone falls silent.

I look at Wyatt, for signs that he's joking around, but the eyes that look back at me are genuine. I think of the answer to Wyatt's question, but I can't say that one word out loud.

Nothing.

Or nothing that can't wait. Stephen has made new a life without me in less than a week; Dad is ecstatic that I'm doing so well over here; and Teresa doesn't give two hoots what I do. As for my job at Carmichael Music, I only have one if I stay here.

I look at Rachel and Wyatt; at Gerry who winks at me; and then at Casey.

'Pleeeeeze stay, Alice,' he says. He must be serious because he's stopped eating to speak.

Then everyone falls silent to wait for my answer.

I steel myself to do something I haven't done for years: to take a chance, to step into the unknown and, just for once, live as though I wasn't afraid of what the future holds.

'I'll stay,' I say.

Summer

CHAPTER 24

It's Casey's birthday today, and in celebration of this event I've decided to make him a traditional English cream tea. We're having cucumber sandwiches, freshly baked scones and a proper Victoria sponge cake filled with strawberry jam and buttercream. I'm currently making the cake in Wyatt's kitchen. He offered the use of his KitchenAid mixer (a free-standing model resembling the British Kenwood Chef, only bigger), and I quickly agreed before he had a chance to change his mind.

Casey is outside riding around on his new dirt bike, given to him earlier by Wyatt.

'Isn't it a bit dangerous?' I said worriedly when Wyatt unveiled it to the two of us in the barn.

'No,' said Wyatt.

'No,' said Casey. 'How fast does it go?'

It's a beautiful sunny June day, the house windows are open and all that can be heard is the buzz of Casey's bike as he does wheelies in the field with a couple of his friends. It will get hotter and more humid as the day goes on, but at ten o'clock in the morning it's most pleasant. It's now the school summer holidays, and Casey spends every day here looking after Mary Lou and pestering me for toasted cheese sandwiches. I did suggest to Casey that he might want to invite his school friends to my English tea. 'It would be an interesting cultural and culinary experience for them,' I pointed out. He agreed but said that he'd rather go to Laser Quest in Columbus followed by McDonald's.

I was very sad when school broke up at the end of May for a three-month summer holiday – far too long in my opinion. I really miss the weekly English vocabulary tests, the maths worksheets and the projects. Casey's Plant and Animals of Ohio presentation was quite an undertaking, and I'm proud to say we got an A+. I don't think I'm going too far in saying that my Poisonous Plants slideshow set a new standard in middle-school class talks.

While I play with the KitchenAid, trying it at different speeds, Wyatt is standing on a chair hanging up pale blue crêpe streamers which say *Happy 12th Birthday Kool Kid!* There are seven guests coming, and Heidi. The seven proper invited guests are Casey, Wyatt, Bruce, Dolores, Rachel, Baby Dale and me. Heidi will turn up anyway. I asked Casey if his grandparents would like to come, but he shook his head. 'Grandpa's busy on the farm and Grandma's busy making stuff,' he announced. 'She makes her own bread and cakes and jam and honey and she makes her own soap.'

Even though there are only seven people who have been formally invited, Rachel has insisted that we decorate the house. American women are obsessed by decorating, which is not things like painting and wallpapering. No, they go on and on about decorating for the holidays. The holidays are Thanksgiving, Christmas, Valentine's Day, Easter, plus all birthdays and the fourth of July (which naturally I've decided in advance not to celebrate). At Easter they hang Easter flags outside their houses, stick wooden painted bunnies in their gardens and drape brightly coloured plastic eggs from the trees. British people give each other one Easter egg, but

Americans give each other huge baskets of chocolate which they call candy. It all takes a bit of getting used to.

(American women are also obsessed about shopping at the mall, how many steps they walked that day to lose the weight they put on eating the baskets of candy, and what the best ever recipe is for brownies.)

Rachel dropped off the box of decorations yesterday and told Wyatt to put them up. 'I'll bring a plate of brownies,' she called out as she left. When you're invited to a party in Ohio, you're expected to bring your own plate of food – another confusing thing that you get used to. If it's a savoury item, it should contain spinach.

In order to make my traditional English tea, I'm wearing a white, crisply starched Williams-Sonoma apron that I found hanging behind the kitchen door. All Wyatt's kitchen utensils are made of shiny stainless steel (at home we have the black plastic bendy kind), and I haven't put anything in the bin – which is tastefully hidden inside behind a door that looks just like a kitchen cabinet – because I'm having such fun with the waste-disposal unit. This must be what it's like to be Nigella Lawson.

It's as I'm taking the butter out of the fridge that the telephone rings. I glance at the number – it's Larry, Wyatt's agent.

'Larry,' I call out to Wyatt. I already know what he's going to say.

'Can you get it?' he says.

I give Wyatt a rebellious look as I go ahead and answer the phone. 'Hello.'

'Alice, it's Larry!'

Thanks to the fact that Wyatt avoids talking to him, Larry and I are now quite good friends. Every time I'm in the house and Wyatt sees it's Larry calling, he picks up the phone and hands it to me, mouthing 'I'm not here.' I'm sure Larry must be suspicious.

'How's it going?' says Larry affably. As usual he doesn't wait to hear my answer. (People in shops and offices here are always asking 'How are you?', and until Wyatt pointed out that this was a form of greeting, I made an effort to give them a detailed reply.) Larry runs on excitedly, 'Now this one he's going to say yes to.'

Larry always says that. Almost every week he calls up with a request for some company wanting to use one of Wyatt's songs in their latest advertisement. Wyatt always says no.

'OK,' says Larry. 'You've got to help me here, Alice. *This* is classy. *This* he'll like. *This* he'll say yes to.'

'What?'

'Non-alcoholic beer! They want to use "Moonshine". It's a genius idea. Seven figures.'

I press the phone to my apron, look up at Wyatt and whisper. 'Moonshine. Non-alcoholic beer. Seven figures.'

'Nope.'

'I'll try, but I doubt it,' I relay to Larry.

'You're killing me here, Alice. This is big-time exposure. We're talking first showing of the ad during the Super Bowl next year.'

'Super Bowl ad,' I repeat to Wyatt. I gather this is quite a big American football game. A bit like our British FA Cup.

Wyatt looks even more bored and shakes his head. He can't speak because he has a drawing pin in his mouth.

'I'm sure he'll give it his fullest consideration,' I say brightly to Larry.

'You're a sweetheart, Alice,' says Larry, who is never downhearted. 'Talk to you later.'

I put the telephone down. 'Poor Larry,' I say. 'Shouldn't

you just tell him that you're never going to do any advertising deals again?'

Wyatt takes a drawing pin out of the side of his mouth. 'I have told him,' he says distractedly. He's twisting the crêpe streamer before fastening it. 'He doesn't take any notice.'

Larry is not one of those high-flying Hollywood agents. Wyatt told me that he operates out of a back office in Nashville. Wyatt is his biggest client. When he got famous, Wyatt didn't drop Larry and change agent, which must have been a big relief for Larry because he still gets ten per cent of Wyatt's royalties.

While the butter softens, I take out the flour and baking powder. I'm using a British recipe faxed to me by Carolyn. Unfortunately, Americans don't use scales to measure things out. You would think that they would have invented kitchen scales over here by now, but instead they use different sizes of cups. So I'm having to do a bit of guesswork to convert the recipe, but I'm sure it will be fine. I very precisely measure the baking powder as instructed by Carolyn, who has sampled my cooking in the past. 'It's the raising agent, Alice,' she said twice. 'Don't forget it.'

I'm just about to add the baking powder to the flour when the phone rings again. I carefully place the spoon back in the pack to remind myself to add it. It's Mr Horner. He calls every day about this time.

'I called you at the cottage but there was no reply,' he says, sounding a little put out. 'So I thought I'd try you here.'

'Good morning, Mr Horner,' I say.

'Weather hot enough for you?' he says with a chuckle. He used to say weather cold enough for you, but now he's switched. There are only two types of weather in Ohio – freezing cold or really hot.

'Now, about the Settler Float . . .'

I tuck the telephone under my ear and begin sieving flour. This could take some time. Mr Horner is organizing the Settler Float for the Barnsley Festival parade. Various members of the Historical Society will be dressed up as early settlers. It's the same every year, and, as usual, Mr Horner has cast himself as William Armstrong, the founder of Barnsley.

'. . . So,' Mr Horner says, 'do you think you could obtain some shiny black shoes with a brass buckle? I imagine they still wear them in London.'

I do hope Mr Horner never actually visits London, because he'd have a terrible shock in Piccadilly Circus.

'I'm sure I can find some,' I say, putting down the sieve and reaching for my notebook.

Mr Horner is now telling me about his costume. 'And I need some black tights,' adds Mr Horner. 'I've located the three-corner hat and the frock coat.'

Wyatt is blowing up balloons and mouthing blah, blah, blah at me and making a yapping mime with his fingers and thumb. I frown and wave my finger at him in a passable imitation of Mr Horner.

Then Mr Horner starts on about the latest page of the Barnsley Historical Society website. I'm adding new pages to the Barnsley Historical Society website as soon as Mr Horner can draft them – which is not very fast, as he's something of a stickler for checking his facts. Finally Mr Horner finishes. 'I think that's all for now. Good-day to you!'

I replace the telephone and add *buckled shoes* to my 'Settlers' Float' list. On the preceding page is my 'Party' list for today, and on the following page my 'Stephen' list. Despite the miles that separate us, I continue to remind Stephen to collect his dry-scalp medicated shampoo from Boots and to stock up on corn plasters at the same time. The last item on the Stephen list is *guttering quotes*. Stephen has asked me to research the cost of economy-grade plastic guttering at five different UK building suppliers.

'I cannot cope, Alice. My tractor-tyre case has reached a critical juncture,' he said wildly in our most recent once-a-week telephone call.

'I expect you have to tread carefully,' I quipped.

'What?'

The guttering quotes are needed for tonight's meeting of the residents of the flats where we live. Originally it was a big Victorian house, but it was converted into four flats a few years ago. The owners of the other three flats get on really well together and often have barbecues in the summer. We can see them from our kitchen window. Stephen is most vexed at the quotes that have been obtained for the repair of the guttering. 'They are extravagant to the point of profligacy, Alice. I'm relying on you.'

I obtained five quotes and emailed them to Stephen. He has promised to let me know how things go tonight and warned me that he 'won't be taking any prisoners'.

I watch as Wyatt jumps off the counter and begins unravelling a plastic *Happy 12th Birthday* banner which Rachel has instructed him to hang across the window. He's wearing a grey T-shirt and a pair of sun-bleached khaki shorts. He's humming some tune under his breath. Not one of his songs. I'm now familiar with all of Wyatt's albums, which I listen to in the car, purely for research.

Wyatt peers into Rachel's box. 'Right, that's it. I'm taking Casey and his mates for a birthday breakfast. Are you coming?'

I'd love to, but I have a cake to make plus two dozen scones and a batch of sandwiches. I shake my head. 'Say hello to Nancy and Dolores for me.'

I've been bowling most nights with Nancy and Dolores. I

was drafted in as the fifth member of the Barnsley team for the Mid-Ohio Ladies Ten-Pin Bowling League after Dolores took longer than expected to recover from her knee replacement. Even though Dolores couldn't play, she still turned up to support the team – Americans take bowling very seriously and say 'There is no "I" in team' a lot. The Barnsley Belles achieved a respectable third-place position. I have the team-member trophy on my mantelpiece in the cottage.

Wyatt hesitates. 'An hour wouldn't hurt.'

'I'm on a very tight schedule,' I say crisply. 'Time is of the essence.'

'All right,' Wyatt sighs. 'See you later.'

The door slams behind him and I turn my full attention to my Victoria sponge. I'm very anxious that the sponge rises properly. In the past this has been an issue for me. So now I begin whipping the cream and sugar really well so as to incorporate more air into the mixture. I have no doubt that Heidi will arrive at some point during the afternoon, and it's my patriotic duty to show off British cooking to its best advantage.

I lick my finger, which is OK because I've lost weight in the last three months. Helping Casey in the barn and having the time to go to the gym with Gerry has really helped. We go three times a week and share Lauren, his personal trainer, who's a redhead with muscly arms. Gerry has only been able to get back on the treadmill in the last couple of weeks. It turns out Bruce was wrong about the toe not being broken. Lauren didn't look very pleased to see me the first time I turned up. After we left the gym, I looked Gerry in the eye and said intently, 'Gerry, is there anything going on between you and Lauren?'

He looked at me with innocent hurt. 'No, Alice. Would I lie to you?'

Anyhow, I can't fault Lauren's professionalism. She makes me do twice as much as Gerry and I'm becoming noticeably more trim and toned.

As I add the sieved flour to the butter and sugar, I feel a profound sense of well-being come over me. The sun is shining, a warm breeze is blowing across my face and the smell of meadow-grass fills my nostrils. It's funny, but I always feel happy and relaxed when I'm in Wyatt's house. All is well with the world. I'm beginning to realize what Dr Vaizey meant when he told us that whatever happens in life, everything will work out for the best.

With a serene smile on my face I gently fold in the dry ingredients exactly as Carolyn instructed me. I allow myself to picture Heidi's face as Wyatt tucks into my Victoria sponge.

'Hmm, Alice,' he says deliriously, 'this is the best cake I've ever tasted!'

CHAPTER 25

An hour later and my spirits have sunk even more than my cake. How can this be! My cake is most definitely not OK. My two cake tins each contain what appears to be a pancake. At the thickest point, I estimate each pancake to be no more than half an inch, and that's being optimistic. I'm close to despair. No, I am in despair.

I think I forgot to add the baking powder.

Who can I ask for help? Wyatt only knows how to cook breakfast, Rachel admitted to me that she always uses a *Betty Crocker* cake mix for her brownies and Bruce, who's a chef, will say that my cake hasn't risen for a reason.

It wouldn't be so bad if I was in Britain. My cake would look normal there. But here in the USA, most cakes have three or even four layers with yet more height achieved by the addition of icing in between each layer and on the top and sides. Honestly, how can we compete?

I must remain positive. I take a deep breath and ask myself the question, 'In this situation, what would Dr Vaizey do?' I close my eyes. He's sitting in his brown leather armchair smiling at me warmly with what I think is more than a hint of affection. 'Alice,' he instructs me calmly, 'take back your powder – your baking powder! Slice each of your two cakes in half down the middle. Then sandwich them together with lots of buttercream to make half a four-layer cake. Then lie about what happened to the other half. It's better to be dishonest than allow that cow Heidi to make a fool out of you.'

I open my eyes. Wow! Dr Vaizey has really changed in the three months I've been in Ohio. He's become a lot more relaxed and worldly-wise. I reach for my knife.

Two hours later and I've made half a really impressive cake. It's just tall enough to qualify as an American cake, even though I didn't make enough buttercream to ice the top. Never mind, I sprinkle on some sugar. Also, there's been no time to make the scones, and the cucumber sandwiches are not quite as dainty as they're supposed to be. I haven't had time to change into my summer dress, put on any make-up or wash my hair either. But the main thing, I reassure myself, is that I've made a half a birthday cake.

Dolores is the first to arrive, limping in on account of the ongoing problems with her new knee. 'Oh, Alice, lovely cake,' she says. 'Have you had a little nibble already?'

'Hmm.'

She brings out two Tupperware containers. 'Spinach dip,' she says, 'and some brownies.' She looks around the kitchen and nods approvingly. 'I see you put Wyatt to work.'

Dolores is Wyatt's cleaning lady, but really she's in charge. Once or twice I've caught him sneakily tidying up before her arrival. After Dolores insisted on coming back to work, Wyatt made me promise not to help her with the cleaning.

'If Dolores can't manage, I'll do it myself,' he said firmly. 'I want you to promise, Alice,' he said sternly.

'I promise,' I said, but I crossed my fingers behind my back. As soon as he goes out I get to work on the windows and floors. Honestly, did he expect me to just sit there when there was cleaning to be done?

Dolores is a happy sort of a person who dotes on Madison, her granddaughter. 'She's the one who's going to turn this family's fortunes around,' Dolores says, 'when you help her win *Barnsley Idol*.'

Sometimes Dolores goes into introspective mood as we clean the windows and she looks out of the window on to the rooftops of Barnsley. 'Honestly, Alice, I don't know where I went wrong with Madison's mother. I took her to church every Sunday and we read the Bible every night. There was no TV during the week and I banned that *Cosmopolitan* magazine from the house. Then as soon as she turns eighteen she ups and runs off to California with that no-good waste of space.' The no-good waste of space is Madison's father, about whom Dolores refuses to divulge further details. Dolores always shakes her head at this point. 'Why wasn't Barnsley exciting enough for her?'

Dolores is not a gossip, but sometimes she lets slip tantalizing bits of information. Gerry and Heidi, she told me in passing, were high-school sweethearts. 'Ooh, he led her a terrible dance. But I'll say no more about it.'

When I heard that, I was very grateful that I'd kept my relationship with Wyatt on a purely professional level. Never mind love triangles: I could have become one corner of a tumultuous love square with Heidi, Gerry and Wyatt.

Naturally I confined myself to cleaning the ground floor and didn't venture upstairs to Wyatt's bedroom. Oh, all right, I did take a peek once. It's a very manly room, with a big oak double bed, an antique chest of drawers and a walk-in closet (which is what Americans call a walk-in wardrobe) full of very manly clothes like jeans and flannel work shirts.

Now Dolores is unwrapping her brownies. Next Rachel arrives with Baby Dale, and then Bruce arrives holding a really impressive puff-pastry circle thing.

'It's filled with goat's cheese, sundried tomatoes and spinach,' he explains.

Next Wyatt comes in from the back field with Casey and his two friends Connor and Jackson. I'm so touched that Casey has had a change of heart and decided to invite his pals!

'You don't have to eat the British stuff if you don't want to,' I then hear Casey say to his friends in a not quite low enough voice as they barrel in through the kitchen door. 'There'll be proper food, too.'

Wyatt sends them off to wash their hands and serves everyone drinks. Then Casey opens the rest of his presents – I gave him a pair of jeans from Abercrombie & Fitch, and Dolores gave him a book of Bible stories – while I chat in a relaxed fashion to Bruce who, it turns out, once worked in the kitchens of the famous New York Carlyle Hotel. He says it's famous, I've never heard of it. 'It was hard work but an excellent training, Alice. Nothing went out of that kitchen that wasn't perfect. If I say so myself, I became renowned for my egg-white omelettes.'

Bruce is not so bad. He does take all his AA stuff really seriously, but that's a good thing because alcoholics are forbidden from gossiping, and I've worked out that he hasn't told Wyatt about the Gerry-Pledge-bedroom incident.

Yes, everything is perfect, and I begin to relax and enjoy myself.

Then Heidi turns up.

She's wearing a white sundress which shows off her golden tan, high-heeled strappy sandals which her feet do not splay out of, and a pair of Ralph Lauren sunglasses pushed up into her hair. Of course she's had all day to get ready, now that she's on school holidays. She clicks into the kitchen, announces her arrival with a loud 'Hiiiiii' and then catches sight of me. For a moment she stands stock-still. I eye up the huge round Tupperware container she's carrying, and she stares at my apron.

Her lips purse.

'That apron looks familiar, Alice. I wonder why? Oh, it's mine.' She moves closer to me. Then, taking advantage of the distraction afforded by Casey opening his present from Bruce – a grooming kit for Mary Lou – she hisses at me, 'Wearing another woman's apron. Is there nothing you Brits won't stoop to?'

Before I have a chance to reply, Casey dashes over to me carrying a brush aloft. 'Look, Alice. It's just what I've always wanted.'

Heidi has a fixed smile on her face as she goes over to the kitchen table, contemptuously pushes my Victoria sponge to one side and, with a flourish, unveils the tallest cake I've ever seen.

'It's a triple-layer, three-chocolate Devil's Food Cake sandwiched with whipped cream and iced with white chocolate buttercream icing,' she says casually. 'I hope you like it, Casey. It was a last-minute idea I had.' She looks at my cake. 'Just as well.'

Casey's name is elegantly iced on the top next to a marzipan cow standing in a field of vermicelli grass. Casey has made a beeline for the kitchen table, Connor and Jackson on either side, and now all three of them are staring wide-eyed and hungry at Heidi's cake.

'Can I have a bit?' says Casey.

'Can I have a bit?' say Connor and Jackson.

'Have some goat's cheese and spinach pastry circle first,' says Wyatt quickly.

Heidi turns round and walks slowly back to me, like a shark approaching a cod. She gestures to the table. 'So this is your little British cake, Alice.' She gives a fake smile. 'How charming. I see you didn't put frosting on the top. What a simple touch!' Then she frowns melodramatically. 'Where's the other half?'

'I think Alice had a little bite before we got here,' says Dolores helpfully.

I see Wyatt and Bruce exchange glances at that. 'You ate half a cake, Alice?' Bruce says querulously.

'No!' I can feel myself blushing. I have to explain – and I only have a few seconds to do so before Bruce diagnoses me with an eating disorder.

'It's a British tradition,' I say. Hopefully no one will ask any questions.

'What's the origin of the tradition, Alice?' says Heidi.

'It's historical,' I say. 'How's your knee doing, Dolores?'

Dolores looks a bit surprised at this, probably because she told me all about her knee during yesterday's cleaning session.

'You look much better, Dolores,' says Heidi brightly. 'Now, Alice. You were going to tell us about the British historical tradition for serving your guests half a cake at a birthday party.' She gives a high laugh. 'It seems almost unbelievable. I'm sure you'd like to explain this to us?'

'Gosh, Alice, how interesting,' says Rachel as she sits with Baby Dale, feeding him banana. 'Do tell us more!'

My mind has gone a complete blank. Disconnected British history facts flash before my mind.

Queen Victoria.

Henry the Eighth and his six wives.

The Spanish Armada.

It's hopeless. Nothing is working.

Magna Carta.

Plague.

Yes, that's it! Plague! 'It's related to the plague,' I say confidently.

'The plague,' echoes Bruce, putting down a cucumber sandwich and peering at my cake.

'The plague,' I repeat aimlessly. I can't remember the date. 'The plague of olden times. Some estimates say that half the population perished. So when they held a party, half the guests didn't turn up because they'd died. So they started making half a cake.'

'Wow,' says Bruce. 'That's a really interesting historical fact, Alice.'

'Hmm,' says Heidi. 'I've never heard of it.'

'It's not something we British talk about much. But it's a proud tradition of ours. Henry the Eighth observed it for the birthdays of all his six wives.' I can see Wyatt giving me a long, hard glance. But I'm in too deep now to turn back. 'Traditionally all children's birthday parties in Britain begin with a moment of silent contemplation to remember those who did not survive the plague.'

Dolores puts down her plate, laden with pastry circle, sandwiches, brownies and spinach dip. 'Ooh, Alice. I feel awful eating with you suffering like that.'

Rachel is always very attuned to people's feelings. 'Oh my gosh, Alice. You must think we have no manners.' She reaches up and grabs Wyatt's plate. 'Put that sandwich down, Wyatt.'

Bruce comes over to me and lays his hand on my shoulder. 'I'm so sorry, Alice. Please – go ahead.'

'What?'

'We need to have a moment of silent contemplation.'

'Oh yes, Alice,' says Heidi. 'Then you can say a few words to mark the occasion.'

'Gather round,' says Bruce. 'Let's hold hands!'

We form a circle. I'm holding Casey's hand and Bruce's. I clear my throat. 'We will now observe a traditional British moment of silence.' I say. Maybe they'll forget about me saying something.

'Before you speak,' adds Heidi.

I close my eyes. There's total silence apart from Casey next to me scuffing his foot on the floor. My mind has gone totally blank. The only image I can summon up is that of Bob eating a prawn toast talking about the plague. We stand there for one minute and then another. Bruce coughs. Heidi coughs.

I open my mouth and close it. Right, I'm just going to have to let go and say whatever comes into my mind. I open my eyes. Everyone has theirs closed and is staring at the floor, apart from Wyatt, who's grinning at me. I stare at him in blind panic, like a rabbit who's been caught out telling a huge lie. I'm totally paralysed.

Then Wyatt says casually, 'Haven't you forgotten something, Alice? The last time I saw this done there was a dance.'

'A dance,' I repeat weakly.

'Yes,' he says matter-of-factly. 'A dance of celebration by those who survived the plague.'

I don't have time to think before he starts whistling 'Greensleeves', comes at me across the room, links his arm in mine and twirls me round, depositing me at Bruce's side, who follows suit. Dolores limps over to take Heidi's arm, and after a moment's hesitation, Rachel with Baby Dale on her hip links arms with Casey. Connor and Jackson look at each other and dive out of the room. Then we all swap partners and go another three rounds.

Bruce is beaming. 'Alice, thank you for sharing your British historical tradition with us. It's been an honour.

You've really inspired me to visit Britain. I expect you have lots more of these customs.'

Wyatt interrupts me before I can say more. 'Lots more. But right now it's time to eat some delicious cake.' Wyatt takes hold of Casey's arm and steers him to the table. 'I expect you want a piece of *both*, don't you, Casey?' Then he looks hard at Casey.

'I'll take a piece of both, please,' Casey repeats dutifully, never taking his eye off Heidi's marzipan cow.

CHAPTER 26

Later, after everyone leaves, Wyatt and I take down the decorations. Heidi didn't want to go, but Wyatt said that Casey needed a lift home. It's these little touches that make me sure their relationship is the real thing. Wyatt would never trust me to drive Casey anywhere.

Wyatt unpins the streamers and hands them to me.

'That was a really good party, Alice.'

'Thank you,' I say, concentrating on rolling up the streamers for the next time I host a twelve-year-old boy's birthday party.

'Yep, I think Casey really enjoyed it. You've done a lot for him, Alice.'

I don't reply because I'm steeling myself to pop the balloons.

Then I turn my attention to my cake, most of which is still sitting on the kitchen table. All of Heidi's got eaten. Casey, Connor and Jackson tore the marzipan cow apart limb by limb.

I reach for my Victoria sponge. Is it my imagination or has it sunk a bit? No, it has sunk. I head for the bin.

'You're throwing it away?' says Wyatt.

'Yes. I think it would be the kindest thing. Put it out of its misery.'

He gives me that grin.

'I think I forgot the baking powder,' I say sadly.

'It tasted great,' says Wyatt almost convincingly.

I give him my who-are-you-trying-to-kid look and scrape it away. Then I start loading the dishwasher. Wyatt grabs some plates and helps.

'No! You have to rinse them first,' I say, wrenching them from his grasp.

'Sorry. I forgot they needed washing before they went in the dishwasher.'

I ignore him.

'So,' says Wyatt, leaning against the kitchen counter. 'What do you think of my choreography skills?'

I can't help but smile. 'I was very glad of them. But I'd say they were like your song-writing skills – a bit rusty.'

'Ouch.'

This is another ongoing topic of light-hearted jesting between us. But underneath our repartee there's a serious undertone. As I rinse out the coffee mugs, I reflect that I still haven't accomplished what I came here to achieve – Wyatt writing again. True, I've made some progress with seeking out local talent. As I informed Brent recently in a lengthy email, the Scott County Maintenance Crew have reformed with a new drummer and revised songbook, venturing into the nineties with an ambitious cover version of 'Wonder-wall', and Madison is making huge strides. Brent replied, telling me not to bother writing every week, an update every six weeks would be sufficient. But despite these successes, still I feel a nagging sense of dissatisfaction.

Wyatt begins eating grapes from the bowl on the kitchen counter. 'I'd say you have your work cut out here in Barnsley without worrying about me.'

'You're the reason I'm here,' I remind him.

He shrugs. 'I'm the reason you came. I'd say you've made quite a mark here on your own.'

Oh yes, I'm sure. My Half-Cake probably merits a page of its own on the Barnsley Historical Society website – *Plague comes to Barnsley!*

'Have you finished clearing up?' Wyatt says hopefully.

'No. I have to wipe the floor,' I say, opening the cleaning cupboard and pulling out the Swiffer WetJet Power Mop. (It's new, a present from me to Wyatt. 'I'm speechless,' he said when I handed it to him.)

Wyatt shakes his head. 'No you don't.'

'Yes I do.'

Wyatt manfully takes the Swiffer WetJet mop from my hand and puts it behind his back, holding me at bay as I grab fruitlessly at it.

'We're going to participate in an American tradition,' he says firmly.

'What, leaving your kitchen floor dirty?' I say petulantly.

'No, drinking iced tea on the porch and watching the sun go down.'

'All right,' I say reluctantly. 'But I have to put my insect-repellent spray on first.' I'm a martyr to mosquitoes.

We walk through the living room and out on to the porch, which overlooks a small vegetable garden and a field below. It's very easy to grow things here because the sun shines every day, and then it rains for a bit until the sun shines again. Wyatt has planted peas, beans, corn and carrots, and I helped with the herb garden. It took us all morning because I insisted on spacing the plants with a tape measure. Despite this, he turned to me at the end and said that seeing how I'd transformed the cottage had inspired him to work on the farm again. Obviously he was just being polite.

It's a beautiful scene: the setting sun and the view of the

woods beyond, the whole experience marred only by the strong chemical repellent smell emanating from me.

Wyatt sits down and gestures at the fence. 'I need to make that repair permanent.'

Mary Lou keeps breaking through the fence and eating the herb garden. She particularly likes basil. Mary Lou is a very greedy cow with a sweet tooth, which I blame on Casey, even though he categorically denies feeding her Oreos.

'So,' Wyatt says, sitting back and stretching out his legs. 'How are things with Stephen?'

Honestly, I don't know why Wyatt bothers to ask me about my very dull life in London. Of what possible interest could it be to him? Stephen and I continue on an emotional rollercoaster, talking once a week and exchanging twice-weekly emails. As Stephen says, we don't want to get into the habit of picking up the phone willy-nilly or we may lose track of time and money. I believe that a reconciliation with Stephen may yet take place, now that Andy and Jennifer have moved out to a flat in Coulsdon (although agreement has yet to be reached on apportionment of the telephone bill).

'Actually, tonight's residents' meeting got very heated,' I tell Wyatt. 'Stephen sent me an email afterwards. He accused the residents' association secretary of fiscal impropriety verging on fraud.'

'Wow.'

'Hmm. There's more. Then he proposed a vote of no confidence.'

'A vote?'

'Yes, all four of those present would have voted. But the secretary agreed, narrowly averting a constitutional crisis.'

'Quite a drama.'

'Stephen said he'd write more tomorrow, but he had to

go and make an Ovaltine to settle his nerves.'

'So,' says Wyatt, staring out at the field, 'does Stephen have any plans to come over?'

I suppress a derisive laugh. 'No. I think a decision on our future will be postponed until I get back. Stephen has a fear of flying.'

'I thought he had a fear of heights?'

'He does.' I count off on my fingers. 'Heights, flying, shellfish, dogs, tunnels, excessive speed and horses. Well, neither of us likes horses.'

'Then you should go riding with me,' says Wyatt turning to me. 'That would get you over it.'

I roll my eyes. 'You mean as I'm hurled to the ground I'll be cured?'

'You won't fall off. I guarantee it.'

'Oh, look,' I say, pointing at Mary Lou and Billy the Goat, who are standing at the fence. 'They're trying to join us.'

'Don't change the subject,' Wyatt says. 'I'm not giving up.'

'That's easy for you to say,' I announce defensively. 'You don't know what it is to be that scared.'

'Nope.' He shakes his head as if to agree with me. 'I mean, walking out on stage in front of thousands of people – that's a breeze.'

'That's different. You don't fall off a stage.'

'I did. Twice.'

'Really?'

'The second time I broke my leg. Had it in plaster for six weeks. My ex wasn't very pleased about it. We were supposed to go to Barbados at the end of the tour.'

I have no idea who this ex is. Wyatt occasionally lets slip something about his ex, but I've come to the conclusion that this 'ex' is in fact a collection of girls: unless there's one person out there who was both an ex-New York Giants cheerleader and a Julliard-trained classical pianist who grew up on a Texas ranch, a Californian hippie commune and the outskirts of Swansea. I think the Swansea one was the British Airways air hostess. It's difficult to keep track.

Wyatt pauses. 'Actually, I think my main fear was of letting people down. It wasn't just me up there. It was the band, the crew, and the people at Carmichael Music. My producer and manager. The irony is that when I quit, I left them all high and dry.'

'What happened?'

'They got other gigs. And I've made it up to them since I got sober.'

'Made it up to them?'

'Yeah. Got in touch with them. Reimbursed them if they needed it.'

I'm intrigued. 'How did they react?'

Wyatt shrugs. 'They were all cool about it. Told me to stay sober and get ...'

'What?'

He sighs. 'Get back on stage.'

'Ha!' I say triumphantly. 'You see.'

'Yeah,' Wyatt says. Then he turns to me with a devilish grin. 'Well, how about this? I'll sit down and write a song if you'll get up on a horse and come riding with me.'

I open my mouth and close it again. 'That's not fair,' I say.

'Yes it is.'

'No it isn't.'

'That's the deal. Take it or leave it.'

'Your song and me getting on a horse have got nothing to do with each other,' I protest.

'True. Is that a no? Pity. I was feeling quite inspired. You know,' he says, waving his hand. 'Nature, fields ... barns.'

'Oh, shut up,' I say. A series of images flashes through my mind. In the first I'm flying through the air, hurled from a galloping, bucking stallion. In the next I'm in Phoebe's office. 'Alice, no one else could have done this. Please be my executive vice-president.'

'I'll think about it,' I say to Wyatt. That will give me time to work out what Dr Vaizey would do.

'Hey,' says Wyatt. 'Maybe I could write something about my Swiffer mop.'

'Oh, stop it,' I laugh. It's unbearable. I aim a playful punch at his arm. He grabs my wrist – showing very good reactions – then lets go. Stephen would have rubbed his arm and sulked a bit if I'd done the same to him.

(It's odd, but when he lets go I feel a bit disappointed.)

The sun is setting now, sending out a golden glow across the fields. This is the nicest time of day here.

'So what's happening at Carmichael Music?' Wyatt asks.

Search me. The only person I have any contact with is Bob, and he's gone quiet on account of what he calls a tricky sub-plot in his new thriller.

I clear my throat. 'They say that they have every confidence in you, and that you continue to be critical to their whole worldwide plan.'

'Really. And I thought I'd been written off.'

'Oh no,' I say with passion. Wyatt was never written off by Graham and me. 'Don't forget we signed you, Wyatt. And loyalty is key to our corporate mission statement.' I have no idea if this last part is true, but I'm not about to dampen Wyatt's spirits now that he's talking about writing again.

Now we're on the subject of Carmichael Music, I tell Wyatt about Bob's new thriller set in the offices of a multi-national music company. I don't know why, but Wyatt shows a keen interest in my English friends, family and colleagues. Over the past few weeks I've ended up telling him about the staff at Carmichael Music, the members of the anxiety support group, and one evening I told him all about Dr Vaizey until I looked over and noticed he'd fallen asleep. I've also told him bits and pieces about Dad, Valerie and Teresa. Not about Mum, though.

'Interesting concept,' says Wyatt after I finish summarizing Bob's thriller. 'Software designer turned private eye.'

'Bob thinks the future of fiction lies in high-tech crime.'

'Does he have an agent?' Wyatt asks.

'No,' I concede, 'but he has a subscription to the *Radio Times*.'

I decide to take advantage of this conversational opportunity. 'So how did you get started?' I ask. Wyatt never says much about that.

'Started?'

'In music. Was it your parents who encouraged you?'

'Nope. They're not what you'd call musical. I had a teacher at school ... Miss Horner.'

'Miss Horner!' This is news to me. Wyatt's never talked about this before.

'Yep. Mr Horner's sister. She was a tough one. She made me stay behind and practise the piano every day. And she used to rap my hands with a ruler if I got it wrong.'

I knew someone had to have done that.

Wyatt shrugs. 'It worked.'

Sometimes I have to remind myself that things in Barnsley are a little more rough and ready than in New Malden.

'Then when I went to high school I started playing guitar and got in a band with the boys.'

'The Scott County Road Maintenance Crew.'

Wyatt nods. 'Chris and I wrote songs.'

'Chris?' I say, surprised.

'He's a really talented songwriter. But he always sings cover versions. The problem is he doesn't believe in himself.' For some reason he gives me a long, hard look at that point.

'Anyway,' he continues, 'when I left school, my parents wanted me to go and get a farm job. That was when Miss Horner stepped in.'

'She talked to your parents?'

There's a pause. 'No,' Wyatt says dispassionately. 'There wouldn't have been any point in doing that. No, she gave me the money for my bus ticket to Nashville.'

It takes me a moment to take this in. 'She must have been so proud of you,' I say warmly.

'Maybe.' Wyatt stares out into the darkening sky. 'She died a few years back – when I was up to no good. I didn't even take the time to send her the money and pay her back for the bus ticket.' He turns to me and his expression is grim. 'What do you think of that, Alice? That's what fame really does to you – it turns your head and makes you believe that you're the centre of the world. I think she must have been pretty disappointed.'

I want to deny this, but something in Wyatt's tone makes me stay silent.

'That's the problem, Alice,' he continues. 'There are some things you can't put right.'

It's dark now. Wyatt stands up and leans on the wooden rail of the porch. It seems natural for me to join him. Together we look up at the stars.

'Sometimes, when it gets really dark, about three o'clock in the morning, you can stand here and see shooting stars,' says Wyatt.

We stand there in the silence.

A long time ago I decided that Mum could see me wherever

she is. I think, as she looks down on me now, standing on this porch overlooking dark countryside and the lights of the town beyond, in this place so far from home, that Mum would be happy for me. Even though it isn't quite real and it won't last, even though it's not so long now until I go back to England, even though I still haven't accomplished all that I set out to achieve. In spite of all these things, I think she's looking down on me and smiling.

Wyatt moves closer to me and puts his arm around me. For a few seconds I let myself lean against him, against the hardness of his body and his warmth. If I look at him I'll know whether this is a companionable gesture, two good friends standing together, or whether it's something more. And then I feel afraid. Because right then I admit to myself what I've been trying to ignore for some time now – that I do want it to be more than just friendship. I think I'd rather not know than feel the pain of disappointment. It's better to have a little of something than all or nothing. It's better to be safe than take a risk and feel the pain. Isn't it?

I move away and turn back to the table without looking at Wyatt.

'I'll take these glasses in,' I say.

Then I walk away back into the house, towards the bright light of the kitchen.

CHAPTER 27

It's two weeks later and I'm driving to the Barnsley Stay-at-Home Mother's Group in order to give my monthly Baby Whisperer talk. The sky is cloudless and the fields are now sprouting bushy soy plants and leafy sweetcorn. On the outskirts of Barnsley, the expansive lawns of the ranch-style houses are bright green and weed-free. As I drive along in my Avis Ford Focus, now on a long-term hire contract, I exchange waves with strangers as they go up and down on their ride-on lawnmowers. Everyone does this. Some of the old people sit out on the porches all day long and salute the passing cars.

I have so far given three talks to the Barnsley Stay-at-Home Mothers' Group and I'm growing in confidence both as a public speaker and as a childcare expert. Carolyn writes the talks for me. Today we move on to feeding, a topic which I have been anxious to avoid, but Carolyn has insisted.

I turn into Rachel's road, which is a cul-de-sac of six modern houses situated on a new housing development. As I park the Ford Focus, I regret not having a black London cab like Supernanny. The houses are like new ones in Britain, brick with fake architectural touches like gables and leaded windows. But it's not really like Britain, because when you stretch your arms out you can't touch both houses at the same time. Each of the houses in Glenn Close have really big lawns, double garages and kitchens that are about the size of our flat back in Southfields. Everything here is named after John Glenn, by the way, the famous earth-orbiting astronaut. There are already several cars parked in Rachel's driveway as I walk to the front door and press the bell.

Rachel is chairperson this year, and that's the reason why I've been unable to come clean about not being the Southfields Baby Whisperer. It would mean that Rachel would lose face in front of the group. Rachel welcomes me with a big hug and leads me into the kitchen. 'No need to introduce you, Alice.'

'Hello, Alice,' say Brandy, Candy, and Tammy in unison. Sometimes I get a bit confused, and I'm still not sure which child belongs to which mother. But I know what to expect. Everyone has brought a dish to share and everyone says beforehand that they won't eat anything. Brandy is unwrapping a strawberry pie. 'You use sugar-free Jello,' explains Brandy, who has previously confided in me that she's considering gastric by-pass surgery. If she were British, Brandy would call herself fat, but over here no one is fat. They're 'heavy'.

I know everyone by now. There are about ten stay-at-home mothers, all dressed in beige shorts, T-shirts and sensible sandals. The babies are much more stylish: the boys wear little blue shorts and white polo shirts, and the girls wear frilly pink dresses with matching ribbons tied round their heads.

'Alice!' rings out a very familiar voice. It's Dolores, who has arrived with her granddaughter Stacey. Stacey is Madison's sister. She had a baby six months ago, interrupting her final year of high school. The father was the captain of the Barnsley High School football team, and Dolores doesn't have many good things to say about him. Baby Tiffany stands out from the other babies in distressed denim with diamond stud earrings. Some of the other mothers are a bit cool towards Stacey, but I like her.

We see quite a bit of each other because she's often there for Madison's singing lesson, bouncing Baby Tiffany along to 'Hit Me Baby One More Time'. (I tape-record Madison and Wyatt tells me what to say.) I'm now Madison's official voice coach and visit her twice a week at her mother's home in the Barnsley Glade Mobile Home Park. I've never met Madison and Stacey's father. Apparently he's working away from home on a permanent basis.

Last to arrive is Sara, who fancies herself as Barnsley's intellectual because she carries Baby Hillary in a Guatemalan swing and drives a Honda hybrid.

Sara greets me a little coolly. 'Good morning, Alice,' she says with a curt little nod as she gets out her spinach flan. She has very short hair and she's wearing baggy trousers in a tie-dye fabric. At my second talk, Sleep Solutions, Sara took issue with my very reasonable suggestion of a bedtime routine. 'I think it crushes a child's spirit to tell them that they have to obey an essentially arbitrary bedtime,' she protested, looking anguished. Fortunately everyone rolled their eyes at this point and Brandy changed the subject to talk about the South Beach Diet.

I decide to rise above this episode. 'How are you, Sara?' I say warmly.

To my surprise, Sara shoots me a furtive look in response to this question. 'Do you have any experience of daycare, Alice?' she whispers.

No, because I don't have any children and I'm not the Southfields Baby Whisperer. But I'm an old hand at this now.

'What exactly is the issue, Sara?' I say earnestly, tilting my head to one side in an empathetic way.

'I'm thinking of going back to work,' she says, so quietly that I can hardly hear her. She holds up Baby Hillary's plastic teething keys and says sadly, 'I used to be a graphic designer and have money of my own.'

'I won't say a word.'

'Let's all sit down, everyone,' calls out Rachel. This could take some time. As soon as anyone sits down they have to get up again to stop their child hitting, crying or sticking a crayon up its nose.

To show willing, I go into the living room, where Rachel has pushed back the furniture so that we can all sit in a circle.

Rachel's house is open-plan, but the modern style ends there. The curtains are edged with thick cream lace, the sofas are covered in tartan throws and there are ornaments on every surface, including a set of Civil War soldiers lined up on their own set of shelves. But more than anything else, there are photographs: Rachel has them taken at J. C. Penney's Portrait Studio every month. Baby Dale is pictured as a newborn in black and white sepia, and then in various guises including a cowboy, an Easter chick (all-in-one yellow fluffy suit with a beak on his head) and in patriotic pose in a red, white and blue romper suit with a Stars and Stripes bandana round his head. Then there are the wedding pictures of Rachel and her husband Brian. I'm trying to stare unobtrusively at Wyatt – the only one who looks natural in the photograph despite the fact that his mother has obviously made him wear a suit – when I hear a familiar voice at my ear. 'Alice, I couldn't miss your talk.'

I swing round. It's Heidi.

'Now that I'm on vacation, I'll be able to come to all of

them,' she continues. 'Until you leave, of course. When is it that your visa runs out?'

It's in three months' time. I concentrate on unpacking my Healthy Options flashcards out of my handbag.

But Heidi is not to be put off. 'I hear you're quite the expert.' She draws closer to me. 'Which is an achievement, Alice, given that you have no children yourself and no qualifications.'

She sits down right opposite me and calls out, 'I'm sure you can handle anything we throw at you!'

After several false starts for dashes to the potty, we're at last all seated in a circle with the babies playing in the middle and the toddlers running laps around the outside. It's quite noisy but I'm used to these conditions now.

'Feeding is a subject about which we all tend to worry too much.'

There's a murmur and some low asides. This is a good sign. At my first talk – Developmental Milestones – everyone started talking amongst themselves after five minutes, which let me off the hook very nicely. But then Heidi says keenly, 'Do give us more details, Alice. You're the expert!'

'Weaning can be a stressful time,' I recite from Carolyn's lecture, which I've memorized. (Notice how we neatly jump over the whole topic of breast-feeding.)

'What age can they have finger foods?' asks Heidi intently.

Hah! If she's trying to catch me out, she's going to have to do better than that. Confidently I reel off the first-year diet recommendations of the American Academy of Pediatricians. Then I reel out one of my catch-all phrases. 'Don't be a slave to developmental milestones!'

There are nods of agreement all round. 'Don't be a slave to developmental milestones' is my top all-purpose phrase. It's all going very well, and with a bit of luck one of the toddlers will have a tantrum soon, setting off a chain reaction during which no adult speech is possible.

'I like those jars,' says Stacey. 'Baby Tiffany loves her custard dessert.'

Sara speaks up. 'You should think about home-made food, Stacey. You can mash up some avocado.'

Stacey wrinkles her nose. 'That green stuff?'

'It's a superfood, Stacey,' says Sara irritably.

'Perhaps some avocado mixed into the fruit dessert,' I suggest quickly.

'What about celeriac?' calls out Heidi. 'What age can they have that, Alice?'

I have no idea, so I ignore her and hold up my carefully constructed food pyramid, hand-drawn using all twelve of Casey's Crayola colours. 'Let's talk about proteins!' I say enthusiastically.

'Or potato salad,' calls out Heidi. 'What age can they have that?'

'That is *so* fattening,' says Brandy to Tammy, both of whom are eating a piece of cinnamon coffee ring. 'But you can't have a cookout without it.' A cookout is what American people call a barbecue.

Stacey looks up as if Brandy has made a point of major paediatric importance. 'Yes, Alice. What age can they have potato salad?'

'It depends on the ingredients,' I say, playing for time. 'Unknown ingredients can be dangerous and cause allergic reactions.'

There's a buzz of conversation. 'Dangerous' is always a useful word to throw in, inducing mild panic and generally causing my audience to forget the original question. Dr Vaizey would have his work cut out here.

'Have you ever had to deal with an allergic reaction?' asks

Heidi. 'Perhaps you could tell us some anecdotes from your days working for London celebrities?'

There's now a buzz of excitement. 'Unfortunately I'm covered by a confidentiality clause.' There's a murmur of disappointment. 'I can tell you that Simon Cowell is very nice in person.'

Stacey frowns. 'Has he got kids?'

Search me. 'He has a very big extended family,' I assure her.

'Oh, come on,' chips in Heidi. 'Surely you could tell us something about your jet-set occupation!'

I can see exactly where this is going. If I'm not careful, I'll be publicly unmasked as a fake. I head her off. 'Heidi, I'm very impressed by your interest in this subject.'

'Not at all.' She smiles at me warmly. 'One can never be too prepared. I think instilling a love of good, properly prepared food in children is so important.'

Our eyes lock. She and I know exactly what she's talking about: the recent events surrounding Casey's birthday cake.

'So what about … cake?' says Heidi, apparently on the spur of the moment. 'Or does that depend on what country you're in?' She smirks. 'I know your British cakes are very different from our American ones.'

Undaunted, I hold up my fat diagram and begin to describe the chemical composition of trans-fats.

Heidi turns to Sara and says loudly, 'I can only assume that they don't have baking powder in Britain.'

'Really?'

Heidi shakes her head. She holds up her finger and thumb close together. 'I gather the fashion is for dense, rather dry sponges.' She turns to me. 'Isn't that right, Alice?'

The group are now looking at me, slightly puzzled.

'I think British cakes would stand comparison with any found here,' I say defensively.

'Perhaps we should put that to the test?' snarls Heidi.

I assume she's asking a rhetorical question. 'Any time.'

Heidi pauses for a moment and then claps her hands together. 'I know! What about the Cupcake Competition at the Barnsley Festival?' Heidi is talking as though this idea has only just come to her. 'Every year there's a competition to judge the best frosted cupcakes. Why don't you enter it, Alice? Then we'll have a chance to sample one of your wonderful British recipes.'

It seems to me that she says 'wonderful' with heavy irony, but no one else seems to notice. Everyone is looking at me expectantly, even, it seems, Baby Hillary, who, now I come to notice it, has a very intense glare. Rachel, though, is shaking her head at me.

As I'm thinking of an excuse, Sara interrupts irritably. 'I think we need to get back to the topic, Alice.'

I feel a wave of relief wash over me. 'Yes,' I agree urgently.

'What is your opinion on breast-feeding into the second year?' continues Sara.

No!

'Oh, surely we don't have to go into all of that,' says Brandy irritably, wrinkling her nose. 'We're not living in the Stone Age any more.'

Sara reddens. 'If you think it's primitive to breast-feed your baby, then you've been brainwashed by multinational corporations who've invested millions into promoting formula.'

Oh my gosh, it's all going off. Carolyn called me the night before my first talk to read me the Riot Act. 'Promise me that you will never, ever discuss breast-feeding or smacking. Not if you want to make it out of there alive, Alice.'

'It's the mother's choice,' I say, but no one pays any attention.

Brandy has coloured. 'Just because you read the *New York Times* doesn't mean you know everything, Sara.' Brandy looks pointedly at Baby Hillary, who is dressed a little bizarrely, it has to be said, in a brown cotton kimono thingy. 'Children can be very cruel to kids who look different.'

Sara looks furious at that. 'Do you really feel qualified to talk about a healthy diet, Brandy?' she retaliates.

Brandy reddens even more. But it's not over. She clears her throat. 'Perhaps you'd like to take the opportunity to clear up a rumour, Sara.' She pauses. 'Your car was seen parked outside the Kiddie Care Daycare Center.' She says this in the same tone one might use to refer to a brothel or pawn shop. 'You *are* the only person in Barnsley who drives a Honda Hyphen.'

There's a collective gasp. All eyes turn to Sara. Oh my gosh, they're going to take her outside and shun her. She'll have to leave town and never speak to any of her family again.

But then a crisp, school-teacherly voice cuts through the awful silence.

'Ladies,' says Heidi, 'haven't we forgotten something?'

We all look at each other. Have we? Now Heidi has the floor.

She turns to me. 'So what's it going to be Alice?' I can tell that she's savouring every moment of this. 'Are you going to accept my friendly challenge to uphold your country's honour and enter the Barnsley Cupcake Competition? Or are you going to admit defeat here and now?'

I have no choice. 'Yes, great idea,' I say meekly.

Heidi sits back contentedly. 'Good for you! We need to

shake things up a bit. I mean, it's so boring having the same winner five years running.' She gives a self-satisfied laugh and picks an imaginary hair off her top. 'I'm beginning to find it a little embarrassing!'

CHAPTER 28

'Heidi's been the Barnsley Cupcake Champion five years running,' says Rachel disconsolately. 'She always gets what she wants.'

We're washing up in the kitchen at the end of the meeting. Everyone else is still in the living room, apart from Heidi and Sara, who made their excuses and left soon after the abrupt end of my talk. I never did get to use my healthy food flashcards.

Heidi got up and shook my hand, squeezing it really tight. 'No pulling out now, Alice,' she said laughing. 'We wouldn't want everyone saying you weren't up to the task!'

I straighten Rachel's tea towel. 'Oh, I'm sure it isn't that important,' I say. 'It's only a cupcake competition.'

'Alice,' Rachel says slowly. 'You might want to start practising. Quite a few people turn up for it.'

'Oh?'

'About a thousand. The whole population of Barnsley.'

I need some fresh air at this point, so I gather up my posters and take them out to the car. Then I go back in to say goodbye to Rachel. I hear Baby Dale screaming and Rachel's voice cooing and I realize she's upstairs trying to convince him he needs a nap. As I hesitate in the hallway, wondering whether to disturb Rachel, I hear Dolores' voice ring out loudly from where she's sitting in the open-plan living room.

'That Wyatt needs to make an honest woman out of her. She's ideal for him – everyone can see that.'

'Maybe he's not the marrying kind,' says Stacey.

'People say he's a bit unreliable,' comments Brandy. 'Though I wouldn't throw him out of bed.'

There's a gale of laughter. The moms can get surprisingly bawdy. It must be a sugar high.

'It would take a strong woman to keep Wyatt Brown on the porch,' says Candy.

I feel my stomach turn over.

'Folks should keep their opinions to themselves,' says Dolores primly. 'He's had his wild days, true enough. But that's all in the past. In my opinion he's ready to settle down. And she's the girl for him. She'd make a wonderful wife and mother – she's a natural with children.'

Of course. Heidi is not only the hometown girl – she's a teacher as well. I stand there feeling miserable, inadequate and British.

'But are you sure she wants him?' asks Brandy.

'Sure?' Dolores says dismissively. 'It's obvious.'

Yes, it is. From the very start – when we met that first snowy day in the Blue Ribbon Diner – Heidi didn't look happy at the idea of me staying at the cottage. Since then she's used every opportunity to warn me off and make me look bad. And on the whole she's succeeded.

I can't bear to hear any more. Without waiting to say goodbye to Rachel, I creep back to the front door. As I silently close it behind me, I hear Dolores' last words on the subject. 'And as for her cooking . . .'

I get into the Ford Focus and proceed slowly back to the farm. Even the sight of endless acres of soybean plants does nothing to lift my spirits. I cannot stop thinking about the cupcake competition. I can predict exactly how events will unfold: I'm standing next to Heidi in the big white Barnsley Festival tent. The clapping of the crowd has gone on seemingly for ever following the announcement of her historic sixth consecutive cupcake win. Then Wyatt unexpectedly steps forward from where he's been standing unnoticed at the back of the crowd. He's wearing a white collarless shirt, breeches with braces and a brown felt hat which he takes off with a polite nod in the direction of the lady domestic-science teacher. His sleeves are rolled up to show his deeply tanned and muscular arms. A hush descends over the crowd. He strides with quiet confidence to where we cupcake competitors are standing and casts a polite but cursory glance in my direction. 'Well done, Alice. A brave effort.' There's a desultory round of applause. Then he turns to Heidi. 'You've made me and the whole town of Barnsley very proud today.' Jubilant cheering erupts. Little children jump up and down excitedly waving flags, and an old lady takes out a lace handkerchief to dab a tear away from her eye. 'So here, in front of these fine townspeople, I want to ask you to be my wife.'

Heidi gasps, blushes prettily, tilts her head and looks up at Wyatt coquettishly. 'My word, Mr Brown. I'm sure I don't know what to say.'

Wyatt puts his hand on his heart. 'I ain't got much,' he says. 'A few good horses, a barn and some land over the hill. But I promise that I'll be a good and true husband to you. And, if the Lord sees fit, a firm but fair father to our children. Six, I hope.' Wyatt clears his throat. 'So what do you say, Miss Heidi?'

'I say I do, Mr Brown!'

Everyone throws their hats up in the air and someone

with a conveniently located fiddle starts playing as the young men and women of Barnsley dance an impromptu jig. The old lady nods at them approvingly. 'She'll be heavy with child by the spring.'

By the time I reach the cottage, I'm doing my deep breathing – I haven't needed to do that for three months now. Desperate measures are called for: I get on my hands and knees, spread newspaper over the kitchen floor and clean the oven.

After an hour – the shelves are shining like new – I'm feeling well enough to go online and print out the Martha Stewart cupcake recipe. Soon I'm feeling worse. There are so many decisions to be made: vanilla or chocolate cupcake? Plain or patterned paper cases? Buttercream or fondant icing? Or should I say frosting, which is what Americans call icing. I need to pull myself together, so I break Stephen's once-a-week telephone-call rule and ring him for some much-needed moral support.

He sounds surprised to hear from me. 'Alice? Is everything all right?'

Before I have chance to answer, he continues. 'Wait a minute, I'll go into the bedroom.' Then there's a muffled noise as if he's holding his hand over the receiver.

'Stephen, what's going on?'

It's been difficult for us to communicate over recent weeks, given Stephen's busy schedule of board-game nights.

'Nothing,' he replies shiftily.

I strain to make out the sound in the background. *Clack, clack, clack.*

'What is it?'

He gives an unconvincing laugh. 'I can't hear anything. Maybe it's the line.'

Clack, clack, clack. Whirr, whirr, whirr.

'Stephen,' I say insistently.

There's a deep sigh. 'I suppose you were going to find out sometime.' He hesitates. 'It's Zara's knitting machine.'

This doesn't make any sense. 'But you said Andy and Jennifer had moved out.'

There's an ominous pause. 'They have,' he says deliberately.

The implications of this last statement take a moment for me to grasp.

'It just happened, Alice,' says Stephen defensively. 'Something clicked between us.'

Stephen has just cracked a joke, but I know it's not intentional. '*How long has this been going on?*' I shout at him.

'It's difficult to say. I've been trying to find the right moment to tell you.'

An awful image enters my mind. 'Are you sleeping with her?'

'I'm not at liberty to answer that,' Stephen says coolly.

'You bastard!' I'm devastated. How could two members of the anxiety support group conspire to do such a thing?

'I never meant for things to turn out this way,' says Stephen, as if it's all some unfortunate accident.

I'm even more furious now. 'So when you were shagging Zara, how did you think it would turn out?'

'I'm sorry you have to descend to that level,' says Stephen haughtily. 'If you must know, Zara and I are soul mates. Over the past few weeks we've become inseparable. It was my idea to buy the knitting machine, and it's transformed Zara's life. She's now able to earn a regular income from the comfort and security of her own home.'

'It's my home,' I protest.

'Actually, I'm going to take your possessions to the New Malden Self-U-Store.

I'm struggling to take this in. 'You don't waste any time, do you?'

But Stephen sounds unabashed. 'Space is at a premium now that we have the knitting machine.'

I slam down the phone, fling myself on the bed and burst into tears. I can't help it. Even though Stephen has annoyed the hell out of me for years, I'm still really upset. I've been dumped for someone even crazier than me. It's so unfair! And the fact is that being dumped by someone is a surefire way to make them instantly appear tons more attractive. Suddenly I really miss Stephen and all his familiar habits: the way he stacked the mugs in the cupboard with the handles all pointing forty-five degrees to the right, and the very precise way he folded up the end of the toothpaste tube.

I can see them now in the flat, Stephen massaging Zara's shoulders as she turns out another Fair Isle sweater. Lovingly, his tongue darts over her neck. He's wearing a dark green velvet smoking jacket and holding a menthol cigarette in a holder, despite the fact that he doesn't smoke. Zara is in a twenties flapper-style cocktail dress. 'Do you ever think about Alice?' says Zara a little jealously. Stephen gives a high-pitched laugh as he twirls his handlebar moustache. 'You silly little thing. She couldn't hold a candle to you, *my dahling*. We'll never speak of her again. Promise!' Then they clink martini glasses and retire to the bedroom.

I fling myself on to my front. It's London Fashion Week. The Stephen and Zara show is the must-have ticket of the collections. Naomi Campbell is wearing a knee-skimming figure-hugging cream Arran sweater and Elizabeth Jagger is warmly wrapped up in a mauve angora turtleneck. Flash-bulbs go off and hardened journalists rise to their feet and cheer as Stephen and Zara, dressed entirely in black mohair, emerge on to the runway at the end of the show amid a posse of scarf-toting models. Their subsequent stock-market flotation makes them overnight billionaires.

I turn on to my side, curl up in the foetal position and start doing my deep breathing. But before long I'm in my Surbiton bedsit talking to the cat about my day at the library and the letter I'm composing to the Prime Minister outlining the shortcomings of the Dewey decimal system.

It's hopeless trying to relax, so I get up and go out into the barn. Casey will be there by now and we've fallen into the routine of an afternoon chat. Then he comes in for his tea, which is generally about the time Heidi arrives.

I find Casey brushing Mary Lou. Mary Lou is now a local celebrity. Last week she won not only the Dairy Prize at the Scott County Show but also the Overall Supreme Champion, beating two sheep and a goat into second, third and fourth positions respectively. Casey and Mary Lou were in the *Scott Sun* newspaper, and there's been talk about sending her to the Ohio State Show next year.

'Hi, Casey. How was school?'

I pat Mary Lou and am rewarded with a low moan. Mary Lou is a very sociable cow.

There's no reply. Instead I notice Casey rub his eyes on the bottom of his T-shirt. I look more closely, and with horror I realize that Casey is crying.

I go over to him and gently touch his shoulder. 'Casey, what is it?'

Casey shakes his head. 'It's private.'

'Has something happened at school?'

He shakes his head.

'At home?'

He shakes his head.

This could take some time.

But then I see Casey look up at Mary Lou and his eyes water once more.

'Is it Mary Lou?'

I think I know what this is about – the pressure of the Ohio State Show. 'Casey, if this is about the State Show, there's nothing to be worried about. It's not about winning or losing. It's the taking part,' I assure him unoriginally.

'She can't go!' he exclaims. 'Grandpa is going to sell her.'

I'm stunned. 'But she's a natural winner.' This is true. Believe it or not, Mary Lou knows when it's show day. As soon as the trailer pulled up she lifted her head and walked proudly up the ramp, just like she does in the show ring. 'Why?'

'Grandpa said I couldn't tell anyone.'

'Well, I'm not anyone. I'm your friend.'

Casey cracks. He'd be a useless spy. 'It's them vet's bills.'

'Oh.'

'We owe a lot. It's bills for when we had the herd. Grandpa's been trying to pay them off. The thing is, we've had a letter from the court. The vet's suing us for thousands of dollars.' Casey slumps. 'Grandpa says selling Mary Lou is the only way out.'

What a day this is turning out to be. I've been challenged to a cupcake-making competition, dumped in favour of a professional knitter and now a much-loved cow is under threat of sale. Whoever said that life in the Midwest was dull has never been to Barnsley.

'Does Wyatt know?' I know that Wyatt would help out in a flash.

Casey shakes his head. 'I told you. Grandpa says we've got our family honour and we can't tell anyone our private business.'

Whether it's a reaction to the events of the day or just the devastated expression on Casey's face, I feel a surge of fury towards Grandpa – a man who puts his own stubborn pride before the feelings of his kith and kin. Oh my gosh, I'm beginning to sound as if I belong here.

'You have to promise not to tell anyone,' says Casey anxiously.

'Cross my heart and hope to die, stick a needle in my eye.' He looks reassured by this.

'Don't worry, Casey,' I say firmly. 'We'll sort something out.'

He looks at me. 'Grandpa says there's no other way.' Then he squints at me. 'Why are your eyes all red?'

'They're not.'

'Yes they are.'

Oh, all right. 'Actually my boyfriend and I just broke up.' I force myself to be positive. 'But I'm looking on the bright side. Everything works out for the best. That's how you have to think about the situation with Mary Lou.'

But Casey is not to be put off. 'Why did he dump you?'

Why is he assuming that I was the one who was dumped? However, he's right. 'Because he met someone else. I think it was the distance between us.'

'You mean he forgot all about you when you weren't there?'

I make a mental note never again to discuss my love life with a twelve-year-old boy. 'Pretty much so.'

'Well, I think he's a loser,' says Casey, 'and I'm sure he'll be sorry!'

I give him a hug. 'You're right.' I think about telling him more about Zara – like how she has a compulsion to suck the chocolate off Kit-Kat fingers, and how she started keeping her eye make-up in the freezer after she heard about eyelash mites. Then I remember that I'm the adult and he's the child. 'Casey, what we have to do now is think of a plan to save Mary Lou,' I say as cheerfully as I can manage.

Casey turns and looks up at me in that trusting way children have. 'Really?' His face is suddenly filled with hope. 'Can you save her?'

I have no idea, but I can't let him see that. Instead I play for time. 'Did we sort out your Kentucky project?'

He nods.

'Did you get an A+ on Plants and Animals of Ohio?'

He nods.

'Then we'll find a way to keep Mary Lou,' I say with conviction, 'and a way to take her to the Ohio State Show,' I add recklessly.

His face lights up. 'Wow.'

He jumps up and says excitedly to Mary Lou, 'We're going to win the State Show!'

I'm already regretting saying that last bit, but it's too late now. Casey is pointing at Mary Lou's Scott County Show Supreme Champion Rosette. 'You're going to have a huge rosette pinned up there,' he assures her, pointing at the barn wall. 'Alice is going to solve all our problems!'

He throws his arms around Mary Lou's neck and buries his face in her velvety coat. Just then Wyatt comes into the barn. As he approaches, Casey shoots me a warning look and puts his finger on his lips. I nod. I did promise, after all.

By the time Wyatt reaches us we're looking casual in the way that bad actors do: I've got both hands in my pockets and am staring at the ceiling, and Casey is whistling to himself whilst scuffing his foot around the floor.

Wyatt clearly isn't fooled. 'What's up?' he says, looking from me to Casey and back again.

Then we both speak at once.

'Nothing,' I say.

'It's Alice,' says Casey. 'Her boyfriend's dumped her.'

I can't believe it! The disloyalty!

But Casey is grinning at me, unabashed. 'Alice said he forgot all about her and he's going to be sorry.'

'That wasn't exactly what I said.'

Wyatt looks at me questioningly.

'Stephen and I have mutually decided to take a break,' I say in a dignified fashion.

'But you said he dumped you,' Casey reminds me helpfully.

Wyatt takes a moment to absorb this news. 'I'm sorry, Alice. Is there anything I can do?'

'No. Really. I'm fine,' I say, but as the words come out my voice wobbles a bit and I realize I do feel a bit in shock.

'You could make us something to eat,' says Casey. 'That would help Alice. We could have toasted cheese sandwiches.'

Wyatt is looking hard at me. 'Good idea. You finish up here, Casey, then come on in.'

Then Wyatt takes my arm and leads me out of the barn.

'I'd offer you a brandy if I had any,' says Wyatt as I sit down in the kitchen.

Actually I could murder a nice glass of wine. But I shake my head vigorously. 'I'm sure alcohol will only make my problems worse,' I say diligently, repeating a line from *Enable YOU*, a book which has, up to this point, proved to be of very little practical assistance to me.

Wyatt raises an eyebrow. 'Alice, you don't have to say that for my sake.'

Actually I do, because I can't exactly go on about how nice a chilled glass of Chardonnay would be right now.

'Coffee would be great,' I say enthusiastically.

He begins to make a pot.

'I'm really sorry, Alice,' says Wyatt. 'I kind of feel responsible.'

'Responsible?'

'Yeah. If you hadn't come over here, you guys would still be together.'

It's odd, but even though I'm still reeling from the break-up, there isn't any part of me that regrets coming to Barnsley.

'No,' I say firmly. 'It wasn't about me coming here.' I can't leave Wyatt thinking that he's somehow to blame. 'Actually, Stephen got together with Zara.'

Wyatt swings round. 'The nutty knitting woman?'

'Yes,' I confirm.

Wyatt shakes his head. 'Unbelievable.' He takes a pack of cheese slices out of the fridge and starts assembling Casey's sandwich. I sit back and watch him as Travis nuzzles up against my leg. It's clear that Wyatt's afternoon's work with Bruce must have gone well, because Wyatt starts to hum a few bars of 'Pretty Woman'. I expect he's inspired to hum this by the song he's writing about Heidi, which is understandable, given that she's the woman he's destined to marry.

It's also odd, but sitting here with Wyatt, I don't feel nearly so bad. Maybe it's the aroma of toasted cheese that's triggering my endorphins? Wyatt hands me a cup of coffee, Travis wanders off to go and hunt for sandwich crumbs and Casey bursts through the kitchen door. 'I'm starving!'

Soon Wyatt is dishing up toasted sandwiches and I'm getting Casey a large glass of milk. Casey demolishes his first sandwich and looks up expectantly at Wyatt for a second.

'You have hollow legs,' sighs Wyatt, making another.

Then Casey starts telling us in some detail about the time Mary Lou got mastitis. It's surprisingly interesting. It's amazing how much my perspective has changed in the three months that I've been here. This morning I found myself looking hopefully out of the window for rain, because I know the farmers need it for the sweetcorn to fill out. Tornadoes are another cause of increased weather monitoring, though so far we've avoided taking refuge in the cellar. I've also learnt to be newly vigilant at night. No one ever gets mugged in Barnsley, but danger lurks at every turn: rabid bats are quite a worry here, and this year the skunk population has reached a record high.

Who would have thought that I could feel a part of Barnsley so quickly? I sit back in my chair and wait for Wyatt to talk me into having a toasted cheese sandwich. I could almost relax right now and let myself think what it would be like if I were to live here all the time. I look across at Wyatt, at the familiar outline of his broad back, at that longish hair which suits him so well, at his hands, now darkly tanned from hours outside on the farm. I look around the kitchen and realize that more often than not I eat breakfast, lunch and dinner in here. And then my eye falls on Casey and I know that it's not only Wyatt I'll find it hard to leave behind.

And then I pull myself to my senses. I can't think that way. I won't allow myself, even for a moment, to dream. I did that once before, and when our hopes were shattered, when everything we thought was going to be all right turned out to be terribly wrong, then I realized how dangerous dreams could be. 'It's just a routine check-up,' Mum said the night before her hospital appointment. By then it had been two years since the operation and the chemotherapy and the radiation. Mum and the doctors had covered everything, or so we thought. I'm not sure I even said good luck to her in the morning. I'd got complacent, you see, and if Mum was nervous, she never showed it. When I got home from school,

239

Mum and Dad were sitting in the living room. They'd forgotten to put the lights on.

'Alice, it's come back,' Dad said quietly.

I was shocked, but I think I gave a little nervous laugh. 'But they can make it go away again.' It wasn't a question. It was what I wanted to believe.

Then Mum spoke. 'It's in my bones, love.'

That was when I vowed to give up dreams. Sometimes I think that was when I gave up hope. But now I look over at Casey, and as he looks back at me I see the trust in his eyes that he has for me, the faith that somehow I'm going to save Mary Lou and make everything all right. No, I haven't given up hope. Not for Casey, anyway. I resolve that tomorrow I will go and see Grandpa.

CHAPTER 29

It has taken me a week to summon up the courage to visit Casey's grandpa. As you can imagine, various scenarios have come to mind regarding my visit, most of them ending with me being chased off the ramshackle premises by a gun-toting white-bearded loon in denim dungarees. 'Lady, I ain't accepting *charidee* from no one. Now take yourself back to the big city and don't be fillin' young Casey's head with yer foreign ways.' I pull away at high speed to the sound of clucking chickens.

I pull into the farm and see that the ramshackle yard is littered with broken-down bits of farm machinery: plough parts, seed spreaders and, to the side, a tractor propped up on blocks because both back wheels are missing. They lie to the side, thick weeds growing up through the centres. There's a sign propped up against the wall: *This Way To The Maize Maze!* Of course, Grandpa still cuts a corn maze every year. I park the car and make my way to the house, a knot of fear in my stomach.

I've never been very good at what Dr Vaizey called 'dialogues of change'. He was always encouraging us to have dialogues of change at every possible opportunity, in which we assertively stated our needs and established goals for growth. Jennifer got a round of applause when she returned a mouldy avocado to Spar, an event which she subsequently credited with marking the beginning of a new era of personal freedom. (I can't recall Zara ever completing the dialogue of change assignment, though I suppose the conversation in which she asked Stephen if he would like her to take her knickers off more than qualifies. But I'm not bitter.)

The farmhouse, which I guess is a hundred years old and built from reddish-orange brick, hasn't been repaired for years. A deep crack has opened up in the peeling, weather-beaten door, one worn shutter is half hanging off its hinges and I see that the iron guttering is sinking alarmingly along the front of the house. As I look further up, I see that the top of the chimney stack has fallen away and a couple of the slate roof tiles are missing.

'What do you want?'

The door has sprung open and Grandpa is scowling at me. I know it's Grandpa because he's got a bushy white beard and he's wearing high-waisted denim dungarees over a collarless plaid work shirt.

Before I have a chance to answer, he continues, 'If it's about Casey, he's at school and the nurse says he's as fit as a fiddle. If you're from the public health about my wife, she's sleeping and she can't be disturbed.'

'Actually . . .'

'And if you're from the court, I've got nothing to say to you.'

'It's about Mary Lou,' I say quickly. 'I'm Alice Fisher. I'm staying at Wyatt Brown's farm. Perhaps Casey's mentioned me.'

Grandpa looks at me, if anything, more suspiciously. 'No. He ain't said nothing about you.'

I hope that I've concealed my surprise at this. I try to look pleasant and casual but also businesslike and professional –

like a trainee social worker. 'Perhaps I could come in?'

He regards me for a few seconds, then nods his head and opens the door. I think this cautious acceptance may have something to do with the outfit I purchased specially for the occasion from the mall: long dark blue pinafore dress, red turtleneck and low-heeled black Mary-Janes. Wyatt looked at me quizzically as I left today, but I'm still adhering to my promise to Casey to say nothing about the threat of sale that hangs over Mary Lou's head.

Before Grandpa has a chance to change his mind, I dart in. He leads the way into a small lobby with dark wooden floorboards. Ahead I can see the living room. It's heavily shaded by faded bottle-green curtains hanging from brass rings. I glimpse a hard-backed sofa with wooden arms, above which hangs a brightly coloured oil painting of The Last Supper. There's a rocking chair and small tables covered with lace doilies, family photographs and an oil lantern. The house has that smell of old people: a mix of wax furniture polish, dust and boiled cabbage.

'Grandma's having a rest,' he says, jerking his head towards the stairs, which are wooden with a thin, threadbare strip of purple carpet running up the middle. I'm surprised: Casey has assured me that Grandma is a very busy person, always cleaning, baking and doing good works for the poor.

I expected to go into the living room, but instead he leads me into the kitchen. It's the same as those museum rooms where they recreate a 1950s house: the sink is cast-iron, the chunky-doored refrigerator has a curved top with 'Frigidaire' spelled out in metal letters and the table is topped with linoleum with a metal strip around the edges. I also notice that the kitchen counters are covered in crumbs, the sink is full of washing-up and the floor looks as if it hasn't been washed in weeks. It's odd: Casey hasn't said anything about Grandma being unwell.

I sit down on one of the pale wooden chairs with red plastic padded seats.

I clear my throat. Then I clear it again. 'I'm here about Mary Lou. Casey says that you're planning to sell her.'

I look up at Grandpa for confirmation of this, but he stares back at me impassively.

'I understand from Casey that Mary Lou could win a prize at the Ohio State Show next year. So I was wondering if we could work out a way to keep her. I know how much Casey loves Mary Lou.' I take a deep breath. 'I'm sure that Wyatt would help out if he knew that help was needed.'

Grandpa's head jerks up. 'Wyatt Brown? That ne'er-do-well? What's he got to do with anything?'

I feel a distinct sense of unease. I choose my words carefully. 'He's very keen on helping the community.'

Grandpa snorts. 'Wyatt Brown abandoned his parents,' he begins counting on his fingers, 'his church and this town to drown in liquor and chase loose women.' He slams his fist on the table. 'I ain't accepting charity from the devil.'

Goodness. Clearly in Grandpa's eyes Wyatt is somewhat worse than a bad boy. But why, then, is he letting Casey keep Mary Lou at Wyatt's farm?

Unless Casey hasn't told him?

'Mary Lou's fine where she is,' Grandpa says firmly.

Which is where, exactly?

'Mr Horner can keep her until market day,' he says briskly.

I feel a jolt of pity for Casey. He's had to keep everything secret.

As I look round the kitchen, I notice the packaging from a frozen ready-meal macaroni cheese poking out of the kitchen bin. The fruit bowl is empty. It dawns on me why

Casey is always hungry. And as I watch Grandpa rise to his feet, this proud old man desperately trying to manage on his own but determined not to admit defeat, I also understand why Casey has told me a collection of stories about Grandma and her baking: he's been brought up never to admit defeat either.

Grandpa sticks his chin out defiantly. 'Good day to you.'

'But what about Casey?' I say, having no option but to stand up too. 'He loves Mary Lou. He spends hours with her every day. That's what he tells me,' I add quickly.

'Good day to you.'

He shuffles out into the hallway. I follow him. But I'm not ready to give up yet. 'Look,' I say. 'If it's Wyatt who you object to, then what about the rest of the town? If Mary Lou won a prize at the State Show it would be an honour for Barnsley. Surely there wouldn't be any harm in letting the town help?'

He stops. 'Help?'

I share his confusion at what I'm saying, but it's too late now. An idea springs to mind. 'We could hold a benefit concert,' I say. 'A bit like Live Earth.'

'Live Earth?' he says, bemused. 'Is that a farming co-operative?

'Something like that,' I say. 'They hold fund-raising events.'

'Like garage sales?'

'And concerts. There's no reason why it couldn't be for a cow. People could sing!'

'Sing?'

'Yes. Like the Scott County Road Maintenance Crew.'

I seem finally to have caught his attention, so I continue at a pace. 'And there could be other exciting events. Mr Horner could recite poetry and we could roast a pig!'

'But it's charity,' he objects mulishly.

'No! It's a return to the spirit of the old Midwest when neighbour helped neighbour and wagons formed a corral at sundown.' I'm on a roll here, so I don't dare pause to catch my breath. 'When all the women gathered round to help a new mother with her baby and men heated baked beans over an open fire. It isn't charity, it's neighbourliness.'

'Sounds like charity to me,' he says with a shake of his head. 'Folks knowing that we can't pay our bills.' His voice drops at this point and I realize that this isn't an admission he had meant to make. His cheeks redden slightly. Then his eye falls on a photograph hanging on the wall. It's a family portrait like the kind Rachel has done. Grandpa and Grandma are sitting, Casey is to the side, and on the other side stands their son and his wife. Their dead son.

'That's something that can happen to anyone,' I say softly. 'No one would think the worse of you.' I gesture out of the window. 'It can't be easy keeping up the farm all on your own.'

His gaze turns to the window. 'Time was when we had two hundred head of cattle and corn stretching as far as that hill.' His voice trails off. 'I did it all for my son, you see. Now we're holding on for Casey.'

I look around the farmhouse, now noticing the thick dirt on the windows and the layers of dust on the furniture. I wonder how long they can hold on for. But I know that there is nothing more I can say, that I have done as much as I can.

Grandpa has opened the front door. 'We can manage,' he says stiffly.

I reach down to pick up my handbag from the hall table.

'Wait!' It's a woman's voice, so quiet I can barely hear it, but there's a strength in it that makes me swing round. There, clutching the oak banister, stands a tiny white-haired figure swaddled in a tartan dressing gown. I recognize Grandma from the family photograph, but goodness she's aged. Casey once had a Grandma who cooked and baked and sang, but the woman in front of me bears no resemblance to her.

'I heard it all, Father,' she says.

She looks at me with her pale watery eyes. 'I presume you're the English girl who's staying at Wyatt's.'

'Yes.'

How does she know that? I must look puzzled because she says stiffly, 'I still go to church. And you know Casey?'

I hesitate. 'Yes,' I say slowly.

'And you've met Mary Lou?'

'Yes.'

She fixes me with an intense stare and there's an almost imperceptible nod of the head. 'I think I understand.' She pauses. 'Let her help, Father.'

His chin juts out. 'You want everyone knowing our business, Mother?'

'It's for the boy,' she responds calmly.

I hold my breath. In the silence that follows, I can hear the heavy ticking of a grandfather clock.

He turns away. 'No.'

I look at Grandma and read the grief in her eyes.

'Wait!' I call out. 'Actually it's for Mary Lou. I mean, technically speaking.'

At this, Grandpa stops in his tracks and slowly turns. But before he has a chance to answer me I continue.

'The benefit wouldn't be for you. It would be for Mary Lou.' Some deeply buried phrase of Stephen's comes to mind. 'She would be the beneficiary of the trust.'

I pause for breath.

Then Grandma's voice rings out. 'There you are then. It would be a proper trust. All legal. For the cow.'

She's offering Grandpa a way out, a face-saving solution whereby he can accept help, and I can see from the way he's rubbing his beard that he's considering whether to take it.

'You give me your word that it would be for Mary Lou,' he says sternly.

'I give you my solemn word,' I say with all the sincerity of someone taking their marriage vows.

He looks from her to me. 'Very well.'

CHAPTER 30

I'm feeling the pressure of organizing a fund-raising benefit for a cow. No one has shown any interest at all. Mr Horner is preoccupied with the Barnsley Festival, Dolores is focusing on her new diet and exercise regime – this one she's going to stick to – and Madison says she will 'get back to me' to let me know if she's available to sing. The cheek! This must be what it's like to be Bob Geldof. No wonder he swears so much. As for Wyatt, he's painting the barn with Bruce and I can't get a word out of either of them. The only person who shows any interest is Casey, who asks me every day how much money I've raised.

It's Monday morning and I'm sitting at the kitchen table in the cottage looking disconsolately at my 'Concert for the Cow' list when Gerry strolls in carrying two cups of coffee in Styrofoam cups and a small box of Krispy Kreme doughnuts.

'Don't tell Lauren,' he says with a wink. Gerry always looks very coordinated. Today he's wearing a pristine white Gant polo shirt, tan Bermuda shorts and brown leather Tod's deck shoes. He's the smartest person in Barnsley by a mile.

He pulls up a chair at the kitchen table. 'So what's up, kid?'

I shake my head. 'I just don't know where to begin with

this benefit for Mary Lou. No one's interested – they're all thinking about the Barnsley Festival.'

Gerry nods. 'So hold it two or three weeks after the Barnsley Festival and get people to think about it then.'

I'm horrified. 'Two or three weeks! Surely that isn't long enough. Projects like this need months of detailed planning.'

'This is Barnsley, Alice. After the Barnsley Festival ends there's nothing scheduled until next year's Barnsley Festival.'

I realize this is true.

'Besides,' Gerry continues, taking a bite out of his dough-nut, 'there's nothing to it.'

I harrumph in irritation. 'There are a hundred details to be finalized and major decisions to be debated. The venue, for example.'

'High-school gym,' says Gerry matter-of-factly. 'It's obvious.'

'Why?' I say, puzzled.

'Because there isn't anywhere else.'

I write down *high-school gym*.

'Just call up the principal or ask Mr Horner,' he says.

'But Mr Horner's the retired principal,' I object.

'Yeah, but his son-in-law is the principal now.' Gerry takes a drink of his coffee, puts his cup down and strokes my knee under the table. 'Besides, they've got lighting and a sound system there, so you don't have to worry about that.'

I write all this down. Gerry is making it seem quite easy.

'Acts?'

'The Scott boys. Madison. And Mr Horner on his accordion.'

I look up. 'Mr Horner?'

'He does "Somewhere Over The Rainbow". It's a real tear-jerker. Oh, and get the moms to do something. Brandy can belt out that one from *Flashdance*. Just keep her away from the tequila till afterwards.'

I write that down. 'Food?'

'Sheriff Billy's barbecue ribs and Dolores for the rest.'

'Drink?'

'Scott County Maintenance Crew.'

'Ticket sales?'

'Sheriff Billy again. He gets around town. He'll handle all the money for you.'

'Raffle?'

'Heidi's your best bet there. She's very persuasive. The raffle can double your money.'

My Pentel rollerball hovers over the paper. The last thing I want to do is involve Heidi. But on the other hand I need to raise as much money as possible. I think of Mary Lou and write down *Heidi*.

'The only other thing is to keep Logan's brother away from the beer.' He gets up and squeezes my hand. 'That's it. Let's retire to the sofa.'

Really. It's ten o'clock in the morning and I'm stone-cold sober. 'I think I ought to be getting on with my list.'

Undeterred, Gerry grabs me and spins me round. I can now see Wyatt and Bruce sitting on the top of the barn roof. I'm rather disappointed to see that neither of them is wearing a safety harness. (I was the employee representative on the Health and Safety Committee at Kingston Council, and what I heard in those meetings has stayed with me to this day.) I hope they can't see Gerry lunging at my neck. Despite the fact that Wyatt is destined to be with Heidi, I still don't want to be seen as a foreign woman of loose morals. I fend Gerry off. 'I've got work to do.'

'It can wait.'

I dodge to the other side of the kitchen table, where Gerry

starts circling me. 'Let's play a game,' he says teasingly. 'I know – the fox and the bunny rabbit. I'll be the fox.'

'No thank you.'

'You know, you'd look really great in a bunny costume,' says Gerry, his eyes glinting.

'I don't think so.'

'The farmer and the milk maid?'

We continue to circle the table until I grab my notebook and make a dash for the door. 'I'm off to see Mr Horner. I don't want anyone else to book him before I get there,' I cry out over my shoulder as I flee to my car.

Three hours later and I've provisionally allocated all the tasks as Gerry suggested (though everyone told me to come back after the Barnsley Festival to remind them). I should say nearly all the tasks. One name has not been ticked off – *Heidi.*

I think of Mary Lou – and her future as a McDonald's product if I fail in my task – as I park my car outside Heidi's house. She lives round the corner from Rachel's house on Armstrong Road, named, I presume, after the famous moon-landing astronaut Neil Armstrong.

She's very surprised to see me. 'Alice,' she says, clearly confused, and at that moment I realize why Andy McNab, the famous SAS soldier turned best-selling novelist, places such emphasis on the element of surprise. She isn't wearing any make-up and she's dressed in cut-off denim shorts and a baggy T-shirt. This might have put me at a further advantage had I not been dressed identically. In my escape from the cottage I didn't have time to change out of my morning cleaning clothes.

'What a pleasure,' she says flatly, looking me up and down very slowly.

I adopt my most professional tone. 'I've come to see you

about the benefit concert I'm organizing for Mary Lou.'

It takes her a moment to compose herself. 'Why don't you come in?'

As I step into her hallway, I also understand how Andy McNab must have felt in enemy territory. Like him, all my senses are now in an elevated state of awareness. Immediately I identify the scent of a Glade 'Clean Linen' plug-in air freshener. I note that Heidi's stripped-wood floors are spotless, as is her gilt-framed hall mirror and brass light fitting.

'Come into the kitchen,' she says coldly. 'No, on second thoughts, come into the living room.' She turns to her left. 'Here,' she says, gesturing at a wooden rocking chair. 'Sit there.'

I don't have much choice but to do as she says. I can't see why she's making me sit here rather than on the comfortable two-seater cream oatmeal sofa or matching easy-chair in the corner.

'I'll make coffee,' she says, disappearing.

I sit back and try to relax, but the wooden bars of the chair dig into my back. Instead I perch forward and carry on my reconnaissance of the room. I have to admit it's very nice. At either end of the sofa are two square cherry-wood tables, each with a brass table-lamp with cream pleated shade. Small ornaments are placed on the tables and mantelpiece, the kind of thing you buy in museum shops – a brass ballet dancer, an abstract sculpture of entwined circles and a small carved olive-wood box.

'I won't be a moment,' Heidi calls out from the kitchen. 'I'm just grinding the beans.'

A whirring sound follows. Above the sofa is a watercolour painting of racehorses charging for the finishing line, and on the opposite wall there's a set of framed aerial photographs:

a hot-air balloon race, a tropical island and Paris. The room is perfectly composed.

'I would offer you some freshly baked lemon and poppy-seed muffins,' she says, popping her head round the door, 'but Wyatt would never forgive me. They're his favourite.' Then she disappears again.

The carpet is cream and spotless. Try as I might, I can't spot a single speck of dust or trace of a cobweb. I feel heavy-hearted as Dolores' words come back to me – *she's the girl for him. She'd make a wonderful wife and mother.*

Heidi returns with a tray covered with a starched white linen cloth, two china cups, a cafetière of coffee, a milk jug, sugar bowl and some chocolate-chip cookies. Then she hands me a lace-trimmed napkin ironed into a perfect rectangle. It's a shame, really, that Heidi and I aren't gay – we'd be ideally suited.

'Chocolate-chip cookie,' she says. 'Home-made, of course.'

'No thank you.'

'Really? I got the impression you liked your cakes, cookies and desserts.'

I will rise above this. 'I've come to ask you to organize the raffle at a benefit concert to pay Mary Lou's vet's bills,' I force myself to say.

She ignores me. 'Alice, come and look at these photographs.'

What photographs? She gestures behind me. I look around and notice for the first time a gleaming mahogany sideboard covered in silver-framed photographs.

'Come on,' she says sharply.

I get up.

'Here, this is me cheerleading,' she points. 'This is me ski-ing in Michigan. This is my first horse. Here's my family at my graduation.'

But I'm not looking at any of them because I've already seen the biggest photograph located in the middle, the one that Heidi is reaching for right now.

'And this is me and Wyatt.' She picks up the photograph. 'Here, I'm sure you'd like to take a closer look.'

I know I shouldn't take it, but I can't help myself.

'We had it taken when Wyatt moved in. It's by the front door of his house.'

I can see that. Wyatt is standing with his arm around Heidi, smiling at the camera. She's wearing a short yellow summer dress. She's staring up at him adoringly, her hand on his chest. My stomach turns over.

'I organized all the move for him,' says Heidi, 'and celebrated his house-warming with him.'

I can't think of anything to say. My mouth has gone dry.

'Wyatt begged me to move in, but I told him that we needed to take our time. What's the rush?' she laughs.

I need to sit down. I hand back the photograph. 'Very nice,' I manage to say.

'Thank you. Would you like to see my albums?'

'Another time.' I sit down heavily. I have to change the subject. 'So how about the raffle?' I can only manage short sentences.

'Delighted to,' she says warmly. 'Anything I can do to help Casey. He's like a son to Wyatt and me.' She takes a sip of her coffee. 'I'll sell those tickets like my life depended on it, Alice, don't you worry – everyone will get to hear from me!'

Ten minutes later – after Heidi has reeled off the names of all the huge prizes she's going to get – I make my excuses. I'm in a sombre mood as I arrive back at the cottage. How right I was to be cautious of Wyatt. I resolve to be pleasant but businesslike in my dealings with him.

It's not until the late afternoon that I catch Wyatt on his way back into the house as Bruce drives off. (I've been in the field with Casey monitoring Mary Lou for sunstroke. 'How much money did you raise today?' was Casey's first question to me.)

'How's the barn coming along?' I call out in a pleasant but businesslike tone to Wyatt across the yard.

'It's coming,' he says curtly. He doesn't stop, so I run to catch up with him by the front door of the house.

He sits down on the doorstep to unlace his work-boots. 'I'm going to take a shower.'

I think he may have a touch of sunstroke himself. He seems a bit off-colour today. I decide to cheer him up. 'Hey, I've got good news,' I say. 'I've sorted out the details for Mary Lou's benefit concert.'

'Hmm.'

'It's going to be at the high-school gym.' I reel off my list of people's names and their responsibilities.

'Sounds like you've got it all under control.'

'Gerry told me who to ask.'

'Really,' Wyatt says coldly, not looking up. 'I saw he was here. As usual.'

'Yes, he was really helpful,' I say positively. 'The only thing that we're short of is musical acts. So far I've got three,' I say.

I should be totally honest at this point and say that I'm hoping Wyatt will offer to do a couple of songs. I really need a headline act and I don't think Mr Horner and his accordion will cut it.

'You'll find someone. I'm sure Gerry can give you some pointers,' he says, getting up and not meeting my eye.

I'm beginning to realize that I need to shut up about Gerry. I take a deep breath. 'The thing is … I was hoping … that you could sing,' I stutter.

'Nope.' Wyatt doesn't hesitate.

I'm sure he doesn't mean to sound so abrupt. 'Just one or two songs,' I say. 'It would really boost the ticket sales. We could definitely charge more.'

'Nope.'

I feel incredibly let down. It's not been the easiest day, I'm hot and tired and I can't work out why Wyatt is being so horrible. 'It's for a really good cause – saving Mary Lou.'

Wyatt looks really pissed off. 'Alice, I'm not in the mood to do karaoke in a high-school gym.'

I'm stung. I feel hot tears welling up. 'It's a charity concert,' I say, hardly able to believe what he's just said. 'I'm sorry if it doesn't match your standards. It's about the whole town pulling together to help one of their own. I thought you might want to participate.'

He stands up. 'I'll give you a donation,' he says, brushing himself down. 'An anonymous donation.'

So Gerry *was* right. Wyatt wants his privacy and he's happy to pay to get it. He plays at being part of the town – but only when he feels like it and only on his terms.

'Don't bother,' I snap. 'We can manage without you.'

Finally he looks at me, holds my stare for a few seconds and then storms into the house, slamming the door behind him.

CHAPTER 31

Wyatt and I avoid each other for two days, during which time I spend a lot of time lying on the sofa listening to Tammy Wynette – there's a woman who understood about heartache – trying to work out my feelings for Wyatt. I decide in the end that I have been a little bit attracted to Wyatt – which explains my feelings of slight jealousy towards Heidi – but this is because of the circumstances of us being forced together virtually under the same roof. The key is to put our relationship back on a purely professional basis. No more iced-tea talks on the porch, no more Sunday brunches and no more fantasies about becoming Mrs Wyatt.

(Yes, there have been one or two of those, but I've been reluctant to commit them to paper. Wyatt proposes after I win the cupcake competition, we get married in an international Barnsley–London celebration, we have two children, a boy and a girl, and Wyatt's next album –*You're Perfect* – is dedicated to me.)

At eleven o'clock on Sunday morning there's a knock on the door.

It's Wyatt. He looks nervous. 'Can I come in?'

'It's your cottage,' I say coolly, holding open the door.

'Thanks.'

He steps in and takes off his hat. 'Look. I've come to apologize about the other day. I was a jerk.'

I pause, but not to compose my thoughts. I've already spent several hours rehearsing my response in the event that Wyatt comes to his senses and apologizes.

Wyatt looks at the floor then out of the window. 'Alice, I just had a bad day. I got the wrong end of the stick about … Anyway, I overreacted.' Finally he looks at me. 'I think you're doing a great thing for Casey.' He stops short. 'I'm really sorry.'

I raise my chin a little. 'I accept your apology and I'm happy to continue our relationship on a purely professional basis.'

He looks a bit surprised at this. 'Oh.' He shuffles a bit from foot to foot. He looks really contrite and I'm beginning to feel a little sorry for him.

I steel myself. 'Wyatt, I'm not a woman to be trifled with. I must insist on firm ground rules for continued contact,' I recite.

'You mean no pancakes?'

'Pancakes are a possibility.' I concede. 'Occasionally.'

'Today?'

I must maintain my boundaries. 'I think that would be rushing things.'

'How about a picnic?'

'A picnic!' I blurt out. I love picnics – almost as much as I loved camping out in our little tent in the garden when I was small (despite the fact that Teresa once put a slug in my sleeping bag).

Wyatt clearly sees an opening. 'We could take a picnic up to the woods.'

'What would be in it?'

'Sandwiches, potato salad and apple and cinnamon muffins. Heidi dropped them off earlier.'

I crack, which I think is forgivable in the circumstances. 'I suppose so.'

'I'll get the food.'

Wyatt goes off to the house while I grab my rucksack and, in a carefree manner, throw in my sunscreen, sunblock, insect repellent, sunglasses, notebook, pen and my antiseptic handwipes.

Ten minutes later we're ready to go. I meet Wyatt in the yard, where he's standing next to Nelson. Nelson is Wyatt's new horse, the one he rescued. Nelson is very old and slow and addicted to grass. I can't understand why he's saddled up.

'By the way,' says Wyatt. 'You're riding.' He throws me a cowboy hat. 'You'll need that, too.'

'I'm not riding and I'm not wearing this,' I say, looking at the battered brown hat.

'You'll get sunstroke.'

I put the hat on. 'No riding,' I insist. As I do so, I remember our deal. If I go riding, Wyatt promised to write a song. I look at Nelson, who has to be twenty feet tall. It's impossible.

Then I think of Phoebe. She's holding the new song in her hand. 'Alice, this is a masterpiece. I knew you could do it! And since I have no children and no prospect of ever getting married, I'd like to groom you as my successor as Worldwide President of Carmichael Music. I'm planning on retiring next year.'

I take a step closer to Nelson. He whinnies and I retreat five paces. I fold my arms and shake my head.

'OK.' Wyatt holds up his hands in surrender. 'You don't have to get on him. But Nelson's very sensitive. He's going to have his feelings hurt.'

'He is?'

'Definitely. Just go up to him, hold the saddle and tell him that you like him.'

'What?'

'We don't want him getting depressed. He might stop eating. And never start again.'

I go up to Nelson and do as Wyatt says. 'I'm sorry I'm not riding you,' I say. 'It's nothing personal. It's me, not you.'

'Hold his saddle at the front and get close to him. Be friendly,' instructs Wyatt.

I do as Wyatt says. Before I know it, he's grabbed hold of my knee, pushed my bottom into the air and hoisted me on to the horse.

I cling to Nelson's neck as he prances about and snorts. 'Get me down!' I squeal.

'Sorry, can't do that,' says Wyatt, grinning at me.

'He's about to bolt!' I screech.

'He's tied up,' says Wyatt.

'He could untie himself with his teeth,' I wail.

Wyatt ignores me. He undoes the reins and walks ahead of me. Oh my gosh, it's so high up here, and really bumpy.

'Try sitting up,' he says after five minutes. 'You'll find it more comfortable.'

After about half a mile, I've eased myself into a seated position with both hands clenched on the saddle. At one point Wyatt starts walking a bit fast, but once I shout at him in a panic to slow down, he resumes a slow amble. If I wasn't so nervous I might feel awkward about impersonating an empress of the ancient world out and about with her personal slave, but I'm too worried to think about that.

In front of me Wyatt is whistling happily. When he turns round every so often to check on me, he looks really happy, which is odd, given that he's used to galloping around at high speed.

It's cool and silent here under the huge oaks, elms and maples with only the sound of birdsong and the breaking of twigs underfoot. We do not speak because I have to concentrate on staying on. Then we reach a shady glade by a stream.

'Right,' says Wyatt, 'off you get. Just take your feet out of the stirrups and swing your leg off.'

I slither off and Wyatt catches me. I'm so happy I throw my arms around his neck. First flying. Now a horse – can it be long before I go swimming?

'That's my girl,' he says.

While Nelson slurps greedily at the stream, Wyatt unpacks the picnic. With relish, I take a bite of a delectable apple and cinnamon muffin. My goodness, they're good. It's such a shame that Heidi can't see how much I'm enjoying them.

Wyatt stretches out on the grass and waves his hand around. 'Bet you haven't got anywhere like this in London,' he says.

'No, I say. 'Just thousands of years of history and the finest museums in the world.'

He rolls his eyes. 'So where would you rather be right now?'

'Bread roll?' I say in response.

'Ha. I knew you'd be converted.'

'Converted to what?'

'Barnsley. I could tell the first day I met you that you'd fit in.'

I'm taken aback. I can't believe that Wyatt noticed that. 'I'm surprised,' I say. 'I thought maintaining your Dork multiple personality took up all your attention.'

He grins at me. 'When you picked up your suitcase in the

hallway – all snooty like – I knew you had guts.' He picks at a sandwich. 'And I was right,' he says.

'Anything else you'd like to tell me you've been right about?'

'Sure, but there wouldn't be time. Let's just say that you've fitted in pretty well.'

It's just as well that I'm committed to being businesslike, because right now this scene could easily be misinterpreted as a romantic assignation. We're lying side by side on the blanket, staring up at the sky through the trees. Looking at Wyatt, it's hard to believe that this is the same man who refuses to rent out his land to the farmers of Barnsley. Maybe, I tell myself, they have lots of land and don't really need it. Yes, that's it.

'So tell me about the concert,' says Wyatt. 'I see Gerry's been helping you.'

'Our relationship is purely friendship,' I assure him, even though Gerry would like it to be more.

'Good,' says Wyatt, and he looks very cheerful indeed. Then he tells me about the time he first sang in a Nashville bar and I tell him about the time I first added toner to the Kingston Council photocopier. I became so expert at clearing paper jams that I was soon put in charge of scheduling all routine maintenance appointments.

We stay there for about two hours chatting about our respective careers. When we get back, Wyatt takes Nelson into the stable and gives him some water and rubs him down while I take the saddle back to the tack room.

Wyatt comes in. 'I'll clean that later.'

'I'll do it now.'

'Oh, for God's sake,' he says, taking my hand. We go hand in hand into the house. In the living room the late afternoon sun is streaming through the windows, a gentle breeze is lifting the edge of the Sunday papers on the table and the air smells of meadow-grass. Wyatt leads me over to the sofa and pulls me down next to him.

'I really like you, Alice. Everything around here feels different since you arrived.'

I can't pretend that this conversation is businesslike.

My mouth has gone dry and my hands are very slightly trembling. Now is the time to get up and walk away. I look into Wyatt's eyes, and as I do so I realize that I'm not going to do that, that I'm not just slightly attracted to Wyatt and that I need to stop lying to myself. We sit for a few long seconds, each of us looking at the other as if for the first time. Wyatt runs his fingers over the top of my hand and at that moment everything in the room and beyond ceases to exist, everything except Wyatt and the colour of his eyes and the warm, rough touch of his hand. He moves towards me and I mirror him.

I'm not thinking now at all, just responding to this irresistible pull. I catch the scent of his breath as he moves closer and the soft brush of his lips across my cheeks. He reaches out and pulls me close. I know that we're about to kiss, and when we do, nothing will ever be the same again. Our lips meet, mine part and I feel the softness of his mouth.

Then the doorbell rings.

I feel Wyatt stop moving. 'Maybe they'll go away,' he says calmly.

I glance down at my watch. I see what the time is and my heart feels as though it's actually sinking. It's half-past four – about time for Heidi. She never goes away.

Sure enough the bell sounds again, seemingly louder and more impatient. I imagine her holding it down with a pink manicured finger, her mouth set in a hard, lipglossed line. With a touch of relief, I register that at least she has come to the front of the house – usually she walks straight in through the kitchen door.

Wyatt is still motionless next to me. Then the bell rings for a third time. He sighs and gets up wordlessly.

I watch him walk to the door and I'm glad that Heidi can't see me from the doorstep. Hastily I sit up and smooth down my jeans.

The voice at the door is familiar, of course, but it takes me a few moments to place it, as if my mind is struggling to catch up with events. So it's still a shock when Wyatt appears a few seconds later.

'Alice, you've got a visitor,' he says, and even Wyatt can't quite conceal the surprise in his voice.

'Hello, Alice.' Stephen walks into the room and drops his Milletts rucksack on the floor.

I'm so blindsided I can't speak. I try to, but the words won't come out.

Stephen looks at me with an adoring expression I have never seen before. 'Alice, I had to see you.'

He turns back to Wyatt. 'I had to see her,' he repeats earnestly.

He hurries over to me. 'Alice, I made a terrible mistake. I know that now. And you would be well within your rights to tell me to leave.' He stops, clearly thinking this last comment over in his mind. 'I should clarify that last statement. I'm referring to your *moral* right, not your legal right, obviously. As the owner of the property, Mr Brown has the *legal* right.'

Wyatt and I exchange glances, both of us clearly bemused by Stephen's unannounced arrival and his impromptu legal lecture.

Stephen coughs. 'The point is, I want you to take me back, Alice. I want us to have a secure life together, inclusive of children. Yes, you heard me right. One or possibly even two children.'

I hear what Stephen is saying, but it doesn't register. I keep looking from Stephen – who is wearing his smart-casual summer outfit of Primark lightweight non-crease trousers and short-sleeved taupe shirt – and back to Wyatt, who is standing motionless in the doorway. Stephen seems like a visitor from another world, like an actor who has wandered on to the set of the wrong play. I cannot for the life of me work out what he's doing here.

Wyatt begins to speak. 'I'll leave you to it,' he says, gesturing at the front door.

'No! Wait!' exclaims Stephen urgently, addressing a somewhat startled Wyatt. 'I would be honoured if you would remain as a witness.' He turns back to me. 'Alice, I expect you're wondering what I'm doing here,' he says. At that moment, unfortunately, I begin to get an idea.

He continues, 'I think that sometimes actions speak louder than words.' Stephen sinks to the floor on bended knee. He pulls a small red velvet box out of his pocket. Oh, hell!

'Now for the words. Alice Fisher, will you marry me?' He opens the box with a flourish, wobbling slightly as he balances on one knee. 'It's gold with a real diamond,' he says proudly, as if this were something unusual. 'Here,' he hands it to me. 'Small but perfectly formed,' he chuckles.

I'm squinting at the ring when Wyatt clears his throat. 'Congratulations to you both,' he says, apparently warmly. 'I'll be in the barn.' He sounds really sincere.

Then he turns and leaves, the door slamming behind him, leaving me all alone with Stephen and my engagement ring.

'So,' says Stephen eagerly, planting a wet kiss on my cheek, 'What do you say?'

I can't help myself. I've finally got my ring – just not the right man. I burst into tears, at which point Stephen leaps on to the sofa and cradles me in his arms. 'It's all right, darling. Stephen's here. Everything's going to be all right now.'

If I could speak through my gulps, I would tell him that everything was all right until he arrived, ruined the most romantic moment of my entire life and started referring to himself as Stephen, which always sounds super-creepy. Obviously Wyatt is going to step aside like the gentleman he is and leave me in the weedy arms of Stephen. As if on cue, Stephen runs a clammy hand up and down my cheek. 'There, there, Alice. I'm here now. I can tell it's been a nightmare for you here. But trust me, your luck is about to change!'

CHAPTER 32

It's seven o'clock the same evening and I have so far managed not to answer Stephen's question or to put on the gold and diamond engagement ring, as he keeps calling it. In answer to Stephen's proposal, I suggested that we have a nice cup of tea. Stephen quickly put it back in its box, slipping it back into his pocket. He pats it from time to time to make sure it hasn't got lost. Then we retired to the cottage, where Stephen promptly fell asleep on the sofa. About an hour later – with the sound of Stephen snoring in the background – I had an uninterrupted view of Heidi pulling up in her car, letting herself into the house by the kitchen door and emerging five minutes later with Wyatt. They went over to the stables and took out Rascal and Flatts.

Now Stephen and I are sitting in the kitchen, or at least I'm sitting in the kitchen: Stephen is hunched over the kitchen counter laying out his pills.

'Benefiber chewables, slow-release iron, multivitamin and an Airborne,' he counts. He looks up worriedly. 'Or do you think I should skip the multivitamin if I'm taking the Airborne?'

Oh, it's just like old times. We had exciting discussions like this every weekend: 'Shall we descale the kettle or vacuum the car?'

'I'd skip the multivitamin,' I say.

I can see he's making an effort. He's brought presents purchased at Gatwick airport: a copy of this week's edition of *Woman's Own*, a Union Jack refrigerator magnet and a giant bar of Toblerone. I accept them gracefully, refraining from pointing out that I haven't read *Woman's Own* for years and that I don't eat Toblerone, much as I would like to, because the nougat bits get stuck in my molars.

I watch as he pops his pills, then he comes over and sits next to me, pressing his knee against mine. It feels very odd. We still haven't discussed where he's going to be sleeping, and I'm damned if it's going to be next to me.

'I still can't understand why you didn't get my emails,' says Stephen for the umpteenth time, shaking his head. 'I sent you several,' he adds, sounding a little wounded.

'I honestly didn't get any of them,' I protest, and as I say this I realize that if I'd known Stephen was planning this, I would have forbidden him from coming.

'It's better this way,' he says. 'I should have come before. If I had, none of this would have happened. I'm sure you must be lonely here,' he says earnestly, gesturing at the yard out of the window. 'At least now that I'm here you can have some fun for a week.' He reaches over and takes my hand. 'I want to make it up to you, Alice.'

I can't meet his eye. 'It's too late for that, Stephen.'

He grips my hand harder. 'Zara was just a moment of madness. Literally.' He shakes his head. 'I had no idea what she was really like.'

'So that's why you've come running back to me,' I say bitterly.

'No,' he says with genuine-sounding emotion. 'Being around her made me appreciate what a wonderful woman you are. And how much we have in common: our love of hiking, our commitment to home ownership and our chemistry.'

'Chemistry?'

'Physical chemistry,' he says, squeezing my knee so that I jump and spill my coffee over the table.

'Just as well,' he says, getting up in search of a dishcloth. 'You never used to drink coffee after four p.m.'

No, and I never used to be about to kiss Wyatt Brown either. I'm in a maelstrom of emotion – torn between intense physical desire for Wyatt and irritation at Stephen, but also feeling duty-bound to hear Stephen out because I can see that he's really making a superhuman effort. He has, after all, got on an aeroplane and paid for a taxi from Columbus airport.

'So tell me about Zara,' I say stiffly.

Stephen runs his hand through his hair. 'The basic problem was that if she drops a stitch she has to unravel the whole jumper and start again.' He pauses. 'It's a compulsion. It's the same with everything: it all has to be done in a very particular order, and if it's not she has to stop and start all over again.'

'But why would that bother you?'

Stephen colours slightly. 'Some things we used to do together,' he says, looking out of the window. 'But we don't need to go into that.'

'What do you mean?'

'It's not suitable for discussion.'

'If you want to get back together, you have to be honest with me, Stephen. Totally honest.'

He's staring at his feet. 'All I'll say is that there are times when starting all over again from the very beginning – i.e. getting dressed and sitting back down on the sofa – can be very frustrating for a red-blooded man. I wouldn't be at all surprised if it hasn't caused some long-term psychological damage. That's why we never slept together.'

'You never slept together!' I say, astonished.

'I explained all of that in my emails,' Stephen says patiently. 'Anyhow, the final straw came with an extra-large cable-knit cardigan. It was a special order and could have catapulted us into the lucrative outsize market.' He takes a sip of his coffee. 'British women are getting bigger, which presents a major business opportunity. Anyhow, Zara was casting off, dropped a stitch, and before I knew it a day's work was reduced to a ball of wool. When I very reasonably pointed out that time is money, she accused me of being insensitive and unplugged the machine.' He shakes his head. 'You know I can't cope with emotional scenes. It was no surprise I felt a migraine coming on and she wasn't at all sympathetic. In fact, she went to bed and started watching *Doctor Who* with the volume turned up.'

'*Doctor Who*?' I say, aghast. 'I thought Dr Vaizey told her to give away her DVD collection.'

'She bought it back on eBay. She watches at least four episodes a day.' Stephen rolls his eyes. 'She says if she doesn't keep up by watching it every day, she'll forget the dialogue and she won't be word-perfect.'

I can't help it. I have to know every detail of Stephen's sordid but unconsummated affair. 'What about the Kit Kats?'

He rolls his eyes. 'She lied about that too. I found them under the bed.'

'No chocolate?'

'Not a bit. All sucked off. Twelve wafer fingers all lined up. I reckon she does three packs a day.'

Stephen walks over to the sink and rinses out the dish-cloth. 'I never had any time to myself. When I wasn't disinfecting the kitchen utensils, I was driving her around to her lymphatic drainage appointments.'

He carefully aligns the edges of the dishcloth and folds it neatly over the rim of the sink. It's hard to believe that I once found this habit endearing.

'But that's enough about Zara. Let's talk about you, Alice. How have you survived in this backwater?'

'It's been a challenge,' I say semi-truthfully.

'I'm sure.'

He comes over and grabs my hand. 'Let's make ourselves more comfortable, shall we?' Without waiting for a reply he pulls me to my feet and leads me to the living room. 'I think we should make up on the sofa.'

But I've stopped listening to Stephen – who has begun yet again to describe his time prostrate on the aeroplane aisle floor engaging in self-hypnosis – because out of the living-room window I can see Heidi and Wyatt returning from their ride, galloping side by side across the open fields. I stand still, resisting Stephen, who has sat down and is trying to tug me on to the sofa next to him, instead mesmerized by the sight of Heidi, who looks every inch the accomplished horsewoman. It might be my imagination, but I could have sworn she was laughing while looking in the direction of the cottage.

'Stephen. I don't want to make up,' I say, as I lose my balance and collapse next to him.

'I made a terrible mistake, Alice,' he says earnestly, embracing me. 'I was lonely and missing you. I fell into the arms of the nearest available woman. And believe me, Alice, she made the play for me.'

I struggle free. 'What?'

'Oh yes. She made it very clear that she wanted me.' He can't resist a smug little smile of recollection at this point. 'It was little things at first – always offering to lend me money in Monopoly. She was the hunter and I was her helpless prey. But I've learnt my lesson. I believe that we can emerge a stronger team from this.'

'It was an affair,' I protest, 'not some team problem at work.'

'But it's over and now we're together again. You don't have to make any snap decisions. Just spend a week with me – surely that isn't too much to ask?'

I suppose that he isn't being totally unreasonable. I can hardly send him straight home again: for a start, he simply isn't up to it. Stephen was given a very stern talking-to by the First Officer, who said that he was obstructing the exit gangway and breaking international airspace regulations.

'You'll have to sleep on the sofa,' I sigh.

'Anything you say!' He begins unpacking, taking out his wash-bag from which he produces a packet of water-sterilizing tablets and takes them into the kitchen. 'You can never be too careful,' he calls out. 'I brought Germolene, too. I wasn't sure about the quality of American antiseptic cream.' He comes back and begins rifling through his ruck-sack. 'I might take a short nap,' he says, pulling out his essential sleep kit: Boots wax earplugs and a pack of Breathe Right nasal strips. 'I don't suppose you have blackout cur-tains here,' he says. 'So I took the precaution of purloining the airline-issue eyeshades.'

He pulls them on and begins testing the position of the elastic – under, over and around the ears. Thank God no one can see us now.

It's then that the door opens. 'Hiiiii!'

I have never seen Heidi look so happy. She bounds into the living room and beams at us. She's glowing in her jodh-purs and black leather riding boots, teamed with quite a tight white shirt which is unbuttoned so you can glimpse the top of her white lacy bra. I look from Heidi to Stephen, who is slowly detaching the eyeshade from his ears.

'You must be Stephen.' She greets him like he's the answer to her prayers. 'Wyatt told me that Alice's boyfriend was visiting. What a fabulous surprise!'

But then, on second thoughts, I suppose he is the answer to her prayers.

Stephen gawps at her. I can see he can't make up his mind whether to stare at her boobs or her teeth. He folds the eyeshade carefully in half and holds out his hand. 'Pleased to meet you.'

She seizes it. 'And it's so fabulous to meet you at last!' Heidi gushes. 'Alice talks about you all the time.'

I do not. I haven't mentioned him for weeks, and even then it was only in passing.

'It's so obvious that she's been pining for you,' Heidi continues. 'That's why she always looks so down in the mouth.'

Stephen turns to me, looking pleased. 'Pining, eh?'

'Alice has made a brave stab at things here,' continues Heidi, 'but it's clear to me that she belongs back in Britain, by your side.'

'Really?' says Stephen, sitting down and putting his arm around me while I continue to sit bolt upright.

Heidi nods vigorously. 'We women notice the signs of a woman who's missing her soul mate. I expect now that you're here, Alice will make more effort with her appearance.' She turns to me, looking me up and down. 'Are you taking her back with you?' Heidi asks Stephen hopefully.

I've had enough. I detach myself from Stephen's arm. 'No, he's not. I have a lot of important work to do here. My contract has a long time left.'

'Four weeks, isn't it?' says Heidi. 'Not that anyone's

counting,' she adds with a fake laugh. 'But you arrived at the end of March on a six-month visa, which by my reckoning means you have roughly twenty-seven days left here before you become an illegal immigrant and liable to be deported by federal government agents.' She gives another little laugh. 'Assuming someone tipped them off about your presence here.'

'There,' says Stephen reassuringly. 'Not long now till you're safely back in Southfields.'

Oh goody.

'Don't worry, Alice,' says Heidi warmly. 'We won't forget you. I'm sure Wyatt and I will sit by the fire during the cold winter months and share happy memories of your time here.' Heidi looks at her watch. 'I must dash. I mustn't keep Wyatt waiting. We're going out to dinner,' she tells me with a triumphant expression. Then she fixes Stephen with a toothy smile. 'I can't tell you how good it's been talking to you. Now I'll leave you two to have a lovely cosy night in together.'

Then she's gone, virtually skipping out of the room. I slump back, Stephen moving in unison with me so that his arm is still around my shoulders. But I'm not thinking about Stephen. I'm positive that Wyatt and Heidi are going out for a lovey-dovey, post-coital dinner. I can't get the image of Heidi and Wyatt riding together out of my mind, cantering through the woods until they find a leafy glade to tie up the horses and lie together on the patchwork rug that Wyatt has thoughtfully brought, together with a bottle of sparkling apple juice and a punnet of succulent strawberries. Heidi reclines elegantly on the rug, her blonde hair fanned out, the late evening sunlight causing it to shine like burnished gold. Wyatt feeds her strawberries, which she manages to eat gracefully despite lying flat on her back. Then she cups a hand to her ear. 'Wyatt, is that the sound of a waterfall?'

She scampers to her feet and looks through the trees, where a two-hundred-foot waterfall has magically appeared. Soon they are naked under the cascading water, Heidi's long, tanned, cellulite-free legs glinting like burnished copper. After a protracted kissing session, Wyatt fetches the towel he has thoughtfully brought, wraps her in its fluffy white folds and carries her back to the rug, which he's able to do because she's so slim and doesn't comfort-eat. Then they make passionate love by moonlight, even though it's only six o'clock in the evening.

Stephen snuggles up closer to me. 'She seems very nice. They say Americans are friendly, and it's obviously true.'

'Oh yes, she's a real treasure,' I say sourly.

'So you've made at least one friend,' says Stephen patronizingly. 'That's good. Maybe we could invite Heidi and Wyatt out to dinner one night.'

'No!' It's all too much. After the waterfall sex, Wyatt is bound to propose and Heidi will be showing off a gigantic diamond, sapphire, ruby and emerald ring.

'Why ever not?' says Stephen puzzled.

'Because ... because ... Because she'll try to get my cupcake recipe,' I say.

'Your cupcake recipe?' Stephen repeats, frowning.

'Yes, it's top-secret. Heidi and I are competitors in the Barnsley Cupcake Competition.'

'Is that a big deal in Barnsley?' says Stephen.

'Yes, it's a very big deal,' I assure him. 'There's a lot at stake. Heidi has won first prize for the best frosted cupcakes for the last five years running. She's determined not to lose to me.'

'Why?'

Because each of us desperately wants to impress Wyatt with our cooking ability and beat the other. But whatever has passed between me and Stephen, I'm not about to admit that. He's liable to confront Wyatt, challenge him to a fight and end up flat on his back with a nosebleed. Not because Wyatt would actually hit him. No, Stephen would faint before it got to that. 'Because . . .' I pause, trying to think of some plausible reason for our rivalry. 'Because I'm a foreigner.'

Stephen looks perplexed. 'But this is a nation of immigrants.'

'But I'm British,' I point out. 'Heidi is passionate on the subject of colonial oppression. Don't mention the Boston Tea Party,' I say, shaking my head. 'She's liable to get physical. She's a teacher, so all that eighteenth-century taxation stuff is really exciting to her.'

I see that Stephen still looks confused.

'And there's a very substantial prize for the winner,' I improvise.

It's a twenty-five-dollar gift voucher for a bar meal at the Barnsley Tavern, plus you get your photograph in the *Barnsley Messenger*.

Now Stephen looks more animated. 'Cripes. Is it sponsored, then?'

I nod. 'By the Barnsley Seed and Corn Wholesale Co-operative. So you can see there's big money at stake here. And it's next weekend.'

'I take your point. This is no time to be collaborating with the enemy.' Stephen rubs his chin thoughtfully. 'Maybe this is something I could help you with?'

Now it's my turn to look confused. 'How?'

'Didn't I ever mention it? I used to do all the birthday-cake icing in my parent's restaurant. I've got a very steady hand and I can ice a perfectly straight line. Not many people can do that,' he adds proudly. 'Oh yes, Alice. When it comes to fancy scrollwork, I'm your man!'

CHAPTER 33

It's Wednesday morning and quite honestly I don't know how I would have got through the week so far without Stephen and his hour-by-hour colour-coded Cupcake Planner. On Monday we had a strategy session, on Tuesday we undertook the drive to Columbus to purchase equipment from Cake Universe, Ohio's largest retailer of cake and cookie decorating supplies, and tonight we begin testing six cupcake recipes. We're trying three vanilla recipes, two chocolate and a lemon, which is our flirtation with the wild side. I'm mentally exhausted. Yesterday we had to decide whether Tuesday's trip to Columbus should be marked on the Cupcake Planner in blue ink for 'research' or brown ink for 'planning'. In the end we just couldn't decide, so we invented a new yellow category, 'retail operations'.

As we finished loading up the boot in the car park of Cake Universe, Stephen surveyed our supplies. 'Sixty disposable icing bags. Twenty bottles of food colouring. And two hundred multicoloured paper cases.' He lifted his head high, thrust his jaw forward and slammed the boot shut. 'Let battle commence!'

We will not actually be exhibiting two hundred cupcakes – this number is to allow us what Stephen calls a comfortable margin of error in both baking and frosting. Note that we're making a special effort to use the American word 'frosting' lest we alienate the judges by slipping into British-speak. Stephen also thinks it's important that I look as much like a native middle-aged inhabitant of Barnsley as possible, so tomorrow we're going in search of a baggy Halloween sweatshirt. Yes, it's weeks to Halloween, but preparations here are well under way, with the locals hard at work decorating their houses and themselves. Orange sweatshirts with pumpkins are à la mode, and on the way into Barnsley the houses are decked out with black plastic cauldrons on the driveways, witches hanging from the trees and fake cobwebs stretched across the front doors. Plastic gravestones all over the front lawn are also very popular.

Right now we've finished breakfast and Stephen has set out the Cupcake Planner on the kitchen table. Each hour that has passed has a neat horizontal red line drawn through it. Next to it is the competition rules, and next to that the all-important frosting design sheet. It was Stephen's idea to obtain a copy of the competition rules, and he has applied his finely honed legal mind to its complexities. Stephen personally filled out my entry form and hand-delivered it to the Barnsley Town Council offices, which are the size of a Portakabin. The woman at the Leisure and Recreation desk (who also does Planning and Schools, because Barnsley isn't very big) said it was the first time that anyone had ever insisted on a receipt for a Cupcake Competition entry form. But apparently she was very nice about it – it's very informal in the Barnsley council offices. She had a scented candle burning on her desk in the shape of a portly white ghost and a bowl of Halloween candy.

Stephen told me how he charmed her with his British accent into giving him some inside information. There are so far nine entries, including Heidi's and mine, and the judges are Mr Horner, the Mayor and a woman who teaches domestic science at the high school. I stayed at home practising buttercream stars, roses and swags with my new twenty-five-nozzle piping set. As Stephen says, with our limited manpower and the fact that we are operating in enemy territory we have no choice but to fight a guerilla war of lightning strikes.

Right now we're conducting an intelligence briefing.

'We have to assume that in the event of a draw, the science teacher will vote for Heidi,' says Stephen, tapping his retractable pencil on the kitchen table. 'That leaves the Mayor.'

'I'm going to the diner today to get some inside information . . .' I continue.

'. . . While I continue the design process,' concludes Stephen. 'Be careful out there, Alice. Walls have ears!' He gestures out of the window in the direction of Wyatt's house.

I have to admit that we make a formidable team. I also have to admit that Stephen is right to be cautious about Wyatt. I know that he wouldn't deliberately give away our plans to Heidi. But he might inadvertently let something slip. For this reason we have adopted several counter-espionage tactics gleaned from Stephen's favourite author, Andy McNab, the famous SAS soldier turned best-selling novelist. The all-important design information is kept in a folder cunningly labelled 'Stephen's airline ticket', and we'll be baking the cupcakes tonight to afford the us the cover of darkness. Naturally we have a codeword – Operation Martha.

Stephen runs his fingers over the A4 page of competition rules and sighs. 'It's very shoddy drafting, but fortunately that works to our benefit.' He quotes: 'First prize will be awarded to the entrant who in the opinion of the judges has submitted the best selection of home-made frosted cupcakes. A minimum of six must be submitted.'

He's not reading this, mind you, he's reciting it, because by now he knows all the rules by heart. 'Nowhere does it say that the entrant *herself* must handmake the cupcakes,' he says, shaking his head. 'An elementary mistake, but one which allows me to assist you without fear of liability.' He leans back. 'Consideration will be given to both taste and appearance.' This is another quote. He shakes his head. 'But in what proportion? Ten per cent taste, ninety per cent appearance? Or vice versa? It's scandalous that the judging criteria are not set out in writing. The losing parties could appeal to the Ohio State Court on the grounds that the rules were insufficiently clear.'

The word 'losing' makes my stomach turn over.

Stephen sighs. 'It's imperative that we try all six cupcake recipes tonight. If we start at eight o'clock, we should be finished by four a.m. I'm not saying it's going to be easy, Alice. But who dares wins.'

I wonder what Andy McNab, the SAS soldier turned best-selling novelist, would say if he could see us now.

I look across at Stephen and feel for the first time a pang of affection for him as he takes a ruler and red pen and crosses out the 8 a.m. to 9 a.m. Wednesday hour on the planner. He has thrown himself into this enterprise with real enthusiasm and grappled with some deep personal fears along the way. I drove to Cake Universe. But several times he took a deep breath and let go of the handle above the door.

Stephen puts down his pen and then I notice that his expression has changed. Curiously, it's best described as one of relief combined with physical pain. It's an expression I know well from our prior travels together.

I know it's important to keep his spirits up at this crucial time. I look at him encouragingly. 'Any luck?'

He pauses. 'I'm cautiously optimistic.'

Right. I grab my BlackBerry and stand up. 'I'll leave you to it.'

Time is of the essence here. I should explain at this point that Stephen has always been a martyr to irritable bowel syndrome, and that transatlantic travel has played havoc with his all-important routine, which at home takes the form of him retiring to the bathroom at seven a.m with a copy of the *Spectator*. What a blessing that they sell Actimel in the USA. They sell All-Bran, too, but Stephen brought his own box with him.

I dart for the door, shoving in my BlackBerry and handbag. I won't be able to come back in for at least twenty minutes. If Stephen gets nervous or is interrupted, he could face further days of discomfort.

'Wish me luck!' he calls out as I open the door.

It feels like we've never been apart.

CHAPTER 34

I make myself comfortable on Mary Lou's hay bales and take out Carolyn's first draft of my next Baby Whisperer lecture, 'Potty-Training Without Tears'. Wyatt's truck has gone from the yard, and not for the first time since Sunday I wonder if he's avoiding me. We haven't spoken since then, the fateful day of Stephen's bended-knee proposal. I expect Wyatt is enjoying some uninterrupted time with Heidi. Probably he's looking back on our near kiss as an aberration, a last fling before he settles down with the girl of his dreams, and feeling relieved that he had such a lucky escape. When I think about it, which I have been doing quite a lot, I wonder if we even were really going to kiss or whether I invented the whole thing in my mind.

I force myself to concentrate on Carolyn's lecture notes. As I reach the third paragraph – The Debate Over Pull-ups – a call comes in. It's Bob. At last. He's calling with Simon Cowell's telephone number!

'Hello!' Bob is shouting, even though it sounds to me like he's standing next door. 'Can you hear me? Over and out.'

I reply as I always do. 'Loud and clear, Bob.'

'Good.' He sounds unusually cheerful. 'Just ringing up to hear how the lovebirds are getting on!'

'The lovebirds?'

'I thought I'd leave it a couple of days for you to, ahem, shall we say, "get reacquainted".'

'Do you mean me and Stephen?'

'The very same.'

'How do you know he's here?'

Bob adopts a really irritating mysterious tone. 'Let's just say I make it my business to know.'

I'm getting a very nasty feeling. 'Bob,' I say suspiciously, 'have you been reading my emails again?'

'It's my job to review the network emails, Alice. But it seemed an appropriate moment to play Cupid.'

Finally, it all makes sense. Like one of Bob's thrillers, a missing piece of the puzzle clunks awkwardly into place.

'Bob, did you delete Stephen's emails to me? The ones telling me that he was coming to Barnsley?'

'No. I blocked them. They're still in the system. Which technically means that I delayed them. I knew otherwise you wouldn't let him come.'

I'm livid. 'He had an affair,' I hiss. 'I had every right to tell him not to come.'

'He didn't actually do the dirty deed,' says Bob dismissively. 'He deserved a second chance. You did leave him behind to follow your own career dreams, Alice. Zara was an accident waiting to happen.' He sounds completely unrepentant at this outrageous invasion of my privacy and meddling in my love life.

'Accident! He didn't trip up and land on her.'

'He sounded very sorry in his emails.'

'I wouldn't know that, would I?' I snap. 'I didn't get the chance to read them. Why do men think that saying sorry makes it all OK?'

'Alice, Alice,' he sighs. 'Man is the hunter. It's his nature to roam. Think of James Bond. His womanizing ways haven't

284

stopped him saving Queen and country on countless occasions.'

'James Bond is a fictional hero,' I point out furiously, 'and he doesn't bear any resemblance to Stephen. You had no right reading his emails to me and I absolutely forbid you to do it again.' I'm about to tell him that I've a good mind to report this to Phoebe when I realize that I still need Simon Cowell's mobile number, and also that Bob is my only ally at Carmichael Music. 'How could you do such a thing?' I gasp.

'I just wanted a happy ending,' he says forlornly. 'It's not as if you had anyone else on the horizon.'

So he's been reading my emails to Carolyn, too. I'm about to explode.

'Besides,' he continues. 'There's your dad and Valerie to consider. Two break-ups in one week would have been very hard on them.'

I stop short. I have no idea what he's talking about. 'What are you talking about?'

'Teresa and her hubby,' he says impatiently. 'Surely she's told you? You're sisters.'

I'm stunned. 'I haven't heard anything.'

'It's her hubby and that lady boss Sandra. Turns out he wasn't at the Birdathon after all. They were at the Reigate Holiday Inn.'

'You mean ...'

'Afraid so. He's flown the nest, so to speak. He's shacked up with Sandra and they've both jacked in their jobs. They're going to go round the world tracking the lesser-tufted sand-piper. I think that's what it's called. He says he wants the house put on the market. Teresa's devastated – says all that stencilling was for nothing.'

I can hardly take this in. 'When did all this happen?'

'A couple of weeks ago. So you see, that's why I thought it best to let Stephen come and for nature to take its course. You don't realize how much your dad worries about you. As I said to him, Alice isn't getting any younger. He agreed that Stephen would make a good provider.'

I cut him off. 'Tell me about Teresa.'

'Turns out hubby's been carrying on with his fancy woman. He was never doing overtime. It was the credit-card statements that were the giveaway.'

'Hotel receipts?'

'Presents from the RSPB online shop.'

'Why hasn't anyone told me?'

But as soon as I say this I know why – pride on Teresa's part and Dad not wanting to worry me.

'We think she's still not really accepted it. She's told the twins that Daddy's repairing a telephone mast in Scotland and he won't be back for a while.'

I sit down on Mary Lou's hay bale and collect my thoughts for a moment, only half listening to Bob as he fills me in on the rest of the story. '. . . She may have to move in with your dad and Valerie in the short term,' he finishes.

I bring myself to my senses. 'I'm coming home,' I announce. It's clear that my family is in crisis and I belong at their side. No, I belong centre-stage!

Immediately the scene comes vividly to mind. I take a taxi straight from the airport to Teresa's house. She opens the door. Moving boxes are scattered over the floor and her face, which has aged at least ten years, bears an expression of quiet despair. Next to her I look tanned and self-assured, a world traveller and all-round sophisticated person.

'I expect you've come to gloat,' she says bitterly as she surveys the boxes wherein lie the wreckage of her life. She lights a cigarette because she smokes now in her misery, and the yellow smoke blows up around her now grey and lifeless hair.

'No,' I say graciously. 'I've come to help, Teresa.'

She looks at me suspiciously. 'Why would you want to do that?'

At this point the sun comes out, framing my head in a halo of light. 'Where there is untidiness I have come to bring order, where there is low self-esteem I bring positive affirmations.'

'But, but ...' she stutters. 'How could you forgive me? I've been a terrible, spoilt, foul-tempered, attention-seeking, stencil-obsessed and all-round less talented sister.'

She breaks down, flinging herself into my arms and begging for forgiveness, which I freely bestow. 'I forgive you, Teresa,' I say nobly, stroking her head.

'Alice,' she says, looking up from where she sits on the floor clinging to my parka, 'I only acted like that because I wanted to be like you.' She wipes snot from her reddened nose. 'I've always felt like second-best.'

'It's understandable,' I agree. 'Would you like me to teach you how to be more like me?'

'Oh, Alice. That would fill the big, empty hole in me. It's what I've been searching for my whole life!'

I'm brought back to the present by Bob asking me, 'Well, what do you think?'

'What?'

'About the storyline?'

Oh hell, he's been recapping the latest chapter of his thriller. 'Tell me again,' I say. 'It was so riveting I couldn't take it all in.'

'Really? OK. Phyllis the evil female tycoon has just fallen into the arms of Rob, our hero. He subdues her on her desk, where she happily performs every sexual favour he has ever dreamt of. As they recline – she's telling him how well-endowed he is and how much she admires his prowess as a lover – they're attacked by agents from the Canadian secret service bursting through the Japanese screens which surround her desk.'

Parts of this scenario sound faintly familiar, but still I'm lost. 'Right.'

'The Canadians are the mystery third party, you see. No one will ever think that they would want a nuclear warhead. Anyway, I've got to go. If you can think of any more feedback, let me know.'

And then he rings off before I have a chance to remind him about Simon Cowell's telephone number. I sit back and close my eyes for a few moments. It's obvious what I have to do next: go home with Stephen on Sunday and forget all about Wyatt and everything that has happened here. Mary Lou gives out a quiet moan. 'It's OK, I tell her. Heidi can take over the benefit. She'll do a great job,' I assure her, patting her on the neck. She moans again. 'I promise,' I say, but she doesn't look convinced. I try again. 'It's like this, Mary Lou. I belong back in England. My family are there. And now that Stephen has made all this effort, I feel that I have to give him a second chance. Besides, I think that Wyatt and Heidi will be very happy together.' I give a big sigh. 'I'm not getting any younger, Mary Lou, and at the end of the day, Stephen will make a good provider.'

I get up and look around the barn, remembering the first time Wyatt brought me in here. It seems an age away. I think about that first snowy day and how terrified I was on my way to the diner. I remember going into the cottage for the first time and all the things I didn't know when I came here: that petrol is called gas and in summer tea has ice in it; that crickets chirp louder when it's hot and dairy cows are milked twice a day; that a buckeye is a tree and that field mice can play havoc with your sweet potatoes. I realize that I don't want to leave, but I have to; that I still want Wyatt, but I can't have him; that I shouldn't give Stephen a second chance, but I probably will. It isn't that I've given up on my dreams – it's just that right now, my dreams have given up on me.

CHAPTER 35

I feel a jolt of pure horror run through me. 'What do you mean, Heidi wasn't at school today?' I say, aghast.

Madison doesn't turn round from where she's changing the CD in her boom-box. 'I think someone said she had a migraine,' she replies distractedly.

It's Friday afternoon, less than twenty-four hours before the Cupcake Competition, and this is a crushing piece of news. My mouth has gone dry and I feel sick to my stomach, though this may also be because I've eaten nothing but cupcakes for the last forty-eight hours.

As far as dirty tricks go, calling in sick the day before the Cupcake Competition is as bad as it gets. This has destroyed one of our top tactical advantages, as listed by Stephen in our 'Top Tactical Advantages' list – time.

Madison turns back to me. We're having a final practice session in the trailer before tomorrow evening's *Barnsley Idol* competition, to be held in the gym of the high school.

'The thing is, Alice,' Madison says, not meeting my eye, 'I want to change my song.'

'But we've spent weeks rehearsing "Hit Me Baby One More Time",' I say, astounded. And I have to be honest here and say that if I never heard that song again I'd be very happy. I suspect this is also the view of the inhabitants of the Barnsley Glade Mobile Home Park, who have shared in our ups and downs, our hopes and our tears on account of the fact that the air-conditioning unit broke down a month ago and we have to rehearse with the door and all the windows open.

Madison's mouth sets in a stroppy pout. 'I want to sing Whitney Houston's "I Will Always Love You". I know it's a last-minute change, Alice. But I have to go with my artistic instincts.'

I'm caught off guard. We've reached a stage with 'Hit Me Baby One More Time' where Wyatt listened to my recording of Madison's performance and pronounced it 'not bad'. But I'm not sure Madison's voice is up to the level of a Whitney power-ballad.

'Why on earth do you want to change your song?' I say.

Madison blinks. 'I have to follow my own vision.' She swallows. 'Whatever you think, Alice.'

Is she firing me as her manager?

'But you've got that song perfectly,' I protest.

'I know.' Madison looks out of the window at the peeling side of the neighbouring trailer. 'But I have to listen to my heart.'

I suspect there's more to this than meets the eye. 'What does Logan say?'

She bursts into tears. 'I'm sure he's seeing Brittany. Grandma Dolores saw them. They were bowling together.'

'That doesn't mean anything.'

'He was letting her use his bowling ball! He never let me do that.' She starts crying. 'I have to get him back, Alice.'

I'm tempted to ask why. But this is not the time to get into deep emotional conversations. 'So you want to sing this for him?' I say as neutrally as possible.

'Yes! Listen, I've been rehearsing.' She blows her nose,

puts on the CD and starts singing the opening line. But first we have to get past the first syllable, which takes about ten seconds. Madison makes the letter *I* stretch and stretch till I think it will never end. She does the same at the end. 'You-ooh-ooh-ooh-ooh–ooh-ooh.' On and bloody on.

Madison has a good voice, don't get me wrong, but as Simon Cowell would say, 'Madison, you're a sweet girl, but that song's too big for you.'

I have visions of Madison being booed off the *Barnsley Idol* stage in a hail of root-beer bottles.

'Madison,' I begin. 'It's quite late in the day to change song—'

'And I want to perform some of my own material,' she pouts, ignoring me. 'All the top artists write their own songs.'

'I know that.' I can see what that Spice Girls' manager went through.

She pulls out a sheet of A4 lined paper. I can see lines of big, loopy writing with drawings of hearts, arrows and bowling balls doodled round the side.

She begins to sing.

> *Shattered dreams*
> *Faded hopes*
> *I gave my heart*
> *Now it's broke*

She sounds like Dido on Valium.

> *Vale of tears*
> *Vale of tears*
> *Vaaaaale of Teeeeears.*

'OK,' I call out.

'But there's more,' says Madison, offended.

'I think we need to call Wyatt.'

Ten minutes later and he's here in his pick-up.

'Alice is trying to get me to compromise my artistic integrity,' are Madison's first words to him as he steps into the trailer. I'm seated on the mustard-yellow cushions that line the back of the living area around a Formica table marked with cigarette burns and covered with newspapers and an empty Kentucky Fried Chicken bucket.

I roll my eyes, get up and prepare to defend myself, but Wyatt signals to me to sit down.

'You do work for a record company, Alice,' says Madison, 'and as such you're the enemy of creativity.'

I'm outraged. This is the girl who's spent the last five months pestering me for Simon Cowell's telephone number and hanging on every word of my office anecdotes.

'She won't let me sing my own material,' whines Madison. 'She's suffocating me, Wyatt.'

'Excuse me,' I say.

But I don't get any further than that because Wyatt cuts across me. 'Let's hear the song, Madison.'

I sit seething in the corner while Madison clears her throat. Then she wails through verse one. Please let it be over soon. I'm expecting Wyatt to stop her, but she drones through verse two.

> *The future's dark*
> *Love has gone*
> *Only one way now*
> *Down, down, down*
> *Vale of tears*
> *Vale of tears*
> *Vaaaaale of Teeeeears.*

Then she takes a deep breath to embark on verse three.

Despair—

Wyatt puts up his hand.

'But there's six verses,' objects Madison.

'I think we get the general idea,' he says.

Madison grasps her sheet of lyrics. 'I can't sell out. And I won't!'

Wyatt nods.

'It's my destiny to perform. Of course no one understands that round here.'

Wyatt nods.

'Sometimes I think this is all a terrible mistake,' she says, waving her hand at the window and to the neighbouring trailer, separated from ours by waist-high weeds and an enormous television aerial jutting out of the side. 'I don't belong here.'

Wyatt nods.

Madison runs a hand through her long blonde hair. 'You can't imagine what it feels like to be an artistic-spirit person in this dump of a town.' She sighs. 'The problem is that my talent has so totally isolated me.'

'I see your point,' says Wyatt.

I'm livid. Wyatt needs to tell Madison a few home truths about the limits of her talent, the hard-nosed realities of the music business and why she should obey me unquestioningly. I fold my arms and look sulkily out of the window at the weeds.

'I think what you're saying,' continues Wyatt, 'is that you want to be the best you can and give the performance of your life so that you win *Barnsley Idol*. You want to give a performance that will get you noticed, give you valuable publicity and set you on the road to commercial success.'

No, she isn't saying that at all.

Madison springs to her feet. 'Oh my gosh, you understand!'

'Right,' says Wyatt. 'If I were you, I would open with "Hit Me Baby".' He shrugs. 'Madison, you and I know it's one for the audience.'

'Uh-huh.'

'Like you say, Barnsley's not the place for your talent. Your song would be wasted on them. Hold it back. Give it an airing when you get into the studio. It's always a good idea to keep something in reserve.'

'Yep, that's what I think,' says Madison.

I make a snorting noise from the back of the trailer, but they both ignore me.

Wyatt gets up. 'I'll leave you to it.'

I follow him out to the sounds of Madison singing 'Hit Me Baby'.

Despite my resentment towards Madison, I do feel relieved. Dolores would never forgive me if anything bad happened to Madison on stage. 'You were very persuasive,' I say to Wyatt.

He shrugs. 'I could have told her the truth about the song. And about the music business. But she wouldn't have listened.' Wyatt shoots me that half-smile and my stomach flips a somersault. 'Any more than I would have listened when I was her age. She's going to have to get the door slammed in her face a hundred times before she listens. You should have heard my early stuff.'

'"Moonshine"?' I say sceptically.

'"Moonshine" was about my five-hundredth song, Alice. It didn't come easy.' He gestures at the trailer. 'Either she'll survive the rejections, get lucky and make it. Or she'll give up, come back here and work in the diner for the rest of her life.'

'Thanks for coming down,' I say.

We're standing in the trailer park. Half the cars are propped up on bricks with no wheels and there's a strong smell of fried fish on the breeze. But I'm in no mood to rush.

'Madison doesn't get it,' says Wyatt contemplatively. 'She thinks that if she's famous she'll feel different. But when it happens – when you go into a record store and your album's at number one – you don't feel any different. You spend all that time and effort thinking you're going to feel so great when you finally make it – but when you do you find fame isn't all it's cracked up to be.' He looks at me. 'Does that make sense? Living your life thinking that if something was different you'd be all right?'

It makes perfect sense. 'Yes. That's how I've felt my whole life since Mum died. That if she was alive everything would be all right.'

Why am I saying this now? I've never talked to Wyatt about Mum. Why now, in the most unlikely place at the most inopportune moment? I should be at the cottage with Stephen.

Wyatt holds my gaze. 'But it is all right, Alice.'

He turns away and gets into the pick-up truck. Then he leans out of the window. 'You're all right, Alice. That's what I mean.'

CHAPTER 36

The day of the Barnsley Festival Cupcake Competition has finally dawned. Stephen and I are close to physical and emotional collapse. I wouldn't be at all surprised if Stephen is diagnosed with post-traumatic stress disorder. When the piping bag broke at half-past midnight last night – destroying half an hour of fine letterwork – Stephen was close to giving up. He had been in a state of heightened anxiety ever since I insisted on popping out earlier to watch the *Barnsley Idol* competition.

'This is no time to desert the battlefield, Alice,' he said petulantly.

I went anyway and was there to see Madison sing 'Hit Me Baby One More Time', beating a ten-year-old violinist, an old man with a harmonica and a fat bloke who sang '*Nessun Dorma*' very badly.

We're preparing to load the cupcakes into the Ford Focus when Gerry pulls up in his Mercedes. Robert Palmer's 'Simply Irresistible' is blaring out of his car stereo. Stephen is sweeping out the boot of the car with a dustpan and brush lest any specks of dust lodge themselves in the buttercream.

'Hey, babe!' Gerry calls out to me. 'I got in from Vegas last night.' He gives me a playful slap on the bottom. 'Hell, I've missed you.'

Stephen emerges from the boot of the car. 'I don't believe we've met,' he says stiffly.

'Gerry Armstrong,' Gerry says, unabashed.

'This is Stephen,' I say.

'I'm Alice's fiancé,' Stephen says coldly.

Gerry is not in the least put off. 'Hey, you're the guy she dumped at the airport. Good to meet you,' he says, shaking Stephen by the shoulder.

Stephen recovers his balance. 'If you'll excuse us,' he says, looking like he's swallowed a lemon, 'we have work to do.'

'No problem,' Gerry says, winking at me.

Stephen bustles into the cottage where four large boxes of cupcakes are waiting to be loaded into the car, plus a sheet of rolled-up poster paper on which Stephen has painstakingly marked out our master diagram. It's a 100 per cent accurate scale drawing.

Stephen takes a deep breath. 'Let's take it steady,' he says. 'No sudden movements.'

He reaches out his hands to the first box then pulls them back. Beads of sweat have broken out on his brow. He takes another breath. 'If any of the buttercream touches, the whole thing could blow,' he whispers.

Gerry strolls in. 'Need a hand?'

I gesture to him to be quiet. Stephen has sat down and now has his head between his legs.

'We're preparing to move the cupcakes,' I explain. 'They're very delicate. Stephen's particularly worried about the buttercream rose.'

At that moment I hear Wyatt's truck pull up. The door slams and he comes in through the open cottage door. 'Hey, you missed the Festival parade.'

Then he catches sight of Stephen. 'Everything OK?'

'Fine,' I say. 'How were the floats?'

'Same as last year.'

'And the year before,' echoes Gerry.

I look anxiously at my watch. The Cupcake Competition is at noon, directly following the judging of the Best Pet Chicken (Owner Under The Age Of Ten Years Category). 'I need to get these in the car.'

Wyatt and Gerry step forward and each pick up a box and carry them out to the car.

'Are you planning on marrying that guy?' says Gerry, exchanging glances with Wyatt.

I feel compelled to defend Stephen. 'All British men are like that,' I say. 'They're very sensitive on account of the damp climate.'

'I'd stay here if I were you,' says Gerry, and for the first time ever Wyatt and Gerry exchange an American-man-bonding look. Then they go back for the other two boxes.

By the time we reach the Festival, Stephen has recovered somewhat and feels able to carry in the rolled-up paper master diagram. I carry in the boxes. On the way to the Festival marquee, I dodge crowds of people as I pass stalls selling apple pies, barbecued pork sandwiches and hotdogs. The tent is like a big top. There are lemonade, beer and cake stalls at one end and a grand display of six pictures by the Barnsley Artists' Group at the other. The Cupcake Competition is set up in the middle. We are the last to arrive and make our way to our table. We have only ten minutes to set up, though. Stephen was insistent that we arrive at the last minute so as to retain the element of surprise. 'Never underestimate the potential for re-icing,' he said gravely.

The other competitors and Heidi are already there, but I can't see what she's done because there are so many people grouped around her table admiring her cupcakes.

Stephen unrolls the paper with our carefully drawn

outline. Then, with no word exchanged between us, we begin setting out the cupcakes with carefully choreographed movements. We do not need to speak because we practised this ten times last night using dummy cardboard cupcakes. Four minutes and forty-two seconds was our best time. I arrange eight blue frosted cupcakes to mark the Pacific Ocean, while Stephen sets out the white cupcake Rockies and Appalachians.

One or two people have noticed us now and have started to drift over.

Next I set up the Great Lakes and Atlantic Ocean, while Stephen works on the Gulf of Mexico.

'Hey, it's a cupcake United States,' someone shouts out.

'Come and look at this,' yells someone else.

'What?' It's a high-pitched, anxious voice. It sounds like Heidi.

'Wow, it's America,' says a little boy in wonderment.

'Wow, it's America,' says an awestruck little girl.

Now we're well into the states themselves: there are fifty individually iced cupcakes each portraying the state flag or a famous landmark.

'Excuse me,' says Stephen, carefully placing Alaska (brown bear) over the head of the small boy, who appears overcome with excitement and is jumping up and down.

'It's a bear!' he cries out in delight.

Oh my gosh, this must be what it was like to have been Walt Disney.

I work on the tricky New England states, starting with Maine (lighthouse) and working my way down. I had suggested a teapot for Massachusetts to commemorate the Boston Tea Party, but Stephen shot the idea down. 'This is no time for frivolity, Alice. There will be time enough for jesting when the battle is won.' So instead we did the Massachusetts state flag.

There are now about thirty people jostling to see us.

One figure pushes her way to the front.

'Did you do all this yourself?' asks Heidi nastily.

'Don't be stupid. That ain't no man's handiwork.' It's Sheriff Billy. 'Any fool can see that takes a woman's touch,' he says, pointing at Stephen's immaculately crafted White House which adorns the Washington DC cupcake.

I quickly slot in Florida (an orange), Arizona (a cactus) and Texas, which has a yellow rose that took Stephen four attempts to get just right. 'I won't let it defeat me, I won't,' became his mantra.

I look up. Heidi has retreated and is standing alone behind her display. The five other competitors look on bemused. With two minutes to go, the tent is packed with people and most of them are around our cupcakes. I slot in Nevada (a casino chip) and hop over to see Heidi's display. The first thing I notice is how small it is. Only twelve cupcakes. True, the country music theme is quaint enough – there's a guitar, a cowboy hat and a fiddle – but the game's over and she knows it. Our eyes meet. But she looks away first.

We wait nervously as the tent fills up, Stephen dabbing his brow with a tissue. Soon the tent is packed. The judges form a line. They make cursory comments at the others before coming to my display last. I stand behind the frosted United States in my orange Halloween sweatshirt, a cauldron on the front and a witch on a broomstick on the back, teamed with a below-the-knee denim skirt. It was Stephen's idea to add the flesh-coloured tights and open-toed sandals.

Then Mr Horner addresses the crowd. 'The winner is Miss Alice Fisher.'

Deafening applause breaks out. I have never been the winner of anything before! Mr Horner turns to me. 'Wait until we put this on the website. Alice, you've taken the Cupcake Competition to a new level,' he says, beaming.

I'm given a brown sash with *I ♥ Barnsley* on it and an envelope containing my prize-winning twenty-five-dollar voucher for the Barnsley Tavern. I'm feeling very elated. I can't see Wyatt, though, only a tent packed full of cheering Barnsley folk.

Then I have my picture taken for the *Barnsley Messenger*.

'Would the runner-up like to be in the picture?' the photographer asks Heidi.

'No.'

I feel a surge of affection and gratitude for Stephen. Later he comes up to me. 'I think we pulled off a significant victory today.' Then he taps the envelope I'm holding containing my Barnsley voucher. 'And a significant profit, eh?'

'Hmm,' I say before I'm conveniently rescued by Dolores. I never did get a chance to tell him exactly how much the prize money is.

'Alice, you're a genius,' Dolores says. 'Is there anything you can't turn your hand to?'

I'm about to list all of them when we're interrupted by Rachel and Baby Dale, who's dressed as an ear of sweetcorn in preparation for the Best-Dressed Baby Vegetable Competition. 'Congratulations, Alice!'

She admires the cupcake America. I can't stop myself. 'Where's Wyatt?'

'Oh,' she says, peering at the Idaho potato, 'He's talking to Heidi.'

Sure enough, I look over and see them deep in conversation.

At my side, Stephen has struck up a conversation with Mr

Horner. 'I've always been fascinated by nineteenth-century ploughing rights, too!' exclaims Mr Horner.

Heidi catches me staring and drags Wyatt over.

'Alice, well done *you*!' she says warmly. 'What a great high to go out on.'

'Out?'

'Well, you're leaving in three weeks, aren't you?'

I've been trying to forget this.

'When your visa expires and you must leave the country,' she reminds me.

Stephen hears this and puts his arm round me. 'Why don't you just cut your trip short and come home with me tomorrow, darling?'

'What a good idea,' chirps Heidi. 'How romantic! The two lovebirds flying back to Britain together.'

'I have to organize Mary Lou's benefit first,' I remind everyone.

'Oh, I'm sure there's nothing to it. I'll take care of all of that for you. Just think, you could be gone tomorrow,' suggests Heidi eagerly. 'How wonderful.'

'I don't think so.'

'Why not?' says Stephen a little sharply.

I think frantically. 'Because ... because ... it would cost hundreds of dollars to change my ticket,' I say. 'And I'm certain Carmichael Music wouldn't reimburse me.'

'Better to stay on,' says Stephen quickly. 'I can wait for you.'

At that moment a loudspeaker announcement is called out for the judging of the Best-Dressed Baby Vegetable competition and we all go off to support Rachel and Baby Dale. Rachel made the costume herself and has hand-sewn over one hundred yellow felt niblets of corn and three large green leaves on to the hood.

An hour later Baby Dale has secured first place Baby Vegetable (second place, twin chilli peppers), Casey and Mary Lou have predictably won Best Cow, and the tractor-driving demonstration has just finished. I have failed to persuade Stephen to go and look at the Clydesdale horse parade. 'They could break free, Alice. Imagine!' he said with a shudder. He wipes his brow for the hundredth time. 'I need to sit down in the shade.'

Back in the tent all our cupcakes are melting.

'Let's announce that we're giving them away,' I say to Stephen.

'Giving them away?' he repeats, horrified. 'Surely a dollar each. That's a profit of over seventy-five dollars, counting the oceans.'

'It doesn't work like that here,' I say crossly. 'You can't sell your display.'

'I don't see why.'

But I've already shouted out. 'Free cupcakes, free cupcakes,' and this being Barnsley, they've all gone within a minute.

I can see that Stephen is sulking, but unlike the old days, I have no patience for him now.

'Snap out of it,' I say crossly, next to our demolished display. Then I relent a little. 'Let's go and get something to eat. We could get some iced lemonade and a cinnamon roll.'

'But we have food in the fridge at home,' he says, puzzled, 'and I've got an awful headache. I think I may have sunstroke.'

I know that there's no point in trying to talk him round. He's got his martyred expression on and there's no reasoning with him when he gets like that.

'All right,' I sigh, 'let's go home.' And we get into the car and pull out of the car park just as the Barnsley High School

Band strikes up Stevie Wonder's 'Isn't She Lovely' for the cheerleading display. I was really looking forward to it.

When we get home, Stephen goes for a lie-down on the sofa. Despite much pestering, I have not allowed him into my bed. I find my BlackBerry and go out to the barn to call Dad and tell him about my win.

I call the home number and Teresa answers. 'Alice. What do you want?'

'I'm very well, thank you,' I say. 'I was calling to speak to Dad.'

'He's at Tesco.' There's a pause. 'I suppose you've heard about me and Richard.'

This is the first time we've spoken since I heard the news from Bob.

'I have. I'm really sorry.'

'So am I,' Teresa says bitterly. 'But I'm determined to be civilized for the sake of the children. I'm spending the afternoon here while Richard packs up his things from the house.'

'Is there much?'

'Just his clothes and his bird books. I'm keeping the rest.'

'Well, I'll be back in a few weeks,' I say. 'We can go out somewhere.' Maybe this will be a new start for us, I think hopefully.

'I can't think where,' says Teresa. 'So what's been happening?' It sounds as though she's yawning.

I tell Teresa about the Cupcake Competition, about the Concert for the Cow and about Stephen's surprise proposal.

'I suppose you jumped at it,' she says.

'No. I haven't accepted him,' I say with dignity.

'I'm surprised. You always seem so desperate.' She gives a little sigh. 'Mind you, marriage isn't all it's cracked up to be. Anyway, you've been on the shelf for so long now you must be used to it up there.'

Then she rings off.

When Stephen wakes up, he's in a foul mood. 'Let's have leftovers tonight for dinner. We'll need to tighten our belts,' are his first words.

'Oh, for goodness' sake,' I snap, 'the Cupcake Competition was *fun*, Stephen. Doesn't that count for anything?'

'Fun doesn't pay the bills, Alice,' he says pompously. 'I only hope the prize money will adequately compensate us for the decorating supply outlay,' he spits.

'I'm sure it won't,' I say with abandon.

It's very odd, but it's almost as if I want an excuse to have a row with Stephen.

'It's a twenty-five-dollar voucher for the Barnsley Tavern.' I extract it from my handbag and tear open the envelope. 'And,' I read out gleefully, 'it's only valid on Tuesday evenings between six and seven o'clock.'

Stephen has gone pale. 'Let me see that.'

He snatches it from me. 'I don't believe it.' He reads it several times. 'How could you do this, Alice?'

'Do what? We won!'

'For what,' he says, running his hand dramatically through his thinning hair. 'We're out of pocket, Alice. We've made a loss.' He gestures at the roll of paper and the empty boxes. 'And there's not even any stock left. You gave it away,' he wails. 'Oh my God, this is exactly what it was like when my parents lost the restaurant.'

He said the same thing the last time we got the electricity bill. And when the car insurance went up.

'No it's not, Stephen. It's a few cupcakes, not a restaurant – and no one's going bankrupt, because we both have jobs.'

He ignores this. 'I expect you to pay me back.'

'Bugger off.'

'Alice,' he says, mortified. 'I must insist that you take your lead from me in financial matters. Otherwise I cannot see a future for us.'

'Well, I can see the future, and it looks bloody miserable to me.'

Stephen looks at me appraisingly. 'I don't believe your change of heart has anything to do with me. How could it? I think there's more to this than meets the eye.'

'There is?'

'I'm not blind, Alice. That Gerry chap clearly has designs on you.'

'He has designs on everyone,' I say dismissively.

'So there's nothing between you?'

'Not really.'

Stephen looks outraged. 'I demand the return of the gold and diamond engagement ring.'

'Fine,' I say, pressing it into his hand. 'I hope you kept the receipt.'

'Of course I did. And there's a thirty-day no-quibble money-back guarantee. What would I have done if you hadn't accepted?'

'I think you ought to go now,' I say with dignity. 'It's over.'

'Yes, I think I should,' says Stephen, preoccupied with carefully inserting the ring in his wallet. 'It is.'

He hesitates. Has the reality of what he has thrown away hit him?

'Can you give me a lift to the airport? I'll spend the night there. I hate to think what a taxi would cost.'

Stephen sent me an email to say that he had arrived home safely. He literally spent the night at Columbus airport, stretched out on the seats by the departure gate. He told me pointedly that he had economized by taking sips from the public water fountain and eking out a Starbucks blueberry muffin for dinner and breakfast. That was the last I've heard from him.

It's two days until the benefit concert for Mary Lou – and two days after that, my visa runs out. I'm sitting at the kitchen table as I do every morning, ticking off my master list. But it never gets any shorter. There are no fewer than three pages of items to be ticked off.

If it hadn't been for Gerry, I don't know what I would have done. Ever since he found out that I've broken up with Stephen he's been ever more solicitous. Last week he even took me clothes shopping. 'I had a big win – I mean *deal* – last week,' he said, looking me up and down as I stood there in my comfy shorts and T-shirt. 'I can't think of a better way to spend it.'

In between times he has been at the cottage every day, arriving at ten a.m. like clockwork.

'The good news,' I tell him this morning, 'is that we've sold two hundred and fifty tickets. And Heidi is set to double that with the raffle. The bad news is that the concert itself is going to be a catastrophic disaster.'

'Hmm,' says Gerry pensively. 'Two hundred and fifty tickets. I thought this was going to be small-scale.' Funny, but he sounds a bit put out. 'Surely that's more money than you need for Mary Lou?'

'Oh yes. We'll clear the vet's bills just from the bar takings. We're going to have a huge surplus to give to Casey's Grandpa. He can use it towards the farm. Assuming I don't have to use it for my medical bills when the irate crowd of concertgoers turns on me.'

So far I have failed to drum up any more acts, although there is the possibility of the Barnsley Kindergarten Choir doing a song, as long as it's not past their bedtime.

Gerry ignores this last point. 'But the money's just for Mary Lou?'

'No. Stephen drafted the trust before he left. He wrote it so that the funds can be used for the benefit of Mary Lou and/or any other farm animal. It's watertight.'

(Stephen was glad to break off from the cupcake icing to do a little agricultural trust drafting. 'So relaxing,' he said, turning over a clean page of his A4 pad.)

'Casey's grandpa can use the money for anything on the farm,' I continue. 'I suspect he's got other bills he needs to pay, too.'

'I see,' says Gerry slowly. He leans back. 'I'd be careful if I were you, Alice.'

'Careful?'

'This is a small town. If Casey's grandpa suddenly comes into a fortune, it could cause some raised eyebrows. Folk may get jealous. He makes a pretty penny from that corn maze, don't forget.'

'I see.' Somehow I find it hard to believe that a corn maze

is a major money-making operation. I suck the end of my rollerball. 'I don't think there's much I can do about what people say.'

'Don't say I didn't warn you.' He gets up. He hasn't touched his doughnut.

'You're not leaving?' I say, looking surprised. He normally starts squeezing my knee about now.

'Yep,' he says abruptly. 'Business to attend to. See you later, Alice.'

And then he's gone, without trying to talk me into bed – that's never happened before. Maybe he's preoccupied with one of those big business deals. I return to my list for that evening's final planning meeting of the organizing committee to be held at the high-school gym. It's the meeting at which all the important decisions and loose ends are going to get tied up, and I've reminded everyone that attendance is compulsory. Naturally I haven't involved Wyatt – deep down I'm still a tiny bit wounded from his high-school karaoke remark, even though it's turning out to be eerily correct.

That night I arrive early at the high-school gym to find Heidi and Madison already there. They're deep in conversation, but stop short when they see me.

'Go on,' says Heidi to Madison encouragingly.

'I think I should perform my own material on Saturday,' pouts Madison.

I roll my eyes. 'We've already been over this, Madison. People want songs they can dance to.'

'I don't think one or two of Madison's compositions would be unreasonable,' suggests Heidi.

'Oh, all right.' I don't have time for another round with Madison, who has turned from high-school wannabe to diva overnight. Mr Horner has arrived with his accordion, followed by Brandy, who is clutching her filofax, and Dolores, slowly bringing up the rear.

'The Scott boys said to tell you they can't make it,' puffs Dolores.

'Why?'

'It's Thursday. That's karaoke night at the Barnsley Tavern,' says Dolores as if it was obvious.

'Oh, should we postpone?' says Mr Horner worriedly.

'Hmm, maybe we should,' agrees Heidi.

'No! It's two days to go until the concert,' I exclaim irritably. 'We have to sort everything out tonight.'

'Are you all right, Alice?' says Heidi solicitously. 'You seem a little tense.'

I'm about to shout at her that of course I'm bloody tense when I catch myself and do my breathing. Focus on one positive fact, Dr Vaizey tells me as he sits in his leather armchair. Yes! At least everyone apart from Heidi is wearing their T-shirt. It's white with black Friesian splodges and 'Concert for the Cow' printed on the back on a brown cowpat.

'How many am I catering for?' says Dolores, sitting down heavily.

'Not many, I'm sure,' cuts in Heidi. 'I can't imagine many people want to come.'

'Actually,' I say smugly, 'Sheriff Billy has already sold two hundred and fifty tickets. He's making extra barbecue sauce,' I say to her with a triumphant glint in my eye.

Heidi can't stop her mouth turning down.

'I'm not surprised,' says Madison. 'It's because I won the *Barnsley Idol* competition. Everyone knows I'm singing.'

'I have to get the potato salad done tomorrow night,' says Dolores, who's in charge of main courses. 'I'll make the cornbread on Saturday.'

'It would have been much easier if the Mom's Group had been handling *all* the catering,' says Brandy. It has been an ongoing point of contention that the Moms are doing desserts while Dolores and Nancy are doing the main courses. 'We're offering a choice of five desserts including cream brew-lee,' she says.

'Really,' says Heidi, smirking. 'I've never heard of cream brew-lee.'

'Oh, do you think that's a wise choice of dessert?' says Mr Horner worriedly. 'This is no time for innovation, Brandy.'

'No, Mr Horner.' Brandy swallows. 'I'll take it off the menu.'

It's like this whenever Mr Horner speaks. They all used to be his pupils and cave in straight away.

'My main concern is the music,' I say, taking charge.

'What about a nice apple pie?' says Dolores.

Brandy rolls her eyes. 'Boring,' she says under her breath.

'*Boring*, did you say, Brandy?' pipes up Heidi loudly.

'Anyone heard what the Scott boys are playing?' I say hastily.

'Me,' says Heidi. 'I run into them when I'm out getting raffle prizes. So that's about three times a day.'

It strikes me, not for the first time, that Heidi is determined to make the raffle the only successful part of the whole evening.

'I'm encouraging them to do more contemporary material,' she continues.

'What's that then?' says Brandy suspiciously.

'Oh, don't worry,' says Heidi. 'They'll still accompany you for *Flashdance*. If you insist. I always think it's such a brave choice, Brandy. No, they're going to do some more up-to-date bands for the younger ones. Oasis, Green Day, Nickelback.'

'Do you think that's suitable?' I exclaim.

'Let's think outside the box, Alice,' says Heidi. 'You can't take those parental advisory stickers too seriously. Maybe some Snoop Dogg would be fun!' She smiles at me.

Madison interrupts. 'It's only fair that I get top billing,' she says, examining her fingernails. 'I did win the *Barnsley Idol* competition.'

'I'm aware of that,' I say testily.

'How about a nice peach cobbler?' says Dolores. 'You can't beat that.'

'Peach cobbler!' chuckles Mr Horner. 'That reminds me of the time—'

'Who's getting the plates and napkins, then?' interrupts Brandy.

Everyone is now talking at once.

'Oh, Alice, did you forget the plates and napkins?' asks Heidi.

'The Mayor and his lady wife were present ...' says Mr Horner to himself.

'And we'll need a team to clean up afterwards,' sighs Brandy.

Then Sara arrives. 'Sorry I'm late! I had to express milk for Hillary before I left.'

Brandy tuts and I look over anxiously at Mr Horner. But he's still talking. 'The time came for speeches ...'

Sara is in charge of decorating the gym. She pulls out some drawings. 'I thought a multicultural world farming theme.'

We gather round to look at the drawings. 'What are those?' points Brandy.

'Tribal masks.'

'But we're having balloons,' says Dolores anxiously.

'Not exactly. I thought we could substitute vegetables made of papier-mâché.'

'That'll get them rolling in the aisles,' says Brandy. 'What are we going to do – dance round a compost heap?'

'Actually, I'm planning a recycling sculpture,' says Sara, pulling out another diagram.

'... The peach cobbler was burnt to a cinder! Oh my goodness, how we laughed,' continues Mr Horner in the background.

I close my eyes. I'm beyond anxiety. I'm hurtling towards a breakdown. I really don't think I can take any more.

Heidi sits back and snorts. 'Oh, Alice. I can honestly say I can't wait for Saturday.'

CHAPTER 38

'Alice! It's Dad.'

I look blearily at the alarm clock. It's four o'clock in the morning.

'It's four o'clock in the morning,' I say, yawning as usual.

'Is it? Are you sure? Oh well, you're awake now,' Dad says brightly as usual. 'We're worried about you. Stephen told us all about it.'

My heart sinks. This is the last thing I want – to have to explain the break-up to Dad.

'No need to say anything,' says Dad airily. 'Stephen told us all the details. He said that he couldn't see a future with you, and the kindest thing was to let you go.'

I'm about to correct Dad but he continues. 'He came round and left your things in the garage. He said the prices at the New Malden Self-U-Store were preposterous and the garage was perfectly adequate. Don't worry, they're covered up with a tarpaulin so they shouldn't get too damp.' He clears his throat. 'Anyway, I was hoping you could do me a small favour.'

I'm barely awake. 'Dad. Can it wait?'

'I'd rather it didn't.'

'Is it about Teresa?'

'In a manner of speaking,' he hesitates. 'I'm calling to tell you the happy news that I have asked Valerie to be my wife and she has graciously consented.'

I sit up in bed and let out a small shriek. 'Congratulations! Oh my gosh. When's the wedding?' My mind is whirring. I'll have to get something to wear. I'm sure Dad will want me to be his right-hand woman.

'Next week.'

'What!'

'Hmm. We had a choice, you see. We could either get married in front of all our family at New Malden Register Office. Or we could go to Barbados and get hitched on the beach in an all-inclusive two-week package. We opted for Barbados.'

'I see.'

'Obviously we're disappointed that you both won't be there. But we'll take lots of photos,' he says cheerfully. 'Anyhow, can you tell Teresa?'

'No.'

'It would be so much better coming from you,' he says earnestly.

'I don't see why. Anyway, hadn't you better tell her soon – before she moves in with you?'

'Oh no. There's been a change of plan. She's staying in her house now. She says Richard will have to carry her out of the matrimonial home in a box.'

'I thought things had been amicably agreed in a civilized manner?'

'They had. Then Stephen got talking to her. She was here when he dumped your stuff in the garage. She's had a change of heart since then. He's forbidden her to leave the house in case Richard slips in and changes the locks. She gets all her shopping from that Tesco website now, and I take the boys swimming at the weekend.'

'How long was Stephen at your house?' I ask, bemused.

'Oh, about six hours. We all sat down over dinner and he talked us through the ups and downs of your relationship.' He clears his throat. 'So you'll tell Teresa,' he says hopefully.

I'm struggling to take this in. 'Why do I have to tell her?'

'You're her sister. Please,' he says.

I have changed in these last few months, and even with Dad I'm not the pushover I used to be.

'I really think it's your job to tell her.'

'You're right. It is. But you'll do it so well. I knew I could rely on you, Alice.'

I didn't mean—'

'Let me know how it goes. Anyway, it's an expensive call. Look after yourself and don't forget to put on your suntan lotion. Byeeee.'

I can't get back to sleep after that. My mind is overwhelmed by a series of random, disconnected worries. Over the years of our relationship, Stephen has become privy to several sensitive confidences. He knows all about the loan I took out to pay for electrolysis on my upper-lip moustache, the time I went on a date with the Kingston Council wheel-clamping supervisor and ... No! He couldn't have told them that my top-secret childhood ambition was to be Suzi Quatro, and that I used to practise 'Devil Gate Drive' in front of the bathroom mirror wearing Mum's lipstick?

After an hour of tossing and turning, I get up and iron my shorts and Friesian T-shirt. I wear it at all times in order to set a leadership example to the others. Then I make a cup of coffee and sit in the living room to do my morning meditation. But I can't get the prospect of going back to New Malden out of my mind. As I look around the cottage – at the CDs now in alphabetical order, at the immaculately swept fireplace, at all the carefully dusted nooks and crannies – I'm taken back in time to when I first arrived here. It's incredible, but in less than six months it has come to feel like my real home. I can hardly believe I'll be leaving in a week. I must be very stressed out by the concert because I burst into tears. I must look on the bright side: very shortly I will be back in New Malden, living in the back bedroom of Dad and Valerie's house with my possessions in the garage below. I burst into tears again.

To cheer myself up I go out to see Mary Lou in the field. Soon she'll be back in the barn for the winter. She looks up at me from the far side of the field, regards me with her sad eyes and puts her head back down to munch grass. Even Mary Lou doesn't seem herself. Normally she would come over, but today she seems listless and out of sorts. As the end of September nears, the days of scorching humidity have given way to the first cold breaths of autumn and the late nights have turned chilly. Maybe she needs a cow blanket? That's an idea – I'll get one for Casey as a goodbye present. But the thought of leaving Casey makes me feel all depressed again.

'Hey! Shouldn't you be out selling tickets?'

I jump with surprise as Wyatt steps off the porch and walks across the garden towards me.

He's brought his coffee too and holds it, leaning on the fence.

'Late start today,' I say. 'I'm meeting Sheriff Billy at the diner at ten o'clock to get an update on the ticket sales.'

'Rumour has it you can get off a speeding ticket if you buy two tickets,' says Wyatt.

That would not surprise me.

Wyatt gestures to the woods. 'The first leaves have begun to turn,' he says. 'Shame you won't be here to see it.'

'Yes,' I say distractedly. My mind is on the concert again.

I start wondering how to turn the topic to the dearth of musical talent. I can't come right out and ask Wyatt to sing – look what happened the last time I did that – but if I drop enough heavy hints, perhaps he'll volunteer?

I clear my throat. 'The Scott boys are thinking of trying out some new material,' I say.

'The red maples, they're really something,' says Wyatt.

'Nickelback,' I blurt out.

'People think you have to go to New England to see fall foliage, but we've got it here in Ohio.'

'And Snoop Dogg,' I say loudly.

'And when those pines get the snow on them, they're really something.'

Oh, for goodness' sake. How can I get him off the subject of leaves? I'm going to have to be more direct. 'I think the music may be a disaster and we'll need more acts,' I say, trying to sound hysterical. Surely he can detect my desperation? How can he not get the hint?

Or is this the hard-nosed Wyatt that Gerry warned me about, the Wyatt who won't rent land to the farmers of Barnsley because of his selfish desire for privacy?

'Any word from Stephen?' he says.

'Stephen? No!' I say, unable to conceal my frustration. Who cares about Stephen? I've got a three-page to-do list and the concert's tomorrow. 'I'll never get it all done,' I wail. 'I'm really worried about the music.' How much more of a bloody huge hint can I drop?

'You'll work it out,' says Wyatt, taking a leisurely sip of his coffee. 'You always do.' He turns to me. 'Pancake?'

I could almost scream. Instead I straighten my T-shirt and sigh theatrically. 'I haven't got time for pancakes. Some of us have got work to do.' And then I flounce off back to the cottage.

Really – when it comes to men, do you have to spell things out in bloody big capital letters?

At ten o'clock I'm waiting for Sheriff Billy in the diner. Celeste has come over to say that he's running a little late on account of a driver who got stuck in a ditch after he swerved to avoid a skunk. It's a motoring hazard over here.

I'm sitting opposite Mr Horner because he insisted that I join him. He's wearing his Friesian T-shirt with a buttoned-up cardigan over the top and a lightweight beige woollen scarf.

Mr Horner has been telling me about his latest idea for a web page – *Barnsley Roof Tiles Through The Ages* – but, try as I might, my attention has been wandering.

'You don't seem yourself today,' he says.

'I'm fine,' I say unconvincingly.

'Is it about Wyatt?'

I can't conceal my surprise. Mr Horner smiles to himself and wipes the corners of his mouth with his napkin. 'Wyatt's a good man.'

'Is he?' I say before I can stop myself.

Mr Horner looks at me in surprise. 'Have you two had a quarrel?'

It's impossible not to tell the truth, the whole truth and nothing but the truth to Mr Horner. 'No,' I say. I take a moment to compose my next sentence because Mr Horner is a stickler for grammar. 'I was hoping that he'd offer to sing at the Concert for the Cow and I'm disappointed that he hasn't volunteered his musical services.'

'I see. We're all hoping for him to sing, young lady. He will – when the time's right.'

'You mean when the time's right for him.' This comes out sounding really bitter. I realize that I do want Wyatt to sing – not just for his sake but in order to help me.

'Whatever do you mean?' says Mr Horner, putting down his piece of toast.

I hesitate. 'Well, what about his land? I heard that he came back to Barnsley after he had been away for years, outbid all the farmers for the Buckle and Braid farm and then refused to rent out the lower fields.'

Mr Horner looks scandalized. 'Whoever told you that misled you most grievously.'

I shake my head. 'I don't think so.'

'Allow me to tell you the facts,' says Mr Horner. 'Wyatt bought that farm to *help* the village of Barnsley.'

'How do you know?'

'Because I called him and asked him to buy it.' Mr Horner sounds quite put out. I need to shut up or he's going to make me write out *I must not contradict Mr Horner* five hundred times.

'Gerry Armstrong wanted that land to build on. His family thinks they have a God-given right to build all over Barnsley. They're the ones who built all the new houses.'

'You mean where Glenn Close is.' That's where Rachel lives. Then something else dawns on me – the name of Heidi's road. 'And Armstrong Road?'

'Yes, it's named after Gerry's family.'

I feel almost light-headed.

'His father wanted to put five hundred houses up. We in the Historical Society were beside ourselves. It's long been rumoured that there is a Native American village buried up in the hills. One day we hope to excavate.' His face lights up. 'Come to think of it, we ought to have a web page about that. What do you think?'

'Great idea. Tell me more about the houses.'

'Wyatt was our last hope. No one else could match the Armstrong family money. Wyatt drove all night from Texas to get here with minutes to spare. Gerry Armstrong was there bidding for his father. He thought he had it all wrapped up. His face was a picture when he saw Wyatt.'

I'm feeling sick. Gerry has told me a pack of lies.

'Wyatt bought the land.' Mr Horner takes a bite of his toast. 'Of course he didn't rent out the land to the south – it's wetland. It's too soggy to plough. In fact that was another of our concerns. The Armstrongs wanted to build on it, risking flooding in the village during heavy rains. Not that Gerry cared about that.'

I sit back, stunned.

Mr Horner gives me a hard look. 'I can imagine from whom you derived your information. Not the most reliable of sources,' he says, pursing his lips. 'Any more questions?'

I do have one more question – one that I've wanted to ask for some time. 'Wyatt told me that Miss Horner taught him the piano. I was wondering what your sister thought about Wyatt ...' *and his drinking*, I nearly say. I stop myself just in time ... 'and his later career?'

Mr Horner doesn't hesitate. 'She was very proud of him. After she retired, she kept a scrapbook of cuttings about him. Whenever he was on the television, she would ask me to videotape it for her. She knew he wasn't the poster-boy for clean living. But she used to say that when he'd got his wild ways out of his system he'd come back to Barnsley, buy some land and settle down. She was right.'

Mr Horner leans forward. 'And as for Gerry, I wouldn't count on him too much. He's been seen up at the boy Casey's farm. Rumour is he made the grandpa a knockdown offer for the farm. Apparently Gerry's father's got tired of bailing out his gambling debts and has told him to make some money. He hasn't given up on those five hundred houses.'

'Gambling debts!' I manage to say. 'He hasn't got any gambling debts.'

'None that he's told you about, maybe. Gerry can't get a card game in the whole of Ohio thanks to his reputation. His father's paid off his creditors more times than I've had breakfast at this diner.' Mr Horner folds his paper napkin into a perfect square and places it to the side of his plate. 'Plenty of people have been taken in by Gerry Armstrong, including a good few pretty girls.' He wags his finger at me. 'Alice, I'm glad that you're the sensible type who would never get taken in by that ne'er-do-well.'

It's the night of the Concert for the Cow and it's half an hour until the doors open. The gym is a riot of muted colour – brown, beige and green – thanks to Sara's eco-friendly and recyclable decorations. There are cardboard cut-out cows hanging from the ceiling, cowpat-shaped brown banners tacked to the walls, and next to the stage, Sara is currently arranging a display board with information about sustainable agriculture. The Barnsley High School football team is busy placing tables around the edge of the room, and on stage the Scott County Maintenance Crew is tuning up.

I'm reasonably calm. As long as I keep looking at my list, I'll be fine. I tick off *Gym decorations*, take five short breaths in and one long one out, and move on to the next item on my list: *Tell the Scott boys to sing songs people like and want to dance to.*

I click over in my new black high heels – one inch; any higher and I start to stagger – and wave them over. I'm wearing my Monsoon black dress and, frankly, I have to say that I'm feeling a little overdressed. When Wyatt told me that everyone would be in jeans, I thought he was kidding.

But before I can reach the stage, Mr Horner intercepts me. 'We have a problem, Alice,' he says worriedly. 'I'm scheduled to open the concert with my trio of accordion favourites, but I see I'm double-booked to man the ticket desk at the same time.' He waves the ticket-desk rota at me.

I'm horrified! How can this administrative mistake have occurred? I look at the list and see that Logan has swapped his name with Mr Horner's. I know why – Madison has instructed him to videotape her performance. Logan's currently at the back of the gym setting up his camera on a tripod.

I sigh. 'I'll ask Brandy to open instead,' I say. 'I'll put you on before Madison.'

Is there no end to my work! I'm beginning to realize what Donald Trump must feel like running all those businesses, and why he needs all those apprentices to help him.

I hurry back to the Scott boys.

Chris looks up. 'Hey, Alice, we're cool. Don't worry about us.'

I stop dead. I really need to warn Brandy about the change in the order of acts – but on the other hand, I should double-check with the Scott boys what they're planning to play.

No, I must let go. This is a learning opportunity to trust! I nod at Chris. 'OK.' Then I scoot for the door.

'Heidi's gone over everything with us,' Chris calls out.

For a moment I falter. I must have misheard, surely? My mind clears: he means that she's sold them some raffle tickets. What other explanation could there be? There is no possible reason that she would involve herself with the music side of the evening.

Reassured, I hurry off to the cafeteria to find Brandy. We're holding the musical entertainment in the gym and serving food in the cafeteria. It's not an ideal dinner venue – the fluorescent strip lighting is rather harsh and the walls are lined with recruiting posters for the US Marines. As for the spare-rib barbecue, Sheriff Billy is outside barbecuing on a tatty patch of grass by the bins. As I make my way along the corridor, I pass Moms' Club members scurrying in with huge foil containers of desserts, Celeste carrying in Tupperware containers of Sheriff Billy's secret-recipe barbecue sauce and Casey zipping back and forth with paper plates. I follow Nancy through the cafeteria double doors; she's carrying what looks like a bucket of potato salad. On closer inspection I determine that it's a bucket.

However, in contrast to the gym, the school cafeteria is at least a proper riot of colour: yellow, pink and purple. Dolores put Madison and her friends in charge of decorating.

They squeal as they see me come in.

'We love this colour scheme,' says Madison.

'Isn't it awesome?' says Leeanne.

'We do it all the time,' says Madison, shifting her gum to the other side of her mouth. 'We did it for Brittany's birthday and my birthday and Leeanne's birthday and ...'

'The yellow is for the accent colour,' interrupts Brittany earnestly. 'We do three pink balloons for every yellow.' A confused expression crosses her face. 'Or is it four?'

Madison and Brittany have made up after Brittany explained that she only went bowling with Logan because he wanted to ask her all about Madison so he could be a better boyfriend, an explanation Madison has accepted somewhat uncritically in my private opinion. But I'm not saying anything to her in case she writes a song about it.

There are crêpe streamers criss-crossing the room, all the tables are covered in purple paper tablecloths and Madison is placing candle holders on every table. 'Leeanne made them,' she tells me. 'You'd never guess they were Pepsi bottles covered in scrunched-up tissue paper.'

I think you might, actually, but it's too late to organize

anything else. Besides, the Concert for the Cow is a rather casual affair. I had thought that people might dress up for a Saturday-night music and dinner event, but this is Barnsley, where things are a bit different from England.

Before I left, Wyatt took me to one side. 'There are three things you need to know, Alice. First, it says seven-thirty on the invitation. That means people will start arriving at seven-fifteen. Second, this is Ohio, which means you can never have too much food. And third, whatever you do, don't let Logan's brother near the bar. Not if you want any beer left to sell.'

Then he wished me luck and said that he might pop in later.

Madison, though, has made an effort with her appearance. She twirls around for me in a plunge-neck bright pink T-shirt, denim miniskirt and white platform shoes. 'It's my new stage outfit. I wanted to look classy, Alice. Like J-Lo.'

Behind the serving counter, Dolores is looking flustered. 'Excuse me,' she says loudly to Brandy, bumping her out of the way with her bottom, and setting down a mountain of sweetcorn. 'Alice, I have to have more serving space.'

'So do I,' says Brandy.

I see the problem. There are mountains of cornbread, piles of sweetcorn and more buckets of potato salad all jostling for space with acres of brownies and strawberry cheesecake.

I decide to ignore the space problem and brief Brandy on the change of acts.

Then I feel a hand on my bottom.

'Hi there.' It's Gerry. 'I brought a prize for the raffle.'

It's a basket of fruit.

He lowers his voice. 'Though there's only one prize I'd like to get my hands on tonight.'

I take a step back and look at him haughtily. Then I point at the basket. 'A Trojan horse, I presume?' I say with a heavy dose of irony.

Gerry looks puzzled. 'No, it's a basket of fruit.'

'I'm speaking metaphorically,' I snap. 'The Trojan horse was made to look like a gift, but really it was filled with soldiers ready to attack. I think the analogy is clear enough.'

Gerry squints at me. 'You what?'

It's hopeless. I drop the ironic tone. 'I hear you've been trying to get Casey's grandfather to sell his land to you and you don't want this evening to be a success at all. You've been lying to me all along.'

Gerry blinks, looks guilty and then rearranges his features in a picture of innocence. No wonder he's useless at gambling. 'Me? Never! I swear to you.'

'How could you?' I hiss.

As I prepare to tell Gerry that he's no longer my friend, Heidi interrupts us. She's wearing a black cocktail dress: a little lower-cut than mine, slightly shorter and perhaps a mite tighter.

Gerry stares from one of us to the other. 'Hey, you two could be sisters.' He looks like a cat surveying a bowl of cream. 'Maybe the three of us could go hang out together later.'

'Oh, shut up,' Heidi and I say in unison. She poses on her high heels, about two inches higher than mine, waving a pack of raffle tickets at us. 'So far we have over a thousand dollars in pre-event ticket sales.'

'A thousand,' repeats Gerry, his face falling. He catches my eye. 'Great!'

'Well, come along, Alice,' says Heidi in a very friendly tone. 'The doors are open. You ought to go into the gym and take all the credit.'

An hour later I'm wondering if I've misjudged Heidi. Perhaps I was cynical and untrusting in thinking she wasn't on my side. The concert is going very well indeed. The Barnsley Kindergarten class did a brave rendition of 'Yellow Submarine' and Mr Horner's accordion rendition of 'Edelweiss' brought Dolores to tears. 'I've got fifty ears of sweetcorn to peel, but I wouldn't miss this for all the potato salad in Ohio,' she said, blowing her nose.

Now Madison has just finished 'Hit Me Baby One More Time', and the dance floor is packed.

'You see,' I say smugly to Heidi who has suddenly appeared by my side, 'everything is going according to plan.'

'Yes, it is,' she says warmly.

Then Madison embarks on 'Vale Of Tears'. I'm horrified. She didn't mention this to me.

> *Shattered dreams*
> *Faded hopes*
> *I gave my heart*
> *Now it's broke*

For a few seconds people try to dance, then give up and return to their tables. By the second verse, half the room has hurried off to the bar. As soon as it ends I call Madison over to the edge of the stage.

'Let's take a break, Madison,' I say.

'But I've got another song I wrote,' she protests. 'It's called "Heal My Inner Child".'

I ignore her and wave over the Scott boys. I'm amazed to find that I'm not going to pieces, despite the fact that an eerie silence has fallen over the gym.

'We need a crowd-pleaser,' I hiss to Chris.

He looks a bit puzzled. 'We've got the playlist.'

What list?

There's no time to find out more. The drummer and guitarist have begun. Oh my gosh, it's 'Wonderwall'. And it's truly awful. I realize at that moment what a very good vocalist Noel Gallagher is, because the Scott County Maintenance Crew version should never be heard in public again.

At last it ends and Chris grasps the microphone. 'I want to thank Alice for helping us discover our true creativity and break out of the mould. This one's for you, Alice.' The Scott boys raise a cheer. Maybe it's all going to be all right. I wave at them.

It takes me a few seconds to recognize the first few bars of Green Day's liberal protest song 'American Idiot'.

I'm struck dumb as Chris wails into the microphone.

But not as bemused as the audience, several of whom are wearing hunting camouflage jackets.

'*I'm not part of a redneck agenda . . .*' cries out Chris.

'I didn't pay good money to hear this trash,' storms a large red-necked man next to me. 'He ought to be shot.'

'And so should that English girl,' someone else adds.

'Do you think she's a spy?'

'Could be. She's from that Europe country after all.'

Oh no. I'm now in danger of not making it out alive. The number of people leaving in disgust is now matched by those coming in to see what all the fuss is about. Finally Chris comes to the end of the song. I say a silent prayer. What we really need now is a good, foot-stomping anthem to get everyone on their feet.

Chris grabs the microphone. It lets out one of those awful shrieking whine noises.

'Hello, Barnsley!' he shouts out. No one responds. The atmosphere is mutinous.

There is now silence broken only by murmurs. People are

shooting hostile glances in my direction. 'Twenty bucks for this,' I hear someone say contemptuously. 'Some concert.'

I'm feeling desperate. There's only one thing I can think of now. I close my eyes. 'Please, Dr Vaizey,' I say, 'What do I do?'

Dr Vaizey appears. He's sitting in his leather armchair, rubbing his chin thoughtfully. 'Hmm. An interesting question, Alice. I don't have any experience of fund-raising events in Barnsley. I'm afraid you're on your own on this one.'

And then he's gone.

'That English chick should give people their money back,' I hear next.

'Who's Dr Vaizey?' the woman next to me says to her husband.

Out of the corner of my eye I see Logan's brother slipping out of the door in the direction of the bar. Well, that's it then. When the booze runs out they're going to barbecue me.

Now there's nothing but the sound of disgruntled comments. A few people have even started pulling on their coats. The Scott boys are frozen on stage.

And then there are footsteps. It's the sound of a man's boots. I can't see whose they are. But then a figure appears on the steps leading up to the stage.

It's Wyatt.

He's wearing the same old work shirt he's had on since this morning, the jeans he wears for doing the yard work, and it doesn't look like he's brushed his hair for a week. I can hardly believe my eyes. He goes up to the band, claps Chris on the back and takes hold of the stand.

'I need a band!'

There's a roar from the crowd, Chris stands graciously aside and the Scott boys take up their instruments. Amid the sound of clapping and cheers, Bruce bustles over to me.

'We were supposed to be going to a meeting, but Wyatt insisted on coming here,' he says, looking horrified. He points at Wyatt on the stage. 'Is this wise?'

'Yes. Very.'

'I think I ought to stop him. I'm going up there.'

I grab Bruce's wrist. 'No, you can't.'

'This could take him straight back to a relapse.'

'Yes, it could.' I realize now that I'm not thinking about me, despite the fact that Wyatt is about to save my skin. 'I also know that you can't protect him for ever. This is what he does, Bruce. This is what he spent years learning to do, ever since he was a little child. And he has to get up there and learn to do it sober. What better place is there than in front of the people who love him?'

Bruce says nothing for a few seconds. 'You're right.'

We both turn to look at Wyatt.

He's up on stage and he looks totally relaxed. 'Let's get this party jumping,' he says as the Scott boys take up position. 'Anyone feel like going down to the creek for a little … Moonshine?'

'*Moonshine*!' the cry goes up, and the Scott boys strum out the first chords.

Then Wyatt starts to sing. '*Take a little walk …*'

The gym has gone crazy. Everyone has taken to the dance floor and people are pouring back in through the doors.

> *Take a little trip in the moonlit dew*
> *Down by the creek*
> *Thinkin' it through …*

When the chorus begins, the whole gym joins in.

> *Maybe come and see you*
> *Maybe come and see you*
> *Hell, I've got the Moonshine Blues*

I feel relief wash over me. Then I catch sight of Heidi in the corner. Her mouth is turned down and she isn't making any effort to look happy.

Wyatt finishes 'Moonshine' and starts on the other tracks on that first album: 'Small Town Girl', 'One Long Night' and 'Never Have To Guess'. After a while he slows it down for 'Losing You'. I feel a lump in my throat. People are coming up to me now, congratulating me on a great evening, but all I want to do is stand alone at the back of the gym and listen to Wyatt.

Is he up there helping me? Or helping himself? Is this what he needed to sing again – to come back home, to the people he knows, in a place he feels safe? I'd like to think he did it for me, but I know that singing is in his blood.

The gym is packed now, Wyatt has made the stage his own and people are singing along to the final lines of 'Losing You'. When it comes to an end, Wyatt takes a long drink from a water bottle. 'And here's a new one. I wrote this just the other day after one of those late summer evenings on the porch. It's called "Take My Hand".'

Wyatt slips on his guitar and the Scott boys stand back. It's just him and the guitar now, alone on stage in a soft pool of light. He sings.

> *When you feel you're all alone*
> *When your heart has no place to turn*
> *When your love has no home*
> *Take my hand*

Take my hand
Hold on tight
Let me lift you up
Over the pain
Over the past
Into my arms

Let me take you to that place
That words cannot reach
Don't let go, feel us fly
Don't wonder any more, up into the sky

Take my hand
Hold on tight
Let me lift you up
Over the pain
Over the past
Into my arms

When he finishes, there are a few seconds of silence – because it's brilliant and no one wants it to end. The melody is one I've never heard before but I feel I've known it all my life. And he sings it in a way that no one else could come close to imitating.

I suppose everyone will think it's a love song. But I know better. It's about alcohol, of course, just like 'Losing You'. It's about the seductive power of drink. Yes, that's it. I suppose Wyatt wrote it after a night sitting alone on the porch when he was briefly tempted to have a drink.

After Wyatt has finished, there's a thunder of applause that I think will go on for ever. Bruce appears by my side. 'That's his best ever. I guess he got inspired,' he says with a smile.

'Oh yes,' I agree. 'The credit's all yours, Bruce.'

He gives me an odd look at that point. I watch as Wyatt comes off the stage, the Scott boys strike up Kool and the Gang's 'Celebration' and Heidi rushes up to Wyatt, throwing her arms around him and clinging on to him as people surround him.

I don't think I could get to Wyatt if I wanted to. There must be three hundred people in the gym. And in any case, I pull myself back to the moment. I remember what this night is all about: not me or Wyatt or anyone in this room. It's about a young boy who's got a dream to take his cow to a show. And right now I need to go and count the ticket money to find out if we've made that dream come true.

CHAPTER 40

It's almost noon. I'm in bed in the cottage and I've just been woken up by the door of a car slamming. I bet it's Bruce come to check up on Wyatt. It takes a little while for me to come round. By the time we finished clearing up last night, it was four o'clock in the morning (I couldn't leave the cafeteria floor unwashed). I didn't fall into bed until five.

I never did get to speak to Wyatt: Heidi was glued to him like a human barnacle. We made over ten thousand dollars. Casey was there when Sheriff Billy called out the total. Everyone who had helped started clapping, and Casey gave me a huge hug. 'Thank you, Miss Alice. You saved Mary Lou's life.' I must say I did cry a bit at that point. It turns out that my life has not been without significance after all.

Now I hear another car pull up, two doors slam shut and the sounds of greetings and loud laughter. I throw on my crumpled Friesian T-shirt over my Marks & Spencer navy-blue tracksuit bottoms, go down the spiral staircase and peer out of the kitchen window. I can't believe my eyes: the yard is full of photographers and people holding notebooks.

Someone catches sight of me and a shout goes up. 'Look – a woman!'

I hear random shouts.

'*Who is it?*'

'It's his girlfriend.'

'It's his shrink.'

'It's his mother.'

What! I duck down and shuffle on all fours to retrieve my handbag from where it's hanging on the back of a kitchen chair. I pull out my Avon powder compact and stare at my reflection. I look exhausted. My skin is grey with tiredness and I have black rings under my eyes where the remnants of my mascara have smudged overnight.

Then they start banging on the door. 'We'll give you the best offer for an exclusive interview,' they all shout.

What on earth is going on? Can Mary Lou really be that famous? I shuffle across the room and quickly bolt the door. I can hear them outside milling around. I listen to the conversation, trying to work out what they're doing here.

'We saw Wyatt on YouTube at midnight, got straight in the car and drove all night.'

'Yep, we were here at six a.m.'

'Some of the guys from the New York papers are turning up now. They must have caught the first flight out.'

'Did you speak to that teenager who took the video?'

'Logan? We've all spoken to him. He's been hanging out at that Blue Ribbon diner. That boy's a good cameraman.'

'That boy's a fool. If he hadn't posted it on YouTube he could have made a fortune.'

I think I've worked out what's happened. I go on my hands and knees into the living room, locate my BlackBerry, switch it on and call Wyatt. He answers straight away.

'Hell, Alice, are you all right? I left a message. Stay where you are!'

'Is this what I think it is?' I say.

Wyatt sounds furious. 'Logan was recording Madison.

337

The little jerk decided to record my new song, too. Then he posted it on YouTube last night.'

I can't believe how quickly this has got out. 'Only last night!'

'Yeah, apparently about midnight. Some of these guys are music press, but most of them are from the gossip sheets.'

'What do they want?'

'An interview,' he sighs. 'They want to know why I've suddenly decided to sing again after spending years as a reclusive drunk. Look, I'll come out later. I need to get my head together. Just lay low. They'll go once I've spoken to them.'

'OK.'

'Alice, stay out of the way,' says Wyatt firmly. 'I don't want you caught up in all of this.'

He rings off. I suppose the best thing to do is use the time to pack. My visa runs out tomorrow and I fly out in the evening. The horrible thought strikes me that I might not see Wyatt before I leave. In fact, I might not see Wyatt ever again. I feel overcome with a horrible, aching sadness. He'll go on with his relaunched life of international superstardom and I'll go back to routine clerical work in New Malden.

Which reminds me – I still haven't called Teresa to tell her about Dad. Hmm. Maybe in a little while.

I go upstairs and begin packing with no enthusiasm whatsoever. Every time I empty a drawer or pull out a hanger I feel worse. Mind-numbing routine activity always used to take my mind off my worries, but today it isn't working. All I feel like doing is curling up on the sofa with a tub of ice cream watching a weepy movie – like normal women do. The more I think about it, the better that idea seems. So I drag the duvet down the stairs, fetch a tub of Ben and Jerry's from the freezer and settle down to watch the Lifetime channel Sunday movie. It's about a woman who discovers that her husband is not at all the successful doctor he appears to be, that he harbours a dark secret from the past and that he's having an affair with her best friend's teenage daughter. The plot is always the same.

After the film ends – the husband dies conveniently in a car accident leaving the wife free to marry her nice lawyer – I'm feeling a bit better. I even feel good enough finally to make that call to Teresa. It's just plain silly to be afraid. If she has issues with Dad and Valerie, then she's just going to have to deal with them. How far I have come on my journey of self-awareness!

'Teresa, it's Alice,' I say assertively.

'Who?' There's a giggle and a splutter. I look at my watch. It's early evening in the UK. Surely she hasn't been drinking?

'Have you been drinking?' I say suspiciously.

'No.' More laughter follows. 'Only a teeny-weeny, itsy-bitsy bit. The twins are with Richard.'

I can hear a man's voice in the background: '*Wine boxes are such good value.*'

I must have misheard. 'Teresa, I'm calling to tell you that Dad and Valerie are getting married.'

'Really? At least there'll be one wedding in this family, Alice. Or should I say … Suzi.' Then she sniggers with laughter.

I hear the man's voice again: '*No need to order pizza. Let's make sandwiches from leftovers.*'

It sounds a bit like Stephen. No, it can't be. 'They're getting married in Barbados,' I continue.

'Fine.' Teresa sounds as though she has other things on her mind.

Then I hear the man again: '*And later we can have half a bar of Dairy Milk.*'

'Teresa, is that ... Stephen?'

'Yes.' She doesn't sound in the least contrite. 'He's here helping me put my affairs in order.' There's a round of raucous laughter.

I'm aghast. 'Let me speak to him.'

Stephen comes on the line. 'Alice, you never told me your sister was so much fun.' He sounds very jolly indeed. 'No wonder you were always so jealous of her.'

In the background Teresa is singing 'Devil Gate Drive' in a poor impersonation of Suzi Quatro.

'Are you two ...?'

'Yes, we are an item,' Stephen says happily. 'Teresa says I'm just the kind of honest and reliable man she's always wanted. I'm sorry, Alice, but it's too late now. You let a good thing go and you're just going have to live with that.'

Then he puts the phone down.

I'm in shock. I retreat to the sofa. Family occasions with Teresa have been bad enough in the past. What is Christmas dinner going to be like sitting across from my ex-lover with Teresa, twirling an imaginary moustache?

At least things can't get any worse, I console myself. I rewrap the duvet around me as I try to banish the image of Teresa and Stephen choosing kitchen tiles together.

It's about five minutes later that I hear a loud woman's voice outside. 'Gather round. Pay attention please.' She sounds like a schoolteacher. I rush to the window.

It's Heidi. She's standing on Wyatt's doorstep in her smart navy-blue suit. It looks as though she's spent all day putting on her make-up and curling up the ends of her hair. All the journalists have gathered round her. She's holding a clipboard.

'I'm Heidi, Wyatt's friend and spokeswoman.' She clears her throat. 'Thank you all for coming today. Wyatt was pleased to help last night at a fund-raising event to assist a cause close to his heart – animal welfare. No decision has been made about his new song. He asks you to respect his privacy and that of those closest to him at this time.' She puts down the sheet. 'I will take questions now.'

'What was this concert?'

'I can tell you all about that. I was there organizing it.' Then she's off, giving them every detail. 'Casey is very close to Wyatt and me.'

'What is your relationship with Wyatt?'

'No comment.'

'Is he drinking?'

'Certainly not!'

'Who's that girl in the cottage?'

'No one important.'

'Is she his girlfriend?'

'No,' snaps Heidi. 'She's a junior employee of Carmichael Music assigned to low-level administrative tasks. Anything she tells you should be treated with the utmost caution.'

'So are you Wyatt's girlfriend?'

Heidi gives an enigmatic smile. 'Let's just say we go back a long way.'

Then she hands out a sheet. 'This has my contact numbers on it. Below you will find a list of local bed-and-breakfast establishments. There will be no further comment today.'

Now why didn't I think of that?

I watch furtively as the journalists disappear and Heidi lets herself into Wyatt's house.

What am I going to do? Two choices present themselves: I can stay here and clean the cottage while Heidi takes all the credit for the concert and seduces Wyatt, or I can go and talk to him honestly about how I feel.

I'm in an agony of indecision.

I close my eyes. It takes a little longer than normal, but Dr Vaizey comes to mind. He's sitting in his leather armchair, but for the first time I notice that his hair is white at the sides and he's very slightly blurred around the edges. 'Alice, you were always my favourite patient,' he says, sounding really old. 'Now, you were asking about Wyatt.'

I'm straining to hear him. Alarmed, I realize that this is because his voice is fading away.

'I suggest . . .' he says.

But I can't hear him! His lips are moving but his voice has gone. At the same time the blurred edges around him start getting worse. They're eating him up! In horror I watch as Dr Vaizey disappears before my eyes. Soon there's nothing left but his armchair and a box of Kleenex.

He's gone, and I know that he will never be back. I'm on my own. I sit down and devote a quiet moment to the memory of Dr Vaizey.

It's time to make a decision all by myself.

CHAPTER 41

Two hours later and I'm ready. My make-up is flawless and my hair is as straight and full of volume and shine as I can get it. I'm wearing my new 542 Levi's, my new white J. Crew shirt and a pair of black leather boots that actually zip up over my jeans. I've always wanted a pair of those, but the zip used to get stuck halfway up my leg before. I look really stylish, probably because Gerry chose it all on our shopping trip.

I take a deep breath and walk confidently over to the house in the fading light of the late afternoon. I know exactly what I'm going to do. I'm going to ask Heidi to leave us alone and then tell Wyatt precisely how I feel. Then, when he says he just wants to be friends, I'm going to be heart-broken for the rest of my life and live in unbroken monotony back in the UK.

But just as I'm about to open the front door, I glimpse the lights of a car coming up the driveway. I stop to look more closely but I don't recognize it because it's a long, black limousine and there are none of those in Barnsley. It pulls slowly to a halt. I see now that there's a chauffeur at the wheel. Then both back doors open simultaneously. On my side a long, slim leg emerges and a foot descends on to the gravel in what I guess is a Jimmy Choo shoe.

Oh my gosh – it's Phoebe. And Brent emerges from the other side.

They stand in the yard and look around, bewildered. It's like a scene from *Star Trek* when the crew land on an alien planet.

I rush over. Should I curtsey? 'Miss Carmichael,' I say, resisting the impulse to go down on one knee.

'Alice,' she says with more enthusiasm than I've ever heard before. 'How nice to see you. Take me to Wyatt. I've come to take charge.'

'We took the personal jet,' Brent says to me smugly. 'So convenient.'

Then Phoebe marches off, lets herself into Wyatt's house with Brent and me jogging behind her and, on seeing that the living room is empty, goes straight into the kitchen, where Heidi is sitting at her laptop, typing.

Phoebe takes off her black leather gloves and throws them on the kitchen table. 'Coffee. Black. No sugar.'

Heidi looks understandably perplexed. 'Who are you?'

Phoebe ignores this. 'Where's Wyatt?' she barks.

Heidi hesitates. 'He's ... resting.' Heidi and I exchange glances. There's a big football game on this Sunday afternoon and I'm guessing he's down in the basement watching it.

'This is Miss Phoebe Carmichael,' I explain to Heidi. 'As in Carmichael Music.'

Phoebe walks round and peers over Heidi's shoulder at her laptop screen. 'My goodness. It's years since I've seen a computer as old as that. Look, Brent.'

'Do they still make the parts?' Brent twitters.

Heidi gets up. 'I'm Heidi,' she says, holding out her hand. 'I'm running things for Wyatt.'

Phoebe puts her hands on her hips and raises an eyebrow by way of a response. 'Can I have that coffee now?'

'I'm a very good friend of Wyatt's,' Heidi says more confidently. I can see she's fighting back. 'Alice can make it for you.'

'Alice is with me,' counters Phoebe. I wonder if I should get under the kitchen table. They're looking daggers at each other now. But Phoebe isn't blinking. 'So what is your business and public relations background, Helga? Harvard or Yale?'

Incredibly I feel compelled to pipe up in Heidi's defence. 'Heidi's a teacher.'

Phoebe smiles. 'How very worthy. We mustn't keep you from your important marking any longer. Goodbye.'

'I'm not going anywhere,' says Heidi obstinately. 'You don't have any right to march in here and tell me what to do.'

Phoebe snaps. 'I think you'll find I do. Wyatt is under contract to my company. I will produce his next album. I will handle the whole operation.' Phoebe switches off Heidi's laptop and snaps it shut. 'Don't you have something to construct out of a toilet roll and a paper doily?'

She draws closer to Heidi. Oh no. I think she might be about to eat her. 'It's time to let the professionals take over.'

Heidi looks as if she wants to speak, but no words come out. Instead we watch as Phoebe pulls out her BlackBerry and Brent begins bringing in stuff from the car. Soon the table is covered with two laptops, a fax machine, folders, rolls of paper and a file saying 'Wyatt Brown Marketing Plan'. Finally Brent picks up Heidi's laptop and handbag and heads for the door. Heidi doesn't have any option but to follow him.

I stand there for about ten minutes as Phoebe makes an urgent call to her massage therapist, arranging to fly her in from New York. With dismay I work out that Phoebe is planning to be here for some time. At last she turns her attention to me. 'Excellent work, Alice. Well done. I want you to know that you're a vital part of Team Wyatt.'

'Thank you.' Oh my gosh, this is it. The promotion!

'This is what I need. Decaffeinated coffee, soya milk, Evian water and some power snacks. She pauses. 'Sunflower seeds, raisins and wheatgrass,' she rattles off. 'Do you think you can remember that?'

There's no chance of getting that in Barnsley.

'But—' I don't get a chance to finish before Brent grabs my arm and hustles me out of the door. 'Drive safely!'

Three and a half hours later I return from my trip to Whole Foods in Columbus. I let myself into the house. Phoebe, Bruce, Wyatt and Brent are gathered round the kitchen table. Bruce is cooking omelettes and Phoebe is laughing as if she didn't have a care in the world. None of them acknowledge me as I walk in, burdened down with four brown-paper carrier bags. Fearful of getting the wrong thing, I bought all possible variations.

'My God, this is fabulous,' says Phoebe, eating her omelette.

'I learnt how to do them at the Carlyle Hotel,' says Bruce.

'I never would have believed that I could come to Ohio and get the best egg-white omelette I've ever tasted. Alice,' Phoebe calls out, addressing me for the first time since I've come in, 'You didn't tell me what a wonderful place this is.'

I'm preoccupied with loading the fridge with soya milk in plain, vanilla, chocolate and low-fat varieties.

'Some more emails would have been helpful,' adds Brent. 'We really were in the dark, I'm afraid, Wyatt.'

I swing round. 'I did—'

But Phoebe cuts me off. 'Let's not dwell on the mistakes of the past.'

I look to Wyatt, but his expression is completely blank. He's observing the scene and making no effort to defend me. I pull out a chair to sit down, but Phoebe holds up her hand.

'Alice, I need you to clear out the guest cottage. Wyatt's told me all about it – it sounds like the perfect office for me.'

I'm incredulous. 'What?'

'It's all right. If you must, you can stay there until you leave for London tomorrow.' She turns back to Wyatt. 'Our elite team fly in tomorrow from New York. Brent's arranging to house them in a luxury trailer in your yard.'

Surely Wyatt is going to object to that!

But he says nothing.

Miserably I shift from foot to foot.

'Would you like something to eat?' says Bruce kindly.

'No,' says Phoebe. 'Alice is on a very tight departure schedule.'

Still Wyatt says nothing. So much for his Midwestern hospitality. I watch as he leans over and refills Phoebe's glass with water.

She turns to me and smiles patronizingly. 'We're relying on you to clear that filing backlog, Alice. And update the internal telephone directory.'

I can't think of anything to say, so I stand there awkwardly. I just can't take it in that Wyatt isn't saying anything to fight my corner.

'Do you need something, Alice?' says Brent impatiently.

I can't even bring myself to answer. There's an awful silence. No one speaks. It feels as though the ground is giving way beneath me. Wordlessly I manage to walk out of the kitchen and open the front door before I burst into tears. Nothing could ever have prepared me for Wyatt rejecting me so humiliatingly.

As I'm stumbling, blind with tears, across the yard, I

bump into someone. It's a short person, who grabs hold of my arm. 'Miss Alice! Come quickly!'

I rub my eyes. It's Casey. He looks terrified. His face is pale and his eyes are wide-eyed with fear. 'It's Mary Lou,' he cries out. 'I think she's dying.'

CHAPTER 42

An hour later and I'm kneeling with the vet next to Mary Lou. She's lying in her stall, her breathing is laboured and her eyes are dull. Casey, his face tear-stained, is huddled next to me.

'It's pneumonia,' says the vet, putting away his stethoscope.

'She caught it at the Barnsley Festival Show, didn't she?' says Casey.

'Probably,' nods the vet. 'It's been going around.'

Casey bursts into tears again. 'I should never have taken her. It's all my fault.'

'It's not,' I say, holding him tight. 'Everything's going to be all right.'

The vet clears his throat and casts me a warning glance. 'Let's walk to the car, shall we?' he says heavily. 'You stay here, Casey.'

Outside, the vet talks to me in a low voice. 'It's touch and go. I've given her an injection, but if it's viral there's not much we can do. If she makes it through the night she'll be OK.'

'What can we do to help?'

'Try getting her up as much as possible to walk around and clear the lungs. Keep the straw bone-dry – you don't want her getting too hot. And keep encouraging her to drink.'

'Anything else?'

He looks grim. 'She's got it bad. Time will tell.'

I go back into the barn, where Casey is looking distraught. 'I'm not leaving her.'

'And I'm not leaving you,' I say firmly, even though I would give my right arm to be in Wyatt's kitchen now finding out what's going on. But I suppose I already know – Phoebe is taking all the credit for my work.

'We're going to stay here all night with Mary Lou and look after her.'

'Is she going to live?' says Casey quietly.

I swallow. 'I don't know, Casey. But we're going to give her the best chance we can.'

He nods. 'I get it.' I go over and hug him at that point. He's being so brave and grown-up.

The next few hours pass in a blur. It takes all our energy to rouse Mary Lou to her feet, one of us walking her round while the other cleans out her stall. At midnight I go in search of blankets for the night. I know Wyatt has some in his hall cupboard. As I approach the house, I see the limousine has gone and the lights in the house are still on. I feel a huge sigh of relief – right now I really need to speak to Wyatt.

But as I let myself in, the first thing I hear is Phoebe talking in a low voice to Wyatt. 'I never gave up on you. That's why I sent Alice. She's my best. Of course, we'll need to move you on to someone better now.'

'I see,' says Wyatt. 'Go on.'

He doesn't sound as if he cares at all.

'Alice has taken you as far as she can, but it's time for someone a little more ... inspiring to take over now.'

'Uh-huh,' says Wyatt.

I feel the shock of betrayal. He isn't making any effort to defend me at all. He's letting me be pushed out of the way and he sounds as if he doesn't give a damn. How could he? It's then that I notice there's low music playing on the stereo, and when I look in the kitchen I see that Brent's things have gone – Phoebe must have sent him to the bed and breakfast alone. I begin to have a horrible suspicion about exactly what is going on in the living room.

I listen as Phoebe continues. 'I will personally take charge of every aspect of the new album. Provisionally we think "Take My Hand" should be lead song and title to follow on from the single release. We thought a North American twenty-five-city tour to begin with, followed by Europe and Asia.'

She pauses. 'I want you to know how much I respect and admire you. I think we could have a very good working relationship.'

That's it. I can't help myself. I peek round the corner into the living room. It's much worse than I expected. Phoebe is sitting right next to Wyatt. Her glossy hair is shining in the glow of the table lamp and her skirt has ridden right up her perfect thighs. I watch as she lays a red manicured hand on Wyatt's knee. 'And I'm in no hurry to leave.'

'Let me play you some more material,' Wyatt says. 'I'll get my guitar.'

What new material? He didn't tell me anything about that.

Wyatt gets up and comes out into the hallway as I dart back into the kitchen.

I lean back against the wall as I hear his footsteps on the stairs, feeling desperate and utterly alone. How could I think we were close when all this time Wyatt was working on a whole album that he never told me about? And now he's about to share it with Phoebe – and very likely his bed as well.

I can't bear to hear any more: I gather up the blankets and slip silently out of the door. Then I lose myself in the exhausting physical struggle of rousing Mary Lou, Casey and I dozing on and off through the night.

The next morning I wake up next to Mary Lou. I stay still for a moment, then feel the soft rise and fall of her rib cage. She made it through the night! I get up, careful not to wake Casey, who's asleep next to me.

It's seven-thirty in the morning. There's no coffee in the cottage – I've cleared out all the cupboards and cleaned the kitchen from top to bottom in preparation for leaving today. So I don't have any choice but to let myself into Wyatt's house, much as I would like never to see him again in my life. The kitchen table is covered with papers, artwork and sheets of figures. I glance at one – *Wyatt Brown Projected Worldwide Sales*.

'What are you doing up?'

I jump out of my skin as Wyatt comes in.

'Nothing.' I step away from him, partly out of justifiable hurt at his behaviour and partly because I'm wearing the same clothes I've had on since yesterday.

Wyatt sniffs. 'Can you smell a cow?'

I sniff too. 'No,' I lie.

I suppose Phoebe is upstairs, smelling fragrant, and he has come to make her breakfast in bed. He's dressed, though, in jeans and a work shirt. I resolve to leave right now.

'Where have you been?' he says suspiciously.

'In the barn,' I say, making my way to the door.

As if on cue, Casey wanders in, bleary-eyed.

'What's been going on?' says Wyatt.

Casey looks up at him with a hint of reproach in his eyes. 'Mary Lou was really sick last night. The vet came and Alice saved her life. Again.'

I don't have any choice but to stop and tell Wyatt about Mary Lou. 'But she's fine now,' I conclude.

'You should have called me,' says Wyatt crossly.

'Alice said you were busy,' cuts in Casey, sounding a bit hostile.

'I would have left,' responds Wyatt as if it was obvious. He turns to me. 'I knocked on the door of the cottage after Phoebe left last night but there was no reply.'

My heart skips a beat. But then I remember that Phoebe is the type to get up and leave promptly after sex in order to get a couple of hours' work done. And I have every line of their conversation in my head – about the album Wyatt was working on that he never told me about.

'Really,' I say coldly. 'I have to pack.'

'What?'

'Yes, to make way for Phoebe's elite team,' I say even more coldly.

There's no chance for Wyatt to reply because Bruce walks in holding a home-made loaf of bread. He looks about hopefully. 'I thought Phoebe might want breakfast,' he says brightly.

'She'll be here in an hour.' It's Brent, who's followed Bruce into the kitchen. 'I'm here to get things ready for her,' he says, sounding flustered.

Wyatt looks around his kitchen: at Casey, who's making himself a bowl of cereal, at Brent, who's checking his emails, and at Bruce, who's loading the fridge with breakfast supplies.

'Alice, come on.'

'I have to—'

He cuts me off. 'Now.'

He grabs my hand, opens the door of the truck for me and then walks briskly round to the other side. 'There's only one place we can get any privacy in this damn town.'

CHAPTER 43

The corn maze is exactly what you would expect: a huge field of sweetcorn cut into a maze of pathways.

'Casey's grandpa cut it over the weekend,' Wyatt tells me as we screech to a halt in the yard of Casey's grandpa's farm. 'He'll open it up in a couple of weeks.'

We've been speeding along wordlessly, me holding on to the door for dear life, only letting go to wave to Sheriff Billy.

We get out and walk over to the entrance to the maze. Casey's grandpa is there putting up a big, weather-beaten sign. 'Morning. You two come to take a peek?' he says.

'If that's all right with you, sir,' says Wyatt.

The sign says

MAIZE MAZE
No smoking
No running
No cussing
No immorality
No cutting through the corn!!!

Wyatt leads the way into the maze. It's impossible to see anything except walls of ripe corn, the fat ears ready to be harvested and the leaves yellow and withered from the sun.

The ground feels soft and damp under our feet.

'Where are we going?' I say.

'To the centre, of course.'

'But I'm supposed to be on my way to the airport!' I wail. 'My visa runs out today.'

'It's not a problem,' says Wyatt.

I don't think US Immigration is going to take that attitude. I look behind me to get my bearings. Oh, hell! Sheriff Billy has followed us: he's standing at the entrance to the maze, talking to Casey's grandpa. I should never have waved at him: all criminals make a fatal mistake, and waving to a policeman was mine. I look on in horror as Casey's grandpa points into the maze, obviously giving Sheriff Billy directions to me. He's going to arrest me! I'm going to be fingerprinted and sent home handcuffed to my plane seat. What am I going to do when I need to use the bathroom?

I hurry after Wyatt.

'Alice,' he begins.

'Shhh. He'll find me,' I whisper.

'Who?'

Panic has gripped me. I start to run, overtake a startled Wyatt, take a left turn, then a right and then a left. Or was it a right? All sweetcorn looks the same.

'Alice,' I hear Wyatt call out.

I'm now totally lost. 'Shhh,' I whisper.

'Is that you?' he yells. 'Alice, stand still,' Wyatt instructs me. 'I'm coming to find you.'

'Where's Sheriff Billy?' I call out over my shoulder as I run deeper into the maze.

'Giving the benefit money to Casey's grandpa?' I hear Wyatt reply. He sounds quite a distance from me.

'No, he's come for me,' I hiss. 'The bell tolls for me! Don't you understand?'

'No, not really.' I can hear Wyatt getting closer. 'Alice, will you damned well stand still.'

'I'm an illegal immigrant. I have to run and hide.'

Wyatt sounds unperturbed by my confession. 'No you're not. Phoebe's got it all sorted out.'

'Phoebe,' I spit as I hurry on into the maze. 'She's no friend of mine. She'll say anything to get you to do what she wants.'

'I know that. I'm not a complete idiot.'

He's very close now, so I take a chance, stop running and slow down to a walking pace. 'I thought you liked her,' I call out. 'I thought you wanted to give "Take My Hand" to her.' As I say this, all the feelings of hurt and bewilderment that I felt last night when I overhead Phoebe and Wyatt come back just as intensely.

'No,' says Wyatt. 'She's the last person in the world I'd give my song to.'

I don't stop to think. I just feel betrayed and confused. 'So why did you tell her you'd written an album? You never mentioned it to me,' I blurt out.

Too late I realize that I'm going to have to tell Wyatt about my eavesdropping. 'I came into the house to get some blankets,' I begin. Then I call out everything I overheard, hoping I'm shouting in the right direction. 'Then I went back to Mary Lou,' I conclude.

I think I just glimpsed Wyatt through the corn.

'I haven't written an album,' Wyatt says patiently. 'I only wrote one song.'

Now he sees me. We peer at each other through three feet of sweetcorn.

'Then what did you play Phoebe?'

'"Vale of Tears".'

'What!'

'I had to. It was the only way I could get rid of her. I had to convince her that she didn't want my next album.'

'Did it work?'

By way of a response, Wyatt starts singing 'Vale of Tears'. Except that he makes it much drearier than Madison ever did. '*Shattered dreams, Faded hopes ...*'

'Oh my God,' I say, desperate for him to stop.

'Then I told her that my next album was a journey into the misery of the human condition, with a couple of songs about possible salvation tagged on the end.'

'What did she say?' I ask, stunned.

'She said she would need to speak to her creative people. Then she started hinting about releasing me from my contract. My guess is she's already drafted papers to get Carmichael Music out of producing my next album.'

'But what about "Take My Hand"? Surely she wants that?'

'Not after I told her that I planned to do a new version with a 1980s techno theme. That put her right off. Then I told her that I could only read very simple words on account of being brought up in Barnsley, and that if she wanted any contract changes I'd need you to stay so that you could read things out to me and help me sign my name.'

I'm flabbergasted. 'You told her you couldn't read! And she believed you?'

'Yep. She's from New York. She probably thinks everyone in Ohio struggles with reading. Phoebe called her lawyers there and then and ordered them to get out of bed and extend your work visa. She's so desperate to get out of that contract she even gave you a pay rise.'

It takes a few seconds to take all this in. My mind is whirring. Can it really be that simple – that I can just stay and work with Wyatt?

No. In my life things are never that simple. For a start, Wyatt has now disappeared from sight and is urgently trying to find a way to reach me. Then there's the fact that I want to do more than work with Wyatt. As I listen to him pace up and down, I think back to the day he took me riding, when we lay in the shade of the trees talking like old friends, when we went back to the house and we so nearly kissed like lovers ... I know that I can't go back to living in that old place where I didn't take risks. It used to feel safe, but now it feels suffocating. I have to know how Wyatt feels and I have to tell him how I feel, too. And it's not only Phoebe I have to find out about.

'Damn,' says Wyatt. 'This maze is impossible.'

I take a deep breath. I have to start somewhere. 'What about Heidi?'

'What about her?' he says, a little bemused. He's opposite me now.

'She was helping you deal with the journalists,' I say, skirting round the issue. I force myself to get to the point. 'I thought there was something between the two of you.'

'Heidi's just a friend,' Wyatt says distractedly.

I'd like to believe that, but then I recall that photograph of the two of them in her house. 'I'm not sure she sees it that way.'

'Heidi will end up with Gerry,' he says simply. 'Heidi's never had any designs on me. She's been fantastic – she helped organize my move, she threw a housewarming party ...'

A *party*. So it wasn't just the two of them.

'... But we're like brother and sister,' he concludes.

I'm about to correct him when I think better of it. 'You're right.'

But I still have some questions. If there's no album and

Wyatt doesn't want to record, then why did he write 'Take My Hand'? 'So why did you write "Take My Hand"?'

Wyatt doesn't say anything for a moment. 'I can't tell you if I can't see you.'

He's referring to the wall of corn three-foot thick that's separating us.

'I'm going to cut through,' he says.

'No,' I screech, horrified. 'The rules say you can't cut through!'

'To hell with the rules. I'm coming through.'

'No!' I shout. 'If one of us is going to get into trouble, it's better that it's me. The worst they can do is deport me.' I take a step forward. The corn is surprisingly hard to push through.

'Alice,' Wyatt says. 'Take my hand.'

He reaches out and I grasp it. He pulls me towards him and I follow. And when I get to the other side, neither of us breaks our hold. He looks away, then looks back at me.

'Hell, I never expected this,' he says.

I say nothing, seeing that he's searching for the right words.

He pulls me closer to him. 'I mean, I never expected to feel like this. I never thought I'd meet someone like you. I guess I planned on coming back to Barnsley and living a quiet life. Then one day you drive up in a snowstorm and turn my world upside down.' He gives a low whistle. 'Alice, you really took me by surprise.'

Wyatt, still holding my hand, starts walking slowly through the maze. 'You got a hold of me from the start. I fought it all the way: backed off and tried to forget you, acted cool, acted like a jerk, but whatever I did I couldn't get you out of my mind.'

It feels so easy, walking hand in hand like this.

'You're the real thing, Alice. I've lived in a messed-up world full of fakes for years now. But I can still spot someone who's honest, someone who's got integrity and does the right thing – and doesn't stop to count the cost. I saw that from the start when you sat in my kitchen with Casey and helped with that school project of his. There wasn't anything in it for you, but you gave it your best shot. There aren't many people who do that.'

He hesitates. 'Before you, I could always walk away. I fell in love but I fell out again pretty quickly. And right from the start I didn't want that to happen with you. I didn't want to fool around with you.'

He stops once more to gather his thoughts. I gather mine. Everything is clear now. I feel happy and peaceful, and for the first time in a long time I know for certain that everything is going to be all right.

Wyatt begins to speak again and his voice is full of warmth. 'You came to this small town and you changed things. You changed Casey. You made him happy – not just because of Mary Lou, but because you treated him like a mother would. You changed Mr Horner. You've given him a new lease of life. You got the Scott boys rehearsing again. You've been a friend to Rachel. And Dolores never stops telling me how you're the girl for me.'

'She does?'

'She's a big fan of yours. You've got a lot of them in this town.'

Somehow we've found our way to the centre of the maze. We slip through the last pathway and find ourselves in a circle of corn. Casey's Grandpa has put a peeling sign there: *The End*.

'But you changed me, too. You made the ordinary things good again. You made me want to paint the barn and ride the horses, you made me want to dig the garden and go for walks in the evenings. And yes, you made me want to sing again.'

He looks up at the sky and then back at me.

'I wrote "Take My Hand" for you, Alice. I wrote it because that's what I think about you.'

'Me?' I say, a little bemused, thinking back over the lyrics.

> *Let me take you to that place*
> *That words cannot reach*
> *Don't let go, feel us fly*
> *Don't wonder any more, up into the sky*
> *Take my hand*
> *Hold on tight*
> *Let me lift you up*
> *Over the pain*
> *Over the past*
> *Into my arms.*

I feel a shiver go down my spine.

Wyatt draws me close to him. 'I love you, Alice. I'm asking you to stay and be with me.'

The air is still and warm. I can hear the distant hum of a tractor and smell the sweet scent of pines. In our circle of corn we are quite alone. We stand together, feeling each other's embrace, holding each other's gaze, in a place where no one else matters. I realize that being here with the person I love makes it the most perfect place in the world.

'I'll stay,' I say. 'There's nowhere else I'd rather be.'